Cady couldn't see it in the [ ]
was there.

A delta-winged Mirage 2000 fighter jet—coming fast, several thousand feet above and nearing cannon range.

Cady rolled his Harrier hard left, gaining airspeed, but losing altitude. AGL 420. Swerving left and right, zigzagging.

The hard place was right below him, and the rock was coming down fast.

He had visual contact in the rearview. The Mirage's cannons began blinking, white and hot. Only a thousand yards behind him.

The Harrier wasn't an ideal air superiority fighter—but it could stop on a dime.

Cady slammed the nozzle lever full back, rotating the nozzles to their forward positions. The Harrier abruptly cancelled her forward flight and stopped nearly dead in midair.

The Mirage jerked upward to avoid a collision and shot over the Harrier.

Slapping the nozzle lever forward again, Cady armed his AIM-9L Super Sidewinders and fired Number One.

The missile whisked off its launch rail, its Rocketdyne solid-propellent motor bringing it to Mach 3 in seconds.

The Mirage rolled right, climbing in afterburner, trying to escape.

The Sidewinder pursued, closing, curving upward, zipping right up the enemy fighter's tailpipe.

A mini-nova erupted over Antarctica's white wasteland far below. A bouquet of orange, yellow, and red ballooned quickly. Only debris flew out of the huge fireball, spinning and tumbling toward earth.

There was no parachute.

WILLIAM H. LOVEJOY

WHITE NIGHT

ZEBRA BOOKS
KENSINGTON PUBLISHING CORP.

ZEBRA BOOKS are published by

Kensington Publishing Corp.
850 Third Avenue
New York, NY 10022

Zebra and the Z logo Reg. U.S. Pat. & TM Off.

First Printing: June, 1994

Printed in the United States of America

This one is for Jane.

ACKNOWLEDGMENTS

Conversations I had many years ago in Nebraska with Don Lowe, who had spent military time on the frozen continent, sparked my interest in it. Then, in 1989, I read M.E. Morris's superb novel, *The Icemen,* and my curiosity was rekindled. And Jon McIntyre, who spent three seasons on the ice, was gracious enough to loan me his journal and his many hours of videotape. My wife Jane probed the libraries for me.

I thank them all.

PEOPLE

UNITED NATIONS SHIP *U THANT*

COMMAND

Cady, James "Shark," Colonel, Commander Air Group

Monmouth, Samuel, Captain, UNS *U Thant*

Eames, Theresa Jeanne, Major, Combat Information Center commander

George, David, Lieutenant Commander, SEAL team leader

Adams, Charles "Shaker," Major, landing officer

Este, Giovanni, Captain, air controller

Purgatory, Eddie, Captain, meteorological officer

21ST SUBMARINE DETACHMENT

D'Argamon, Jean, Commander, 21st Submarine Detachment

Moritz, Oscar, Lieutenant, *Calais* pilot

Suretsev, Ivan, Second officer, *Calais*

Magnuson, Erik, Electronics and ordnance technician, *Calais*

Arnstadt, Rolf, Lieutenant Commander, *Dover* pilot

1ST SQUADRON (Gypsy Moths)

Anderson, Phillip "Flip," Wing executive officer, Squadron commander, Gypsy Moth Two

Olivera, Miguel, Lieutenant, Gypsy Moth Three

Stein, David, Lieutenant, Gypsy Moth Four

Sifra, Solomon, Captain, Gypsy Moth Five

Mikkelson, Jasper "Tiger," Lieutenant, Gypsy Moth Six

2ND SQUADRON (Tiger Barbs)

Travers, Jake, Major, Squadron commander, Tiger Barb One

Nakamura, Nikki, Captain, Tiger Barb Two

11TH HELICOPTER ATTACK SQUADRON (Falcons)

Baker, Archie, Major, Helicopter wing commander, Falcon One pilot

Decker, Henry, Lieutenant, Falcon One gunner/copilot

12TH HELICOPTER TRANSPORT SQUADRON (Copperheads)

Makarov, Mikhail, Seahawk pilot

Alhers, Gail, Seahawk pilot

Hammond, Tex, Seahawk pilot

ANTARCTICA

BRANDEIS BASE
Andover, Paul "Zip," Meteorologist
Brelin, Gustav, Geophysicist
Metier, Jacque, Station leader
Oliver, Ruth Anne, Ecologist

UNITED NATIONS PEACEKEEPER COMMITTEE

OPERATIONS COMMITTEE
Bentley, Sir Charles, United Kingdom, Chairman
Highwater, Julia, United States
Albrecht, Justin, Denmark
McNichols, Cameron, Defense Intelligence Agency analyst

FRONT FOR SOUTH AMERICAN DETERMINATION

LEADERSHIP
Silvera, Juan, President, Front for South American
 Determination
Fuentes, Ricardo, Administrative assistant and adviser

JAGUAR SQUADRON
Suarez de Suruca, Emilio, Commander of air operations,
 Squadron commander

PUMA SQUADRON
Tellez, Roberto, Squadron commander, Puma One pilot
Ramirez, Jesus, Puma One radar intercept officer
Ramon, Alberto, Puma Four
Salazar, Enrico, Puma Five

FSAD NAVY
Enriquez, Diego, Commander of sea operations, Captain,
 San Matias
Montez, Dante, First officer, *San Matias*
Estero, Carlos, Second officer, *San Matias*
Mondragon, Umberto, Navigator, *San Matias*
Encinas, Jorge, Captain, *Marguerite Bay*

27 NOVEMBER

Shark Cady scanned the cockpit instruments automatically, paying particular attention to the status of the Reaction Control System (RCS). The system would be crucial in the next few minutes.

Upon reflection, he thought, *perhaps* it would be crucial.

Provided he found a need for it.

At the moment, his priority was less that of anticipating the landing than attempting to stay aloft.

The familiar instrumentation of the cockpit was more comforting than the view outside the canopy. The blue-gray scuzz that swirled past the windscreen was his close-up view of what the meteorologists at Howard Air Base in Panama had called low overcast. It was low, all right. His radar altimeter read 212 feet above sea level, and he hadn't broken out of it yet. In fact, he had been encased in it for the last quarter-hour and for the last eleven thousand feet of his descent.

It wasn't a common, everyday, lazy overcast, either. This one was hyperactive, alive with a gusting wind that was undecided about the direction it wanted to take. Cady estimated that the gusts, primarily out of the northwest, might be hitting sixty knots. He fought to maintain his heading with the stick and rudder pedals, and he had tried trimming in a little rudder and aileron to counter the main drift, but every time he thought he had it set, the crosswind shifted direction by a few points.

Since he was trying to maintain a heading of 255 degrees, the wind was interfering with his flight, slowing his ground speed, though he was showing 430 knots on the True Air Speed (TAS) indicator.

The headwinds affected all aspects of his flight, including the other item that was about to start bothering him: the read-out for his fuel state.

Twenty minutes left.

The Harrier III could easily ferry itself 1400 miles, flying clean and with the auxiliary fuel tanks slung on the wing pylons, if the pilot babied the throttle. The Rolls-Royce Pegasus Mk 105 vectored-thrust turbofan produced 21,750 pounds of thrust, but if a cautious pilot didn't use all of it, all of the time, a journey such as this should have been a cake-walk.

Cady had been conservative with his fuel consumption, even resisting the urge to go supersonic for the long stretch out of Panama, but his weatherman had been more optimistic than realistic, and an hour out of Panama City, he had encountered the strong headwinds.

Like the weatherman, though, James "Shark" Cady was also an optimistic man, and he assumed that once he broke out of the overcast, he would find something more than a few million acres of barren Pacific Ocean.

With his left hand, he found the big ball of the throttle handle and retarded it some more, lost speed to four hundred knots, and reduced his altitude to 150 feet above the sea.

The buffeting didn't seem to abate, but his visibility may have increased by about ten feet, which wasn't a great deal of help.

His primary UHF radio was already dialed into 290.10 megahertz, with the scrambler cut into the circuit, and he pressed the transmit stud on the stick with his thumb.

"Beehive, Gypsy Moth One."

The air controller, an Italian by the name of Giovanni Este, came right back to him, his voice tinged with a metallic echo as a result of the encryption equipment.

"I have you, Gypsy One. Go ahead."

"Beehive, do you have any idea where you are?"

"Of course, One."

"Well, then, do you know where I am?"

"I have a fair idea," the controller said. "I would be more positive if you would squawk me with the appropriate modes and codes."

Cady switched his Identify Friend or Foe (IFF) transponder to active, setting the modes to transmit his position and altitude. He skipped mode one, which would provide a unit designation for friendly forces, and mode four, which told the world he was military. Este already knew that. The transponder identified his blip on the air controller's radar screen.

"It is as I thought, Gypsy One. I show you at one hundred and fifty feet, bearing one-six-one, forty-five miles. You are flying awfully low, Shark."

"I'm looking for the sea."

"You will find it, but not before you leave the fog."

"Wonderful. What are your conditions, Beehive?"

"Winds from the northwest, gusting to forty-five knots, barometric pressure two-nine-point-six-five and falling, visibility a quarter-mile."

Cady reset his barometric altimeter.

"How about your heading?"

"The ship is making sixteen knots on a heading of two-six-one. Come left two points, Gypsy One."

"Left two." Cady made the adjustment, but the crosswind wanted to push him off the numbers.

"Your conditions are not ideal," Cady told Beehive.

"In other circumstances, I would divert you. Say your fuel."

There wasn't a diversion air field within a thousand miles.

"I've got all of sixteen minutes," Cady told him.

"Well, we will hope for the best, then."

Cady appreciated such strongly-worded support.

Losing more altitude, to a hundred feet above the sea, and reducing his airspeed to 250 knots, Cady finally saw the ocean surface. It wasn't serene. He estimated that the seas were running twelve-foot swells, and the wind was whipping the tops off the waves, creating a moving kaleidoscopic pattern of white and gray that constantly shifted to the southeast.

The tunnel of his visibility had extended. Este was more-or-less correct, he thought. At times, he could see almost a thousand feet in most directions. Little caverns of fog-free clearing zipped by, nearly doubling that distance, but then rapidly disappearing.

Eight minutes later, he located the ship. Because of the visibility limitations and his altitude above the sea's surface, he didn't have an early warning. It appeared abruptly, emerging from the haze like a phantom vessel.

Most aviators in his fuel and weather situation would have been dismayed at the sight. She wasn't a massive aircraft carrier. She was a massive crude oil tanker, classified as an Ultra Large Crude Carrier (ULCC). One of the giants of the sea, she was 1,350 feet long, and in comparison, she was 300 feet longer than the U.S. Navy's *Enterprise* class of aircraft carrier. With a beam of 170 feet, she was eighty-two feet narrower than the flight deck of an *Enterprise* though her hull was actually forty feet wider than the hulls of the carriers. The draft was thirty-six feet, and her registry with Lloyd's of Lon-

don stated that she was capable of on-loading 750,000 tons
of crude oil.

The hull was black as night, with blunt bows that savagely
leveled the seas ahead of her. The stern was squared-off, and
a white superstructure aligned with the stern rose seven decks
above the main deck. With visibility restricted as it was today,
those on the bridge deck—the sixth level—could not see the
bows.

When he found her plowing through the angry seas, her
wake a widening vee of churned water, Cady bled off more
power, and came up on her stern. He couldn't see the bow,
and he couldn't yet read the six-foot-high gold letters spaced
across the stern, but knew they spelled out *Cornucopia*, and
below them, smaller letters suggested her home port was
Marseille.

She had turned into the wind, which was no mean feat.
Turning or stopping the beast required miles of ocean, time,
and preplanning.

"Gypsy Moth One, Beehive."

"Go, Beehive."

"You are cleared for approach and landing. Give us a little
more room than usual, please."

"Wilco, Beehive. Gypsy Moth One on approach."

"Go to two-eight-six-point-five, Gypsy One."

"Gone." Cady punched the keypad for his secondary channel, calling up the frequency he had preset.

"Gypsy Moth One. I'm with you, Shaker."

"Got you, Shark. There's some buffeting. Be cool."

"Wilco."

With an aircraft carrier, Cady would have had a landing
approach system to help him get on the deck—flying the
"ball," to guide his descent. Because of the mountainous superstructure spread across the stern of the *Cornucopia,* he

lined up parallel to, and a hundred feet off the starboard side of the vessel.

He came in slow, at 150 knots, deployed his flaps for increased lift, and as the stern letters of the ship became legible, he punched the landing gear button. He felt the bicycle gear—nose and main wheels both located in the fuselage—thud into the down-and-locked position, but checked for green lights, anyway. A quick glance out either side of the canopy reaffirmed that the outrigger gear—the small stabilizing wheels on long oleo struts—had deployed successfully from the high-mounted wings.

As he lost more speed, he added power, then grabbed the nozzle lever, which was located inboard of the throttle, and began to ease it backward. The Harrier III, like other late models of the Harrier, had been outfitted with a computerized stability system which removed some of the dangerous aspects of the transition from flight to hover, and vice versa. Still, the act of abandoning reliable wing-lift for the posture of standing on one's own engine exhaust increased the adrenaline flow.

Drawing back on the nozzle lever turned the four side-mounted exhaust nozzles downward—and even slightly forward if he wanted reverse thrust. The aircraft slowed dramatically as he passed to the right of the superstructure, noting the pale blobs of faces through the bronzed bridge windows turned toward him. The engine RPM climbed as the power of the turbofan was vectored downward. Within seconds, Cady was moving at a walking speed, slowly advancing ahead of the superstructure and still alongside the ship. As requested, he gave her more clearance than normal. When something went wrong, the wind pitched him over into the sea, the captain preferred that he not take the ship with him.

Once he cleared the superstructure, he had an unobstructed

view of the centered catwalk that extended the length of the deck several feet above the maze of piping and tank hatches that covered that open deck. He couldn't see the far, bow end of it, though. It disappeared into a shadowy, shifting fog. The catwalk was thirty-five feet wide, conveniently wider than the thirty-foot wingspan of the Harrier II, as well as the twenty feet spread between its outrigger wheels.

He also had a fair view of the landing officer, dressed in a fluorescent yellow vest and helmet, standing midway down the deck on a small, railed platform to one side of the catwalk. A large trampoline-like netting was suspended next to the LO's platform. It was a place of refuge into which he could jump if something unexpected happened on the catwalk. The yellow vest whipped wickedly in the wind. The LO held two red-lensed flashlights for signaling, and his communications headset kept him in touch with Cady.

Charles "Shaker" Adams was their best landing officer, and Cady had automatically assumed Adams would be in control of a landing in these weather conditions.

Ocean spray was rocketing upward, splattering droplets against the canopy. Cady had to continually balance the attitude of the aircraft against the ebb and flow of the wind turbulence. Because he was no longer on wing-lift flight, his controls had switched to the Reaction Control System, small thrusters on the wingtips and tail which managed pitch, yaw, and roll. He dipped the right wing lower, as much from habits learned in F-4s and F-14s as from the need to fight the crosswind.

"Easy now, Shark," Shaker Adams said. "Match speed."

Cady glanced to his left and saw the yellow cross laid out on the catwalk. He vectored the nozzles forward slowly until his forward movement coincided with the cross.

"Good, man, good. Now, let's come to your left."

A stream of denser fog shot over the bows, shredding into

patches and striding its way down the deck. The yellow cross blurred. Cady eased in some left rudder, the RCS eased the tail around, and he advanced the nozzles momentarily. The Harrier moved in toward the ship, passed over the starboard gunwale, and approached the catwalk. He kept his eyes on Adams and the flashlights.

"All right, Shark, couple more feet. Bring the nose around."

He added some right rudder, and the nose swung into alignment with the catwalk.

"Right on! Almost. I need a couple more feet left . . . there you go! Set her down."

Cady eased back the throttle, reducing the nozzle velocity, and the Harrier began to settle.

A blast of wind raised the nose.

He corrected quickly with the RCS.

The Harrier settled lower, lower, and then the landing gear banged as he chopped the throttle.

Five crewmen in yellow vests scrambled onto the catwalk, surrounding him, hooking lines into the tiedowns. Shaker Adams came trotting down the catwalk, coming out of the vaporous fog like an errant specter, propelled by the wind at his back.

Cady shut down the engine, then his electronics. He unclipped the oxygen and communications umbilicals, then the G-suit hose. After releasing the harness for the Martin-Baker ejection seat, he found the snap-pin on its short chain and safed the seat. He unclipped his oxygen mask and cranked open the canopy. It slid backward on its rails, and he stood up in his seat.

The air was damp and salty, but it tasted sweet after his hours of stale oxygen. The mass of the ULCC took away most of the ocean's movement, and Cady felt as if his airplane was resting on solid ground. By the time he removed his helmet,

Adams was standing next to the cockpit, below the high wing of the airplane.

"Welcome back to the *Cornucopia,* Shark."

"It's good to be back, Shaker," Cady said and grinned.

He knew it wasn't really the *Cornucopia.*

28 NOVEMBER

If Captain Samuel Harrison Monmouth, United States Navy, were ever to be immortalized, which he didn't expect, a large, square block of marble would be required. Dressed in his tailored uniforms, he appeared to be one vertical mass from spit-polished shoes to shoulders. Latched to his shoulders by a thick and short neck, his head was squarish, with a lantern jaw and grim mouth. Lively blue eyes tempered the harshness of his mouth and flaring nose. He was fifty-four years old, and though some accused him of dyed vanity, his hair had actually retained the same black tint that had appeared at age one.

Monmouth was a superb listener. Even people he didn't really have an interest in spilled their life stories and their tribulations to him. He listened, and he filed the information away for future reference in a mind that categorized easily and retrieved readily. His ability to remember people and names and facts, and to cull vast amounts of data rapidly and analytically, made him a popular and effective decision-maker.

From the time he graduated from the United States Naval Academy, Monmouth—a native of Maine and the Atlantic Ocean—had had one goal in mind. He would one day command a battleship.

He was afraid now that the battleships would all be retired again before he had the chance.

He was also amazed that he had been selected by the Chief of Naval Operations (CNO) himself to command an oil tanker.

Not that she wasn't a unique tanker; the image just did not quite conform to the one he had envisioned for himself thirty years before. At that time, too, he had thought that he would always belong to the United States Navy. His father had been a Navy man in World War II. His grandfather had been a Navy man with action in the Great War, and though he wasn't certain about his great-grandfather, it seemed prudent in family gatherings to suppose that he had also been a Navy man.

Now though, Captain Monmouth, still an active commission in the U.S. Navy, belonged to the world. It was sometimes difficult to suppress the nationalistic fervor with which he had been imbued and take on the universal morality and ethics with which he had been charged. It was a responsibility in which he could take pride, but frequently, it was also a balancing act.

As commander of the United Nations Ship *U Thant*, named for a former UN Secretary General, Monmouth found himself in command of diverse and shifting philosophies, cultures, and personalities. Bringing them together and herding them in approximately the same direction could be considered a world-class magic act. And in the other direction, he reported to a command structure composed of equally divergent cultures and personalities. He often pictured himself as a traffic director at the center of an hourglass, attempting to capture a thousand grains of truth and channel them into one path; even though once they passed through his hands, they would immediately follow their own courses once again.

Monmouth often awakened with that picture hanging in front of him, and it took a few moments to shake it.

He had almost completed the breakfast that had been delivered to his quarters when he heard the rap on his door.

"Come in."

The door swung inward, and Colonel James Cady and Major Archibald Baker stepped inside and came to attention.

"As you were, gentlemen. Pour yourself some coffee and sit down while I finish my muffin. Blueberry, if you want one."

"Thank you, sir," Cady said, "but I've already eaten."

The two men filled mugs from the plastic pot on the serving cart and took seats on the couch against the bulkhead. One of the more agreeable aspects of commanding a ULCC could be found in the living accommodations. The *U Thant* had been designed by a Japanese shipbuilder, and it had been eighty per cent complete when it was purchased by the United Nations Security Council and immediately retrofitted. The spartan quarters, with exposed conduits and drab paint, that Monmouth had become accustomed to in three decades of seafaring would not be found on his current ship. Though the crew quarters, which had had to be revamped from the original plan, were somewhat cramped, they were still airy-feeling and cheerful. The interior paint schemes for residential and recreation spaces ran from white to yellow to pale blue. The officers' staterooms—and they were staterooms—on D and E decks generally housed two persons each, but each room was spacious and had a bath shared with the next stateroom. Spaced throughout the superstructure and below decks were wardrooms, lounges, and recreation rooms. The ship was designed to keep her crew happy at sea or in exotic ports where they weren't allowed liberty for fear of disclosing the total number of men and women aboard. In the nine weeks since the ship had been commissioned, his enlisted personnel still had not conquered all of the electronic games to be found in the recreation areas.

His own quarters, on the Bridge Deck, aft of the bridge, with large ports overlooking the water astern, had walls paneled in soft honey oak and were composed of a large bath and bedroom, plus the sitting room in which he was now meeting two of his senior subordinates. The room held a small round table with four castered chairs and the couch and two easy chairs in a conversational grouping. The wood tables and a sideboard against one bulkhead were finished in oak, and the upholstery was tweedy, a dark blue with random gray stripes passing through the blue. The lamp tables and coffee table had dark glass inserts in their tops. Monmouth had hung his personally owned pictures: a large oil painting and a half-a-dozen watercolors of scenes along the Maine coastline. They tended to be moody, storm-threatened scenes, with angry seas pounding the rocks and distant white sails racing for the refuge of harbor.

Monmouth, at his dining table, finished his blueberry muffin, refilled his coffee cup, and leaned back in his chair.

"You cut it a little fine, yesterday, Jim."

Jim Cady produced his infectious grin. "I wanted to make certain everyone was on their toes, Captain."

Cady was a product of the United States Marine Corps. In his early forties, he was hard and fit at six feet and about 175 pounds. Physically, he hadn't changed much from the time Monmouth first met him when they were both assigned to the aircraft carrier *Ranger* during the last stages of the Vietnam hostilities. He had been a kid then, wanting everyone around him to know how good he was in the front seat of an F-4 Phantom. And he was good.

The changes could be seen around his dark and sometimes fiery eyes, where the lines of crowfeet—the pilot's squint—had become permanent. His skin was weathered like a good clapboard seafront house, though in shades of tan rather than gray. The dark hair had streaks of silver in it, working up from his temples, but it was difficult to discern since, like any good Marine, he kept it cropped shorter than the stubble of a freshly mown alfalfa field.

Cady carried the nickname, "Shark," though not from a physical trait. It had been earned during his fifteen missions over Vietnam before the war ended, in the Grenada excursion, and in the Persian Gulf, for the tenacity he had shown when pursuing his prey.

Both Cady and Baker wore flight suits in United Nations blue with the UN emblem embroidered in white on their left shoulders. The only other decoration was their rank insignia sewn with silver or gold thread on the left collar of their flight suits. Like Monmouth with the Navy, Cady still held his Marine Corps commission, but he was on permanent duty assignment to the *U Thant*. He was assigned in a capacity very few Marines might expect to achieve on an aircraft carrier, as Commander Air Group or CAG. He was aboard the *U Thant* because Monmouth had asked for him.

Archie Baker had come to Monmouth from the Royal Air Force, and though he had not had a hand in the selection, Monmouth was content with his lottery. Baker was so thin he was almost emaciated. He emanated thinness. His blond hair was receding quickly except for his mustache, which he trimmed into a pencil line across his solid upper lip.

Baker had learned to fly helicopters on an exchange program with the United States Army, and he flew them sideways, upside down, and in other ingenious ways. He did things with helicopters that Monmouth hadn't known was possible. And he did it laconically, as if the talent could easily go unrecognized. Outside of a cockpit, where instantaneous decisions were a requirement, Baker was given to thoughtful, in-depth consideration of issues. He wasn't verbose, but when he spoke, it was with quiet, informed authority.

"The next time, Jim," Monmouth said, "let's wait out the weather and arrange an aerial refueling."

"The weather wasn't a problem when I took off," Cady defended.

"When you took off from where? Miami?"

Cady had gone stateside to pick up a new Harrier, but with one delay or another—and perhaps it was because Cady was having a good time—he had missed their planned rendezvous a couple hundred miles off Panama.

Cady just grinned.

Monmouth wasn't going to get into a debate over it, so he waved it off with a big hand, and said, "How about you, Archie? Any major problems?"

"None, sir," Baker said. "I've a Seahawk down for a compressor replacement, but that will be accomplished in the next two days."

"All right, good. Let's take our tour."

Once a week, sometimes more often, Monmouth toured the ship with two of his senior officers. Cady and Baker had the duty today. The three of them rose, donned their floppy overseas caps, and exited the captain's stateroom.

The uniforms worn aboard the *U Thant* were a result of Monmouth's careful consideration. Some members of the UN committee wanted their troops to dress in national uniforms, but Monmouth had argued against that, and he had finally prevailed. He wanted a sense of discipline and cohesiveness in his crew, and so the work uniforms like his own and the pilots' flight suits were of UN blue with the single identifying shoulder patch. They were worn ninety per cent of the time, when they were at sea and not likely to be observed by other shipping. The major variant in uniform could be found in the camouflage utilities worn by the SEAL detachment, adapted from a U.S. Marine prototype.

The *U Thant,* however, was also a covert ship, changing her name frequently—currently the *Cornucopia.* The concept behind that, and behind her appearance in the first place, was to make her less conspicuous as she navigated around the world. And when she was near ports or populated shorelines, or heavily travelled sea-lanes where a casual spectator might see them, a civilian "uniform" was in order, and deckhands and officers changed to appropriate clothing. At those times, also, the larger part of the crew was kept below decks. Most people, much less the captain of a passing container ship, knew that even supertankers did not require a crew complement of 750 men and women.

Monmouth led the way down the corridor, which crossed the beam of the ship. On the right were the cabins assigned to senior ship's officers and the chief engineer. When they reached an intersecting corridor, he made a left turn. The spaces along this corridor, and a matching corridor on the starboard side, were dedicated to the ship's operational departments.

At the forward end of the corridor was an elevator and stairwell, but Monmouth went on through the hatchway to the bridge. A petty officer from New Zealand called out, "Captain's on the bridge."

Monmouth put them at ease, then scanned the seas through the massive windscreens that canted top-out around the narrow bridge area that spanned the width of the ship. To the west, he saw a thin clear blue line.

Jacob Ernst, an Israeli and the second officer, had the conn. He was a small dark man with a prominent smile. In his short-sleeved uniform, the hard sinew of his musculature was evident. He was an avid bodybuilder, and he spent many of his off-hours in the gymnasium.

"Good morning, sir."

"Good morning, Jacob." Monmouth indicated the west with a nod of his head. "Are we going to see the sun today?"

"It looks promising, Captain. About midday, I expect."

Monmouth scanned the high-tech digital readouts on the panels below the windscreen, reaffirming what he knew about the ship's position, heading, speed, and other conditions, then turned back to the elevator.

They stepped inside, and without asking, Cady pressed the button labeled, "A Deck." That deck was also the main deck and the flight deck. Below it were Hangar Decks 1 and 2, then Decks 3 and 4. Fore and aft, below decks, were also divided. The aft portion of the ship was devoted to engineering spaces and the nuclear reactor on Decks 3 and 4. Above them, on Decks 1 and 2, were crew accommodations and storage spaces.

When the elevator door parted, the three men stepped out, made certain their caps were firmly in place, then left the superstructure for a narrow catwalk that fronted the superstructure. They used it to walk toward the center of the ship, then turned onto the main catwalk that ran the length of the ship. The wind was strong, still gusting, and Cady gave up trying to hang on to his cap, pulled it off, and stuck it in the leg pocket of his flight suit.

It was a long walk, leaning into the stiff wind, but Monmouth enjoyed it. He kept his head and eyes moving from side to side, searching for anomalies in the appearance of the deck—the equipment that should be present, the things that were not.

Below the catwalk, which with its reinforced substructure was also the flight deck, was a metallic and plastic jungle of tubing, piping, pumps, winches, and cranes in folded repose. The maze would keep engineering and hydraulic people in awe for months on end. And eventually they would discover that it was mostly a facade. The piping went from nowhere to nowhere. Most of the pumps were only fiberglass housings.

"Archie, tell the deck crew to get those cranes up," Monmouth said.

"Aye, aye, sir."

The six loading cranes, port and starboard, were supposed to be in the erect position when flight operations were not scheduled. The deck appearance was important since one never knew when overhead surveillance, by aircraft or satellite, might take place.

Huge rectangular oil tank hatches were spaced along each side of the catwalk, dividing the deck into twelve approximate squares, each hemmed in by the tubing. Those, also, were facades, and the two forward and two aft hatches were in reality aircraft elevators. Other hatches, when folded open, would reveal some damned lethal hardware.

Monmouth turned and looked back at the imposing altitude of the superstructure. The band of windows around the bridge was bronzed, and he could not identify particular faces. They were pale spots in the dark glass. Above the bridge level was what appeared to be another deck, but that was also a phony, made of fiberglass. On top of it were the radar and communications antennas that any seafarer would expect of a ULCC. Just below them, however, encased in the fiberglass deck, was an array of super-tech communications and radar antennas that Monmouth never expected to understand, like the Thorn EMI Searchwater radar. He knew they worked, and that was the important point.

When they reached the bow, Cady pulled open a hatchway and they stepped over the coaming into the forward watcher's "shanty." The seaman on duty came to attention while they checked the compartment. In congested waters, or in bad weather, the shanty was occupied by lookouts in continuous telephone contact with the bridge.

"All right," Monmouth said, "let's check your bailiwick, Jim."

"We could skip it, Captain, since it's perfect."

"After yesterday, I question your judgment."

Cady cleared his throat quietly, and they took the companionway down to Hangar Deck 1. Below them were the magazines, behind solid steel vaulted doors, and Monmouth ignored them for this tour.

As Commander Air Group, Shark Cady was responsible for the people and equipment on the two hangar decks. He led the way through the hatch on Deck 1 and stepped aside to survey his domain. Monmouth knew that Cady was extremely proud of it, though he didn't often say as much.

The elevators took up some of the space, and the rest was densely compacted with the thirteen Harrier III reconnaissance and strike aircraft of the 1st and 2nd Squadrons of the United Nations Air Wing One. One of the aircraft was a two-seat version, utilized to transport important passengers or for training. Tow tractors and start-carts were spaced around the deck. Cranes, engine hoists, tall banks of tool chests, and electronic diagnostic equipment seemed to clutter the bulkheads, but were placed with studied precision. Huge snakelike rubber tubes crawled over the floor, used to vent intake air and exhaust when engines were test-run. Men in the uniform of the day, but with colored vests that denoted their jobs, moved around the deck like random and colorful atoms. Cady was responsible for nearly three hundred men. The overhead fluorescent lighting illuminated the deck to almost day-like proportions, but with a blue tinge.

They took thirty minutes to walk the length of the hangar, stopping occasionally to talk to technicians or to examine aircraft, then went down to the next deck. This space was smaller—slightly shorter and narrower—because of the curvature of the hull, and it contained ten McDonnell Douglas AH-64 Sea Apache attack helicopters and six Sikorsky UH-60 Seahawk helicopters, each capable of carrying eleven heavily-laden troops. They belonged to the 11th Helicopter Attack Squadron and the 12th Helicopter Transport Squadron commanded by Major Archibald Baker, who reported to Cady.

After completing their inspection, the three men took a companionway down another deck. Here, most of Decks 3 and 4 were opened into one tall area. In the center was a moon pool, an opening to the sea in the middle of the hull which could be closed off by massive doors on the bottom of the hull.

The moon pool was fifty feet long and thirty feet wide, and it was currently full of water and two submarines. The whole area felt overly humid.

Commander Jean d'Argamon, who was a Frenchman, met them, saluting Monmouth.

Monmouth returned the salute. "Good morning, Jean."

"Good morning, sir. I was expecting you, and I held off our morning deployment."

In her disguise, the *U Thant* did not have escort vessels, of course, and the mini-submarines, each ten feet wide and thirty feet long, served that purpose. They were capable of limited attack roles, carrying four torpedoes each, but primarily, their job was to cruise ahead of the tanker, with their reconnaissance pods extended to the surface, watching for potentially hostile aircraft or ships. D'Argamon commanded the small 21st Submarine Detachment and reported directly to Monmouth. He was tall for a Frenchman, Monmouth thought, standing close to six-three. With fair hair, quick hazel eyes, and a smooth olive complexion, he was handsome and probably attractive to women. At least, he thought so. He was also frequently obstinate, and normally on the other side of any tactical or strategic planning discussion.

"Go ahead, then, and we'll watch."

The commander signaled a Belgian Navy lieutenant named Oscar Moritz, who was standing near the far sub, and Moritz nodded. He and his two crewmen crossed a short gangway to the small conning tower of the sub and disappeared through the hatch. It was quickly closed, and as soon as a froth of bubbles appeared aft of the sub, indicating her propeller was active, deck crewmen hastened to release the spring lines that held the sub in place.

In a matter of three minutes, the sub matched speed with the ship and slowly sank out of sight into dark waters.

Cady was trying to look at his watch unobtrusively.

"Getting bored, Colonel?" Monmouth asked.

"Of course not, sir."

"All right, then. We've covered the offensive systems. Shall we go see if we've got any defenses?"

"By all means," Cady said. "I'm thrilled at the prospect."

UNS U THANT
1100 HOURS LOCAL

Theresa Jeanne Eames was a major in the Canadian air force, and she had volunteered for a classified program seeking her military occupational specialty, been selected by a review board that interviewed her for four hours, and ended up with this duty. Increasingly, she had begun to think it was the biggest mistake she had made in her life. Her friends, and even her lukewarm family, could only reach her through a New York post office box number. She was out of contact with her world, stranded on a floating semi-palace. She had joined the air force because she didn't particularly care for water, and now water was all she saw.

Born in Montreal, she had a fluent command of the French language, and though the universal language aboard ship was English, she could converse with a number of people in their native or secondary languages. With Jean d'Argamon, her most frequently utilized word was an emphatic "No!"

Educated properly in good Catholic schools, Eames had arrived at high-school graduation with a fine command of etiquette, a well-rounded knowledge of the arts, and absolutely no idea of what she wanted to do with her life.

Her parents, both blue-collar workers, slightly liberal, and peace activists except where it involved French-speaking residents of Quebec, were positive that they had fulfilled their obligation by footing the parochial school bills, and they urged her to find a nice-paying job just as soon as possible so as to help her three younger siblings with their bills. They were appalled when she accepted an air force scholarship that allowed her to get a degree in mathematics at Fordham University, then further disenchanted when they learned that she would actually pay back the advance by devoting four years of her life to warmongering. Her visits home were not cordial even though she was now helping her two youngest brothers with their university tuition.

When she elected to stay in the service, her father almost completely stopped talking to her. She couldn't convince him that the aim of the military was to maintain peace.

Eames didn't look like much of a hawk. At five-four, she was petite and trim. Her figure might have been described as lush in anything other than a military uniform. Her cheekbones were high enough and her eyes dark enough to suggest that her lineage had been invaded with Indian blood at some point. Especially at sea, she wore little makeup, and she kept her hair short enough to simplify its maintenance. Her hands were unconsciously expressive, seemingly always on the move when she talked or particularly when she was at a console in the Combat Information Center.

With her math background, she had gravitated naturally into computer operations with the Canadian Armed Forces Air Command, and she had become highly proficient in managing enormous amounts of information, achieving her majority while serving as a ground control intercept officer. She had never expected to find herself on board a ship at sea, though, and she didn't care much for it. Periodically, she went to sleep in the cabin she shared with Captain Jan Gless, a medical doctor seconded from the Swedish navy, vowing to never again volunteer for anything.

Based on experience and proficiency, she had been selected over two men as the senior officer in command of the CIC, and she knew there were some barely concealed resentments floating around. Naval Lieutenant Luigi Maroni, an Italian with macho instincts, was having the worst time accepting her, but she thought he was coming around. She also knew she was the best-qualified and that she would have to prove it time and again.

While she understood Captain Monmouth's regulations regarding uniform, she was still proud of her service, and she wore small earrings of gold with enameled blue circles enclosing a red maple leaf, the insignia for the Canadian Armed Forces—Air.

The Combat Information Center on board the *U Thant* was on the Bridge Deck, aft of the bridge, in an interior compartment. There were no windows from which the personnel could watch the sea pass by. With their electronic eyes and sensors, the inhabitants of the CIC could see much farther than a porthole and human eyes allowed. The forest of antennas hidden in the deck above, which the technicians who maintained them called Ghost Deck, fed radar signals and intelligence data from dozens of different sources directly to her fingertips. The sonar antennas located in the hull of the ship augmented the information, providing clues about the activity below the surface.

Since there were always rivalries among nations in intelligence gathering, she was a little hamstrung. Her outside intelligence came "on loan" from various sources as needed or begged. She did not have direct links to satellites or other ELINT (Electronic Intelligence) sources. Currently, some section in the American Defense Intelligence Agency had been detailed to assist the *U Thant* on an irregular basis, but the data transfer was a bit primitive, considering some of the sophisticated techniques now available.

All of this data, analyzed and filtered by the CIC computer, appeared on one or more of the three forty-inch multifunction display screens or the two smaller data screens mounted on one bulkhead of the CIC. Below the screens were three consoles, one for the data input technician, one for the Tactical Information Officer (TIO), and one for the Tactical Action Officer (TAO) when that position was in residence.

In the dim red light of the compartment, the symbols on the screen were clear and well-defined by small square boxes next to each symbol. At the moment, the *U Thant,* in the center of the screen, was simply a blue boat-shaped icon. Her box described her heading, speed, and position. To the upper right of the screen was another blue ship icon, and the box identified it as:

> ID: CALAlS
> HDG: 256
> SPD: 27K
> ALT: -656
> RNG: 2.5NM
> POS: 2-12-32N 92-47-21W

To the north was a large aircraft icon designated by the computer from information received from radar, radio reports, and airline schedules as:

```
ID:    BOE 747-QUANTAS
HDG:   88
SPD:   362K
ALT:   30,400
RNG:   56NM
POS:   2-13-13N 92-47-16W
```

It was a disappointing screen, Eames thought, as she stood behind the Tactical Information Officer's chair at the main console. Next to the TIO for this watch, Luigi Maroni was the data entry operator, a Mexican army sergeant.

Cruising this part of the Pacific was Nirvana for those who liked to sleep a lot. For her, it was data-less ennui. At least, when they had been sailing south along Central America, she had been able to play games in the identification business, targeting freighters, yachts, and private aircraft she suspected of drug trafficking. Someday, she hoped, the UN Security Council would turn them loose on those kinds of targets.

The miniature submarine *Calais,* sailing in the point position, had her reconnaissance pod deployed, with the antennas on the surface, but she, too, would be getting the same kind of information.

Boring, boring, boring.

It wasn't her watch, and she had only stopped by on the off-chance that something, anything, needed her attention. Lieutenant Maroni had smiled at her, but somewhat indulgently, she thought, reaffirming the rumor that some people considered her a mother hen.

Well, mother hen or not, this department is my responsibility, and nine weeks after the U Thant *had been commissioned, and after seven weeks at sea, there hasn't been one major. . . .*

The hatchway from the light trap—the CIC was kept in continual red light—opened, and she saw the silhouette she had come to recognize instantly as a result of his frequent visits.

Cady said, "Good morning, Major."

"Good morning, Colonel."

She didn't think she liked Cady very well. Anyone who was called "Shark" affectionately was someone deserving of suspicion. Though he appeared fit and hard-muscled, he also appeared ruthless. Except for their coloring, she didn't see any commonality between them.

Cady glanced at the screen.

"An airliner fifty-six nautical miles away and our own sub," he said. "Not much to get excited about, is there?"

"Not much, Colonel."

He waved her toward the back of the compartment, where four extra chairs were parked, so as not to interfere with the two men at the consoles, though they had their headsets in place, anyway.

"I have a request, Terri."

Her friends called her Terri, and on this ship, there were few who did. She didn't correct him, of course, since he was a superior officer, and she stepped backward a few paces to stay with him.

"I just learned from Sam Monmouth that you once developed gaming scenarios for the Air Command."

"That was a few years ago, Colonel—"

"Call me Jim, will you?"

"Ah, Jim . . . but, yes, I was part of a team that wrote some war games."

"Interactive?"

"Yes."

"Well, look. I've got fifteen pilots, most of whom had never

flown together before this cruise, and most of whom learned
their skills under different philosophies and disciplines. With
our training schedule, they're starting to look like they're on
the same team, but I want to add some stress to their lives.
If we ever get into something hairy, I want to know what
they're capable of doing."

"You want me to program some simulations?"

"I'd appreciate it very much," he said. "I'd buy you lunch
or dinner or something."

"How complicated do you want them to be?"

"You've been watching these guys fly almost daily, Terri.
Why don't you do a rough outline of what you think would
be appropriate, and we can sit down and talk about it."

My God. A challenge, finally.

"How difficult do you really want it to be?" she asked.

"Maybe we could start with a couple, three scenarios with
differing levels of difficulty. And then there's Baker's choppers. Maybe later we can do something for them?"

"Yes, that would be easy enough."

"Great!"

She noticed for the first time that when Colonel Cady got
excited about something his eyes, which were a dark gray,
appeared to lighten and sparkle. In the dim light of the CIC,
they looked as if they were emitting a million tiny shatters of
laser beams.

"How soon would you like to see something?" she asked.

"Ah, we're both in the military. . . ."

"Yesterday. I know." She glanced up at the digital readout
for local time. There were five readouts above the display
screen, each showing different time zones adjacent to the one
they were in, plus Zulu time—the Greenwich Meridian. "Can
we meet at thirteen hundred hours?"

"Great. My office okay?"

"I'll be there."

DEFENSE INTELLIGENCE AGENCY
1720 HOURS LOCAL

Since taking on his new assignment, which was supposed to be only half-time, Cameron McNichols had acquired a whole bunch of new equipment for his office in Arlington Hall Annex.

He'd had to get rid of the small and endearing couch that been holding up the south wall for fifteen years, shift his desk and computer credenza to the wall which had a single window overlooking the Arlington National Cemetery—to keep things in perspective, and make room for the large electronic console.

With its three screens, keyboard, and panels of switches that a training technician had taught him to use, the console had become the center point of interest in his office. It was a much better conversation piece than the old, flower-patterned, and tattered couch. There was, in fact, some degree of jealousy exhibited by his colleagues in the analysis section.

With his console, McNichols had direct access to the National Security Agency at Fort George G. Meade, Maryland. The NSA was the largest intelligence gathering organization in the United States, and with the crash of the KGB, probably the world. It was responsible primarily for monitoring electronic signals—radio, television, microwave telephone—and satellite reconnaissance. The NSA culled the mountains of information it obtained and produced concise hills of intelligence data for a variety of organizations. The Air Force, Army, Navy, Defense Intelligence, and favored allies were recipients.

But McNichols was getting whatever he wanted, when he wanted it, directly. He could delve into the raw data or accept the filtered version. Except for specially encrypted files, he had been granted additional security clearances and had access to all of the written and recorded files, from agents' notes to video, sonar, and radar recordings. There were historical documents and tapes, and in some areas of the world, real-time observations.

Cam McNichols was a civilian and, with twenty-six years devoted to his profession, a high-ranking one. He was in charge of the European analysis section, and since his superiors figured he didn't have enough to do, they had asked him to take on the new project, providing intelligence summaries to the Peacekeeper Committee of the United Nations Security Council. He didn't know precisely what the committee—called the PC in-house—did for action beyond managing the super-secret supertanker they had spent over a billion bucks for, but they had a voracious appetite for information. They asked for everything—and anything—that came into their minds after reading the morning papers.

He didn't really mind the extra load. A widower of three years standing, McNichols wanted both something to fill his hours and the direct access to NSA. He loved data—manipulating it, playing with it, projecting future scenarios from vast compilations of seemingly innocuous facts and observations. The factual information was there—collecting it was just an exercise in human observation or electronic surveillance. The spook masters, and McNichols didn't consider himself one of their number, called it HUMINT (human intelligence) or ELINT.

What was far more important, as far as McNichols was concerned, was the interpretation. What was relevant? What was not? Perceptive people, like himself, with years of background, spotted the differences quickly.

McNichols's hair had departed along with the years. What was left was a bushy fringe that leaped over his ears and circled his head. He augmented it with a full and proud beard in magnificent silver gray that intimidated some people. His eyes, too, a bright green, almost zealous pair of emeralds, could cause hesitation in his conversants. Never considered by anyone at all as a Washington social lion, McNichols generally wore jeans and bright plaid flannel shirts (T-shirts in the summer). He conceded to some necessities by keeping a couple suits in the small closet of his office, just in case he needed to disguise his six-feet-six-inch, 240-pound bulk as a real bureaucrat.

Devoting half his time to the special project had started out as a hobby, but within the first month, he had added another console and two of his subordinates to the hobby task, each of them half-time, naturally. The workload had increased steadily since the people who wanted their information usually ended up wanting more.

And more.

And more.

He was ambivalent about the workload, though. That was his job, and if his product was good, the demand was going to rise. The demand was a reflection of his ability and his credibility.

McNichols had completed an intelligence estimate relative to Basque terrorists for the Army—and what did they want with it, anyway?—a little before five, and not yet hungry enough to go searching for a restaurant—he rarely cooked for himself—had moved over to his console to play for awhile. When he played, he chose anywhere in the world but Europe or what had been the Eastern bloc because those regions were too much like work.

He called up a menu that listed the satellites currently in an active mode, viewing their sections of the world in real time, and saw that a Teal Ruby was in the southern hemisphere, having just crossed the Pole, and since he hadn't looked at the southern hemisphere in a couple weeks, selected it.

It took a few seconds for all the right telephonic cable and microwave transmission connections to be made, and then a sixteen-color image appeared on his center screen.

It wasn't the same as looking at a map in a Hammond Atlas. For one thing, nothing was labeled. For another, atmospheric distortion and cloud cover obliterated parts of lines and curves. The Teal Ruby was capturing direct visual image, rather than infrared (IR) so the things that normally got in the way, got in the way. But McNichols had a practiced eye, and after glancing at the scale being used (printed in the upper right corner of the screen), he realized he was viewing the western coastline of southern South America. The chain of the Andes was obscured by cloud cover, and to the northwest of the continent was another large band of clouds.

The coverage was low. Santiago, Chile, did not appear on his screen. In the upper quadrant was the mass of islands called the *Archipiélago de los Chonos,* caught in a large indentation of the coastline. The lower portion of the screen caught all but the eastern tip of Tierra del Fuego.

With the mouse, McNichols moved a magnifying-glass icon over the area of Punta Arenas and hit the F2 function key. His image zoomed in, and he clearly saw the small town of two thousand or more souls laid out like an irregular chessboard. The nearby national guard air base was what drew his eye, and out of habit, he counted the pairs of wings he saw there.

Oops.

He counted again.

Six aircraft. Four transport types and two smaller jobs.

Didn't seem right.

On his left monitor, McNichols called up another menu, selected "Chile," and on the succeeding menu, picked "Air National Guard."

The inventory of national guard aircraft showed him that, the last time it was checked, in September, there had been fifteen airplanes on hand and accounted for at Punta Arenas. On his right monitor, which he was using as a notepad,

McNichols made a note to himself, and then sat back and followed along with the flight path of the satellite. He didn't have any choice in that regard.

A little later, since the satellite was travelling toward the northeast, with the world turning under it, he checked in on the airport at Santa Cruz, Argentina, which was at the mouth of the Chico River. As the continent bulged, the Atlantic side of his map was just about to go off the screen. Sometimes, he wished he was in a powerful enough position to order satellites repositioned in space, just so his screen maps could be complete.

It was a tiny airstrip, and he counted two airplanes, which wasn't difficult, but when he called up the Argentine inventory, he found that they were short three airplanes.

That wasn't unusual, of course. Airplanes came and went. Some hauled people, some transported cargo.

Some carried guns and rockets and such. Those were the ones he found himself most interested in.

He made another note to himself.

And rode along with the Teal Ruby.

Peeking at airfields every now and then.

29 NOVEMBER

"Weapons. You've got a full two hundred rounds for the two twenty-five-millimeter cannons," Commander Phillip Anderson said, "and you've got four Sidewinders each, just in case you run into an air-to-air situation. Gypsy Moth Five is carrying an IR recon pod. Gypsy Moth Three's got the ECM on her outboard starboard pylon. The bomb load is six Snakeyes apiece on centerline hardpoints. Auxiliary fuel on all craft. Questions?"

Anderson fielded a few questions from his briefing position at the podium in the wing briefing room, located on Deck 1. Cady sat at the back, listening and watching.

Anderson was U.S. Navy, a broad-shouldered and narrow-hipped man who would have been handsome but for the burn scars on his left cheek and temple. He'd picked up those souvenirs when his F-14 Tomcat turned over and slammed into a deck barrier after the failure of his arresting gear. He was a skillful aviator, was gaining a modicum of conservatism along with his age, and served as Cady's wing executive officer in addition to his duties as commander of the 1st Squadron. Major Jake Travers, an Australian, led the 2nd Squadron, the Tiger Barbs.

"Okay, then," Anderson continued, "the weather report.

You've seen it. Blue skies this morning at last, cloudless, and projected to last for a couple days. Visibility limited only by your imagination. A word of caution, gentlemen. The horizon can be deceptive, when all you've got is blue sky and blue ocean. Temp's going to be in the nineties by takeoff, wind's gusting to four knots out of the west, and the barometer's at two-niner-point-seven-six."

Cady paid close attention to his aviators. Only three of the 1st Squadron aviators were accompanying Anderson this morning, and they would go as Gypsy Moths Three, Four, and Five since Cady reserved Gypsy Moth One for himself. Miguel Olivera, out of Spain, was Three; David Stein, an Israeli, was flying Four; and Five would be in the hands of the Egyptian, Captain Solomon Sifra. Capable hands, Cady had so far judged. All of them were jotting notes on their clip-on kneeboards, and he approved of that also. Unlike computers, people found they could not store everything in memory.

After responding to several more questions, Anderson detailed the communications frequencies for command—code-named Jericho, squadron, and air control. Then, he looked to the back of the room and asked, "Any comments, Colonel?"

"None," Cady replied. "Let's go for it."

"Go, guys. Double-check your takeoff weights, please. Let's not have anyone taking a splash."

Carrying their helmets and oxygen masks, the pilots filed out of the room, and Cady got up to follow them, walking with Anderson.

"How are they coming along, Phil?" he asked.

"These are my hard cases, Jim. They don't think as much of each other as they do of themselves, so that's why we're flying together so much."

"Maybe they're putting on an act, so they get more flying time."

"Shit," Anderson said. "You don't, and I don't, believe that one for a minute, boss."

"I'd have done it, in the old days."

"That was you, Shark, and probably me. These guys just don't think they like each other. And they don't like each other because they know the other guy is a worse pilot."

"You still think Stein's the best of the lot?"

"He's hotshit, but the problem is he knows it."

From the briefing room, they crossed a narrow corridor, then exited into the hangar deck. Two aircraft were sitting in the middle of the deck, one behind the other, ready to be shoved onto the elevators, and two Harriers were already on the port and starboard, aft elevators. The squadron members headed for their aircraft, and Cady went along to the port elevator to watch Anderson climb into his bird. The crew chief on Two, a grizzled Brit who was close to sixty, climbed the ladder and helped Anderson with his umbilicals and harness.

The elevator started upward.

After rising two feet, the elevator interlock released and the overhead deck—the phony tank top—began to rise, folding into two sections, and leaning outboard. It was completely out of the way by the time the elevator passed above the main deck and aligned itself vertically with the catwalk. One sailor stepped forward and accordion-folded the protective guardrail on the catwalk. The tow tractor linked to the nosewheel growled, and the Harrier followed it off the elevator and onto the flight deck, turning quickly to line up with the centerline. Yellow-vested flight deck crewmen scurried about, some ducking beneath the wings to pull the red-taped safety pins from the ordnance.

Cady had at one time thought the Harrier an awkward-looking airplane, what with its bicycle landing gear and outboard stabilizing wheels. The high wing was canted downward to each side—the new wing on this model composed of high-strength carbon composite materials. It had a fifty per cent greater fuel capacity than the earlier wing. The horizontal stabilizers had a similar anhedral angle. On these later models, the Harrier III's, the canopy and cockpit had been raised eleven inches to provide the pilot with a better field of view. The nose of the new model was slightly longer and less pointed than earlier aircraft in order to accommodate an ARBS (Angle-Rate Bombing System), a FLIR (Forward-Looking Infrared), the new Blue Vixen radar, and a laser system. The wings and tail contained radar warning systems, and the aft fuselage housed a new flare/chaff dispenser for countering missile attacks. His Harriers and Baker's helicopters were finished in a dove gray that was resistant to visual sighting, and the only insignia was to be found on the fuselage sides—a small UN logo and the aircraft number. If they found themselves in a situation requiring high-profile ID, the ground crews had a supply of giant, economy-size, tape-on United Nations insignia readily to hand.

With the weapons load hanging from the pylons on the drooping wings, she looked especially lethal. Cady had changed his mind about the Harrier. She was beautiful.

She also had more capability than he could take advantage of, flying off the *U Thant*. Up to 9200 pounds of ordnance could be loaded underwing and under the fuselage—16 Mk-82 five hundred-pound iron bombs or ten Paveway laser-guided bombs, for instance, but the takeoff profiles were restricted. Lightly loaded, with her huge flaps and ailerons drooped in the takeoff mode, the Harrier could take off vertically. A fully loaded craft required the STOL (Short Takeoff and Landing) profile, meaning that 1640 feet of dirt, asphalt, or steel runway was needed to get her airborne.

They had had to make some compromises in order to fit the Harrier into the mission profile of the ship. Stepping off the elevator as it began to descend for its next load, Cady looked forward, toward the bow end of the catwalk and their first compromise. The catwalk was already raised by its huge hydraulic jacks into takeoff configuration, creating a smoothly curving ramp—a ski jump—that gave the airplane a decided boost in lift before it departed the ship.

Their second compromise involved weapons load. By reducing the weapons load to four thousand pounds, they had shortened the STOL takeoff run to match what the ship had to offer, provided an adequate safety margin, and increased the combat radius to 550 miles. A fully loaded bird could only manage a hundred miles, with an hour of loiter time.

Compromises had been made, partly because of their lack of airborne tankers for refueling, but Cady didn't believe that, for their purposes, a more flexible aircraft existed. She could carry the weight of ground, ship, or air attack weapons; she could play helicopter; she could make supersonic speeds; and she could handle an air defense role.

A deck crewman in a yellow vest handed him a headset just as Anderson's turbofan was fired up. The headset allowed him to listen in on the aircraft-to-ship dialogue as well as protecting his hearing from the thunderous roar of the Rolls-Royce turbofan.

Coiling his comm cord as he traversed the catwalk, Cady walked aft and turned onto the smaller and narrower cross-ship catwalk, to get out of the direct wake of Gypsy Moth Two.

Halfway down the flight deck, on his railed platform off to the right, Shaker Adams stood up from the canvas sling chair he usually carried with him. He had a hook on his belt from which he hung the chair when the wind was high and his hands were full of flashlights.

With his brakes locked up, Anderson ran the turbofan up to full power, held it for a minute, then backed it down.

On his headset, Cady heard the landing officer, who in lieu

of a catapult, also liked to serve as the takeoff officer, saying, "Who we got there?"

"Gypsy Moth Two, Shaker."

"Okay, Flip"—Anderson's nickname after flipping his Tomcat—"how's she reading?"

"All greens, ready to hop."

"Give me your weight."

"Two-six-five-three-two-oh."

"Run her up and hop to it then," Adams said, offering a snappy and traditional salute.

Behind his canopy, Anderson returned it.

Cady felt the power of the jet engine in the vibration of the open gridwork of the catwalk as Anderson advanced the throttle. He saw the four vectoring nozzles come down to about twenty percent.

Anderson released the brakes, and the Harrier leapt forward, building speed quickly, racing toward the raised lip of the ramp.

The aircraft hit the ramp, nosed upward, left it, and clawed her way into the sky. Anderson immediately retracted his landing gear, and after his speed built up, his flaps.

"Two's away," he said on the radio as the fighter climbed away in a spiral to the left.

Gypsy Moth Three was already being towed onto the flight deck from her elevator on the starboard side, and when he looked down, Cady saw that Four was being chocked in place on the port elevator.

He relinquished his headset to a crewman, turned, and entered the superstructure through a hatchway. Pulling a cigar from his breast pocket, he clamped it tightly in his teeth, then pulled off his sunglasses and stuck them in the same pocket. Cady hadn't smoked in ten years, but he kept a supply of pacifiers around.

He took the elevator to the Bridge Deck, got off, and found

his way to the CIC. Slipping through the light trap, Cady waited a moment for his eyes to adjust from the bright sunlight of day.

Eames was sitting in a cushioned chair at the main console, and she had Anderson ID'd on the screen. A second before she filtered out the image, he saw *Dover,* the second mini-sub, as a computer icon. A hundred and fifty miles to the west was an Air India cargo plane. Several ships were in the vicinity, though none was closer than seventy miles.

Eames had the radio dialogue between the aircraft and the air controller—in the compartment next door—coming in on the overhead speaker.

In less than ten minutes—they were getting better and better at the takeoff sequence, all four aircraft were wheels-up and joining in formation at ten thousand feet. Eames's big screen showed them in the right echelon formation that Anderson had briefed.

Cady slipped up behind her chair.

"Good morning, Colonel."

She hadn't even looked at him, as far as he knew, and she didn't then. She kept her eyes on the screen.

"And a good day to you, Major Eames. How are we doing?"

"They're going through angels ten, on the briefed heading, so the first part's all right," she said.

"When do we do it to them?"

Cady had agreed to her first suggestion at their afternoon meeting yesterday. It was a simple program that she could quickly write and implement, involving only one hostile simulation. It would serve as the starting point, and she would enhance the program in the days ahead.

"Oh, let's give them some distance from the ship," she said. "Do you want a chair?"

"If it's going to take a while, I guess so."

Cady went to the back bulkhead and grabbed one of the

castered chairs parked there. He rolled it up next to Eames and sat down.

She looked at him for the first time.

"I didn't know you smoked."

"I don't. Not any more."

"You don't light that thing?"

"No, but it sure as hell tastes good when I worry."

"Do you worry?"

She was full of questions. He had noticed that yesterday, too, during what was their first real meeting together. He had kind of taken her, though not her position, for granted before.

"In the good old days, all I had to worry about was my own a . . . ah, myself and my backseater. Sam Monmouth has made it possible for me to worry about three hundred bodies, many with minds attached. I don't know whether he was boosting my career or getting back at me."

She smiled at him, and he thought it was for the first time. He glanced at the data input operator, an Irish woman wearing a headset and an enlisted collar insignia that he didn't recognize. She was resting back in her chair, waiting for action, and she gave him a nod.

"Hi," he said to her.

"Hello, Colonel."

"Sergeant . . . ?"

"Trish O'Hara."

"Glad to meet you, Sergeant."

Everywhere he turned, he kept running into more women. Back on the *Ranger,* during the Vietnam era, when it was a bastion of male egotism, they wouldn't have lasted long.

He grinned back at Eames, for lack of anything else to say.

"Is this a career booster, this cruise?" she asked.

"I don't think they'll be very specific in your dossier, Terri, but you can be damned sure that the right people will know all about it."

She shrugged. "I don't know how they handle this kind of classified assignment."

"Generally, they keep it classified. At least, my service does."

He saw her sniffing at the cigar, and when she looked back at her screen, he resignedly extracted it from the familiar clamp of his teeth and dumped it in a leg pocket of his flight suit.

Cady thought he had adapted pretty well to women in the services, but he sometimes resented the fact that it was obviously *he* who was supposed to change the most. His first tour at sea, on the *Ranger*, was vastly different from this one.

Over the speaker, he heard Anderson reporting in, "Beehive, Gypsy Moth Two at waypoint one. Changing course."

"Roger that, Gypsy," the air controller said.

The four symbols on the CIC display all turned left, onto a heading of 322 degrees. They were making 450 knots. While the Harrier could manage 647 miles per hour at sea level, they were cautious about it. At that speed, the turbofan sucked fuel like a hot kid with a cold Coke. While aerial refueling was possible for the fighter, those arrangements with a member air force or navy had to be made pretty far in advance. In their current position, en route to the South China Sea, there weren't going to be many tankers available, though in a pinch, he could probably get some KC-10 Extenders out of Hickam in Hawaii. In the good old days, he could have called Anderson Air Base in Guam. There were a lot of good old days that would be no more. Many active duty pilots in the Navy, the Marines, and the Air Force were being RIF'd (Reduction in Force) and transferred to reserve units as the politicians decided the end of the Cold War called for less vigilance. Those strategies in the United States and elsewhere made the *U Thant*'s mission all the more important he thought. Bringing reserve flyers and equipment back to combat readiness would take a long time. If the American public had thought it took forever to raise the forces necessary to take on Saddam in the Persian Gulf, the next time might seem more like infinity.

"How about now?" he asked.

"Getting anxious, are we? Let's let them get settled in some more. There's nothing like boredom to increase the surprise."

Eames lifted a headset from a hook on the console, pushed the hair away from her left ear, and settled it on her head. She pressed the transmit button on the deck with her toe and said, "Gypsy Moth Flight, Jericho."

Jericho was the code name for the CIC when it was employed as a ground control intercept director.

"Jericho, Gypsy Moth Two."

"Let's go to data link, Gypsy."

"Roger, Jericho. Going now."

The Irish sergeant sat up and flipped a few switches.

Now the four aviators were seeing on their multifunction screens the same data that the ship was seeing. Using the data link precluded the aircraft having to emit their own radar emanations, which drew attention and, possibly, hostile radar-homing missiles.

"What do you see, Two?" she asked.

"I see us, you, and an Air India freight train. There's a few ships spotted around."

"Roger that. Jericho standing by."

They waited twelve minutes, and then Eames said, "All right, Trish. Copy the scene and add Sim-One."

The sergeant copied the real-time imagery on the screen to memory, dumped in the programmed simulation, then brought it up on the big screen.

Eames switched to the intercom and said, "Bridge, CIC."

Monmouth's voice came back, "Bridge."

"Simulation underway, sir."

"Roger."

A small green triangle appeared magically in the lower left quadrant one hundred and twenty miles southeast of Gypsy Moth Flight. It was a hundred miles south of the ship, and it was unidentified on the screen.

Cady depressed the stopwatch stud on his watch.

At their altitude, they had sufficient radar range, but nearly forty seconds went by before anyone noticed the triangle, and Cady noted that it was Solomon Sifra who did. He wrote a note in his battered black notebook.

"Jericho, Gypsy Five."

"Go Five," Eames said.

"I've got a bogie at eight o'clock, one twenty out on our position."

"Attempting to identify now, Five."

Cady watched Eames's hands as her fingers nimbly fluttered over her keyboard. A few identification factors began to appear in the outlined box next to the green triangle on the screen.

"Gypsy Flight, Jericho. We've got an unidentified target at our bearing one-seven-four, range eight-seven nautical miles, speed seven-two-zero knots, closing on Beehive. Go to one-three-zero, full military power, for intercept."

"Roger that, Jericho," Anderson said. "Gypsy Flight going one-three-zero."

"Cut in the Tactical Two frequency, Trish," Eames told the sergeant.

The overhead speakers began to issue the dialogue on the inter-plane frequency used by the four aircraft.

"Damn, Sol, how'd you see that?"

"By keeping my eyes wide open, Flaming Star. It is possible that you might have done the same."

"Flaming Star" was David Stein, the Israeli.

"Can it," Anderson said on the squadron net. "Three, you're losing spacing. Pull it up."

The green triangle on the screen suddenly radiated an "S" symbol, indicating a search radar in operation.

"Range to Beehive now seven-four," Eames broke in. "Bogie is searching on J-band, probably High Lark radar. Tentative ID is Flogger."

"Jesus!" Stein said on the Tactical Two frequency.

"Flogger" was the NATO code name for either the MiG-23 or MiG-27, the MiG-27 being a dedicated ground attack aircraft.

Cady was aware of Eames's little test, and it impressed him. The export version MiG wasn't shipped with the High Lark radar, but with a shorter-range version. No one in the flight questioned her identification factor, though, and Cady wrote another note on his pad.

"That's sneaky," he said to her.

"Yes, isn't it?"

On the screen, Gypsy Flight was now crossing the bow of the *U Thant,* just about as far from the hostile target as was the ship.

The green triangle did not divert from its course.

Eames made the pretext of attempting to contact the unidentified aircraft several times, but got no response.

"Under the ROE," Eames told Anderson, "you are free to engage. Jericho orders weapons released."

The Rules of Engagement provided that the *U Thant's* aircraft could defend themselves, fire if fired upon. The exception to that rule was the event that the ship herself was in imminent danger of being attacked, and the boundary line for that decision was currently one hundred miles.

"Gypsy Two. Copy weapons released and engage bogie."

On the squadron frequency, Anderson ordered, "Gypsies,

take combat spread. Five, you are lead for Four. Take your element left."

"Five," was the confirming response.

The icons on the screen began to separate, and Solomon Sifra led the second element, with Stein as his wingman, on a divergent path.

"Which ones do you want, Colonel?" Eames asked.

"Take the second element," he said.

Tapping the keyboard, Eames changed the course of the green triangle abruptly. It turned off its interception path with the ship and toward an interception with Sifra's element.

At fifty miles of separation, she pressed another key, and the "S" symbol changed to "H," signifying the High Lark radar in attack mode.

"Gypsy Flight," she said, "the bogie's gone to attack radar. Confirm MiG-23."

"Take him out, Five," Anderson ordered.

"Five."

The AIM-9L Sidewinder air-to-air missiles had a ten-mile effective range, and they could attack a hostile craft from all angles.

On the squadron frequency, Cady heard Sifra tell his wingman, "Star, take a greater spacing and arm two. Back me up, now."

"Why don't you back me up?" Stein replied. "I can get this bastard in the first pass. Better, you head on back to the ship."

Cady jotted a note in his book.

The gap between the icons on the screen continued to close, seventeen miles apart.

"Jericho, Gypsy Two."

"Go, Two," Eames said.

"We've got him vectored away from Beehive, now. Do we give him a warning shot?"

Cady wrote another note. Anderson's new conservatism was showing.

"Negative, Two. Engage."

At seven miles of distance, Sifra called Anderson.

"Two, Five. If this guy had Aphids or Apexes, he'd have released on me by now."

"Engage, Five."

"Five, roger."

A few seconds later, an agitated Sifra reported, "Two, there is nothing there. I cannot get an infrared lock."

"What?"

"It is a ghost."

"Gypsy Flight," Eames said, "Jericho. The simulation is ended. RTB."

Anderson's voice was a bit tense as he replied, "Gypsy Two, roger. Gypsies, return to base. Form on me."

Cady almost patted Eames on the back, and then decided that might not be one of his better tactical decisions.

He said, "Thanks, Terri. This is going to give us a few conversational topics."

"I can certainly see that," she said.

BUENOS AIRES, ARGENTINA
1215 HOURS LOCAL

The outdoor tables of the May Day Cafe were protected by large yellow umbrellas, but Juan Silvera had moved his white metal chair out of the shade and into the sun. The heat felt good on his face.

He sat in his chair with his face turned up to the sun and his hands resting on his knees, an image of total relaxation. His eyes were closed, but he was aware of the movements around him, the luncheon crowd beginning to build, waiters slipping between the tables, his guest not yet arrived.

Silvera was wearing a light tropical worsted suit in pale beige, a white shirt, and a figured tie his wife had purchased for him that he thought a little garish, but which she insisted was perfect. Silvera had always been conservative in his appearance, his profession, and his politics.

Until two years before, he had been an army colonel, and he frequently missed the protective coloration, status, and authority of a uniform. His current position as president of the Front for South American Determination did not yet afford him the prestige he had enjoyed as one of hundreds of colonels. There were too many small political groups on the South American continent, some with prominent acronyms and many with obscure images. The FSAD was not an organization that enjoyed household recognition.

Yet.

One of the reasons Silvera had obtained his presidency could be found in his physical appearance. His profile was lean and aristocratic; his bright smile and lively, liquid brown eyes the ingredients of cinema stardom. With smooth, olive skin, dark brown hair that had shaped itself into a decided widow's peak, and slightly pouty lips, he was decidedly photogenic. Though there were a few women who got dizzy when meeting him for the first time, Silvera was mostly faithful to his wife, Lucia. The ruling council of the FSAD, a group of three—including himself—had determined that public relations and a clean, sincere, attractive appearance would be important for the group's spokesman when the television cameras and newspaper photographs became daily aspects of their lives.

Silvera had been selected, also, because in crisis situations, he was unflappable. He did not get excited about many things, much less ordinary little barriers that cropped up in the daily life of a business or an individual. Many of his acquaintances remembered well the time when his son, now twenty years old, struck his head on a railing and fell from a fishing boat into the Gulf of San Matias. With others of his fishing party panicking, and with Lucia screaming to high heaven, Juan Silvera had calmly removed his shoes and his windbreaker, dove over the side, and pulled the seven-year-old to safety.

When he sensed the approach of his luncheon companion, Silvera sat up and scooted his chair back into the shade of the umbrella. He took a sip from the tall glass of lemonade that dripped beads of frosty perspiration on the glass top of the table.

"Good afternoon, Colonel," Emilio Suarez said as he settled into a chair on the opposite side of the table.

Silvera did not really need the military title any longer, but Suarez, who had been an air force major, was enamored of rank. In the FSAD, Suarez had been declared a colonel, and it was that action, more than any other, that had convinced him to permanently associate himself with the organization. Silvera was careful to nurture it.

"Good day, Colonel."

"I apologize for being late, but the traffic. . . ." Suarez waved a hand at the stream of automobiles scurrying down the side street that fronted the cafe. A blue cloud of exhaust was suspended in the windless street above the cars.

"I understand. It is quite all right. I was enjoying the sun."

Their waiter appeared, and Suarez, after a sidelong glance at Silvera's glass, ordered tea. He also ordered the daily special, and Silvera opted for a salad. At sixty-one years of age, he found himself watching his diet carefully in order to maintain an appearance of being in his early fifties. It was necessary for the cameras.

He knew Suarez quite well. The man still utilized his full name of Emilio Esteban Suarez de Suruca, and was part of a well-known, and well-established, aristocratic family that owned vast ranches in northern Argentina. With no head for business, and with no desire to delve in the arts, Suarez had chosen a military life, a selection that had disappointed parents and grandparents, though not his siblings. He prepared himself by obtaining his flying license and jet certification before entering the air force, thereby assuring his selection as a pilot. The man liked to view himself as an exciting, danger-daring buccaneer. And though he was exceptionally capable as a pilot, he was less so as an administrator. His promotions, and his career, had come to a standstill at major and at squadron commander. It was the FSAD that gave him hope for a grander future.

He was in charge of air operations for FSAD, and while Silvera kept a close eye on him, appeared to be handling his duties with extreme efficiency. He was determined to succeed, perhaps as much for the sake of his familial status as for his personal ambition.

Suarez was not imposing as a person. He was shorter than the average Argentinean, and his head seemed oversized for his torso. He wore the droopy Zapata-styled mustache as if it were a badge of honor, but it was plastered on a round, moon-shaped face with great, bovine eyes that peered over a bulbous nose. His slight body, however, was muscular. The man had stamina, and that quality was certain to be necessary in the next weeks.

As soon as Suarez's tea had been served, and Silvera's lemonade freshened, Silvera said, "We are at D-day, plus twenty-three hours. I trust that you will report compliance with the schedule."

Suarez grinned, which was not necessarily reassuring. He said, however, "Absolutely on schedule, Colonel. There have been no breakdowns and no delays, though we expected them. All units are moving exactly as planned."

Silvera smiled, which drew the attention of a shapely blonde *turista* two tables away. "That is wonderful news!"

Suarez looked at his watch. "And in the next two hours the heavy craft will begin Phase One. I will check on them at three o'clock and call you with another report."

"I shall look forward to it."

"We have set history in motion, *Presidente*."

Silvera already knew that.

UNS U THANT
1311 HOURS LOCAL

Jean d'Argamon, commander of the 21st Submarine Detachment, often felt the need to keep his skills current, and frequently he would supplant one or the other of his sub commanders for the eight- to twelve-hour surveillance deployments. This afternoon, he gave Lieutenant Oscar Moritz a break.

D'Argamon and his two crew members, Junior Lieutenant Ivan Suretsev and Petty Officer Erik Magnuson, did the premission inspection together. Suretsev, never certain whether he belonged permanently to the Commonwealth of Independent States Navy or the Russian Navy, was an intense young officer with a great deal of experience in nuclear attack submarines. Magnuson, with a strong Swedish accent, had been a munitions expert prior to his assignment aboard the *U Thant,* and he had had to be schooled in the electronic portion of his duties.

The three of them walked around the moon pool, listening to the heavy hydraulic system as it moved the hull doors into the open position. Only the *Calais* was in the pool, and they surveyed the hull with the care of men who would trust their lives to its integrity.

On the far side, near a workbench cluttered with the tools, diagnostic instruments, and replacement parts necessary to the maintenance of the subs, d'Argamon went carefully over the logs that attested to the state of the batteries, the calibration of the instruments, and the testing of watertight seals. He handed the clipboard to Suretsev when he was done and accepted the ordnance and electronics log from Magnuson. He looked it over.

"Do you see any anomalies, Seaman?"

"None, sir. The depth transponder was changed out, as requested."

"Good. How about you, Lieutenant?"

Suretsev placed his initials on the log form and handed it back. "All is in order, Commander."

D'Argamon scratched his own initials next to the lieutenant's and gave both logs to the petty officer in charge of maintenance.

"Let us sail, then."

All three of them were dressed in the typical uniform of the naval complement—blue jumpsuits with the UN shoulder patch. Beneath the uniform, however, they wore thick woolen underwear. Each also wore two pairs of wool socks with his heavy rubber-soled boots. It could become extremely cold below the surface, even though the submarines were only certified for 2500 feet of depth.

At the edge of the moon pool, d'Argamon stepped onto the short gangway with its safety railing of a chain stretched between stanchions. He crossed quickly and bent to lift the hatch in the conning tower. With practiced agility, he descended the narrow ladder and stood upright on the interior deck. His crew members followed him, and Magnuson pulled the hatch closed and dogged it tight.

The space was confining. Most of the hull was taken up with ballast tanks, the huge trays of batteries, and the torpedo tubes. While there was a utility diesel engine for propulsion and electric generation, the mini-sub operated primarily on battery power. Typically, with average draw on the energy source, the sub could manage a twenty-hour voyage on electric power alone.

Overall, the submarine was thirty feet long and ten feet wide, not counting her diving planes. The compartment housing her crew was much more cramped than that—eight feet long by seven feet wide. The lower portion of the cockpit was in the hull, and the upper three feet took up what, in a normal submarine, would be called the conning tower. It did not rise vertically from the hull deck, however; the bulge on top of the hull was treated aerodynamically, and the shape enhanced the sub's top speed of twenty-seven knots. Emplaced in the forward slope of the tower were three triple-thick, acrylic plastic portholes which gave them a true view of the sea. Their vision could be augmented, when necessary at depth, by inset floodlights which produced six million candlepower. Additionally, a video camera lens with a forty-degree axis of movement was located in the bow, and its image could be displayed on the pilot's and copilot's multifunction screens as well as being broadcast to the mother ship.

There were two seats forward, overlooking a vast array of gauges, digital readouts, and controls. In the aft section of the compartment was a seat facing abeam, ninety degrees to the controller's seats. All three seats were heavily cushioned, attempting to provide the utmost comfort over the long hours of deployment. The aft seat faced a console that governed weapons control, sonar, and life support systems, and behind the console was a miniature head which was nearly impossible to get into unless one was feeling intense bladder pressure.

D'Argamon, as he was known to do, abruptly changed his mind about taking the left seat. He eased into the pads of the right seat, and said, "Ivan, you will be mission commander."

Suretsev grinned and took the left seat.

The commander knew that the Russian did not mind these little trials of his ability in the least. He wanted to prove himself, and d'Argamon suspected that, when his three-year tour of duty was completed, he would volunteer for another. It would give him a sub command and delay his return to the Black Sea and an uncertain future.

They all donned headsets and powered up their instrument panels, and d'Argamon, as copilot, called off the checklist he had displayed on his screen. It took nearly six minutes to run through the start-up procedures, setting circuit breakers and switches, examining readouts for the correct settings. D'Argamon paid particular attention to Magnuson's report of oxygen tank levels and flow, as well as the positive operation of the lithium hydroxide blower, which scrubbed their atmosphere of poisonous carbon dioxide.

Finally, he said, "Checklist complete, Ivan."

"Thank you, Commander." Switching to his radio channel, Suretsev checked in with the air controller who, incongruously, also managed the launch and recovery of submarines. With this assignment, they were definitely exploring new territory and new methodologies. "Beehive, this is Dolphin. We are prepared for deployment."

"Dolphin, the ship is currently making a speed of two-two knots. Proceed when ready."

"Dolphin descending."

Both launch and recovery, when the *U Thant* was under way, could be tricky. The water in the moon pool was essentially moving at the same momentum as the ship, though the water below it was not. As the submarine blew ballast and dove, the pilot had to add sufficient power to the big propeller to match the speed of the ship. Otherwise, diving into the slower waters would bash the submarine back into the ship's hull.

D'Argamon placed his hands lightly on the joystick controls in front of him, prepared to instantly assume control if it were necessary.

It was not.

Suretsev punched the button to blow ballast, grabbed his joysticks, and as the bow submerged and the water level climbed up the portholes, began to ease in forward power. After a count of five, he shoved in full power, and the sub dove out of the belly of the ship.

"Very well done, Ivan."

"Thank you, sir. Magnuson, switch to VLF and deploy the antenna."

"Aye, sir."

The technician changed the communications mode from high frequency to very low frequency. Water did strange things to light and radio signals; it bent them in crazy directions, and the standard AM, FM, HF, VHF, and UHF bands were useless to them until they had the antennas on their reconnaissance pod deployed on the surface. For emergency contact with the ship, they had to rely on the VLF band transmitting through a thin, towed antenna, which was also ultra slow. Communications were accomplished by short telex messages, keyed in by way of Magnuson's console keyboard.

"We will want six hundred feet of depth," Suretsev said.

"Six hundred," d'Argamon echoed and began to set up the adjustments on the ballast tanks so that when the pilot leveled the diving planes, the sub would maintain the correct buoyancy.

The electric motors made very little noise, and the commander could hear Magnuson tapping away on his keyboard, sending the short, coded message that their launch had been successful and that *Dover* could return to the ship for recovery in twenty minutes.

The speed indicator showed that they were making twenty-seven knots, their top speed, moving faster than the *U Thant* in order to reach their station thirty miles ahead of her.

When the depth readout displayed the numerals "-604," d'Argamon relaxed back in his seat and perused the portholes. A grouper flashed past to starboard, and the *Calais* disrupted a school of orange-and-blue fish so quickly that he could not identify them. At this depth, the light of the sun still provided a halfhearted illumination in the clear and unpolluted waters of the Pacific. It was not until they reached depths of 1100 or 1200 feet that their world lost color and changed to inky blackness.

Twenty minutes later, Magnuson deployed the reconnaissance pod which was mounted on the aft end of the hull, between the two rudders. On the end of its fiber-optic, Kevlar shielded cable, the pod rose to the surface to be towed behind them. As Magnuson activated his systems, he announced then, "I have HF radio, sir . . . now radar . . . now sonar."

D'Argamon turned in his seat to look back at the twin screens on the console, one displaying radar data, and the other the sonar readings. Both screens seemed serene.

He twisted a rotary switch on his instrument panel and brought up the radar information on his own multifunction screen. There were a couple of airplanes at the extreme range of the radar coverage, and as he watched, one of Cady's 2nd Squadron aircraft took off from the ship.

"Commander," Suretsev said, "I have the watch."

"Very well, Ivan. I leave you to it."

On the long deployments, the crews tried to relieve each other in order to overcome boredom, and the copilot's seat was often the napping seat.

D'Argamon loved this. If he could not have intense action, he was always relieved to be at sea, or rather, below it. The turmoil of waves was left behind, and the silky smooth subsurface ride was immensely comforting.

The only thing that might prove more interesting, he had often considered, was to bring some lucky lady with him one day.

PUERTO WILLIAMS, ISLA NAVARINO, *CHILE*
1945 HOURS LOCAL

Ahead and below his left wing, Roberto Tellez saw the single narrow airstrip appear out of the haze that gripped the islands below.

It was little used, and it was located on an almost uninhabited island south of the *Isla Grande Tierra del Fuego*. It actually belonged to Chile, though it was south of the half of Tierra del Fuego that was under Argentine control. Sixty kilometers to the south was Cape Horn.

Though summer was fast coming on, the thousands of islands, straits, bays, and waterways were caught in fog and overcast, and they appeared forbidding. It was a fascinatingly beautiful place, hypnotic in the beauty of a random ray of sunshine striking sheer cliffs plunging into the sea and the pale greenery of moss clinging to hard rock. There was also peril here, with treacherous waters and rugged islands that could defeat life in a matter of moments.

Tellez's advance party of pilots and ground crews had arrived hours before, as scheduled, if he believed the evidence of the radio beacon he had been following for the past half hour.

The cloud cover blanked out the airstrip once again, and Tellez checked the right side of his cockpit canopy. The three Tornados were still in formation off his right wing, though the fourth, flown by Alberto Ramon, was almost obscured by the clouds.

"Puma Flight, this is One."

A series of clicks in his earphones told him that each had heard him.

"We will enter trail formation now and then turn to the left for the approach to the field."

Again, he received the microphone clicks in reply.

Tellez banked his big Tornado fighter-bomber to the left and eased back on the twin throttles. The Tornado, designed and constructed by a consortium of companies from the United Kingdom, West Germany, and Italy, and similar to the American F-111, carried Texas Instruments multimode ground-mapping radar and Decca Type 72 Doppler navigation radar. A GEC Avionics terrain-following E-scope allowed him to use an automatic approach mode.

He switched it on and adjusted his mind to following the images. A low series of hills appeared.

He checked his rearview mirror and saw that the others had swung in behind him, though Ramon was out of sight in the clouds.

Rolling out of his turn when he saw what appeared to be the landing strip appear on the radar screen, Tellez backed off yet more on the throttles. The roar of the twin turbofans eased. Automatically, the wings moved forward from the swept-wing position to the landing configuration.

And he broke out of the cloud cover, with the runway in sight some six kilometers ahead of him.

He lined up on it, noting the seven aircraft parked off to one side of the strip.

"It is exactly as I expected it to be," Jesus Ramirez, the radar intercept officer in the backseat said over the ICS, the Internal Communications System. "A large collection of nothing."

"Nonsense, Jesus. It is an exciting frontier. A jumping-off place to stardom and destiny."

"You are an impossible romantic, Roberto."

"I am that," he agreed as he deployed flaps and landing gear. He was landing heavy, with a full load of ordnance, and he needed all of the lift he could muster in addition to an increased throttle setting.

At the last moment, he decided the runway appeared shorter than he thought it was, and he cut the throttles and dumped the air brakes. The heavy fighter settled onto the packed-dirt strip with a trifle more impact than he had planned. He let it run for a bit, then eased reverse thrust in as he passed the parked aircraft.

They were all painted in camouflage colors, and matched his own airplane in tone, hue, and intensity.

They looked magnificent, and Roberto Tellez thought it was going to be a grand, if short, war.

1 DECEMBER

Captain Samuel Monmouth was meeting in his quarters with David George when he was interrupted by a call on his scrambled telephone.

"Hold on for a second, Dave," he said, rising from his chair at the table and crossing to the sideboard placed against the interior bulkhead. There were two telephones mounted on the wall next to the intercom panel above the sideboard, and he picked up the red phone and said, "Monmouth."

"Captain, Communications. You have a priority call from Gold Mine."

"Thank you. Put it through."

He waited while the connections were made. The *U Thant's* international voice and data communications were conducted over twenty satellite channels dedicated to her by the U.S. Defense Department. Their primary system for communications was the Fleet Satellite Communications System (FLTSATCOM) which was composed of four geostationary satellites. As backup, and as the chief data transfer system, the ship was using Milstar. The Military Strategic-Tactical and Relay system was the newest thing in the skies and would eventually supersede all of the older satellite constellations. Milstars were placed in supersynchonous orbits of 110,000 miles in order to increase their invulnerability to antisatellite missiles, and they were nearly immune to electromagnetic pulse and laser attack.

Monmouth recalled the code of the day while he waited, and finally a voice came through, echoing with the effects of the scrambling. Still, he recognized it as that of Sir Charles Bentley, who was the Peacekeeper Committee's chairman of operations, Monmouth's immediate boss.

"Gold Mine," Bentley said.

"Flagstaff," he said, providing his code name for the month, just changed. In January, it would change to something new and bizarre dreamed up by a computer's random search of a dictionary.

"Thursday?"

"Mairzy Doats," Monmouth said, providing the daily-changed authentication code.

"I say, Captain, this seems to be getting faster."

"I suppose it's practice, Sir Charles."

"Yes. Well. It seems as if we might have a problem on the island of Mindanao."

"Sir."

"A bit of communist insurgency. You would think that they might have learned by now that the movement is dead, would you not, Captain?"

"I should think so," Monmouth told him. Every time he talked to the chairman, he found himself falling into the man's speech patterns.

"At any rate, the Philippines president has asked us to stand by, should the need arise for either a show of power or some rather forceful assistance, and the committee has agreed to the request. We're ordering you to take up a position a hundred kilometers southeast of the island."

"I will alter course immediately, Sir Charles."

"Very well. And shortly, you will be receiving a data package with most of the particulars."

They signed off and Monmouth called the bridge on the intercom and ordered the change in course.

He went back to his chair at the table and sat down opposite the expectant face of David George.

"I'd brush up on your maps of the Philippines, Commander, especially that of Mindanao."

"Mindanao, Captain?"

"Sounds like a brushfire to me, but perhaps we'll be needed."

"I'll do that, sir," George said.

Lieutenant Commander David George had been born in Sydney, Australia, but had moved to Los Angeles when he was nine years old, following a father who achieved minor stardom in the movies as a character actor and who was now a director of some note. David George had graduated from the University of California at San Diego where he had become involved with the activities at the Scripps Institute of Oceanography in La Jolla. Eventually, his interest in things sub-seaworthy had led him to the Navy and finally to his command of the ship's twenty-four-man SEAL detachment.

He was a physical fitness freak, an obsession that was essential to his profession, and it showed in the steel-like musculature of his forearms, the hard slabs of his cheeks, and the ropy muscles of his neck. He wore his blond hair short, and his blue eyes were flat, giving away nothing. In one of his father's movies, Monmouth thought, he could have portrayed either the hero or the villain, but probably the villain.

"Let's go on with your report, Dave."

"Yes, sir." There was only a little of Australia left in his accent, but enough that the three members of his team from Australia had taken to him immediately. The others hailed from Great Britain, Russia, Italy, France, Spain, Japan, South Korea, and New Zealand. Technically, of course, they were not United States Navy SEALs, but the SEAL portion had stuck, and now they were UN SEALs.

"We've been utilizing the moon pool, with the hull doors closed, for training sessions, Captain, but that's a trifle confining. What I really need is for the ship to stop for a few hours and let us work at depth."

"How long would you need?"

"Ideally, three hours every other day for a couple weeks. Realistically, sir, three hours any time you can spare it."

"I'll take it under advisement, Dave, and we'll see if we can't work something out."

"Thank you, sir. On weapons training, we've finally got everyone using M-16s and Uzis, though there was a hell of a lot of resistance in the beginning. My ROK marine and my Kiwi have proven to be great buddies, and they've made a superb demolitions team. There's a great deal of competition among team members, but I suppose that's to be expected."

"Anything else pressing?"

"We haven't been able to make any parachute jumps since our two weeks in San Diego. I'd like to arrange that sometime."

Monmouth thought about it.

"How about, Dave, if we loaded you on the Seahawks, took you a couple hours out ahead of us, and dumped you in the ocean?"

George's normally stoic face blossomed with his grin. "That'd be great, Captain, really super!"

PUERTO WILLIAMS, ISLA NAVARINO, *CHILE*
1100 HOURS LOCAL

Unless it was Antarctica, Colonel Emilio Suarez could not think of any place in the world as desolate as this thin strip

of dirt on an island in the land of fire. It was not even suitable
for raising sheep, as they did on the northern part of Tierra
del Fuego, though they went ahead and raised sheep anyway.
On the eastern side of the chain of the Andes Mountains, the
weather was considerably more temperate than the west, but
it still was not a place he would choose to live.

The wind was the worst. It never stopped blowing, or had
not since he had been there, and a thick haze of dust was
continually in the air. All around him were low hills, but they
seemed to offer no protection from the incessant wind. A kilometer to the north was the coast where wind-whipped waves
marked the channel between *Isla Navarino* and *Isla Grande
Tierra del Fuego*. Over the rise to the west and several kilometers away was the village of Port Williams where, according
to his information, 950 people actually lived. He found it difficult to believe that anyone would want to live here.

And he thanked the Lord that their stopover would be short-
lived.

At times like these, Suarez was apt to recall with some
fondness the flat *pampas* where he had grown up. Often, he
would think that he should have remained there, but then he
would also vividly recall his arrogant and superior brothers.
Were he still on the ranch, he would be no more than a hired
man, begging for his share. It was far better to be engaged
in a profession that would have an effect on the history of
the world.

Across the narrow airstrip from him, his air force was neatly
aligned fifty meters off the runway. Behind them, ground
crewmen were attempting to erect tents, and they were having
a difficult time in the wind.

Suarez had to lean hard to his left, into the wind, in order
to remain standing himself.

Still, if he ignored the landscape, the scene he was viewing was fabulous. He had almost come to believe that he would never see all of the aircraft assembled in one spot.

Near the western end of the airstrip were six C-130 Hercules transports for moving the massive amounts of supplies they would require: food, armament, replacement parts, and two of the missile batteries for initial defense. Next to them were parked seven KC-130 tanker versions of the Hercules. They had once been the property of the United States Marines, but through a chain of front companies, had been acquired as surplus, then fully rebuilt for use by the FSAD. There were two more of the aerial tankers, which would not make the final leg of the journey, but serve as their pipeline to the mainland from this island. They had not yet arrived, and if everything went as smoothly and as rapidly as Suarez thought that it would, they would likely be unneeded.

Behind the C-130s was a small mountain of supplies, protected under canvas, and a half-acre of fuel bladders containing jet fuel. This materiel was excess at the moment, the overage they had been unable to load aboard the transports. Subsequent trips would be required to pick it up.

Roberto Tellez's Tornados, the Puma Squadron, were next in line. Tellez had brought four in the day before yesterday, and the last four had flown in this morning. The Jaguar Squadron, which Suarez himself would lead, was composed of French-built Mirages, twelve of them. They were an odd collection of 2000B, 2000C, and 2000P models, in addition to the Mirage IIIs.

Suarez's air force also included several heavy helicopters—Aérospatiale Super Frelons, a Gazelle, and a Mystère-Falcon business jet. Except for the Kamov Ka-27 Helix helicopter assigned to the destroyer, the helicopters would be transshipped partially disassembled and reassembled on-site, and the Falcon was currently at the disposal of President Silvera.

As soon as the fighters had landed, each group within minutes of their prearranged schedule, the ordnance men on board the Hercules transports had begun fitting weapons. Not all of the fighters had been allowed to leave their original bases with weaponry.

Now, Suarez could see that most of the Tornados had been outfitted with four Sky Flash air-to-air missiles, the Cerebus jamming pod on the right wing, the BOZ-101 chaff and flare dispenser on the left wing, four Beluga cluster bombs on outboard wing pylons, and a multipurpose weapons dispenser under the fuselage. The armorers were currently loading twenty-seven-millimeter rounds for the IWKA-Mauser cannons.

The Mirages, except for the C models which did not have fixed cannon, were also having their canisters loaded with thirty-millimeter shells. Since they were to be utilized as strike aircraft, the Mirages were to carry Aérospatiale AS.30 air-to-surface missiles, Matra Magic air-to-air missiles for defense, and Exocet antiship missiles.

Among the stores under canvas were yet more varieties of missiles, including Matra R.530 and Matra Super 530 air-to-air. The melange of weaponry was not as he would have liked it, but his purchases had been defined by what was available through shadowy arms dealers from around the globe.

By evening, Suarez expected to see the one C-130, having depleted its cargo of munitions and other supplies, on its way back to the mainland for another, and final, load of ordnance.

His logistics for this operation were highly complex, and though he had a logistics officer to assist him, Suarez kept a close eye on the operations. He did not want to get very far ahead of his supply line.

Major Roberto Tellez ducked under the nose of his Tornado, spotted him, and crossed the runway to join him.

Tellez, Suarez had decided, was not a complex man. He was a Colombian by birth, but a mercenary at heart. He went where the action and the money were to be found, and his loyalty was to the man with the largest bankroll. That facet of the man's makeup made Suarez nervous, but Tellez's skill was not to be frowned upon. He could fly anything with wings and propulsion, and he flew them all exceptionally well.

Even in the hazy day, with the sun not readily apparent, Tellez wore his large, wire-framed aviator sunglasses. They hid eyes that Suarez knew to be quite cold and calculating. The .nan was about the same height as Suarez, but he was much slighter of frame. In contrast with Suarez's round face, Tellez had a long and lean visage, swamped with overly long black hair that swirled out at his collar. The cheeks were almost sunken, and they were pitted with the scars of acne. He wore an old and battered leather jacket against the chill of the wind.

"The operation is proceeding quite smoothly, don't you think, Major?" Suarez asked.

"Sure, Emilio. People more-or-less are doing what they are supposed to be doing."

Tellez did not take his commission as Major in the FSAD very seriously. He had also criticized the training frequently in the last few months, but the man was not an administrator. He did not understand the difficulties Suarez had had to face in conducting training seminars for ground crewmen, for ordnance people, for cargo handlers, and for others in the absence of a central training site. Their sessions had been conducted clandestinely at night, and in dozens of different locations. Under those conditions, he was fully amazed that they worked together as well as they did now that they had been assembled as a unit.

"You will agree, will you not, Roberto, that my schedule allows for a certain amount of disharmony?"

"True," Tellez said. "It is a damned good thing, too."

"All we need is patience. As the stress levels grow, these men will come together. You will see."

"I am looking forward to it," Tellez confessed, but not, Suarez thought, wholeheartedly.

"And to D-day plus however many hours there are left?"

"That, I am looking forward to most of all."

FALCON ONE
1320 HOURS LOCAL

Cady was having an almost-great time. His problem—one of long duration—since he had played cowboys and Indians as a kid growing up in Billings, Montana, was that, whatever the game he was involved in, he liked to be, not only part of the action, but also in control. He knew that, as a kid playing on the rimrocks north of the city or on the basketball court, he had been bossy as hell. The Marines hadn't been able to train much of that out of him.

He was in the front seat of Archie Baker's Sea Apache, the copilot/gunner's seat, replacing Lieutenant Henry Decker, when he would much prefer to be in the rear of the tandem cockpits, where he could give more orders than he received. That wish aside, there was also the small glitch in that he wasn't certified in rotary-winged aircraft.

Baker had taken him along for the jaunt as a favor, and very likely over the strident objections of Henry Decker.

The twin General Electric turboshaft engines, each generating 1696 shaft horsepower, throbbed as background music. The rotors, at their speed of 180 miles per hour, were simply a silver disk above them.

Though he was seated slightly lower than Baker, Cady had an excellent field of view through the large canopy. If it weren't so light out, he'd have tried out the night vision sensor. As it was, with his borrowed helmet, and with Baker's rudimentary instructions about the Doppler navigation system, the

Litton attitude and heading reference system, and the target acquisition and designation sight, he had his hands full trying to enjoy all of the new goodies at once.

The Sea Apache was the naval version of the U.S. Army's AH-64 Apache, and in place of Hellfire air-to-ground missiles, they had four Sidewinders mounted out on the stub wings. While they could mount 2.75-inch rocket launcher pods or British Sea Skua antishipping missiles also, they were then carrying two Mk 46 torpedoes. Attached to the fuselage almost directly below Cady was a swivelling M230 thirty-millimeter Chain Gun.

The neat part was that whatever weapon he selected, he could aim and fire it with his helmet. If the Chain Gun were selected, for example, whichever way he turned his head, the gun followed along.

He wished he had something to shoot at.

"Having a grand time, are we?" Baker asked over the ICS.

"Damn, Archie. If I'd known you guys were such kids at heart, I'd have flown with you earlier."

"It seems to me. . . ." Baker started to say, then let it dribble off.

"I know. As wing commander, I should have paid closer attention to you earlier. I confess to an anti-chopper bias."

"Now corrected?" Baker asked.

"Now corrected."

"When we get some free time, boss, I'll teach you to fly her."

"I'd like that, Archie."

Baker eased back on his forward speed and let the other choppers catch up with them.

Another Sea Apache, escorting two H-60B Seahawks, pulled into formation with them, all of them to the left of Baker's Falcon One. Cady looked them over. The Sikorsky Seahawks were utilized as transports and could carry up to fourteen combat-equipped troops. These two had their side doors open, and Cady saw Dave George and his SEALs waving at him.

He waved back.

The Seahawk had an elongated fuselage that looked odd to anyone whose first close association with helicopters had come with the combat-proven Huey. The steeply-sloped nose carried a plethora of avionics that Huey drivers wouldn't even have dreamed about.

Cady swung his head back to the front to stare into the distance where one of Baker's Seahawks, equipped as a LAMPS (Light Airborne Multi-Purpose System) chopper, was skimming the surface of the sea. The two LAMPS helicopters belonging to the *U Thant* were capable of the antisubmarine mission of detection, identification, and interdiction. They carried sonar equipment in addition to either mine-dispensing pods or the Mk 46 torpedoes.

The LAMPS and Seahawk helicopters were designated by the code name Copperhead while the rest of Baker's choppers flew under the name Falcon.

"Tally-ho!"

"Come back to me, Copperhead Two," Baker said.

"Got a contact, Falcon One. Sub on heading two-eight-niner, making maybe four knots. He's trying to go silent." The weapons officer on the LAMPS chopper had a Norwegian accent.

"Good job, Copperhead. We'll take it from here."

"Ah, Falcon One, couldn't we just sprinkle a few mines around him?"

"Negative. We're going to take him alive."

Cady grinned to himself as Baker ordered, "Falcons and Copperheads, go to angels one and let's take some spread."

He watched as the other choppers increased distance from them. All of the aircraft, like his Harriers, were painted a flat, low-visibility dove gray that seemed to absorb the rays of the afternoon sun. On the side of each fuselage was a blue-and-white UN insignia and a white squadron and aircraft number designation, but they were designed to be removed quickly for missions charged as clandestine.

They climbed to a thousand feet as they closed in on the LAMPS Copperhead, which was circling an area of empty ocean. The sun shone down on a sea that was almost serene, running three-foot swells.

"Are you certain about this, Copperhead Six?" Baker asked.

"That's affirmative, Falcon One."

"Did you get a copy, Raccoon?" Baker asked.

"Roger," Dave George called back. "Raccoon is ready to take a dive."

"Go," Baker told him.

Baker slowed his forward speed to a crawl and eased off to the side so that he and Cady had a ringside seat for this performance.

The Seahawks hovered above Copperhead Six, who was still circling some nine hundred feet below them.

"Copperhead Six is out of here," the Norwegian accent reported, utilizing some dated American idiom learned from videos in the ship's extensive tape library, and the lower chopper immediately leveled and went into straight flight, clearing the sea below.

As soon as he saw that he had clearance, George gave a hand signal to his second in the other Seahawk, and the SEALs began filing out of the side doors of both choppers.

Each man barely cleared the level of the landing gear before he popped his chute. The pilot chutes streamed out of the packs, followed by the main chute and risers. The scalloped, highly maneuverable canopies were black and difficult to follow as they made the descent, but Cady counted carefully and got twenty-five blossoms.

Like large hawks circling for the kill, the skydivers floated into a revolving formation, gradually closing with the sea. As they got lower, he saw them drop their equipment packs on ten-foot cords and begin preparing for the transition to SCUBA gear.

The first man—George?—almost walked into the sea, the landing appeared so effortless, and within a minute, his chute was floating like flotsam on the surface, and he had disappeared.

One by one, the rest of the SEALs followed the example of their leader, and the choppers lost altitude and took up a large circling pattern over the discarded and deflated parachutes floating on the sea.

"I hope they get the son of a bitch," Baker said on the ICS.

"You don't like d'Argamon much, do you?" Cady asked.

"He's after my girl."

3 DECEMBER

UNS CALAIS
0745 HOURS LOCAL

Two days before, when Jean d'Argamon had been humili-
ated by David George's SEALs, he had also been livid with
anger.

No one had briefed him that the SEALs would be involved
in the exercise. He had fully expected, as in two previous
exercises, to be attacked with dummy mines or torpedoes, and
he had taken up a station one hundred and fifty feet down,
just below a cool layer of water which should have distorted,
if not hidden, his sonar image. He, Suretsev, and Magnuson
had calmly waited for the attack—a series of electronically
produced pops—to pass before escaping to depth.

When the SEALs slapped magnets—simulated mines—on
his hull and David George waved at him through his porthole,
d'Argamon had sworn revenge on someone, probably Baker
or even Cady.

Cady would do something like that—change the rules. He
had noticed that the marine colonel paid lip service only to
some of the regulations.

And yet d'Argamon was forced to admit to himself that he
had become, well, just somewhat complacent. The mission of
the 21st Submarine Detachment had become so routine—one
patrol after another, without surprises—that he himself had

fallen into the rut. He had not scheduled a training exercise for his own people in three weeks.

And over the unvoiced but obvious complaints of his sub crews, he had resolved to change that. There would be a two-hour training session for the off-duty submarine each day.

And so he sat in the Combat Information Center and watched the sonar images picked up by the *U Thant*. Out on the point, the *Dover*, commanded by the German naval lieutenant commander Rolf Arnstadt, was conducting her normal surveillance cruise.

And ten miles ahead somewhere, out of sonar range, Oscar Moritz and the *Calais* waited in ambush.

From here, d'Argamon would wait and see how Arnstadt reacted when he suddenly found himself under attack by another submarine running under a supersilent regimen.

And from here, while he waited, d'Argamon had the opportunity to become better acquainted with the beautiful Canadian, Theresa Eames. He had made certain that he involved her in his training exercises.

She sat in her customary position at the console, and d'Argamon sat next to her in one of the extra chairs. A Mexican sergeant manned the data entry console next to her. The man who had the normal tour of duty, a British lieutenant, sat in a chair near the data entry operator.

He knew his Parisian accent could be charming to some, so he spoke in French. The choice of language also precluded eavesdropping by the other two people in the CIC, and provided, he thought, a sense of intimacy.

"It seems a shame, my dear, that I must force my crews to work in their off-duty time."

Eames replied in French, with that quaint accent of Montreal that was not as cultured as his own.

"And consequently require that you also must work in your own off-time, Commander?"

"Please. I have told you; it is Jean. And to answer your question, we who are committed to the objective do not quibble about the hours."

She took her eyes from the screen momentarily, to glance sideways at him, using her eyes to acknowledge him without turning her head, and he thought the gesture quite sexy.

"You have taken a sudden new interest in training," she said.

He was going to touch her forearm—a tender intimacy—and then thought better of it. The women in American and Canadian military organizations had become very sensitive to what they might interpret as improprieties. Instead, he pressed his hand flat to his own heart.

"I confess, my love, to a degree of complacency of late." He gave her a big smile. "But I have reformed. I have joined Lax Commanders Anonymous, and I am taking the first of my twelve steps."

She did not seem to find his confession or his humor well-placed.

"I thought it was because Colonel Cady's exercise caught you by surprise," she said, confirming his supposition that Cady had masterminded his defeat. She turned once again to her screen.

"Nonsense," he said. "I do not report to Colonel Cady."

"Perhaps he knows that."

"As well he should."

"And perhaps this was his way of sending you a message."

THE SAN MATIAS
0820 HOURS LOCAL

The destroyer had once been employed by the United States Navy, and was designated as one of the *Forrest Sherman* class.

The United States upgraded four of the eighteen originally constructed as *Decatur*-class guided missile destroyers, converted eight to antisubmarine warfare vessels, and retired six. This ship went to the Argentine Navy in 1973, had seen service during the Malvinas war in 1982, and was subsequently mothballed in 1988.

She was in amazingly good shape for a forty-five-year-old, twice-retired ship. Her two sets of Westinghouse steam turbines had been retrofitted, and she could still make thirty-two knots on them. The paint was fresh, and her armament either rehabilitated or replaced. Forward, she mounted a five-inch gun turret, and following the example set by the *Decatur* class of ships, a Tartar surface-to-air (SAM) launcher had replaced the two aft guns. Additionally, the missile-launched torpedo system ASROC was located amidships, and Mk 32 torpedo tubes were located on both sides ahead of the bridge.

At 418 feet of length and forty-five feet of beam, displacing 2900 tons, the *San Matias* was the largest ship in the fleet of twenty-three ships and boats, and she was the flagship of Captain Diego Enriquez.

He was rightfully proud of the restoration. Enriquez had personally supervised the renovation over a seven-month period, just as he had taken special interest in the rest of his fleet which, though not large, was adequate for his purposes.

In addition to the destroyer, there was a small and old frigate, the *Marguerite Bay,* one minesweeper, the *San Jorge,* and sixteen patrol boats of various sizes and origin, known by the numbers assigned to them. In terms of support ships, he commanded three large, though elderly, freighters and one medium-sized tanker utilized as a refueler.

Diego Enriquez stood on his bridge and watched the helicopter approaching. He was sailing, with patrol boats Eight and Eleven as escorts, four miles off the coast and thirty miles south of the entrance to the Rio de las Platas. The shoreline was a crisp green edging to the tranquil blue of the sea. It was a magnificent day, and with very little effort, he could ignore the approaching helicopter and put himself in the boots of Juan Diaz de Solis, who had first entered the Rio de las Platas in 1516. Solis had not left the river, of course, because some of the twenty major Indian groups (hunters and food gatherers) residing along the eastern coast had not been as tranquil as the sea. Still, the man was an adventurer of the highest caliber, and Enriquez liked to think himself the same kind of man.

He was, after all, and if he could believe his mother's recollection of oral history, a descendent of the explorer Pedro de Mendoza, the Spaniard who had led the largest conquest expedition to the New World in 1536. He chose to believe his mother.

His reverie was shattered by the clatter of rotors, and Enriquez stepped through the hatchway out onto the starboard bridge extension to watch the Aérospatiale SA 341 helicopter, called the Gazelle, circle to the stern of his ship, then close on the landing pad. His own helicopter, a Kamov Ka-27, produced in the Soviet Union, and obtained through India, had been pushed far forward to give Silvera's craft space in which to land. After Silvera was returned to the mainland, the Gazelle was to embark on the freighter *Paloma*.

Leaving the bridge under the control of his second officer, Carlos Estero, Enriquez went below to the wardroom and had the coffee poured by the time Silvera was shown in. The president was accompanied by his administrative advisor and assistant, Ricardo Fuentes.

Enriquez had always thought Fuentes a trifle too effeminate—too soft-skinned, too pretty, despite the pencil-line mustache. His soft brown eyes were expressive, perhaps the reason why he had been an aspiring actor for so many years. Why Fuentes should be an expert on administrative matters, when his background was drama, escaped Enriquez. However, as he frequently reminded himself, Eva Duarte had been an actress—though not a very good one—before she became Evita Peron and made such revolutionary changes in social programs. Had he not been in the military, and had he not originated in Chile, Enriquez would probably have been a Peronista.

After effusive greetings, the three of them settled at the table with mugs of coffee.

"Are you prepared, Diego?" Silvera asked.

"I have been prepared for three weeks, *Presidente.*"

"Your stores?"

"Have been embarked. The freighters, as well as the tanker, are moored in San Sebastion Bay. The other ships and the patrol boats are dispersed so as to prevent suspicion, but I intend to join up with the *Marguerite Bay* and the *San Jorge* by early morning. We will be in position by 1400 hours."

"Excellent!"

Even Ricardo Fuentes beamed, though he likely knew that Enriquez was not fond of him.

"The air force is in place, also," Silvera said.

"The weather forecast is not an optimistic one," he said.

"I know. Suarez says it is not insurmountable, however. In any event, we cannot delay the hour. Our air and sea movements may have already been detected by the satellites, and we do not want to prompt any early warnings."

"Perhaps the satellite surveillance has been limited," Enriquez said. "Certainly, the last year has been quiet in this region, militarily. There are other parts of the world to which the watchers will devote their attention."

"That is true, Diego, but still, our movements have committed us, and we must not take faltering steps."

"Sixteen hundred hours, then," Enriquez said.

"Exactly! At that time, we control our own destiny."

Fuentes beamed some more.

BRANDEIS BASE, ANTARCTICA
0955 HOURS LOCAL

Summer was coming, but so far, Paul Andover, known as "Zip" to his friends, who were many, was unaware of it. Outside the Quonset hut, the wind still sped along at sixty miles per hour, and though it wasn't snowing at the time, it might as well have been. The wind created a ground blizzard that turned any landmark, vehicle, or person beyond a hundred meters away pure white.

Because of the one-meter-thick layer of insulation in the roof of the hut, Andover heard the wind as only a dull background thrum. And after so many years on the continent, he didn't really hear it anymore.

Over a twenty-year period, Zip Andover had spent sixteen winters on the ice, working for one consortium or another. He was an accomplished meteorologist, and he had learned in that dozen years that his hobbies were biology and reading. Biology because Christine Amherst, who wintered this year and would stay for the austral summer at the United Kingdom's Faraday Station, was a biologist; reading because there wasn't a hell of a lot else to do in his off-hours. He read anything and everything he could get his hands on, and every resupply party had standing orders to bring him books. For his forty-fourth birthday, Andover had gotten himself reading glasses. He was afraid his eyes were going to go before he had a chance to read all that he should read in this life.

Andover had been born on a sheep station near Broken Hill, New South Wales, and the isolation and dirt had forced him to flee to Canberra, then Sydney, where he got his degree.

He had also picked up an intense interest in the fifth-largest continent and spent several summers as an intern on expeditions to Australia's outposts at Mawson, Davis, and Casey stations, all on the coast of East Antarctica. By some quirk of fate, he had become an expert in his field, as far as Antarctica meteorology went, and he ended up either studying it in graduate schools, writing long treatises about it, or trying to outlast it. He still had the isolation he had been born with, but he had swapped the soil for ice, which was at least cleaner.

Although he carried an Australian passport, Andover really considered himself a native of Antarctica, though there was no such animal. On his trips to other stations, he could encounter a dozen different nationalities, and the territorial claims on the continent were just as diverse. Radiating out from the South Pole, the boundary lines following longitudinal guides divided interests claimed by France, Australia, New Zealand, Norway, Chile, Argentina, and the United Kingdom. The last three areas overlapped extensively, and the territorial dispute had been raging for decades. Even Poland had a presence in the area. The United States and the Soviet Union—now Russia, Andover presumed—maintained bases, but had never claimed, nor recognized, any other territorial ownership.

That was his position. As the continent's leading and only credible citizen—in his opinion, he thought of himself as an international personage. He didn't bother voicing his convictions, however; that would only result in argument and probably ostracism.

While he had worked many of the fifty-two permanent stations on the ice, going with any organization that had the need for his skills and the money to support him, Andover had most frequently spent his time with the Australians. There was an inordinate sense of nationality at each base, and he had felt it when he worked for the USSR one summer, the Americans one winter, the UK the next winter.

This year, he was working for a joint expedition at a brand-new station. A consortium of German, French, United Kingdom, and Italian scientific groups which were particularly concerned about and interested in the greenhouse effect had established the station called Brandeis Base. It was located on the Antarctic Peninsula which stretched for a thousand miles from the primary mass of the continent toward the southern tip of South America. First designated by the United States as Palmer Land for Nathaniel Brown Palmer, who sighted it on November 18, 1820, the peninsula was also called Graham Land by the British in honor of Sir James Graham, first lord of the admiralty when Edward Bransfield of the Royal Navy discovered it on January 30, 1820. It wasn't until 1964 that most everyone decided to call it the Antarctic Peninsula, with the northern portion known as Graham Land and the southern segment called Palmer Land.

So Brandeis Base was situated on the western coast in an area named the Danco Coast of Graham Land of the Antarctic Peninsula, which was an extension of West Antarctica. The bays, coasts, islands, inlets, channels, mountains, and ice shelves of the continent were named for so many different explorers or their sponsors, representing so many nations, that Andover couldn't understand why any nation wouldn't recognize the land as truly international.

Along the western side of the peninsula were a plethora of experiment stations. North of him, in the Shetland Islands off the tip of the peninsula, were stations maintained by Poland, Argentina, Chile, and Russia. On the very tip was Esperanza, an Argentinean venture. A few kilometers south of it was the Chilean base General Bernardo O'Higgins. Brandeis Base was sited seventy-five kilometers south of Primavera, a major Argentine station, and sixty kilometers north of another Argentine base, Brown.

The United States' Palmer Base, on Anvers Island, was 130

kilometers southwest, and the United Kingdom's Faraday station, in which he had a special interest, was 140 kilometers away to the south. That was about an hour-and-a-half, with the top down on a Triumph TR-3 (which he owned, back in Sydney), on a Sunday afternoon. If he wanted to attempt it today, with one of the five Brandeis Sno-Cats, he could plan on around twenty to thirty hours if there were no traffic.

The distances between stations were far greater on the main continent, though some were clustered. The Americans' McMurdo Base, which could really be classified as a town, or at least a village, was a couple kilometers from New Zealand's Scott Base, and they shared facilities at Williams airfield as well as some communications antennas. Close by was the Greenpeace base, which, like Brandeis, was intensely interested in the ozone depletion and the greenhouse effect. The Greenpeace people were much better than the Brandeis people in the matter of recycling, Andover thought. Antarctica was really becoming a dump. Waste and toxic chemicals accumulated over forty years were still sitting in the open at some stations. There were mountains of fifty-five-gallon drums full of discarded fuel, motor oil, and chemicals that no one seemed to know how to make disappear.

The thought of it made Andover angry. He didn't need supposed scientists and administrators from thirty nations coming in to dirty-up his continent.

In his tiny office at the back of Hut 2—there were five, all connected by surplus sewer pipe someone had the nerve to call tunnels—Andover completed his ten o'clock readings of wind speed and direction, temperatures, barometric pressure, and precipitation from the instrument readouts mounted on the wall. He entered the results in his logbook, then left the office, and went down the corridor to the main office. There was no one there, so he pulled on his anorak, popped the tight seal on the door, and stepped into the tunnel.

It was cold in the tunnel, probably around ten degrees Fahrenheit, and he didn't waste time sightseeing. He trotted on over to Hut 3, their primary living area which contained the kitchen, dining area, and the laughable game room. Both of the video game machines had broken down in September, and all of the sixteen people at the station were so bored with them, no one bothered to repair them.

Jacque Metier, the French geologist, was the only one present, sitting at the radio desk, listening to a few words breaking through the static.

"Jesus, Jocko, how can you stand it?" Andover tossed his parka toward a peg on the wall, went to the counter near the kitchen, poured himself a mug of coffee, and dug in the tin box for freshly unfrozen gingersnaps.

Metier turned the volume control down and rotated in the swivel chair to look at him.

"You're getting fat, Zip."

"Not." He snapped a cookie in half and dunked it in his coffee as he took a seat on the frayed leather couch.

"Twenty pounds, at least."

"Fifteen," Andover claimed.

He preferred to think of himself as stocky. At five-ten, he weighed 175, which he would not admit to Metier, was twenty-one pounds more than he had weighed when he checked into the station in March. His bulk went with the full red beard he sported, he thought, gave him a real macho, iceman appearance. When he was fully dressed in his outdoor gear, he looked like a tank.

Metier would have said a butterball.

He worked out every other day in the weight room, but the gingersnaps, chocolate chip cookies, and fudge were taking their toll. He dunked another cookie in his coffee and resolved to add another day a week to his regimen.

At least he didn't look like Metier, the boss of the station, who was positively emaciated in appearance. Scrawny legs, scrawny mustache, a nose so thin it was a razor.

"So, Jocko, you trying to establish new distance records with the shortwave? You talk to anyone?"

"No. Just listening. There's something funny going on, Zip."

"I could use a laugh."

"Primavera's been on the air nearly all morning."

"It's just after ten. That's only mid-morning," Andover pointed out. "They're saying funny things, that it?"

"No. It's just more verbiage than they usually put out. Mostly in Spanish, and I lose most of it. But the patterns are quirky."

"What's with quirky?"

"I don't know. It's almost a code."

"Who they talking to?"

"Brown, Esperanza, Jubany in the Shetlands, the mainland."

"Maybe they're planning a party," Andover suggested.

"Perhaps."

"I hope they invite us."

DEFENSE INTELLIGENCE AGENCY
1300 HOURS LOCAL

"Good afternoon, everyone. Please come in and have a seat. There's some goodies and coffee on the side table, if you didn't get lunch on the plane."

Cameron McNichols, untrue to form, was wearing one of his good suits in his own office.

The room was actually the conference room next to his office. It was capable of handling ten people around the small rectangular table, but he had only three people to entertain.

They had all flown down from New York at his request,

and over their objections. McNichols had prevailed by claiming that he needed his high-tech monitors nearby when he spoke to them.

Sir Charles Bentley grinned his appreciation to McNichols when he saw the pot of boiling water and variety of tea bags stacked on a plate. He made himself some tea with one of the Celestial Seasonings varieties. Bentley had the silvery gray hair that McNichols used to envy. It was full and swept back over ears which jutted a few centimeters too prominently, but which matched his nose. He wore heavy horn-rimmed glasses and had a professorial air about him, but McNichols knew that the man had a nice background with MI-6 (the British secret service), had served in several ministries, had been a member of Parliament, and was now the United Kingdom's ambassador to the United Nations.

Julia Highwater, the United States ambassador, a stylish lady with credentials that included the Harvard Law Review, private practice in a major New York firm, the Justice Department, and the State Department, opted for coffee. In her late fifties, Highwater had auburn hair well-speckled with gray, green eyes that were very direct, and a posture that a West Point grad would be proud to have.

The third person waved away the sideboard and took a seat at the side of the table. Justin Albrecht was a Dane who had been a pillar of the diamond industry before entering politics. He was stout, McNichols thought kindly, maybe five-nine and three hundred pounds. His tailoring did lots for his appearance, though, and he could have been a Danish Orson Welles or William Conrad.

McNichols, who didn't believe in coincidence, did believe in searching for commonality: in data, in people, in life. The common denominators for his three guests were their appointments to the United Nations and their service on the

Peacekeeper Committee, which reported to the Security Council.

The PC was actually comprised of twelve members, with a support staff of another dozen, but these three made up the Operations Committee. What it boiled down to, they had power.

McNichols, in his part-time role, served as support to the committee, and in essence reported to the three now gathering at his table. Sir Charles, as chairman, automatically and quite comfortably took the chair at the head of the table. He waited for his tea to steep and studied the big screen mounted on the wall.

"That is the device which prompted our trip, Cameron?"

"It is, Sir Charles."

"I have a telly in my living room. We could have used that."

Bentley enjoyed playing the ingenue. His spy days and his foreign ministry experience precluded his ignorance of what might be coming over that screen.

"Next time, sir, we'll try that," McNichols said.

Bentley grinned. He had big, horsey teeth.

Highwater said, "You said this was serious, Cam."

"I think it is, ma'am, yes."

McNichols took his seat at the side of the table, where a keyboard rested. Clicking a command into the board, he brought up an image on the screen.

"This is a real-time satellite image," he explained. "It's coming from a Rhyolite in polar orbit, at an inclination of forty degrees."

He knew they didn't understand all of the details, nor probably cared, but they did like hearing the jargon. He had learned that in his short time working with the committee.

"It's a fairly clear day, and perhaps you can identify the

southwestern coast of South America on the right of the screen?"

He waited for the nods, then went on, "I've filtered out the extraneous detail, but the symbol you see on the left of the screen represents the position of the *U Thant.* She's steaming sixteen hundred miles west of the continent, en route for the Philippines."

"How long before she reaches her objective?" Albrecht asked.

"Well, that's what I wanted to discuss with you."

He brought up his recorded series of images and narrated as they appeared on the screen.

"I've gone back to November twenty-sixth and pulled selected archival tapes to put together the data for this session. It's going to jump around a little, because the imagery comes from different satellites, at different times, in different positions and angles of view. The selected region is the southern tip of South America. Also, the imagery is both true video and infrared. Some days were just too cloudy to get high-resolution pictures.

"On the twenty-sixth, three aircraft of the Chilean National Guard, all C-130 Hercules, disappeared from their base in southern Chile." He used the blinking cursor arrow on the screen to point out the base.

The image flickered and died, then a new scene appeared.

"The three aircraft reappeared on *Isla Navarino,* down here." McNichols whisked the arrow southward.

"On the twenty-seventh, a KC-130 tanker was moved from a base near Buenos Aires to *Isla Navarino.*

"On the twenty-ninth and thirtieth of November, and on the first of December, coming from a variety of bases in Chile and Argentina, three more transports, six more tankers, eight Panavia Tornados, and twelve Mirage fighters arrived at *Isla Navarino.*"

McNichols waited for the recorded video and infrared appearing on the screen to catch up with him.

"What in the bloody hell is on *Isla Navarino?*" Bentley asked.

"A small village called Port Williams, a few sheep, and a single ten-thousand-foot dirt airstrip, Sir Charles. I went back almost five months before I found when that runway was lengthened."

The screen finally showed his last picture, which he froze. All of the aircraft were lined up on the north side of the runway, in one neat row. Behind them was a hillock of canvas-protected crates and boxes as well as seventy-two fuel bladders resting on the ground. The scene was vague and hazy, but he had computer-enhanced the image.

"I know what it looks like to me," Highwater said. "What does it look like to you, Justin?"

"Pretty clear, Julia. A war game. An exercise of some sort."

"Ah, come on, Justin," Bentley said. "They wouldn't extend a runway for a war game. It's a damned strike force. If I go back a decade, it looks like the buildup for an invasion of the Falklands."

"Would they attempt that again, Sir Charles?" Highwater asked.

"I shouldn't think so. Cameron, you've got all the analysts. What are they saying?"

"We think it's Antarctica," McNichols said.

Bentley nodded sagely. "Why?"

"Both Argentina and Chile have long claimed ownership. Argentina thinks they have the first discovery rights to the whole continent. From that angle, it's a matter of pride, of historical rights that have been infringed. From the reports of all of the scientific expeditions, we don't think there are significant reserves of minerals or other resources, and of those that are present, the cost of recovery doesn't make economic sense. There is an off-chance that one of the Argentine or Chile bases has made a new discovery of some kind. On first reading, however, I guess we'd say an invasion of the continent would be based on historical rights or economic gain or both."

"Stupid damned thing to do," Bentley said.

"Do you have a recommendation for us, Cam?" Highwater asked.

"Fortunately," McNichols said, "I only provide the data. You all get to wrestle with the significance of it."

"Come on," she said.

"I think I'd suggest that a few of your members have a quiet little chat with the representatives from Chile and Argentina."

"And what else?" Albrecht asked.

"And, if the Philippines thing isn't too pressing, I'd turn the *U Thant* around and head her south."

Bentley looked to his two colleagues. When they nodded, he said, "May I borrow your telephone, old chap?"

UNS U THANT
1150 HOURS LOCAL

Jan Gless was on duty in sick bay, so Eames had the suite to herself. She took a regulation-ordained short—in order to conserve fresh water—but wonderful shower, washed her hair, and was seated in a terry cloth robe, doing her nails, when the intercom buzzed.

She got up and crossed to the bulkhead where it was mounted.

"Major Eames, sir."

"Major, this is Captain Monmouth. What do you know about Antarctica?"

"Antarctica, sir? Not very much, I'm afraid."

"Great, you're more informed than the rest of the people I've talked to, who said they knew absolutely nothing. I want you to give us a briefing on Antarctica at 2000 hours."

"But, sir—"

"Appreciate it, Major. See you in the wardroom."

UNS U THANT
1950 HOURS LOCAL

Shark Cady got off the elevator on Deck 1 and met Jake Travers coming down the corridor.

Travers gave him a grin that was full of happy anticipation. Since early afternoon, when the ship had reversed course so abruptly, the rumors had been airborne like the Red Baron's Flying Circus, performing all kinds of acrobatics. Rumors were the lifeblood of any military ship, of course, and they were all the absolute truth until something new, and possibly more outlandish, started making the rounds.

"Hey, CAG," Travers said, "does this mean the training pays off?"

"Let's hope the training is applicable, Jake."

Travers was one of those irrepressible spirits who approached life as if it were an enormous amusement park. He found the merry-go-round as exciting as the roller coaster. A western Australian who had spent some of his formative years growing up in New Zealand and Bali, Travers had attended Oxford in England, because his father had. He had a command over several languages, all of them spoken with a thick Aussie accent. He was thirty-four years old, but had around fifty years of experience showing in his lively blue eyes. At five-ten, he had thick, rounded shoulders, a barrel chest, and big, big arms. From time to time, Cady had to remind him to have his unruly blond locks trimmed. Jake Travers vehemently detested military haircuts, but they were a necessary evil for a man who liked to fly birds with jet power and lethal payloads.

Selected by Cady two months before to command the 2nd Squadron, the Tiger Barbs, Travers had impressed Cady with his ability to meld his aviators—two Japanese, one Russian, one German, and one Belgian—into a cohesive unit. He hadn't had quite the same problems Phil Anderson had had with Stein, Sifra, and the Kiwi Mikkelson in the 1st Squadron.

They arrived at the wing briefing room and found it jammed with the pilots from the Harrier and the helicopter squadrons. They didn't often brief together so they all knew that something was up. Jokes were flying along with the more preposterous rumors, and the atmosphere was full of vibrant energy. Since space in the ready room was limited, two decks down, the off-duty sub crew and the SEALs would be gathering to listen to the briefing via closed-circuit television. The ship's deck and engineering officers were assembled in the officers' wardroom for another television presentation, and they would pass on the pertinent information to their sections in secondary briefings to the crew.

In the wing briefing room, all of the seats were taken. The room was a private sea of UN blue flight suits.

Travers smiled engagingly at one of his aviators, and the man quickly climbed out of his cushioned chair and offered it to his boss.

Cady made his way to the head of the room, where Monmouth, Eames, and the meteorological officer, a Marine captain named Eddie Purgatory, were gathered, standing in their own discussion group.

As he joined them, Eames gave him a tiny, reluctant quarter-smile. For some undisclosed reason, she didn't like him much, he thought, but maybe she was warming up a little.

Monmouth's smile was even more grim. He didn't like what he'd heard from McNichols, their intelligence source at DIA.

Monmouth had given Cady and the ship's command officers a short briefing soon after he'd gotten his orders from Sir Charles Bentley of the Operations Committee. Directly after that, Cady had talked to McNichols personally.

"We all here?" Monmouth asked.

Cady scanned the faces in the room, the lucky ones in chairs, the less lucky lined up against the back and side walls. His fifteen active and reserve fighter aviators were present, as were Baker and the thirty-one men and women serving as either pilots or copilots of his Sea Apache and Seahawk choppers. Shaker Adams and Giovanni Este, the leading air controller, were in the front row of seats.

The dozen private conversations taking place created a low buzz that permeated the room. From the jubilant overtone of the dialogues, Cady judged that none of the aviators had evaluated the demeanor of their superior officers, all of whom were less enthusiastic.

"All accounted for, sir," he said.

"Let's do it, then."

Cady moved to the podium. He didn't have to call for attention; as soon as they saw him take up his position, the silence became golden.

"Gentlemen and ladies," he said with a smile, "so far this afternoon, I've heard stories that we're going to take out the Colombian cartels, run training exercises against the Andes mountains, and support the return of Pinochet to power in Chile. While the theories are creative, I'm afraid we'll have to discredit them. This is likely to be the first of many briefings you'll have in the next few days, and I'm sure you'll want to take notes."

A fluttering rustle of paper resounded through the room as notepads were opened.

"Captain Monmouth will start us off."

Monmouth took his place at the podium and got right to

the gist of it. "At 1325 hours this afternoon, the operations subcommittee of the Peacekeeper Committee ordered us to Antarctica."

Cady saw quite a few faces take on grimaces as thoughts of cold and ice ran through the minds behind the faces.

"Colonel Cady will outline the known facts about the threat in a few minutes, but let me explain the timing. When we received our orders, we were thirty-seven hundred miles—thirty-two hundred nautical miles—northwest of our new destination. Currently, we are about three thousand nautical miles away, and we're making top turns, thirty-two knots. That puts us ninety-three hours away.

"Flight operations, however, will be initiated as soon as we're within range for the fighters. That will come in about seventy hours."

The faces were mostly bland now. They didn't know what the threat was. Some would anticipate action with heated fervor, and others would use the seventy hours to stew. Cady's job would be to keep them busy enough that neither pot boiled over.

"The full details are not yet known, but it appears to military intelligence analysts as if Chilean and Argentine forces are poised for an invasion of Antarctica," Monmouth said.

Downright puzzlement on most faces.

"If, as the analysts seem to think, the attack comes within the next twenty-four hours, our arrival in the region will come too late to serve as a deterrent. If hostile forces are in place on the continent before we arrive, we are not yet certain of what our role will be. That will be up to the policy-makers, but since the Security Council will likely want to establish the *U Thant*'s credibility as an enforcement unit for the first time, that role will probably be an active one.

"I know I'm dealing with a lot of ifs here, but again, if the hostile forces are counting on forty-five or sixty or ninety days for the world to react to the invasion, time in which they can firm up their defenses, our arrival is going to be a hell of a surprise for them. That's why the powers-that-be made us a covert unit, and that's the reason we exist as a fighting unit. I'm counting on all of you to set aside national competitions and unite as a solid force, supporting the dictates of the United Nations."

Monmouth stepped away from the podium to a short round of applause that seemed to embarrass him.

Eames took her turn, handing a stack of paper to Cady. He noted that the pages were detailed topographical maps of Antarctica, and he handed half the stack to Archie Baker, and the two of them walked back along the sides of the room to pass them out.

"I'm going to tell you about Antarctica," she said, "and I'll start with the good news—summer is just beginning. The seasonal high summer occurs next month, in January."

Some faces sagged in relief.

"That's the end of the good news. The first of the bad news is that summer is not much different from winter. The mean temperatures are about twenty degrees lower than the corresponding latitudes in the Arctic—this is the coldest region on earth. The interior of the continent is much colder than the coastal regions. When it's minus one degree Fahrenheit on the coast during the coldest month, it can be minus eighty degrees in the interior. The Russians recorded the world-record low of minus one hundred and twenty-eight degrees Fahrenheit at Vostok station in the interior in 1983. It is not going to be balmy, and all ship's personnel are to report to Stores within the next twenty-four hours to be issued arctic gear."

Cady passed out the last of his maps and went back to the head of the room. He was pleased with the way Eames's presentation was starting. She had done a lot of research in the time available to her.

"Pilots," she said, "will be especially concerned with the winds on the continent, and Captain Purgatory will be posting met reports every hour on the hour, once we're within range of flight operations, primarily because it is difficult to predict the weather any further ahead than twelve hours. In general, however, the winds are strongest along the coasts. One explorer, named Mawson, called Cape Denison the 'Home of the Blizzard.' Wind forces from the plateau have been measured at two hundred miles per hour."

Jesus, Cady thought, *a hovering Harrier could do two hundred miles per hour in reverse.*

"At the Bay of Whales, in the Ross Sea, one four-year study showed the average wind speed to be eleven miles per hour . . ."

Better.

". . . though the strongest recordings reached sixty miles per hour.

"In Antarctica," Eames continued, "it snows. It snows more along the coast, a little less in the coastal mountains, and the least amount of snowfall is recorded at the South Pole. On average, the coasts receive sixty inches of annual precipitation, and the Pole will get six inches. The snow, however, stays in place; that is, it doesn't melt. Many storms consist of old snow being blown about by the high winds, rather than fresh precipitation.

"The average altitude of the landmass—not counting the snowpack—is six thousand feet, but the average thickness of the ice and snow layer is eight thousand feet, bringing the total average to fourteen thousand feet. The ice cap layer is nearly eleven thousand feet thick in the interior."

Cady could tell that others in the room were having as much trouble as he was trying to picture that much ice. He preferred his in the shape of cubes drowned In Johnnie Walker Black Label.

"While the geographical South Pole is only ninety-two hundred feet high, there are mountain peaks which rise to nearly seventeen thousand feet," Eames said. "The Transantarctic Mountains separate the continent into East Antarctica and West Antarctica, which is essentially an archipelago of islands covered by the continental ice cap. The ice also moves. For example, the Beardmore Glacier begins on the South Pole Plateau and moves onto the Ross Ice Shelf. That ice shelf, ladies and gentlemen"—she glanced at Cady as she put the ladies first—"is large enough that it could hold Spain and Portugal, if they were portable. The ice is in continual movement, sometimes attaining as much as eight or nine feet of progress in a day, and in the case of the Ross Ice Shelf, when the ice reaches the Ross Sea—with cliffs that are one to two hundred feet high on the coast—it begins to break off, or calve, and plunge into the sea to become icebergs.

"The seas, of course, are full of ice, in huge floes or in smaller icebergs, and they are a danger to shipping as they float northward into warmer waters where they melt."

Cady planned to spend most of his time in the air.

"There are about fifty—fifty-two at last count—experiment stations or bases on the continent," she went on, "ranging from the Russian station, Vostok, in East Antarctica at thirteen thousand feet to the American base called Eights in West Antarctica. McMurdo, the U.S. station located on Ross Island, is seven hundred and fifty miles from Vostok. McMurdo is the chief U.S. station, supported through Williams Field, an ice-based airport. Scott Base, manned by New Zealanders, is close by, and the two stations share some facilities. Several miles away is a Greenpeace station. I mention McMurdo specifically since, as the largest station, a small city really, it could well be the prime target.

"In general, the distances between stations are large, and transportation between stations can be an ordeal. All of the primary stations, both permanent and temporary, are noted on the maps passed out to you.

"The population changes with the seasons. Generally, some eight hundred people remain in residence over the winter, and the summer population can triple that number, depending upon the number of expeditions and projects funded by a wide variety of sponsoring organizations.

"With the seasons comes a dramatic change in the hours of daylight. During the austral summer, there is twenty-four hours of daylight. Right now, the sun barely dips below the horizon at its lowest point, and we essentially have light around the clock.

"A number of nations have made territorial claims on the continent, beginning with Argentina, which first established a weather station on Laurie Island in 1904. However, during the International Geophysical Year in 1958, the United States approached the eleven nations participating with a treaty, which took effect a couple years later. The primary points of the treaty prohibit the use of Antarctica for the purposes of war, allow for free scientific utilization, freeze the existing territorial claims, foster international scientific cooperation, and ban nuclear testing or nuclear waste disposal.

"That treaty has now lapsed, but the United States and other countries have continued to observe its caveats, and the international group, the Scientific Committee on Antarctic Research, known by the acronym SCAR, continues to coordinate activities on the continent. For the United States, the National Science Foundation, supported by the U.S. Navy, oversees most of the experiments and expeditions of that country.

"That is the general picture," Eames concluded. "We'll be

providing you with more detail as the situation becomes clearer. Are there any questions?"

She fielded a dozen questions, professing ignorance and a willingness to correct her lack of information on a couple of them.

When she was done, Cady returned to the podium, and using the controls there, dimmed the room lights and activated the big screen on the wall behind him. He brought up the picture of Navarino Island, with its computer-enhanced blowup of the airstrip, that McNichols had transmitted to him.

He went over the types of aircraft pictured—Mirages, Tornados, Hercs, and KC-130 tankers—and pointed out the fact that ground crews were loading weapons at the time the photograph was taken.

"We can't identify the specific ordnance types from this photo, but both bombs and missiles have been mounted," he said.

Baker raised a hand, and Cady recognized him.

"Isn't it possible, Colonel, that they're only preparing for an exercise?"

"It is," he agreed, "and the Peacekeeper Committee considered that angle, Major. Our analyst in Washington seems to think, however, from imagery captured from another photographic angle that the identification insignia on these airplanes has been changed."

"To that of a hostile, but harmless adversary?" Baker said. "You do that at your Red Flag war games out of Nellis."

"Again, Major, it's possible. However. . . ."

Cady brought up his next photo.

". . . this photo was snapped about three hundred miles south of Cape Horn."

He used the electronic pointer controlled from the podium to point out eleven circles on the photograph.

"These ships have been identified as both Argentinean and

Chilean. This is the destroyer *San Matias* right here. Over here is the frigate *Marguerite Bay*, and this is the minesweeper *San Jorge*. The others are large patrol boats, two freighters, and an oiler. All of them are on a course which is projected to end in the Shetland Islands, which are located to the west of the tip of the Antarctic Peninsula. This convoy assembled in a matter of hours."

Cady recognized his exec, Phil Anderson.

"That's not much of a strike force, is it, CAG?"

"They're only gunning for eight hundred people, Commander, a population that is spread out over five million square miles. It's also a population that is unarmed and which could be picked off piecemeal. Antarctica has no defensive capability, unless it's us."

"Right. I forgot."

"Are there any ideas about a specific target on the continent, Colonel?" Travers asked.

"None at the moment. As Major Eames said, DIA seems to think McMurdo would make a choice plum. It's got some thirty buildings, plus a big runway about five miles away, and it's the logistical support point for the U.S. stations at Eights, Palmer, Byrd, Amundson-Scott at the Pole, and Plateau."

"What about aircraft facilities?" Travers asked.

"Most of the bases have at least a short runway plowed out of the ice, but in virtually every case, the transports using them are outfitted with skis. The U.S. Navy flies winterized C-130s with skis which are owned by the National Science Foundation. If you see birds with orange tails, that's them. C-141s and C-5 Galaxies have flown in and out of Williams, also. There are a large number of helicopters, usually Bell Jet-Rangers and LongRangers, used for internal transportation, and they'll normally be finished in orange paint, also. DIA is trying now to get some satellites repositioned in order to get some reconnaissance photos for us, but it'll be a while before we know more."

"Colonel," Terri Eames asked, "is anything being done to notify the people at those stations?"

"About that, I don't know, Major. If our bosses are on the ball, I should think so."

"Could these people be evacuated? Perhaps that would be one of our roles," she said.

"We could handle it with the Seahawks, couldn't we, Major Baker?" Monmouth asked.

"Along the western coast, and if the weather cooperated, yes, sir," Baker said. "I think we'd have a tough time reaching the interior camps without refueling the choppers."

Cady didn't want to get into a brainstorming session just yet, even though he had been considering the refueling problem. The thought passed through his mind that, with the help of the C-130s out of McMurdo, they could just pull everyone off the continent and give it to the Argentines. He wasn't so sure it was worth fighting over. However, other people in much higher places would make those kinds of decisions. And the time for a decision to evacuate, he was sure, had passed some time ago.

"Right now," he said, "we want to prepare for whatever mission the people in New York throw at us. That means prepping our aircraft and our maintenance crews, and getting winterized ourselves. Everybody gets to dig out their manuals and review cold weather operation. As Major Eames mentioned, everyone gets to check out new clothing. At 0600 hours in the morning, I'll have a new duty roster posted, and we'll set up some review classes. Major Baker will cover arctic survival, Commander Anderson will deal with arctic aircraft operations, and Major Travers will take us through the unique aspects of navigation around the poles."

Baker, Anderson, and Travers gave him pained looks. They

were going to have to do some midnight studying to prepare for their training sessions.

"Questions, anyone?"

Travers had the same one Cady had been keeping to himself. "Why in hell do they want it?"

UNS U THANT
2240 HOURS LOCAL

Lieutenant Commander David George and his exec, a Russian Spetsnatz (Special Forces) captain named Gregori Suslov were the first to line up with their squads at Ship's Stores on Deck 4 aft.

Together, they stood at the head of the line of SEALs, making sure every man got everything that was coming to him.

Suslov eyed the shelves on the other side of the counter and said, "Whoever did the planning for this ship was very thorough, David."

"They were that, Gregori. I'll bet you, though, that they were thinking North Pole rather than South when they compiled their list. You've had experience in the arctic, haven't you?"

"Yes. It was near the Plesetsk cosmodrome."

"I did a six-week outing with the army in Alaska once, but it was some time ago. Can't say as I'm looking forward to a repeat of the episode."

Suslov looked puzzled. "Outing?"

"Like camping, Greg, old sod."

"Ah." Suslov turned toward a Brit, a former member of the SAS (Special Air Services), and said, "Be certain of how those boots fit, Sergeant. When we are on the ice, it is too late to find they are too large or too small."

The Brit said, "Aye, sir," but his dark and worldly eyes said, "You boob, I've done this before."

They watched as each man tried on thermally insulated boots or odd pieces of clothing, then signed for his issue. Their new wardrobe was unlike any that would be doled out to others in the ship's company. The boots were designed for combat wear, and the clothing was either white or thin coverings called overwhites to be worn on top of standard issue. They were also issued skis and poles, snowshoes, and backpacks in white. The skis were cross-country in design, though they were wider in order to support the weight of eighty-pound backpacks.

Suslov and George were the last to be outfitted, and they carried their gear up to the SEALs quarters on Deck 3. The detachment was assigned to three large spaces—two squad rooms and one large training and assembly area in which George and Suslov shared a desk in a corner alcove. They didn't get much use of the desk, either, since their administrative clerk had commandeered it. Since George didn't think much of paper-pushing, he didn't mind giving up the desk.

They had the two squads lay out their equipment on the deck in the assembly room and conducted an inspection to make certain everyone had everything he was supposed to have, from white helmet covers to the requisite numbers of spare gloves and woolen socks.

When they were each finished with their squads, George reminded them of an 0600 assembly, then dismissed them. He and Suslov stowed their gear in their lockers and left for the starboard elevator which would take them to C Deck where they shared a stateroom. Traffic in the corridors was dying down as people settled in for the night.

George got a can of grape soda from the small refrigerator, took a long swig, and then sat down to unlace his boots. He loved grape soda, and there was nearly a case of it in the refrigerator. Suslov was addicted to Pepsi-Cola.

Suslov plopped on a chair at the single desk, unfolded the map Eames had provided, and pored over it.

"Do you know, David, that I was unaware of the existence of Russian stations in the Antarctic?"

"Come on."

"It is true. Here is one called Sovetskaya. It is in the interior at three thousand, six hundred and fifty meters of altitude. And here, on the coast, is Mirnyy Base. I do not think my government advertised these well. On the west side is the Bellingshausen Sea. I remember from my history classes that he discovered the continent."

George pulled his boots off and lined them up next to his chair. "Did he really?"

Suslov dropped the map and turned around. "I doubt it. The more I travel and read, the more I have to revise what I have learned."

"That's true for all of us. The history books I read in high school neatly left out a lot of women, blacks, and other minorities. They're being rewritten, or maybe they have been already. I haven't been to school in a long time. I think there's a lot of people in my generation, and the generations that preceded us, that may be ignorant of some interesting history."

"Do you think that we will make an entry in the history books?" the Russian asked.

"I hope to hell not, Greg, old sod."

BUENOS AIRES, ARGENTINA
2355 HOURS LOCAL

The headquarters of the Front for South American Determination was located in a back room of the house that Juan

Silvera leased. It was located in the southeastern part of the city, high on the side of a hill, and it overlooked the broad reaches of the Rio de la Plata.

He thought that he was going to miss the view.

Already, he had sent Lucia for a long visit with her parents in Rosario, leaving the house without a female presence. Ricardo Fuentes was directing the five men who were packing the office. Most of what was there would be going with them, though they would leave a small contingent of men to operate the office as a communications way station.

Silvera sat at the last remaining desk and watched the lights of shipping in the channel. When, at last, it was time, he dialed the telephone number in Santiago, the capital city of Chile.

The connection took some time to complete, but the telephone was answered after one ring. The recipient said nothing.

"Meadowlark," Silvera said.

"Un momentito."

A minute went by before another and deeper voice came on the line. "Chopstick."

"It is a time for decisions."

"And the decision is affirmative."

Silvera broke the connection, then dialed the local telephone number. He went through the same routine, but with different code names, and he received the same response.

Leaning across the desk, he turned up the volume on the large radio resting in the corner of the desk top. Adjusting the squelch, he removed most of the static from the frequency he had keyed in earlier.

The microphone was mounted on a desk pedestal, and he pulled it close, then pressed the transmit stud in its base.

"Jaguar and Ashcan, this is Cheetah."

They were standing by their radios.

"Jaguar," Suarez said.

"Ashcan," Diego Enriquez said. Silvera did not know why he had insisted on that code name.

"Vaya con Dios," Silvera said, "go with God."

4 DECEMBER

The last of the KC-130 tankers took off on the hour, in the slowly gathering light of dawn, and Emilio Suarez stood at the side of the runway, his hair blowing in the cool wind, and watched it retract its landing gear and flaps as it disappeared over the lip of the hill and into the low-lying clouds.

He felt pumped up, every sense alerted. The images around him were sharper than they had ever been. His hour had come.

The publicity would come later, but he thought with great satisfaction of the impact it would have on his siblings on the *Rancho de Suruca*. His sister, who thought of herself as Argentina's greatest undiscovered artist, and his older brother, who *knew* he was the supreme cattleman and business entrepreneur in the country, would learn that Emilio Suarez de Suruca carried a name that would be known the world over.

But that was for later.

"Every man will achieve greatness today, Major," he said to Tellez.

"It could be, Emilio, and then again, who knows?"

Suarez did not like ambivalent people. One took a stand, and one backed it up with every ounce of his being.

"This will go so smoothly, you will not believe it, Roberto."

"Of course."

"Who is to stop us?"

"We're breaking the first commandment of the treaty, Emilio. No doubt someone will become a little angry. The Scientific Committee on Antarctic Research will yelp like a stung dog."

"The treaty no longer exists, and besides, we were not a signatory to it. The SCAR holds no power over us."

"The tradition of that treaty exists, Emilio."

"Yes, but it will be months before they react, and by then we will have established our defenses, our contrite apology to the United Nations, and our terms for ongoing research. That is, if they react at all. This is not the Persian Gulf, with its known and vast oil reserves. This is an ice desert with eight hundred people attempting to live in it. The diplomatic dialogue will last for years, and during those years we will become firmly entrenched."

"Of course," Tellez said again.

The man could be infuriating.

"You do not believe this?"

"I am not a crystal ball gazer, Emilio. And I am not being paid as one. I will do the job for which I am being paid, and we will see what will be."

Suarez sighed and looked pointedly at his watch. "It is time for you to go. Take care."

"Care of what, Emilio? It is like shooting at blind men who have their arms broken."

Tellez spun on his heel and walked down the side of the runway toward where his Tornados were parked. The tufts of grass that had crowded the runway until the FSAD aircraft had arrived in force were crushed now, bent to the ground, and Tellez kicked at them as he walked.

Despite the dozens of ground crewmen and pilots darting around the airplanes, connecting the start-carts, attending to the last-minute details, Suarez had the disconcerting feeling that Tellez was all by himself, sauntering down the apron, walking into oblivion.

He shook off the image and looked for the sun, though because of the overcast skies, it would not be seen from this island today; still, the sky was brightening, and he was determined to have that positive sign be his omen.

Suarez walked the other way, east, toward the transport aircraft. The tents had all been folded and loaded aboard. Parked just off the loading ramp of the nearest C-130 was a mess truck, and he stopped at its lowered tailgate to pour himself a cup of coffee from the huge urn standing on the tailgate. This truck would be the last to be loaded before the transports took off.

He contemplated the huge stack of boxes and crates covered with tarpaulins and guarded by armed men. Suarez knew almost to the ounce what was under that canvas: twenty-one tons more of food, ordnance, and replacement parts. For lack of transport, and for that matter, pilots, the materiel would have to be shipped to its destination in the second wave. The same was true of the fuel. His tankers would return to replenish themselves from the fuel bladders, even as more fuel arrived from the mainland and refilled the bladders.

At 0445 hours, without a whisper on the radios, but with a thunderous roar of their turbofans, the eight Tornados took off, one behind the other. With their full loads of missiles and bombs, they looked as deadly as the pumas for which they were code-named. The heavily-laden aircraft seemed to struggle to clear the hills at the end of the runway.

Suarez went around the truck and stood by its front fender

to urinate. Then he walked back up the runway to his Mirage, stopping along the way to shake the hand of each of his pilots and to wish them Godspeed.

When he reached his own craft, he circled the sleek airplane with his crew chief, examining it for abnormal hydraulic leaks or stiffness in the control surfaces. The delta-winged Dassault-Breguet Mirage 2000 was the sixth aircraft in the Mirage family, but it was smaller and lighter than its relatives. With a single M53-5 bleed-turbojet engine, it was meant to emulate many of the characteristics of the General Dynamics F-16 fighter aircraft. It had taken Suarez many long hours and a great deal of practice to become accustomed to the fly-by-wire control system, but now he thought it superb.

With his knuckles, he thumped one of the 1700-liter external fuel tanks hanging below the wing. The dull thud reassured him.

He was already wearing his flight suit, the pockets of which were crammed with his personal choice of survival items: a folding knife, fishing line and hooks, two water bottles, extra ammunition, and spare sets of gloves and socks. The crew chief helped him fit the pressure suit, the underarm holster with the Smith and Wesson .38-caliber revolver, and the safety harness.

Suarez stood by the nose of his Mirage, cradling his helmet in the crook of his elbow, while the sergeant snapped several photographs for him. He would have a record of this historic morning for his own posterity and perhaps for the edification of his family. Eventually, they would know that he had achieved a plateau they could only look up to.

Climbing the ladder, he checked for the safety pins in the ejection seat, then slipped over the coaming and into the cockpit. He settled into the seat with its built-in parachute and slipped his helmet on. The crew chief helped him with the harness fastenings as well as the pressure suit, oxygen, and radio connections. He accepted the survival pack from the sergeant and clipped it to the front of his harness. It contained a parka, a thermal-layered sleeping bag, an ultra-thin one-man tent, Sterno cans, packets of food, and a life raft. Suarez thought the life raft superfluous. If he, or anyone, went down over the water, they might last for a minute.

He spun his finger in a miniature circle, and the chief slipped down the ladder, took it away, and told his men to activate the start-cart.

The ignition checklist took several minutes, but soon, with airflow provided by the cart, the turbine was spinning, and at thirty-five per cent revolutions, Suarez started fuel flow and ignition. The engine whined into life.

Turning on his radios, he checked that they were on the proper frequencies, but refrained from using them. After returning the salutes of his ground crew, Suarez released the brakes, pulled forward onto the hard surface of the runway, and turned left. He taxied to the far east end, pulling off the strip before reaching the end, then turning 180 degrees to center the airplane on the narrow strip.

Testing the engine by running it up to full power output, he waited while the other eleven Mirages fell into a single long line, just off the runway to his right. He held his hands high, in view of the two ordnance men, so they would know that he would not accidentally touch inappropriate switches or buttons. They ran beneath the wings to pull the safety pins and streamers from the ordnance. Backing away, they signalled his clearance.

When he had received a thumbs-up signal from each of his pilots, he again ran the power up to one hundred percent, released the brakes, then shoved the throttle outboard, past the detent, into afterburner.

The Mirage hesitated only a couple seconds, then surged

forward. It felt sluggish, however, with the load and with the uneven, rippled surface of the airstrip. He watched the air speed indicator with more than a bit of anxiety. The crosswind was gusting slightly to ten knots, and he kept it balanced with the rudder pedals. The aircraft lurched over a rise in the strip, kept gathering speed, reached 160 knots, felt light, then gained another ten knots, and he eased the nosewheel from the ground a few meters from the end of the runway. A split second later, the rumbling of the landing gear ceased, and he was airborne.

He rotated gradually, cleared the hill, and was almost immediately in the clouds. He retracted his landing gear and flaps. Keeping his eyes on the key indicators of the Head Up Display (HUD)—airspeed, altitude, turn-and-bank symbol, he avoided looking through the canopy at the swirling clouds and becoming disoriented. When his airspeed passed 220 knots, he cut off the afterburner in the interest of conserving fuel.

At six hundred meters of altitude, he emerged into blindingly bright daylight and immediately went into a left turn, continuing to climb. Within ten minutes, all of the Mirages had joined him at 3500 meters, forming into a vee-shaped flying group, and he took up a southeasterly heading. Suarez set the pace. While the Mirage 2000 could achieve Mach 2.3, or 2445 kilometers per hour, above eleven thousand meters, not all of the aircraft in the formation were of the same type, and he would balance the need for speed with the requirements of his other airplanes and the consumption of fuel.

The Antarctic Peninsula was but 1400 kilometers away, and he could be there in less than forty minutes, but timing was important. He had had to evaluate the targets, the speed of the tankers, the speed of his cargo transports—which should now be taking off, and the speed capabilities of the fighter aircraft. Suarez jockeyed his throttle until his air speed indicator read 450 knots.

To either side of him, the eleven Mirages of his squadron were neatly aligned in echelon, each airplane stepped up behind the one in front and offset to either the left or the right. It was a magnificent sight. He felt like Napoleon or Ney or Julius Caesar leading his legions into battle.

Suarez was proud of them. He had forgotten to arrange for photographs, but later, after they had settled in at their objective, he would have someone on a C-130 take pictures of the formation for him.

He glanced at the digital chronometer mounted on the instrument panel. Tellez's Tornados should now be leaving the tankers, taking up a course for Anvers Island.

The next forty minutes went by almost too rapidly, propelled by anticipation, and the KC-130 Hercules tankers appeared on his radar scope precisely where they were supposed to appear. Within two minutes, he had them visually. They were at three thousand meters, slightly below, their camouflage paint standing out clearly against the sea.

Beyond the tankers, Suarez could see the northern edge of the distinctive Antarctic Ocean. It was an interesting phenomenon. The deep ocean currents of the Atlantic, Pacific, and Indian oceans ran along the bottom and picked up food-laden sediment, carrying it into the upper regions of the Antarctic seas. The warm waters rose while the colder Antarctic waters began to sink. The line between the cold and warm waters was called the Antarctic Convergence and was evident in a five-degree-Fahrenheit difference in temperatures as well as a visual change between the blue of the tropical oceans and the muddy gray-green of the Antarctic.

The camouflage paint of the tankers would help disguise them from above while they were over the Antarctic Sea, but it was not very useful over the Atlantic. Nor would it hide them on the continent. Suarez thought, however, that it was a moot point. He did not expect to be bothered over the continent by anyone for months, if ever. If the United Nations acted against them, it would take the participating nations several months to mobilize their forces.

He waggled his wings as the previously agreed signal, and the fighters broke formation and aligned themselves with the three tankers designated for this refueling. Afterwards, those three tankers would return to Argentina to be refilled while the other four would trail after the fighter group, prepared to offer vital help if needed. One tanker would remain aloft, flying far to the south to support Roberto Tellez on his special mission.

Suarez backed off his throttle and lost altitude until he achieved the same level as his tanker, which had turned into straight and level flight to the east. With small nudges of the throttle, and watching the director lights on the bottom of the fuselage, he worked his way up behind it, prepared to make corrections if turbulence off the larger aircraft's wings threatened his stability.

The drogue basket was deployed from the tanker's left wing, floating along behind the Hercules some fifteen meters below it. Suarez had practiced this maneuver many times, and his refueling probe entered the basket on his first attempt. The green light-emitting diode on the instrument panel activated, indicating he had a proper connection. He tapped the throttle a little to keep pressure forward on the basket, then clicked his microphone transmit button twice to tell the other aircraft that he was prepared. Jaguar Three moved up and connected with the drogue on the right wing.

In a matter of seconds, 3100 liters of aviation fuel was transferred to his internal tanks. He had not yet utilized his external tanks.

He backed away, rolled the right wing up, and dove away

from the rendezvous. Ten minutes later, his Mirages were in formation again, and Suarez aimed the deadly dozen for the Shetland Islands.

THE SAN MATIAS
0530 HOURS LOCAL

Captain Diego Enriquez, though he expected no opposition at all, deployed his ships as if they were in imminent peril of assault by submarines, aircraft, and opposing marine forces. He was a cautious man when he had to be.

The three freighters and the tanker were in trail formation behind the San Matias, spread far enough apart that a single torpedo or missile would not endanger all three of them. The minesweeper San Jorge was on the point, but so far, she was warning them only of the ever larger and larger icebergs they were encountering. The icebergs floated past them with some kind of intrinsic majesty, some much taller and of more mass than the destroyer.

The turbulent waters of the Antarctic Ocean were running swells of eight and nine feet, and their turmoil was caused by the constant west winds which pushed the surface water from west to east around the continent. The few crewmen exposed to the biting wind on the decks were wrapped in arctic clothing which made them seem twice as large as they were.

The frigate Marguerite Bay, named aptly for one of the bays of the Antarctic Peninsula, had assumed a position at the rear of the flotilla, protecting them from hostile intentions from behind. The sixteen patrol boats were ranged far to the left and right, providing flanking protection.

Enriquez sat in his chair—he had designed it himself—bolted to the deck on the bridge. Standing beside him, watching one of the giant floes go by, were Commander Dante

Montez, who had the watch, and Lieutenant Umberto Mondragon, the navigation officer.

"Do we have a position, Lieutenant?"

"Yes, sir. We are now one hundred and twenty kilometers due west of Livingston Island in the Shetlands. Anvers Island is three hundred and sixteen kilometers ahead, on our bearing one-six-five degrees."

"Very good, Lieutenant. Air traffic?"

"None, sir. At least, none within our radar coverage."

That amounted to 250 kilometers, though the mountains of the peninsula might hide an airplane if it was flying low. Ground clutter returns on the radar had increased, also, with the growing population of icebergs.

He tapped Montez on the arm. "Commander, signal all ships and boats to the new heading of one-six-five, then order a decrease in speed to five knots for the next hour so that the departing boats may refuel."

"Immediately, Captain." Montez left them for the communications compartment, aft of the bridge.

The slower speed would assist Patrol Boats Eight, Eleven, Twelve, and Fifteen as they took on fuel from the tanker. Those four boats would then leave the fleet and head for the Shetland Islands to assume patrol duties.

Another four boats would be ordered on to Anvers Island shortly, as the balance of the fleet turned east and headed directly for the northern region of the peninsula.

Enriquez checked his watch, then said, "Lieutenant, in half an hour, we will want all crews on alert, prepared to go to general quarters at any time."

"I will see to it, Captain."

Now it was a matter of waiting, but the wait would not be long.

Enriquez scanned the skies. He expected to see friendly aircraft at any moment. He did not expect to see hostile aircraft or surface ships for many weeks, but when he did, he was prepared to see that their crews died quickly.

Unlike President Silvera, who seemed to share Fuentes's notion that diplomatic means would solve their coming problems, Enriquez knew from experience that there would be bloodshed.

It would not be his blood staining the gray sea.

PUMA LEADER
0605 HOURS LOCAL

Roberto Tellez was the first to break radio silence.

"Puma Five, One."

"This is Five."

"Your two elements will now deploy."

"Five."

Tellez looked back over his shoulder and watched as the four Tornados peeled away from the formation, rising above it, and took up a heading for Faraday. The British station would not be exempt from this morning's activities.

He had been losing altitude steadily and slowly since leaving the tankers, and he and his remaining three fighter-bombers were now at 1400 meters above the surface. Above him, the sky was amazingly clear. There were a few clouds towering on his right.

Below, it was a different story. The winds were whipping the surface snow into a frenzied ground blizzard, and it was difficult to make out landmarks. Defining Anvers Island was a near impossibility, anyway, since the ice shelf connected it to the peninsula and gave the appearance of a single, solid landmass. He was dependent upon what his Texas Instruments ground mapping and attack radar scanner could tell him about his relationship with the coordinates of the American's Palmer Station on the island.

In this region, also, the Magnetic Pole, which is offset from the geographical South Pole, did funny things to the magnetic compass. In all of the aircraft under his command, Tellez had placed masking tape over the magnetic compasses so that the pilots would not inadvertently refer to them. They would rely on the INS, the Ferranti Inertial Navigation System, and the radio compasses, currently tuned to the transmitter at Primavera, the Argentine station 180 kilometers north of Palmer Station.

Pressing the transmit button on the throttle lever, Tellez said, "Pumas Two, Three, and Four, trail formation, combat spread. Bring your sweep to three-five degrees."

The other pilots confirmed his order as he reached for the manual sweep lever behind the throttles and moved the swing-wings forward to thirty-five degrees, short of their slow-speed twenty-five degrees, but way forward of the high-speed sixty-six degrees of sweep.

He reduced the throttle settings, and the Tornado lost speed to three hundred knots as he banked to the east. Checking the rearview mirror, he made certain that the other aircraft were flying with enough clearance from each other. If they had to descend below the level of the ground blizzard, and lost sight of each other, he didn't want to lose airplanes to midair collisions.

"Pumas, be calm and follow the plan," he said on the radio, then on the ICS to his navigator, "Jesus, take us in."

"If you will turn to the left by two degrees, we will be right on the approach path."

Tellez eased the control stick to the left and took two degrees off the radio compass.

"Right there, Roberto, that is fine. Now, let us lose a thousand meters of altitude."

He continued to follow Ramirez's instructions, and the

ground blizzard continued to loom upward toward them. The closer they came to the surface, however, the more transparent the storm appeared. He began to see solid ice formations through the snow.

"The storm is only sixty meters above the ground," Ramirez reported.

"Good, we may see the target."

"It would be helpful," the backseater agreed. "Here is the initial point. Go to the left ninety degrees."

Tellez banked hard to the left and leveled the wings as he came up on a heading of ten degrees. A quick glance in the rearview mirror told him that the others had followed, though Alberto Ramon, in Puma Four, had drifted far to the right coming out of the turn.

"Puma Four, close it in."

"Closing in, One."

"One minute to target," Ramircz said.

The wind was now nearly directly behind them, and the Tornado picked up airspeed. He countered it by reducing the setting of the throttles.

They were less than a hundred meters above ground level now, and the icy fingers of the storm seemed to reach up for them, but they managed to slip away from its deadly grasp.

Tellez had memorized the aerial pictures of Palmer Station, and though he had never been there, he was certain that he would know every one of the huts and buildings that comprised the base the instant he saw them.

Patches of the ground appeared irregularly.

"Activating laser," the backseater said.

The Ferranti LRMTS (Laser Ranger and Marked-Target Seeker) was in a retractable pod on the starboard side, and greatly simplified the bombing run, which could normally be made in one pass. The navigator would use it to mark the target as soon as he saw it. Once marked, the computer would determine the release point for the bomb load.

"Be certain that you get the right building," Tellez warned him.

"I will be certain, Roberto."

Each of the fighters would release its four Beluga cluster bombs on a designated building. The bombs contained hundreds of miniature bomblets, which would destroy a wide area, even if the target was not hit directly.

He saw the station abruptly, and very close, merely dark images shining through the snow. The huts and snow sheds were spread over a wide area, and they were partially submerged in the snow.

Before he could say anything, Ramirez reported, "I see it . . . have the target . . . committed."

The station flashed past below them, but it was seconds after he had felt the bombs release.

He rolled left and looked back.

The station was already out of sight, obscured by the blowing snow, but the other three Tornados whistled in on the target, released their bombs, and turned to follow him.

He did not see any of the detonations directly, but a sudden blurt of orange illumination, diffused by the snow, suggested that one of the primary targets had been hit.

Tellez thought about making another pass, to assess the damage, then decided he did not want to see it.

"Form up on me, now, Pumas. We will head north at an altitude of three thousand meters."

DEFENSE INTELLIGENCE AGENCY
0615 HOURS LOCAL

So many of the people McNichols dealt with, he knew only by name and the sound of their voices. This one was definitely female, but enchantingly husky, even with the warble of the scrambled satellite communications circuit.

"My name is McNichols. A few people call me Cam."

"Major Theresa Eames," she said.

With that voice, he pictured a tall woman, deep-chested, extroverted. Just right for him.

"Do you know who I am? What I do?"

"Yes, Mr. McNichols."

"Look, Major, this is a whole new procedure for us. Sir Charles wants us working directly, so the pertinent facts don't get filtered out in the communications process. It looks like it's going to get hairy, so let's you and me be buddies. I'm Cam. Can you be Theresa?"

"Terri works, too."

"Great, Terri. I suppose, too, if we lose our secure communications channel, we should adopt a code name."

"I'm Jericho," she said. "You're Pack Rat."

"Pack Rat?"

"I picture you as a pack rat."

"Thank you, ma'am."

"Hoarding all that information."

"Oh, yeah. Okay. Right now, I'm looking at this big screen I have on my wall, and I see a lot of little streaks heading for a big ice cube."

"They're attacking?"

"As we speak," McNichols said. "There's twelve hostiles breaking up and heading for different parts of the Shetlands. We've identified them as Mirage fighter-bombers. Two groups of four, which are Panavia Tornados, are messing around to the south, down by Anvers Island. Hard to tell just now, since my current satellite will only give me direct visual and the aircraft occasionally disappear, but I think one group of four may have just made a pass over Palmer Station."

"That's all you can see?" she asked.

"There's a ground blizzard active on the western coast of the peninsula, Terri. I can't make out details on the ground. I don't see Palmer Station, for instance, but the coordinates are right."

"Have those people been warned?"

"I've got a bunch of my assistants working the phones and radios," he said. "They're making contact wherever they can. Mostly, we're working through the radio operator at McMurdo. Just a sec. . . ."

Jack Neihouse was waving wildly at him through the open doorway to his office, and McNichols slipped his hand over the telephone's mouthpiece. "What have you got, Jack?"

"They just hit Palmer Station, Cam. Four planes, but nobody down there recognized the type or the insignia. Hell, no one really saw the planes, but they heard them."

"Damage, man! Casualties?"

"They're still checking. Four buildings hit and in flames."

McNichols went back to his line with Eames. "Palmer's been zapped, Terri. They count four buildings on fire, and they're looking for casualties."

"Damn it!"

Another of his assistants, Pamela Akins, was signalling to him frantically, yelling, "Arctowski!"

"Hey, Terri, it's going to get hectic here, and we're not really set up as a combat center. I'm going to have to change that, but for now, I'll let you go and call you later, okay?"

"Yes, but hurry. Now, you've got me worried."

"They just hit the Polish station in the Shetlands. I'll call when I've got a full list for you."

McNichols was suddenly afraid that it was going to be a long list.

And he wondered what the hell the diplomats were doing.

BELLINGHAUSEN STATION, ANTARCTICA
0614 HOURS LOCAL

Dr. Igor Stregalov, who had unfortunately drawn duty for this week as steward and was required to oversee the preparation of meals, had been up for two hours.

There was no more thankless job at the station. Poor meals resulted in deriding remarks from the residents, in addition to declining morale. And Stregalov was a scientist, a biologist, not a chef trained in Paris. He ate to sustain energy, not to enjoy, and he detested the kitchen.

In fact, he had slipped away from the kitchen to find his anorak and mittens, then had left the main hut by way of a side door, just to make a quick check on his harem.

Stregalov's harem, so named by his colleagues, consisted of twelve female imperial penguins. The chinstrap penguin was common to the Antarctic Peninsula, and Stregalov had imported the imperial, which did not normally roam, from farther south. He was trying to acclimate them to their new home—a kennel located behind the warehouse—over a period of three months. Then, when he released them, he would determine whether they stayed in place, or if they sought to return to their normal breeding grounds, he would track them with radio-imbedded collars.

He had come to know them well, and each of the magnificent creatures now had her own name: Natasha, Ingrid, Katrinka, and the like. Some of his ladies stood ninety centimeters tall and weighed almost thirty-six kilograms. They were the largest of the penguins. Stregalov was keeping a careful record of their weights, and as he had feared, they had all lost weight in the first days after their relocation, perhaps out of fear, perhaps as a result of depression. The weight loss had stabilized now, and they seemed to be eating better.

He worried about them, and he visited them often. They

were coming to know him, too, especially as a feeder, and they now tolerated him in their pens.

And this morning, as he leaned into the windblown snow and began his three hundred-meter trek toward the warehouse, he heard a strange noise and came to a complete standstill.

At first, he thought it was the moaning of some strange animal. Or the wind.

Then, in seconds, it became mechanical, a high-pitched, rising scream.

Frozen in place, Stregalov whipped his head about, searching for the source of the noise. He could see very little in the snowstorm, not even the warehouse from where he stood.

And then, it was there.

Then gone.

An airplane.

Another.

More.

And the ground erupted beneath his feet, tossing him like a rag doll.

Dazed, he found himself on the ground beside a Sno-Cat.

The ground trembled.

Waves of concussion rolled over him.

A sudden sting in his left arm startled him, and he looked down to see a red stain spreading over the yellow sleeve of his anorak.

The ground convulsed again, his hearing deadened, a great red glow pulsed out of the snow behind him, and Stregalov pulled himself under the Sno-Cat, clamping his right mitten over the wound on his arm.

He couldn't understand this.

And then he thought of his harem, and looked up, toward the kennel.

The warehouse was in flames.

The roar of the airplanes was dying away.

Stregalov rolled out from under the Sno-Cat, leaped to his feet, and began stumbling toward the warehouse, skirting it wide to the right to avoid the flames.

When he reached what was left of the kennel, and saw the charred meat and bloody bodies, he sagged to his knees and cried.

JAGUAR LEADER
0620 HOURS LOCAL

Jaguar Nine checked in on the squadron radio net.

"Leader, this is Nine."

"Nine, Jaguar One."

"We have four off of Arctowski. Six targets destroyed."

"Acknowledged," Suarez said.

He and his flight of four were just regaining two thousand meters of altitude after their bomb run on Bellinghausen, which was a Russian base in the Shetland Islands. The bright red-orange flash of the fuel supply detonating still echoed in his mind. It was a satisfying image.

"Jaguar Five, One," he said into his oxygen mask microphone.

"Five."

"Situation report, please."

"Two minutes out of Signy. All targets hit."

"Understood," he said.

Signy was the United Kingdom station northeast of the peninsula.

He rolled to the right, checking his mirror to be certain his flight stayed with him, then advanced the throttle when his radio compass showed him a heading of 163 degrees. He had followed Tellez's excellent suggestion and masked off his magnetic compass.

Airspeed 670 knots. He had just broken the sound barrier, a reflection of his jubilation.

He held the speed at Mach 1, using precious fuel for seven minutes, then backed off the throttle.

Despite his bronze-tinted visor and the low sun, the view ahead was blinding. The horizon was wavery with blowing snow. Directly below, the landscape shifted like desert sand, which Suarez thought appropriate. Technically, because of the lack of plant life and of precipitation, Antarctica was classified as a desert.

Switching frequencies to the one used by Tellez, he depressed the transmit button.

"Puma One, Jaguar One."

"Puma."

"Your location?"

"Coming in on Primavera," Tellez said. "It's going to be touchy with the wind and visibility."

"We will be there in two minutes," Suarez warned him. "Jaguar out."

He concentrated on lining up for the interception with Primavera's coordinates, and less than two minutes later, picked out the shadowy boxes of the Argentine station in the snow. It helped that he saw Tellez's four aircraft circling the base a thousand meters below him. Swinging his head to the right, he spied the four other aircraft of Puma Squadron four or five kilometers farther south, coming from their sortie over Faraday.

Losing a little more speed, Suarez put the Mirage in a left bank and began to circle as he watched Tellez's first attempt at the runway. Simultaneously he began to slowly descend.

The Primavera runway was 3300 meters long, or was supposed to be, as of November first. Plowed and leveled out of the ice and snow by bulldozers, the hard surface would be uneven, but the narrow strip of PSP (pierced steel planking) that was to have been laid down should accept the fighter aircraft readily enough if they took care. The PSP and the bribe to the station manager, Ortiz, had been expensive, and was listed in Suarez's budget as "Arrival amenities."

He monitored the Puma frequency while he circled, his squadron in trail behind him.

"Primavera, Puma One," Tellez said, calling the station's air control.

"We have you, One. You will have to hold a minute, until we get the snow removal vehicles off the runway. You will have a crosswind from the west at twelve knots, blowing snow, three centimeters of snow drifted onto part of the runway, visibility one kilometer."

Suarez thought the report optimistic as he looked down on the scene. Most aircraft operating in Antarctica utilized skis directly on the ice, but that option was not viable with fighter aircraft which performed much better in the air with their wheels retracted, precluding the use of skis or even of the oversized tires for rough landing strips.

The Tornados, with their large tires and anti-skid brakes, were more suited for rough fields than the Mirages, but they would be taxed to the limit for this airfield, especially with pilots that had never attempted landings in such weather.

The Tornados continued to circle.

"All right, Puma One, we are ready for you."

Tellez, being the superb pilot that he was, as well as a brave man, made the first attempt.

Suarez watched him fly several kilometers to the south on his downwind leg, turn onto the approach, and slow perceptively as he neared the end of the single north-south runway, which as far as Suarez was concerned, was invisible. A white runway hidden in a white ground blizzard. It had been laid out on the north-south axis, contrary to the prevailing west wind, because of the geography. A two hundred-meter high ridge of ice and rock to the east of the base prevented construction of the runway on an east-west configuration, but also diminished the effect of the crosswinds to some degree.

With a suddenness that was startling, six red flares ignited, defining both ends and the middle of the runway.

Tellez's Tornado descended through the top of the ground blizzard, becoming a shadowy form that raced above the surface at 180 knots. It continued to blur as it approached the first two flares, centering itself between them, then became a blob that slowed quickly.

"Puma Leader to Pumas. I am down. There is a high hump on the southern end of the runway, fifty meters beyond the flares. Be certain to fly over it. The steel mat is firm enough, but midway down the strip, the snow cover has frozen into ice. Puma Two, go."

The second and third Tornados achieved the runway successfully.

"Puma Four," Primavera control said, "begin your approach."

"Four," Alberto Ramon responded.

The last four Pumas, the ones that had attacked Faraday, had now reached the base and begun to circle below Suarez's flight. They would be the next aircraft to land since their fuel states were more critical than those of the Mirages.

Above Suarez, he saw four more Mirages beginning to circle. Jaguar Nine, Sancho Amador, and his flight of four had caught up with him.

Suarez was out of position to see very much, several kilometers north of the north end of the runway, and 1200 meters above ground level, but he heard the dialogue.

"Four!" Tellez yelled. "You're drifting left. Correct or go around!"

"I can make it, Major Tellez . . . wheels down . . . correcting. . . . there . . . goddamn it!"

The radio connection was broken, and Suarez cursed under his breath.

He keyed his microphone.

"Puma Leader?"

Primavera control replied, "We have an emergency on the runway. All aircraft continue to hold."

Mary, Mother of God!

One runway, and aircraft continuing to arrive. The third element of Mirages would be here soon, and directly after them would come the cargo aircraft. Then, most of the tankers.

As he turned to parallel the runway, heading south, he peered through the canopy at the space between the flares. He could not see flames, which was fortunate. A burning aircraft would probably melt the ice base and ruin the runway for the rest of them.

"Puma Leader, Jaguar Leader."

"I have you, Jaguar."

"Provide a situation report."

"Four went sideways and collapsed his gear. The airplane did not tumble."

"Can you tow it off the runway?" Suarez asked.

"Affirmative, but we have a little problem," Tellez said. "There are a lot of missiles that were ripped from the pylons. We will have to collect and safe them first. They will have to repair a section of the runway."

The brightening sky that had seemed a positive omen when he took off this morning now seemed dimmer. A long delay could threaten the aircraft scheduled to land last.

He checked his fuel state, which was not yet critical, then switched frequencies and called the lead tanker.

"Esso One, Jaguar One."

"Go ahead, Jaguar One."

"Advance your rendezvous with Primavera. You will probably have to refuel aircraft earlier than expected."

FORTY KILOMETERS SOUTH OF BUENOS AIRES, ARGENTINA
0650 HOURS LOCAL

Aboard his Mystère-Falcon, Juan Silvera drank coffee and listened to the jumbled radio transmissions being monitored by the pilot. He had channeled them over the cabin's speakers, but because of the distance, there was a lot of static, and the voices were difficult to decipher.

Ricardo Fuentes and four more of Silvera's assistants were also listening, their faces intent, as the situation at Primavera became clearer.

"A plane has crashed on the runway," Fuentes said.

"Damn it! I want reports on the attacks," Silvera told him.

"Perhaps we should divert to another airport until it is cleared up," Fuentes said. "We cannot refuel in the air."

"No. Go to the cockpit and have the pilot radio Suarez. I want to know about the attacks."

Fuentes climbed out of his chair and made his way unsteadily up the narrow aisle. He was not a frequent flyer. Silvera did not think he would be a good sailor, either.

Fifteen minutes later, he reeled back down the aisle and collapsed in his seat opposite Silvera. His face was pale.

"All of the bases were attacked as planned and on schedule," he reported. "Suarez says he has everything under control."

"It doesn't sound to me as if everything is under control."

"One of the Tornados was damaged on landing."

Silvera groaned. "That airplane cost eleven million dollars American, and it is a used airplane, yet."

"It is repairable," Suarez said.

Silvera leaned back in the soft cushions of his seat and ran his hand through his hair. He thought perhaps his hair was getting thinner. He knew he was conducting a war, and he knew there would be casualties, but he had hoped to avoid them this early in the game. Major Tellez, the mercenary Suarez had hired, had said to plan on a thirty per cent attrition ratio, but both Suarez and Silvera had thought that number extremely high. If the crash at Primavera was a standard by which to judge the rest of the operation, however, Tellez might be right. And Silvera would continue to lose his hair.

Through the round window next to him, Silvera had a view of blue skies and blue seas. On the horizon ahead were a few puffy white clouds. He tried to envision what was ahead, but found it difficult. He had only been to Antarctica once, to Esperanza Base in the summer of last year, and that had occurred on a rather peaceful day.

"We could, *Presidente,* make the announcement from here," Fuentes said.

"No. I must be on the ground in Antarctica. To tell the world of our feat, while two thousand kilometers away, would be the same as would-be dictators making proclamations from exile. We will not be in exile from our homeland, Ricardo."

He knew that Fuentes, who had never set foot on the continent, would be having difficulty thinking of it as his homeland.

UNS U THANT
0620 HOURS LOCAL

Cady turned the handle on the urn and watched the strong, hot coffee stream into his mug. He let the level rise dangerously close to the top before killing the stream, then carrying it over to the table where Eames, Baker, d'Argamon, and Charley Adams sat.

Adams pulled a chair over from the next table. "Have a seat, Shark. Take two if you like."

"One will do, Shaker."

D'Argamon took the addition of a fifth chair at the table as an opportunity to move his chair closer to Eames. Baker scowled at him.

Cady looked at the faces hanging over their coffee cups. No one was eating breakfast, though Baker had a plate with a partially consumed fried egg in front of him.

"This is a festive gathering," he said.

"You heard about the attack?" Baker said.

"Yes." Monmouth had given him the word earlier. "We didn't think we were going to get there in time to prevent it."

"Terri has received the after-action report from her boyfriend at DIA," d'Argamon said.

"He's not my boyfriend."

"Then, I must be."

She ignored him.

"What's it look like, Terri?" he asked.

"There were five different strikes, Colonel. They hit Palmer and Faraday in the mid-portion of the peninsula. In the northern islands, Arctowski, Bellinghausen, and Signy were attacked."

"None of them were Argentine or Chilean?"

"No. Poland, Russia, Britain, and U.S."

"Casualties?"

"Those are still mostly unknown. The reports, so far, have been compiled from overhead surveillance. Communications have been lost or badly interrupted with all but Bellinghausen, and they've reported two dead and four wounded. Fortunately, the summer season has not gotten fully underway, and the crews manning most of the stations right now are not at their peak populations."

"Not so bloody fortunate for the dead men," Baker observed.

Cady shook his head. He felt extremely saddened by it all. The worst part was that people were dying for reasons that were illogical, or at least deeply hidden. He couldn't see any economic or politically reliable rationale at all behind an Argentinean invasion of the continent.

"Terri," he asked, "you're our resident expert on the continent. What are they after?"

"After?"

"What's valuable?"

She rotated her coffee mug on the table in front of her. He had begun to notice that her hands were always in movement.

"I wondered about that myself, Colonel, and I went through, as far as my security clearance would allow, and McNichols could get me, the data bases of the U.S. National Reconnaissance Office and the Central Intelligence Agency. To date, nothing of strategic or economic importance has been discovered in Antarctica. The scientific community seems to consider the continent as the most worthless on the globe. They have discovered traces of some minerals like gold, silver, nickel, copper, molybdenum, and iron in some of the mountain ranges, but the cost of extracting it is prohibitive. Furbearing seals were completely exterminated by the 1850s, and only haired seals remain. Whaling was the only industry to have made some profit, but that has pretty much died out as a result of quotas and the endangered species designations. The Japanese supposedly operate whaling ships in the waters, still, but they're quite often dogged by Greenpeace boats with cameras. That slows them down."

"You think it's purely nationalistic?" Adams asked.

"Argentina has laid claim, at least to the peninsula, since 1904, Shaker," Eames said. "And so far, the attacks have only taken place on the peninsula."

"My forebears," Baker said, "got there nearly a century earlier."

"Bransfield, in 1820," she told him, "but if my history

serves, the English were only interested in colonies that could produce some kind of wealth."

"Practical bunch, my forefathers," Baker said.

"That's not to say, though," Cady offered, "that some nationalist streak isn't behind it. People commit enough atrocities in the name of it. Look at Palestine, Israel, Lebanon."

He found himself glancing around the compartment for any of his Israeli colleagues. On board an international ship, one learned to be cautious about rash statements.

Eames caught him looking and seemed to discern his mental backpedalling. She gave him a grin.

D'Argamon said, "You're saying, CAG, that the Israelis are uncivilized?"

Baker took him off the hook. "We'll have to pursue this later, Jim. You, Jean, and I have an audience with the boss."

Cady looked at his watch. "That's right, Archie. Let's go."

UNS U THANT
0720 HOURS LOCAL

Monmouth was late for his meeting. Sir Charles kept him on the scrambled phone for forty minutes, and Monmouth's habit of listening to people wholeheartedly prevented him from interrupting an obviously upset chairman.

The others had arrived while he was on the phone, and he had waved them to seats at the table in his sitting room. When he hung up, he studied the picture of a serene Maine coastline on the wall above the sideboard for a few seconds. He owned a house about sixty miles north of where the scene had been painted. It wasn't a big house, but it was well-built and shingled in weathered cedar against the fierce storms that battered the shore. He wished he were in it.

December was a good time for big, hardwood fires in the fireplace.

He turned from the wall to study his unit commanders sitting around the table. Cady was a big and competent aviator, and a fine tactician, but he sometimes shaved regulations almost to the bone. D'Argamon, the Frenchman with an inflated sense of self, was quick on the temper and took offense rather easily, but in the nine weeks Monmouth had known him and watched him, had proven himself fearless and capable. The man hated taking orders, but did so almost to the letter. The Brit, Baker, was affable and easygoing, and Monmouth was impressed with the man's concern for his helicopter crews. Because he reported to Cady, the Commander Air Group, Monmouth hadn't monitored his military skills very closely, but Monmouth would bow to Cady's evaluation, which was excellent. The SEAL commander, David George, could be just a little too gung ho for Monmouth's liking, but if he had to rely on a near-stranger coming through in a pinch, he'd bet on George.

Cady and Baker were wearing flight suits; George was as crisp as fresh toast in starched camouflage utilities; and d'Argamon was wearing the jumpsuit favored by the submariners, but he had, naturally, added his own flair to it in the form of a blue silk scarf wrapped around his neck and tucked into the open collar.

Monmouth watched them silently for long enough to see some squirming embarrassment beginning to appear, then crossed the cabin to sit where he had left his yellow legal pad.

"I think, gentlemen, that I still have reservations about how we're all fitting together, but I also think that, if we're going into battle, I'd just as soon do it with the four of you."

"Are we going into battle, Captain?" Baker asked.

"At this very moment, I'm just guessing, Major, but I

guess the answer will be affirmative. Keep in mind that our entire organization is still feeling its way along an untrodden and dark path. As a military unit, I believe that we're at, say, ninety per cent of our total capability. The civilian command structure, on the other hand, may not yet be performing at that level.

"I am not, I hasten to add, being critical. The Operations Committee is new to this, also, and is understandably reluctant to take a position that may involve fatalities without having the consensus of the entire Security Council. That body will be meeting in the next two hours to discuss the situation in Antarctica.

"In the meantime, our orders remain unchanged. We continue to sail for Antarctica and to prepare to initiate action. The type of action, the strength of it, and the intensity are still open for discussion."

Cady retrieved a black notebook from his breast pocket, opened it, and laid it on the table. Monmouth wasn't certain, but he might remember that same scarred notebook from the *Ranger* days.

"Colonel?" Monmouth asked.

"Until we know the goals of the Security Council, we can't very well fit an order of battle into them, sir. But we do have some short-term decisions to make."

"Such as?"

"We're eighty hours and twenty-six hundred nautical miles out of the target area now. About ten hours from now, I recommend that we start flying combat air patrols, to augment Commander d'Argamon's surface sensors. We don't know for certain that we're still in disguise, as far as the hostile forces know, and we'll be entering a range where they could reach us. Especially if they're still maintaining the base on Navarino Island."

"Good," Monmouth said. "Plan on it. Now, let's assume

that the Operations Committee tells us to drive the hostiles off the continent. What I need from each of you is a general outline of how you would proceed to do that. I will be required by Sir Charles, I'm sure, to suggest a plan of action."

"How soon, Captain?" d'Argamon asked.

"Oh, let's give you an hour."

Cady grinned.

"I'm not asking for an air tasking order, just a philosophy and an outline."

David George asked, "Are we to assume that they are also landing ground forces?"

"Yes, Commander. Assume that. There's a small fleet of surface craft approaching the peninsula, and McNichols, according to Sir Charles, estimates that they will put some kind of force ashore."

"Captain," Cady said, "getting filtered intel isn't going to be helpful."

"Sir Charles has already recognized that factor," Monmouth said. "McNichols will be talking directly with Major Eames, whom I designated."

"All right, good," Cady said.

"They attacked five stations this morning," Baker said. "Do we know if they plan to occupy those bases?"

"No, we don't know, Major. Sir Charles just told me that it appeared as if some of the aircraft were landing at Primavera."

"That gives Primavera a long and hard-surfaced runway," Cady said, "if they're able to handle those fighters. It also suggests that they'll set up a defensive system right away to protect it. Triple-A and SAMs both, probably."

Monmouth would have antiaircraft and surface-to-air missiles as one of his priorities if he were taking over a strange base, too.

"For the time being," he said, "just to facilitate your planning, let's presuppose that Primavera will be their primary base on the continent. If they move it, we can shift our planning."

"We need," Cady said, "to contact McNichols about what to look for."

"Contact, instead, Major Eames, and tell her what you need," Monmouth told him. "Let's not disrupt the channels we've just opened."

George broke in, "Eames told me there's probably around eight hundred to a thousand people stationed around the continent."

"That's what I understand."

"Those people, if they're not at the center of the attacks, have to be wondering what in the hell is going on. I would like, sir, to put a couple of my men in the communications compartment to scan radio frequencies and see if they can't make contact with a few of the civilians."

"Go ahead, Commander," Monmouth told him.

"They have no submarines as part of their sea operations?" d'Argamon asked.

"Not as far as we know now."

"What do we know of their surface fleet, then, Captain?"

"DIA tells us there is one destroyer, one frigate, one minesweeper, and sixteen patrol boats. The convoy this morning included three medium-sized freighters and a large oil carrier or tanker."

D'Argamon smiled. "In ten hours, and two missions, I will take them all out of action."

"You're quite the sharpshooter," Baker told him. "It would take me three missions."

Monmouth liked hearing the optimism, but he would have to be careful to not let it become over-optimism.

"As soon as the two of you have accomplished that," he said, "we'll retire to Rio de Janeiro for recreation. Say a week from now?"

"Fine by me," Cady said.

DEFENSE INTELLIGENCE AGENCY
0900 HOURS LOCAL

What was once a rabbit warren of small cubicles outside McNichols's office had been transformed into a combat center. He had ordered desks, filing cabinets, and computers moved, the five-foot-high partitions shifted to create a large space, and the data-link consoles repositioned. Hating to do it, he had even moved his own console out into the larger space. He was going to lose his privacy when he played games with the world.

Not that he was going to have much time for games for awhile.

Now the two consoles linked to the National Security Agency were placed against the outside wall, with two large screens mounted on the wall above them. Several of his assistants had been placed, along with their desks and computer terminals, in a row behind them. When he wasn't in his office on the phone, McNichols sat at a single desk in the third row.

He felt exactly like the mission director at NASA during a tension-filled shuttle launch.

The technicians rerouting the wires and cables were sweating and flinching every time McNichols yelled at them to hurry.

He had been up most of the night, worrying and waiting for something to happen in Antarctica, and when it did, went into action. McNichols had begun to feel a new loyalty, or at least a shift in loyalties. Where once he served the U.S. military exclusively, he now felt compelled to give his all, and his best interpretation of data, to his masters in New York.

Even if he were only part-time.

One technician was taping cables to the linoleum floor, so people would trip on them, no doubt. Another technician finally slapped two multiline phones on his desk and began to connect them.

"Snap it up, man! You're holding up the war."

"Is there really a war, Mr. McNichols?"

"Won't be, if I can't talk to someone."

"There, that set's ready."

McNichols's first act was to program the first two speed-dialing buttons for the scrambled lines for Sir Charles in New York and for Terri Eames's line in the Combat Information Center on the *U Thant*.

He tried hers first.

"CIC, Sergeant Wilson."

"This is McNichols. Where's Eames?"

"One moment, sir."

It took only fifteen seconds to find her.

"Hello, Mr. McNichols."

"Cam."

"Cam."

"Okay, Terri, we've got a direct line, now. It's scrambled."

"Good," she said. "I need information on the current deployment of hostile forces."

"I haven't been able to get you a direct, real-time data link with NSA's magic boxes. Some self-important engineer told me you don't have the right equipment. When I get a moment in the future, I'll correct that oversight. Right now, though, I've got you a data transfer channel on the Defense Satellite Communications System, and in about three minutes, I'll be shipping you the latest pictures."

"That will relieve some of the hotdogs around here," she said.

"You tell them that I personally identified all the bogies for them, so they don't have to go guessing at it."

"I'll do that."

"Great. Talk to you later."

McNichols punched memory button number one.

"Bentley."

"You're standing on top of your phone, Sir Charles."

"I've been waiting for you to get back to me."

"What's happening?"

"The Council is in session right now."

"Have we learned anything?" McNichols asked.

"We have learned that Chile and Argentina do not know anything about an excursion into Antarctica."

"What!"

"That is correct, Cameron. Their ambassadors have denied any knowledge or responsibility."

"Who the hell's blowing up experiment stations?"

"That's what the Council is trying to determine," Bentley said. "We'll have to be patient, I'm afraid."

"Damn it, Sir Charles! The aircraft and ships came right out of Chilean and Argentinean airfields and waters."

"Those observations were brought up, Cameron, but the governments involved insist that the aircraft and ships are privately owned. None are missing from their own inventories. They say they will investigate the matter for us."

"Jesus! How long will that take?"

"Mañana, Cameron, *mañana."*

BRANDEIS BASE, ANTARCTICA
1020 HOURS LOCAL

Jacque Metier, the station chief, was almost apoplectic because Andover refused to let him play with his radio.

Instead, Zip Andover had commandeered the chair in front of the radio table in Hut 3, which was now populated by all sixteen of the station's inhabitants.

Gustav Brelin, a Dane who was almost as big as Andover,

but hairier, had sided with him, and was helping hold off the crowd of talkative sorts who wanted to get on the air and broadcast their plight, as well as their position, to the rest of the southern hemisphere.

Andover, and thankfully, Gustav Brelin, didn't think they were quite ready for that.

The reports had started trickling in a couple hours before. On various frequencies captured by the big Blaupunkt radio, they had heard cries of alarm from Bellinghausen, a partial plea for help from Arctowski, and a swarm of inquiries from nearly every other station in Antarctica. The static, and the distance from many stations, made listening a chore, and Andover used a headset to improve his concentration. As he heard reports, he jotted notes on a pad, and a succession of people passed behind him, to lean over his shoulder, read his notes, and complain about his penmanship.

Earlier, he had heard the tail end of a broadcast from McMurdo, the large American base, and while he wanted to call them back, he did not. Finally, McMurdo repeated its transmission. He listened carefully, wrote sloppily, and when it ended, shoved the headset aside.

He turned his bulk around in the chair, stroked his beard once, and yelled over the din of excited babblers.

"Hey!"

Slight abatement in conversation.

"Hey!"

When he had their attention, he said, "That was McMurdo. They seem to be trying to take on a leadership role in keeping communications orderly. They're telling everyone to stay off the air and listen for their reports every fifteen minutes. Got that, Jacque?"

Metier wasn't going to listen to either him or to reason.

"Here's what they've got so far," he said, "and they're getting some information from sources in Washington, D.C.

About twenty aircraft, thought to be Argentinean, attacked five stations on the continent this morning."

"Jesus!" someone said.

"Bellinghausen, like we heard earlier, is reporting heavy damage by bombing. There are three dead and seven wounded there. They've lost their steam plant and are asking for evacuation."

"No heat?" Brelin asked.

"Probably not, unless they're burning the huts. Arctowski, Signy, Palmer, and Faraday were also hit, but no one's heard from any of them."

Andover ached to call Faraday, wanted to hear Christine Amherst's soft, safe voice. He wouldn't try, though. When he imposed policy, he lived by it.

"These are Argentines?" Metier asked.

"That's what they're guessing, and as support for that supposition, none of the Argentine stations were bombed."

"Have they talked to the Argentines, to Brown, to Primavera, to Esperanza?" Metier wanted to know.

"Damned if I know, Jacque. They didn't say."

"Call them back and ask."

"They said to stay off the air."

"The Americans are always bullying us, telling us what to do and what not to do."

"I think they've got a damned good point," Andover said. "If we don't get some damned order on the airwaves, nobody's going to know what's going on. Besides, there's a more important point."

"What's that, damn it!"

"Every non-Chilean and non-Argentinean base on the peninsula was hit, except for us."

"So?"

"We're a brand-new venture, Jacque. I don't think they know we're here, or if they do, they overlooked us."

Metier's shoulders slumped.

"And if we go on the air, they'll damned well know we're here."

"And bomb us?"

"Do you want to chance it?"

"No, Zip, I guess not."

"All right, then. Everybody relax. Eat, drink, sleep, whatever. I'll stay on the radio and see what I can find out. This'll pass over, guys and gals."

He tried to believe what he was saying, but wasn't very successful for himself. A dozen of the others, however, dispersed to other huts, and Andover went back to the radio.

Metier ducked into his small office.

Brelin pulled up a chair and sat next to him. It was like having his own bodyguard. He almost asked the bodyguard to dig up some gingersnaps, and then decided he wasn't really hungry.

Warplanes shooting up scientific endeavors.

This wasn't the way it happened in academia or science.

He was getting damned mad, angry about dead and dying people. But he wasn't quite sure where to direct his anger.

He pulled the headphones back in place and started tapping the buttons, calling up the digitized frequencies, listening for voices.

On the frequencies used mostly by the Argentine stations, he heard a few conversations, short ones, in Spanish. That in itself was unusual. Most of the stations used English as a common language.

Quite a few of the stations seemed to be taking McMurdo to heart and were no longer transmitting on the frequencies generally used by the scientific community.

Taped to the top of the radio was a short list of the most-used frequencies, and Andover had jotted down the freq numbers for those where he had heard some other conversations.

Idly, he tapped in 243.0, the emergency channel for military aviation, called the Guard channel, and was surprised to hear a voice.

What was more, it was a voice with a tinge of an Australian accent. A strong dose of American culture had deteriorated it, but it was there.

"Anyone on Antarctica, can you reply to Chestnut?"

It was a strong damned transmitter, judging by the quality of the voice. But it was using a code-name and an emergency channel. Maybe it was a pilot who went down during the raids.

Enemy, then.

Or maybe not.

"Anyone on Antarctica, come back to Chestnut."

Maybe not on the continent.

To Brelin's and Andover's surprise, Andover broke his own policy.

Keying the transmit button, he spoke into the mike. "Chestnut, go to three-three-six-point-five. Call me Bandit."

He hadn't heard any traffic on 336.5, and he thought it would be safe for a short dialogue. He punched in the new frequency and waited.

But not for long. "Bandit, this is Chestnut. Tell me about yourself."

"To hell with that, mate, and I'm not staying on the freq for long. You tell me about you."

"Hey, mate, would I con you?"

"Yeah, man, you might."

PUMA LEADER
1414 HOURS LOCAL

Major Roberto Tellez leveled the Tornado off at fourteen thousand meters, well above the blizzard which was dying out now, anyway, and the altitude above which the speed of sound was constant. It was also the best high-speed altitude for the Tornado.

He checked his right wing and watched as Pumas Two, Three, and Five joined the formation, then advanced his throttles to military power until the airspeed indicated Mach 2.1. The sound of his turbofans was left behind him, and Tellez enjoyed the relative silence.

The radio compass showed his heading as 170 degrees, and he decided to hold it there until the next radio broadcast.

At precisely 1415 hours, he heard the same voice he had heard three times before.

"This is McMurdo Station, United States Scientific Station. As of one o'clock today. . . ."

Tellez dialed the TACAN (Tactical Air Navigation) receiver into the frequency and got a lock on the direction.

Then he checked his armaments panel, then squirmed around a bit for a more comfortable position, and settled in for the long ride.

THE SAN MATIAS
1620 HOURS LOCAL

Diego Enriquez stood with Lieutenant Umberto Mondragon, the navigator, next to the plot at the back of the bridge.

Mondragon was very tall—a sign of a new generation Enriquez often thought—and made the FSAD naval commander feel his lack of stature. Enriquez had once, or perhaps more than once, been compared behind his back to the American comedian Jimmy Durante in terms of his height and his prominent facial feature, his nose. Though his nose and his large-lobed, oversized ears, as well as the ample girth of his waist might provide him with a comic appearance, Enriquez had never once in his life considered himself a humorist, and those who knew him well would certainly not find him comical.

Personally, he considered himself a shrewd strategist, well seasoned at age sixty-two, with over thirty years of experience in the Chilean navy, where he had achieved the rank of captain. As a close associate of General Pinochet, he had been aware of, and had participated in, some of the distasteful but necessary tasks required of those who wished to maintain discipline in a military rife with intrigue and plots. Enriquez could deploy surface-to-air missiles or a Llama .45-caliber semi-automatic pistol equally well, and he had done so. Over the years, nine would-be insurrectionists had knelt before him, their backs to him, and waited expectantly for the last sound they would ever hear.

Enriquez still had the automatic pistol, in a drawer in his cabin, and though his subordinates might not know that, they had heard enough of his history on the grapevine that they gave him absolute obedience, if not loyalty. He was not worried about the crews on his ships and boats—approximately a third of his sailors originated from Chile, a third from Argentina, and the balance from various mercenary endeavors.

"Very well, Lieutenant, tell me."

With a pointer, the lieutenant tapped out the positions of symbols on the plot of the Antarctic Peninsula. "Patrol Boats Eight, Eleven, Twelve, and Fifteen are patrolling the Shetlands. To this time, they have made no contacts. Boat Eight reported seeing a Russian helicopter, probably an Mil MI-8 at 1300 hours; it was headed toward the Bellinghausen station, and it probably came from a Russian ship now sixty kilometers north of the Shetland Islands."

"What? What ship?"

"We do not know the name, sir, but it is probably a resupply ship, and it may be carrying scientists bound for Bellinghausen for the summer."

"Mark it."

The lieutenant placed a silver ship symbol in the approximate location on the plot.

"We want to monitor that ship closely," Enriquez said. "As well as her helicopter."

"Yes, sir," the navigator said and then continued, "down here, off Anvers Island, are Patrol Boats Three and Sixteen. They report no activity, not even radio transmissions from either the Palmer or Faraday stations since Colonel Suarez broadcast his radio warnings for all bases to stay off the air. McMurdo Station, however, continues to transmit."

Tapping rapidly with the pointer, Mondragon said, "The balance of the patrol boats are spaced along the Dacono, Graham, and Loubet Coasts. Here, off Primavera, are the major vessels."

It was such a huge continent, and Enriquez's was such a tiny navy in comparison.

"Signal Captain Encinas on the *Marguerite Bay,* Lieutenant. She is to take up station a hundred kilometers south of us."

"Sir, that is a change in the plan."

"I formulated the plan, Lieutenant. I may change it."

"Of course, Captain."

Enriquez moved forward to the large windscreen of the bridge and stared at the enterprise taking place a half-kilometer away.

The *San Matias* was holding position three kilometers off the shelf ice. Until the missile batteries were in place, she would provide the basic defense of Primavera, which was nearly fifty kilometers inland. Not that he expected the need to rise. He did not think there had been armed vessels or aircraft on the continent in this century, until today. The Russian ship bothered him, though, and as soon as his task was completed here, he thought he might take the destroyer north.

The snowstorm had ceased, and the ice was clearly visible in the wavery daylight, an imposing cliff nearly one hundred meters high, stretching for as far as he could see to the north and to the south. A few large icebergs floated randomly away from the cliff, and the three freighters were aligned ahead of the destroyer, their decks awash with activity. The temperature had achieved two degrees Fahrenheit at two o'clock, a level Enriquez supposed was balmy. Deck crews clad in heavy white parkas were winching pallets of supplies, or of a single vehicle, from the holds, trundling them across decks which were becoming treacherous with sea spray and snow frozen into a thin skin of ice, and wrapping them in cargo nets. The Aérospatiale Super Frelon helicopters, four of them, took their turns hovering over the decks, dropping their cargo lines, and lifting the heavily-laden cargo nets from the decks. The round-trip to Primavera and back took about thirty minutes, and three of the helicopters were engaged in that chore. The fourth helicopter was shuttling vehicles—Sno-Cats and self-propelled artillery—to the top of the ice cliff. By nightfall, a convoy of vehicles would begin wending its way inland. Except for a few first-line-of-defense missile launchers and several antiaircraft guns, the vehicles would go by surface, and the fifty kilometers were expected to require seven or eight hours for the passage.

Enriquez wished he had another dozen helicopters. The offloading was not proceeding as fast as he wished.

Still, there had been no incidents, indicating that his preparations, and the condition of the used helicopters, were excellent. Already, the first surface-to-air missile launcher was in place at the airfield and soon to be operational. When they were done, some forty Russian-made SA-8, SA-9, and SA-11 SAM batteries would be emplaced around Primavera. Additionally, there were twenty ZSU-23-4 Quad Self-propelled antiaircraft guns to be deployed.

It did not seem like much, but considering that there were no hostile forces on the continent, or within several thousand kilometers, it might well have even been overkill.

He spun around and faced the lieutenant. "Mondragon."

"Sir."

"Find Jaguar Leader for me."

"Immediately, Captain."

Immediately took twelve minutes, but someone finally located Suarez at Primavera.

"Your helicopters are arriving right on time," Suarez said.

They were being careful to not use names or other identifying traits on the radio waves.

"As I promised. However, there may be a problem."

"Such as?"

"I have just learned that a Russian ship, probably transporting scientists and supplies for the austral summer, is sixty kilometers north of the Shetlands on a southerly heading. You should detail one or more of your aircraft to a reconnaissance of the region."

Suarez was silent for a long time, then said, "It will have to be one of the C-130s. But I hate to take it out of planned service."

"It is important, and you should probably detail at least two of them, given the limitations of their radar."

"Yes. We are not certain just who is headed this way. It will be done."

PUMA LEADER
1657 HOURS LOCAL

McMurdo Station was over four thousand kilometers away from Primavera, a staggering example of the vast expanse of the continent. At twice the speed of sound, Tellez's flight reached the target area in under three hours. Twice, they had slowed to meet the pre-positioned tankers for aerial refueling. Twice, on the way back, they would do the same.

This was not a trip that would be made frequently, but Suarez had felt, and Tellez agreed, that the example had to be set. Every base in Antarctica would be made to know that they were not out of reach of, and were therefore under the thumb of, the new landlords at Primavera. The proof of perceived invincibility as a result of distance was in the quarter-hour news broadcasts made by the American station at McMurdo.

The Americans were always assuming the superior attitude, and when McMurdo had taken the leadership role in communications, it had sealed a fate that had been planned from the beginning.

The TACAN reported that they were sixty miles away from the station, and Tellez straightened up in his seat, tightened the harness across his chest, and keyed the transmit button.

"Pumas, Puma One."

He received double clicks of the microphone button from each of the members of his flight.

"We will descend now and reduce speed to four hundred knots."

He retarded his throttles and eased in the speed brakes by thirty percent As the aircraft began to lose altitude, he surveyed the landscape. Or more appropriately, the icescape.

McMurdo Station was located on the eastern shore of a large indentation in the continent, near the juncture of the Ross Sea and the Ross Ice Shelf. A few kilometers south was the New Zealand facility at Scott Base. On the ice, six kilometers from McMurdo, was the major airport the Americans called Williams Field. It was an ice and/or snowpacked runway which required most aircraft to be fitted with skis. To the southwest of McMurdo and Scott were the peaks of the two volcanoes, Mount Terror and Mount Erebus, Erebus still an active volcano. The Greenpeace organization had a station in the area, also, studying the ozone layer and the greenhouse effect, but Tellez understood that there was very little inter-action between them and the other two bases. He supposed that Scott and McMurdo were major polluters and the Green-peace people shunned them.

They were under heavy overcast and had been for the last hour. The light of day was still present, but had been dimin-ished considerably, creating a false darkness. Visual clues tended to be deceptive, and Tellez was at eight thousand me-ters of altitude, and down to seven hundred knots, before he picked out the volcanoes. Erebus was easily recognized by the cloud of steam rising above its peak. Except for a few rock outcroppings stripped of snow cover by the wind, the scene was mostly white, though it was also bathed in deep shadow. One had to be careful, especially during a brighter day and during snowfall, to define one's horizon. Often, the sky and the earth blended together, and in the air, complete disorien-tation could result. During high summer, in January, when temperatures might reach the freezing point, a fair amount of the landscape was swept clean of snow, revealing the hardened lava flow from the volcano.

Near the base, darker areas of earth were visible, the result of some melt and of much traffic.

He had been told that a United States Coast Guard ice-breaker would probably be in attendance, breaking up the ice near the station.

He activated his radar and took two sweeps of the area ahead. There were over thirty buildings at the station, com-posed of differing materials. Wood was prevalent because in this environment, it did not rot. Some huts and roofs were of metal, and the radar picked them up most readily. At the airstrip, he received radar returns on what looked like four large aircraft, and a half-dozen smaller ones.

"Pumas, take combat spread."

FISHING HUT #2, MCMURDO STATION
1701 HOURS LOCAL

Tom Detmer, an associate professor of geophysics from the University of California, San Diego, had taken an assistant and a Sno-Cat out to the fishing hut to conduct his next set of measurements.

It was located some ten miles from McMurdo proper, and it was noted chiefly for its large-diameter pipe punched through the ice to the water below. Scientists could access the strange fish that lived in the deep waters below, capture them for study in the station's aquarium, and learn the secrets of the food chain. One of the important aspects of Antarctic research was that it should provide a standard against which judgments about change in the environment and the ecology of the rest of the planet might be made. That had changed, of course, as the humans tromping on the continent had brought about alterations in the Antarctic environment themselves.

But Detmer's objective was not to be found inside the fishing shack. Instead, he was interested in what was straight up.

He had placed his instrumentation and recording devices inside the hut, where they would remain warm, and he had gone outside to set up his laser on its tripod base. When he had it secured firmly in the ice, he stepped back and turned it on. A thin, purple beam of light shot vertically into the gloomy skies. It was almost *Star Wars*, he thought, as he tried to follow the beam into infinity, frustrated by the sparse cloud cover.

Detmer was measuring the size of the opening in the ozone layer.

He turned back toward the hut, then stopped when he heard thunder.

Thunder?

He looked out toward the sea, and in the gloom, he saw shadows. Then more shadows.

Racing toward him.

Low to the earth.

Getting larger and larger, four of them.

Airplanes.

No airplanes had been scheduled to arrive today.

God, they're moving fast!

And then they were over him, and he was astonished to note that they were warplanes, with oblong cylinders hanging from the wings and fuselages.

"Jesus Christ! What in the hell is that about?"

PUMA ONE
1702 HOURS LOCAL

They had been flying with their formation lights on, to help them maintain their separation, and now the lights of the three Tornados on his right flickered out, and the aircraft drifted off farther to the right, attempting to maintain one hundred meters of distance between each craft.

Ahead in the gloom, Tellez picked out a small scattering of lights.

He checked his HUD: four hundred knots of airspeed, 1200 meters of altitude above ground level.

He continued to descend.

The distance to target, still using the TACAN tuned to the McMurdo transmitter, was sixteen kilometers.

"Pumas, arm weapons."

"Two."

"Three"

"Five."

"Take your targets," Tellez told them. "Five, be certain you get the antennas. Take a second pass if it is required."

"Affirmative, One."

He thought that Puma Five, Enrico Salazar, would find the antennas—in a compound on Crater Hill shared by McMurdo and Scott—on the first pass. Their fuel state was so critical, a second pass meant that Salazar and his navigator would not make it back to the tanker.

It seemed to be almost too light out for the destruction that would soon occur. Tellez liked the sun, and he would have appreciated a twenty-four-hour daylight, if it were to occur in warmer latitudes. He also liked tropical climes.

At four hundred meters above the ground, he leveled the Tornado and advanced the throttles enough to maintain four hundred knots of airspeed. He thought that the station was still unaware of their approach. Williams Field might not have radar operating or personnel present.

The ice shelf below would become mesmerizing, if he allowed it. It sped past him in a grayish blur, and he forced himself to concentrate on the lights ahead. Banking slightly to the left, he picked up the floodlights on several structures at the airport.

There were no flight operations underway, and another sweep of the radar defined the parked aircraft. He was certain they would be four of the seven winterized C-130 Hercules transports with orange-painted tails which were owned by the National Science Foundation, but which were flown by U.S. Navy pilots from the VFE-6 squadron. The rest would be helicopters.

He glanced at the armaments panel.

On the ICS, he said, "Jesus, I am selecting two Matra Martel air-to-surface missiles."

"Understood," his navigator said.

The two armaments panel LEDs winked on.

The missiles were mounted on the wing pylons. On the fuselage pylons, he was carrying four JP233 antirunway bombs and four one thousand-pound bombs.

The Martel missiles were guided by either antiradiation or television, and since the parked aircraft were not emitting radar signals, Ramirez selected the television guidance system.

At ten kilometers of distance, Ramirez switched in the first missile's video head, and the image seen by the missile appeared on the small multifunction screens in front of both the navigator and the pilot. Ramirez slaved the second missile to the first, so that it would follow where number one led it.

The picture on the screen was not difficult to decipher.

Ice.

He eased back on the stick.

Lights.

Eight kilometers to go.

The lights intensified in the video image.

Aircraft.

C-130.

Ramirez locked the video eye on the target.

"We have lock. When you're ready, Roberto."

He depressed the commit switch on the control stick head.

Tellez squinted his eyes, to preserve his sight in the twilight, as the first missile, then the second, dropped from the pylons, hesitated, then ignited.

The white fire of their ignition lit the side of his fuselage briefly, then they all but vanished as they leapt ahead, quickly accelerating to their Mach 2 sea level speed.

"Cratering bombs," Tellez said, as he flicked the switch on the armaments panel.

Ramirez said, "Bombs, confirmed."

Through the HUD, he ignored the fiery trails the missiles left behind and searched for the runway.

"Come left, Roberto. Raise the nose a little."

There. Only a smoothly leveled depression in the snow surrounding it, but the darker shadows defined the long line of its near edge.

He jockied the stick up and right until the target reticule found the center of the runway.

"LOCK-ON" appeared on the HUD as Ramirez also found the target.

Tellez pressed the commit stud.

The missiles impacted the first aircraft in the row, and a miniature orange flash, followed by a gigantic red and yellow blossom, filled his windscreen. He tried to ignore it.

Four seconds later, the Tornado surged upward a trifle as the bombs released and the aircraft was relieved of their weight.

Without time to accurately select a target, Tellez banked right, and saw the line of helicopters and several fuel tanks coming up fast.

"Let them go, Roberto!"

"Bombs away," Tellez said and released his last four bombs.

Then he was past, climbing, banking left, looking back.

The runway-cratering bombs had found the center of the runway, erupting geysers of ice high into the sky. The pillar of shattered ice crystals reflected and refracted the red-yellow fire consuming three of the C-130s—two of them destroyed by shrapnel and debris from the missile hits on the first. The last four bombs had been released at random, but one or more of them had slammed into helicopters and tanks, found flammable liquids of some kind, and burst into yet another flower in his bouquet.

And that was just his delivery.

On the near horizon to the south, bright yellow eruptions appeared at Scott Base.

Over toward the American station, Tellez saw yet more explosions, and fires raged randomly through the settlement.

And the radio station, which he was still monitoring, went off the air.

Which was the point of all of this, after all.

PRIMAVERA BASE
1710 HOURS LOCAL

Emilio Esteban Suarez de Suruca took shelter from the wind in the lee of a maintenance hut fifty meters off the long runway and surveyed his domain. Despite his silk thermal underwear, snow pants, and heavy parka, he was still chilled. The frigid air, with particles of suspended ice crystals floating in it from the activity of the clearing vehicles, caught in his mustache and it seemed to crackle when he moved his mouth.

It had stopped snowing, but the Sno-Cats with mounted blades and the three Caterpillar bulldozers were still clearing areas down to solid ice in which to park aircraft. Their crisscrossing silhouettes reflected eerily off the snow and ice pack. As soon as one area was opened, ground crews moved Mirages and C-130s into it from where they had simply been driven off into deep snow to keep the runway open. In the revetments assigned to the Puma Squadron, three of Tellez's operational Tornados were on alert, prepared for almost instantaneous takeoff. The damaged Tornado was raised on jack stands and protected by windscreens, and a crew of ten were making repairs to the landing gear, pylons, and aluminum skin. He had been told that it would be airworthy by morning, but he was doubtful. The freezing temperatures of night made working with metal a struggle. External fuel tanks froze to their pylons, landing struts and wing slats felt brittle to the touch. Propane heaters, with long flexible tubing, were used to warm the work areas and the work materials. Nearby, covered with plastic sheeting and warmed by propane blowers under the sheeting, was Silvera's Mystère-Falcon. It had not been prepared for arctic operation.

With his gloved hand, he stroked his mustache, breaking up the accumulation of frozen ice.

A lieutenant trotted up to him.

"Colonel Suarez."

"Yes?"

"There is a message from Puma Leader. *Conquistador.*"

"Excellent." The assault on McMurdo Station had been completed successfully, and the four Tornados were on their return flight. Other codes would have told him different stories.

"And, Colonel, Nightdog One is ready to take off."

"Very well. Clear the runway of Sno-Cats and release them."

The lieutenant saluted awkwardly in his heavy coat, spun around, and raced back to the hut that served as operations and air control, and for the time being, their headquarters.

Suarez had selected the first C-130 to be off-loaded, renamed it Nightdog, and assigned two flight crews to it. Though their radar coverage would be limited, they would fly a large, racetrack-like oval along the western coast of the peninsula and serve as a surveillance and early-warning aircraft. The cost in fuel would be dear, but Diego Enriquez had been quite correct. It was a necessary change to their plans. Shortly, he would add another Hercules to the task.

He turned from the runway and looked over toward the station, nearly a kilometer away. It was made up of twenty-two wooden and tin huts, some of them connected to each other by jury-rigged wooden tunnels. They were spread out in a random pattern that may have had meaning to someone, though not to him. Most of them appeared to be half-buried in snow. A light haze of smoke from the chimneys of oil-fired heaters rose above them and drifted to the east. Most had lights showing in their small windows.

Tonight, they would be crammed wall-to-wall with the bodies of his pilots and ground crew. By tomorrow night at this time, the size of Primavera Station would quadruple as sixty prefabricated shelters were erected, though in more military and orderly rows.

Several kilometers to the west, on the other side of the runway, he could make out the vague shapes of two Sno-Cats which were fighting through one- and two-meter drifts, attempting to establish the ground-link with the coast. In the next few hours, the first contingent of Enriquez's convoys should be arriving from the coast.

As he watched, he saw the navigation lights of another incoming helicopter. The helicopter was too far away for him to see what prize it had suspended from its winches.

Suarez turned and walked across the packed snow toward the operations hut. The snow crust resisted, then crackled and broke under the tread of his heavy insulated boots.

The entrance door was set in a small ell that projected from the main structure, a cold-lock arrangement. He opened the door, stepped inside, closed the outer door, and then opened the inner door.

The large, open room was buzzing with people: pilots, maintenance chiefs, ground crewmen taking breaks, and station personnel. He would have shooed them out, but as yet, they had nowhere else to go for warmth. And it was warm. A large, oil-fired stove in the back corner burned cheerily. With the overpopulation and the stove, it was almost stifling in the room. Suarez unbuttoned and unzipped his parka and shrugged it off, then pulled the balaclava from his head.

Shouldering his way through the crowd, he made his

way to the worktables set below windows overlooking the runway. The tables were stacked high with radar and radio equipment, some of which he had brought with him. One of his first acts had been to erect a more massive radar antenna high on the hill behind them and get the system activated.

A Chilean captain was in charge of the operations.

"What is the status, Captain Arquez?"

The man looked up at him.

"Oh, hello, Colonel. We are doing very well. I have two SAMs on-line, as well as two antiaircraft batteries. You heard the report from Puma?"

"Yes."

"They are now meeting Esso Four for fuel, and they should be back by 2000 hours."

Suarez glanced at the radar scope, manned by a technician he thought had come to them from Peru.

"The air activity?"

"We show the four helicopters operating from the ships and the single Mirage flying cover. Nightdog is being towed to the runway, and soon, we will pick up Puma flight. There are no other aircraft operating within our coverage."

Their new radar gave them a 250-kilometer range of coverage, which included a portion of the Shetland Islands, though the ridge to the east defeated some of that coverage. With Nightdog participating, the coverage would be extended, though sporadically, dependent on the C-130's position.

"Not even Bellinghausen?"

"The helicopter reported to have landed there has not reappeared on our scopes, Colonel."

"Excellent. Keep up the good work, Captain."

Suarez turned to find the station manager standing beside him. An Argentinean named Ortiz, he had been on Silvera's payroll for six months. It was he who had arranged to have the runway lengthened at the proper time, but Suarez was certain that the man had expected to find himself in supreme authority at the station once the takeover had been accomplished. Instead, he had found himself shunted out of the way as the aviation and electronics personnel from FSAD took control of his station.

"Ortiz?"

"Uh, Colonel, I wonder if you might have a word with the major who is directing the snow clearance."

"What kind of word?"

"He will not listen to me at all, Colonel. He is bulldozing ice in places I have forbidden."

"How about, Ortiz, if I had you taken outside and shot? Would that get you out of my hair?"

"But, Colonel! There are buried cables. . . ."

The lights in the operations hut flickered and died.

UNS U THANT
1835 HOURS LOCAL

Dave George found Cady and Baker in the helicopter squadron's ready room on Deck 3. On the other side of the corridor, through the hatchway to the hangar deck, he heard the scream of a turbine engine being test-run.

In the ready room, several Seahawk and Sea Apache pilots were arguing in one corner, and Cady and Baker were hunched over a large map at the podium.

Cady looked up and said, "Hello, Dave."

"I'd like to talk to the two of you, if you have a minute, Colonel."

"Sure thing. We're just trying to reacquire our map-reading skills."

"There is nothing wrong with my skills," Baker said. "I know a map when I see one."

George walked over to the podium and looked down at the large scale, 1:50,000 map.

"Where'd you find that? I thought nobody had a decent map of Antarctica because there would never be trouble there."

"Eames got McNichols to fax it to her. We had to do some Scotch tape work, to get all the pieces together, then printed off a few. You should have one in your mailbox by now."

"Great."

"Archie and I are going to set up a coded coordinate grid in the hope that we'll know where we are, but the opposition won't."

George leaned over to take a close look at the maze of topographical lines and landmarks noted on the map.

"It's already out-of-date, Colonel."

"The hell it is."

"According to Bandit, it is."

"Who the bloody hell is Bandit?" Baker asked.

"He won't give me his real name, being a suspicious clod, but he and I are countrymen, or were, before I was naturalized. Got some dividers?"

Baker reached into a drawer of the podium and came up with the instrument, handing it to him.

"I made contact with him," George went on, "on Guards channel, then we went off to a little-used freq that he selected. He was damned worried about being overheard and maybe pinpointed. This is Primavera, right?"

"When did you make contact?" Cady asked.

"A little before eleven. And I called him back at three. We didn't talk long, but I'm supposed to ring him up at 1905 hours, again. Damn. He's got me talking like a Brit."

"Was that an insult?" Baker asked.

"Of course, Archie. I let the old accent come out, and it seemed to reassure him enough to give me his location."

George made his measurements, then used a pencil to draw a circle with an "X" in it. "That's Brandeis Base. It's seventy-five kilometers, about seventy miles, south of Primavera. It was established in late February of last year to study the greenhouse effect, and there are sixteen people in residence."

"You checked this?" Cady asked.

"I did, through Eames, with one of the station's sponsors in England."

"You don't think the bad guys know of this place?" Baker asked.

"Bandit doesn't think so, Archie. I'm not making a judgment on it."

"How much did you tell him?" Cady asked.

"I tried to be open, to get his trust, without revealing too much," George said. "I told him about the attacks and the fact that Primavera looks to be their main base, at least judging by the latest pictures DIA has sent us."

Baker said, "Did he ask about the identity of the hostiles?"

"He did, though I told him we weren't sure. And I guess we aren't sure, are we?"

"Not from what McNichols passed on to us," Cady said. "How about us? What did you tell him?"

"That we're friendlies, but that I couldn't give him ID or location on the air. That added to his suspicion, I'm sure. He's got to figure he's one-off in the negotiations. He gave me his coordinates, if reluctantly, but I wouldn't give him mine."

Cady walked around the podium and sat in one of the cushioned chairs of the first row.

"You think you can use this guy, Dave?"

"Damned right, I can. He sounds like an old hand. He'll know the terrain like it's his backyard."

"Seventy miles could be the same as a thousand miles in those conditions," Cady said.

"He said it's rugged as hell, but he's got Sno-Cats."

"How many?"

"I don't know."

"So what do you need from us?"

"Two things. We'll need to plan an assault, using Archie's Seahawks, but first I damned well need to establish myself with Bandit."

"How do you want to do that?" Cady asked.

George told him.

BRANDEIS BASE, ANTARCTICA
1903 HOURS LOCAL

Gustav Brelin had become his watchdog, and he sat close by as Andover tuned in the frequency 336.5. He kept an eye on the clock.

Metier and two others stood behind them, waiting.

"I think this fellow sounds for real," Brelin said.

"Yeah, Gus, maybe. Anything could be a trap, though."

"I can't imagine," Jacque Metier said, "that none of these people know we're here."

"Seems to me, Jacque, if they did, we'd have a few missiles up our asses by now. Sorry, Ruth Anne."

Ruth Anne Oliver was an ecologist from London.

"People have said 'missiles' in front of me before, Zip."

"You've always struck me as worldly, Ruth Anne," he said. They waited.

Precisely at five minutes after seven, the speaker barked, "Bandit, this is Chestnut. You there?"

"I'm here, Chestnut."

"How are you holding up?"

"Lonely as ever. You hear anything about Faraday, yet?" He was getting real worried about Christine Amherst.

"Negative, but we're trying."

"You know McMurdo went off the air?"

"They were hit by four Panavia Tornados, nationality unknown as yet. We don't have a damage report, yet."

"That's a long damned flight from anywhere," Andover said.

"They had to refuel in the air four times."

"I need to know who the hell you are," Andover said.

"Which would blow my security. What I'm going to do, though, Bandit, soon as I can, I'm going to drop you a radio."

"I've got a radio."

"This one has an encryption device incorporated. Once you have it, we can talk."

"That sounds better," Andover admitted. "How soon?"

"It'll be a while yet, but not too long. I don't want to get more specific than that."

"Understood."

"In the meantime, Bandit, don't do anything rash, okay?"

"I'm not Paul Hogan," Andover told him.

UNS U THANT
2315 HOURS LOCAL

As Commander Air Group, James Cady didn't have to share his stateroom with anyone. It was located on E Deck, had two portholes overlooking the portside swish of seawater, one oversized bed, one combination-locked safe, one leather-clad easy chair, one desk with its own chair, and a bathroom shared with the next cabin, occupied by Commander Hermann von

Stein. He was a former German missile cruiser commander who served as the *U Thant*'s first officer.

Cady had taped one of the new maps to the bulkhead over his bed and trained the single desk lamp on it. He sat in his leather chair with his bare feet up on the bed and studied it. It seemed as if he had been studying it for hours.

Which he had.

His last few years, in command positions, had been contrary to his nature, he thought. It required introspection and rumination, and he had always been more spontaneous. Growing up, with a hot-rodded '55 Ford F-100 pickup at his disposal, he had never known what the next turn might bring, though usually it was just more miles and miles of Montana. The best part was taking the turns without planning them, slapping the accelerator pedal to the floor, and listening to the dual exhaust rumble from the twin stacks behind the cab.

He had never taken responsibility with relish, and that was reflected in his failed marriage to Sueanne, who had been unable to cope with his long absences, or worse, the four months he'd spent in the hospital at San Diego after shearing the wings off an F-4 Phantom in a controlled crash landing during a night exercise at Miramar.

Her desertion, his long convalescence, and his increasing command responsibilities had inured him to the fact that he would have to eventually face life as an adult.

He hated it, though.

There was a muted knock on his door, and he called, "Come on in!"

He rolled his head back to look over the top of the chair as the door opened tentatively to reveal Terri Eames.

"Come on in, Terri."

"I don't want to disturb you, Colonel."

"I was just about to have a cocktail," Cady said, dropping his feet to the floor and rising from the chair. "Want one?"

"I don't think . . ."

"Tomato juice or orange juice? My bar's a little limited."

She came on inside and closed the door. "I guess orange juice would be all right."

He opened the small refrigerator, found the pitcher of orange juice, and poured two glasses.

"You have a choice of the big chair, the little chair, or the bed."

She took the chair at the desk, and Cady sat on the bed. She sipped from the glass.

"This is fresh."

"I carry my own oranges," he said.

"I was afraid I might wake you."

"No, I've got two birds from the Tiger Barbs aloft, flying CAP, and I'll wait until they check in the first time before I snuggle up to my pillow."

She looked around the stateroom. "This is nice."

"Just like home."

"My roommate, Dr. Gless, has about three cases of cosmetics with her. They use up a lot of our space."

"Toss 'em overboard."

"She'd be mad."

"I'll toss 'em, and she can be mad at me."

"She might have to operate on you some time."

"That's a very good point, Terri. We'll let her be a glamour puss."

She handed him the single sheet of paper she had been clutching in her left hand.

"I just came from Captain Monmouth on the bridge, and he said to show you this."

Cady took it and spread it out on his knee.

He'd seen a lot of missives from the Operations Committee, but never one quite like this:

NATIONAL SECURITY COUNCIL
UNITED NATIONS

DATE: 4 DEC
TO: CMDR, UNS U THANT
FROM: OPERATIONS COMMITTEE
SIGN: CE BENTLEY, CHAIR
AUTH CODE: WHITE HORSE

PER RESOLUTION 233 OF THE UN SECURITY COUNCIL, 4 DEC, UNS U THANT ORDERED TO RELIEVE OR EVACUATE SCIENTIFIC PERSONNEL FROM STATIONS UNDER SIEGE ON THE CONTINENT OF ANTARCTICA.

SECONDARY MISSION. ENGAGE AND DESTROY OR EVICT HOSTILE FORCES CURRENTLY UNIDENTIFIED FROM THE CONTINENT ASAP.

MEANS: AIR, SEA, OR GROUND FORCES TO BE UTILIZED AT DISCRETION OF CMDR, UNS U THANT.

FORCE: CONVENTIONAL WEAPONS ARE HEREBY AUTHORIZED.

Very few people aboard the supertanker knew that the forward magazines contained, in a locked vault, ten tactical nuclear weapons. They were air-delivered weapons, and he had one of the three keys required to open the vault. Cady was relieved that, so far, they would remain in a locked vault.

"Well," he said, "here we go."

"Yes, here we go."

"You don't sound very eager," he said.

"I'm not, certainly."

"Neither am I," he told her.

"That's funny. I was sure you would be."

5 DECEMBER

Juan Silvera had surprised himself and slept very well through the night, wrapped in the down comforters on the station manager's bed. He had even gone to bed early since the power for the lights in some huts had been out for several hours while the cable cut by the bulldozer was repaired.

He had risen early, dressed, and shaken Ricardo Fuentes, who had slept on the sofa in the living room, awake. Fuentes made them breakfast in the tiny galley kitchen, and they ate it while discussing Silvera's address. He had formulated the heart of it many weeks before, though he had refused to consider it finished until his forces were successfully in place. Fuentes wanted—even came close to insisting—the speech include references to two hundred years of grievances, slights, and injustices attributed to Western and European powers, but Silvera prevailed. It would be simple and to the point; not a two-hour rave that no one would listen to, anyway. Let others read into it what they would. Later, the details would be sifted and analyzed by the commentators.

By eight o'clock, Fuentes had written out the final text and called operations for a clerk to type it up. The text would be faxed to a dozen different media organizations at the same time that Silvera addressed his audience. By going to television and the news bureaus, Silvera hoped to initiate quicker action than he could expect from government bureaucracies.

At eight-thirty, he and Fuentes donned their parkas and gloves, left the hut, and walked the kilometer to the operations building. The wind had abated, and the sky was clear. For as far as he could see in any direction, however, the landscape was dismally the same, a pure and almost virginal white. To the east, the ridge of ice was a blockade that rose abruptly. It had jagged vertical crevasses haphazardly breaking up its broad front, the shadows creating a chiaroscuro pattern that strode off into the far distance.

The two of them trudged along a path trodden by hundreds of boots in deep snow.

"How cold do you suppose it is, Ricardo?"

"When I called operations, *Presidente,* they said sixteen degrees."

"Perhaps it will warm yet more by midday."

"Warmth seems relative," Fuentes said. "One becomes acclimatized."

Silvera could see his breath in the crisp, dry air. He reminded himself to drink more water. At one of his briefings, he had been told that people became easily dehydrated because of the dry cold.

Behind the operations building, rows of prefabricated housing and tents were slowly being erected in areas cleared by the bulldozers. A number of them had active smokestacks, the diesel oil stoves sending bluish smoke straight upward until, sixty or seventy meters above the earth, a breeze caught it and drifted it eastward.

More bulldozers were still clearing parking areas for the aircraft, but most of the fighters had been retrieved by tow tractors from their random parking spots off the runway and organized into rows on the newly formed ramps.

Fuentes opened the door, and they entered into what seemed

to be the overly heated interior of the operations hut. It was still crowded with people.

Suarez crossed the room to greet him. Smiling, he said, "You're looking rested, *Presidente*."

"I slept well, Colonel. And you?"

Suarez was dressed in a recently pressed flight suit and he was freshly shaved with his bandito mustache trimmed neatly, but his eyes betrayed a restless night. They were reddened, and dark circles hung beneath them.

"It was a tolerable night," Suarez said. "Tellez's flight returned safely and the Russian helicopter departed Bellinghausen, but a Sno-Cat clipped a parked Mirage and damaged it."

"Badly?"

"No."

"What of the helicopter?"

"One of our patrol craft intercepted it, but we decided to escort it north. It was returning to the ship."

"And the ship?"

"A resupply vessel named the *Inga, Presidente*. It is holding its position forty kilometers north of the Shetlands."

"Very well. Anything else?"

"Buenos Aires relayed to us the text of a resolution made by the United Nations Security Council."

"Already?"

"Yes, *Presidente*. I, too, was surprised by the speed."

"They are unhappy with us?" Silvera smiled.

"More than that. The resolution calls for our immediate withdrawal and suggests that, if we do not comply, force will be brought to bear. We are to reply by twelve o'clock today, or we will be forcefully evicted."

"Well, first of all, Emilio, we will change the schedule of our address. I will not have my deadlines dictated to me."

"Very good, *Presidente*."

Fuentes did not appear to think the decision was very good. Fuentes had decided on the time of the announcement, and he did not like having his decisions remanded.

Silvera looked around the room and saw that changes had been made. The radar equipment had been partitioned into one corner of the room by curtains. Several desks had been confiscated from somewhere and lined up at the back of the room for various of the operations officers: logistics, maintenance, and ordnance.

"The vehicle convoy from the sea?"

"It did not arrive until three in the morning, but already we have a dozen SAM emplacements operational, and as you saw, some of the living quarters. I must start giving the men longer rest breaks."

"Good. How about radio traffic?"

"We have been scanning all frequencies," Suarez said. "Most of the continental stations are staying off the air since the attack on McMurdo and our warnings to them. There have been continuous requests for information from radio and television stations outside the continent, but we have ignored them. There is one thing, *Presidente.*"

"And that is?"

"There are many amateur radio operators. Ham radios. We did not know about them."

"Tell me," Silvera said.

"There are apparently several located at the field and base stations. At two in the morning, one started transmitting from Palmer Station. I broadcast a demand for silence on his frequency and sent one of the patrol aircraft for a low pass over the station. He has stopped transmitting."

"We knew there would be leakage of some kind, Colonel, so we will not fret over it. What was the gist of his message?"

"A report of seven casualties and three fatalities."

"Either our pilots are not very accurate or their people were in the wrong place at the wrong time," Silvera said.

"We will assume the latter," the air chief said.

"Are the fax machines working?"

"They are."

Silvera turned to his administrative assistant. "Ricardo, you may prepare the document."

Fuentes turned away and went to look for the clerk who was typing the declaration.

Silvera said, "Now, Colonel, show me how this is going to work."

Suarez took him across the room to the curtained-off alcove where the radar scopes had been set up. Shoving the curtain aside, he revealed a tripod-mounted television camera aimed at a leather easy chair. Behind it was a blue drapery and the flag of the Front for South American Determination—a deep gold field topped with a centered row of thirteen blue stars—mounted on a staff.

"It is not much of a television studio, *Presidente,* but we have satellite access scheduled, and we can reach the entire world. The satellite up-link is installed and operational."

"It will do very well, Colonel."

Silvera appreciated a sizable audience, and one or two billion radio listeners and television watchers would do nicely.

NEW YORK, NEW YORK
1020 HOURS LOCAL

Cameron McNichols was uncomfortable. He had bought new black loafers to go with the gray version of his bureaucrat suits, and they pinched his toes. He missed his running shoes.

His assistant, Pamela Akins, sat next to him in the back of the limo that had picked them up at La Guardia Airport and appeared entirely comfortable, and that didn't help, either. She was a matronly fifty-five, with impeccable manners, an imperturbable nature, and three grandchildren.

The driver hummed something McNichols didn't know as they swished along the pavement of the Queens-Midtown Tunnel. He also didn't like tunes he didn't know or tunnels. There hadn't been a tune worth humming since "Bridge Over Troubled Water" or "Hey, Jude," and he thought that tunnels were an infringement of nature.

On the Manhattan side, they emerged into the same light snowfall they had left on the Queens side. It was a miserable day, overcast and depressing. The car's tires squished as they raced through the slush.

McNichols had better things he could be doing.

After some jockeying around, some vile horn blasts at cabbies, and some muttered curses that didn't make a damned bit of difference in the conduct of other drivers, his limousine driver found his way onto the United Nations Plaza, was allowed into the circular drive in front of the thirty-nine-story Secretariat Building, and drew up at the main doors.

"Wait here for us," McNichols ordered the driver. "We won't be long, if I can help it. Come on, Pam."

He got out, pulling his topcoat on, and looked around. There was some activity to his right, at the Hammarskjöld Library, but opposite across the circular drive, the General Assembly Building was quiet. McNichols thought that was inconsiderate as hell. The whole world ought to be up in arms.

With Akins in his wake, McNichols aimed himself at the front doors, passed through them, and headed directly through the building toward the Conference Building, which abutted the high-rise structure and fronted on the East River. Tour groups parted before his bulk, blazing green eyes, and imposing beard like the Red Sea.

The three main councils—Security, Trusteeship, and Economic and Social—had their chambers in the Conference Building, and McNichols supposed from the activity near the Security Council's main doors that they were in session. And well they should be. A couple dozen reporters hung around outside the doors.

He ignored the meeting and the elevators, both of which would slow him down, and took the stairs to the third floor. Pam Akins trailed along, uncomplaining about his pace.

As he reached the third floor, not even panting, McNichols asked, "Why don't you bitch about being hauled to New York, Pam?"

"Whatever for? I haven't been to New York in quite some time. It's a nice respite."

Shaking his head in resignation, McNichols sailed on down the hallway until he reached the offices assigned to the Peace-keeper Committee.

The secretary recognized him from previous visits. "Go right on in to the conference room, Mr. McNichols. They're waiting for you."

Before he did, he used her phone to call his office at DIA and see if there were any recent developments, but there were not.

They entered to find six people seated around the big table.

"Ah, Cameron!" Charles Bentley said. "So glad you could pop over."

Two hundred and fifty miles was quite a pop when he was busy, McNichols thought, but retained his civility. "Good morning, Sir Charles. This is my assistant, Mrs. Akins. Pam, why don't you set up over there?"

She moved to an easel near the head of the table, removed her heavy coat, opened her big portfolio, and got out the charts and enlarged pictures McNichols had printed from his data-base.

McNichols nodded to Julia Highwater and Justin Albrecht,

and Bentley introduced him to the ambassadors from France, Russia, and China, who in addition to the United States and the United Kingdom, were the permanent members of the United Nations Security Council. Others, like Albrecht of Denmark, held two-year terms. The Council was composed of fifteen members, and nine votes were necessary for passage of important resolutions, though any of the five permanent members could scuttle an issue by saying, *"Nyet."* Infrequently, a permanent member would allow a resolution on which it did not agree to pass the Council by abstaining from the vote. The French, Russian, and Chinese representatives also served on the Peacekeeper Committee.

"I know you're in a hurry to get back, Cameron," Bentley said, "so why don't you proceed?"

"Thank you, Sir Charles." Shaking free of his topcoat, McNichols tossed it on a chair at the side of the room, and walked around to stand near the easel.

Akins unfolded the first map and taped it to the board on the easel.

"Antarctica," McNichols said. "All of the current base and field stations are shown, most of them in blue. The stations that were attacked are indicated in red, and Primavera, an Argentinean station, is shown in orange because it appears to have been taken over as the primary base of the hostile forces. Incongruously, we have a single base identified in mauve. That is Brandeis, and it is so new that the invaders seem unaware of it. We would like to keep it that way, so please don't mention it to your colleagues."

"I'd have thought," Highwater said, "that McMurdo would have been a better selection as a home base. It's much larger, and Williams Field has better facilities for aircraft."

"That's true, Ambassador. I can't explain their choice, except that McMurdo is a greater distance from the airstrip on Navarino Island, from where the attacks were launched. Of significance, too, when I checked back on earlier satellite photographs, is that they appear to have had help at Primavera. The runway was lengthened and pierced steel planking was laid down almost a month in advance of the invasion. That was necessary in order to land the fighter aircraft."

"You're calling it an invasion?" the Chinese man asked.

"I think that's appropriate from the evidence, sir."

"You're suggesting," the French ambassador said, "that the Argentines cooperated."

"There's complicity somewhere, sir. I don't know how high it goes."

"How about fatalities, Cameron?" Bentley asked.

"Let me cover this one base at a time, Sir Charles. Pam, let's have the photo of Signy."

If they didn't stop asking questions and let him get on with the briefing, he'd never get back to his console. McNichols had the brief thought that this invasion might be completed while he was out for lunch. They needed him, but they needed him where he could be in contact with the *U Thant* and with his computers and consoles.

Akins taped the enlarged satellite photo in place. It was grainy because of the extreme enlargement and the enhancement, but the scattering of buildings could be seen clearly, along with four gigantic, circular dark spots against the white of the snow.

"At Signy, the most northerly target, we don't know about casualties. The National Security Agency is attempting to make radio contact, as they are with each station, but so far without results. Additionally, a helicopter from a Danish merchantman attempted to approach the base, but was turned back by gunfire from a patrol boat. The boat was marked with the letters, 'F-S-A-D.' As with most of these bases, DIA doesn't know the site plans, but a telephone conversation with a scientist in London, who was on an expedition to Signy last summer, suggests that the communications hut, two supply warehouses, and a fuel depot were lost. Next picture, Pam.

"At Arctowski, there were again four sites bombed, though we're not certain exactly what was hit. A ham radio operator there got a message out to a regular chatting companion in Alabama. They have six seriously wounded by shrapnel and two with minor wounds. The radio operator reported the loss of their main radio antenna and the fuel supplies for their Sno-Cats. Pam.

"This is Bellinghausen. A transport helicopter from the supply ship *Inga* got out with the dead and wounded. That count is now at six dead, nine wounded, four of them seriously."

"Damn them," the Russian ambassador said.

"I agree, sir. The helicopter had to leave six people behind, all in fair shape, and the pilot reports that the base was heavily damaged, though the residential huts were spared. The pilot hopes to attempt a return to the station."

Akins put up the next photograph.

"Palmer Base has reported, again through a ham operator speaking to someone in Saskatchewan, four critically injured and four with minor wounds. They lost their fuel supply, a laboratory, and a kitchen."

McNichols waited while Akins put the next photo on the easel.

"Faraday is completely out of contact."

Bentley frowned, which McNichols took as a sign of his concern.

"Our same source in London, who has also been in residence at Faraday, thinks the damage sites include the operations building, the storage facilities, and two residential huts."

Akins attached the next photo to the easel.

"McMurdo sustained the heaviest damage and also reports via ham radio that there are twelve dead and sixteen wounded. Williams Field was destroyed, with three C-130s lost and one heavily damaged. They lost six helicopters. A Coast Guard icebreaker was attacked with bombs, but sustained only minor damage. The runway is cratered. The antenna complex was destroyed, which also put New Zealand's Scott Base off the air, though Scott apparently suffered only minor damage to supply buildings, as reported so far. McMurdo reports the loss of their fuel and warehouses, and they say that, with rationing, they can last maybe twelve days. There are four-hundred-and-twenty-seven people still at the base, and they've sent parties out to contact fifteen people who were out at nearby field sites.

"The totals to date, without information from Signy or Faraday, are eighteen dead and forty-one wounded."

The faces around the table all reflected deep concern, and McNichols was struck with the new idea that he was glad he worked for them.

"You do see a thread in all of this, don't you, Cameron?" Bentley said.

"There appears to be a commonality, yes, Sir Charles. I don't think residential areas at any of the stations were directly targeted. The attackers were after supplies and communications. The Faraday residential huts were probably an accident. There was a ground blizzard raging at the time."

"And what do you read into that, Cam?" Highwater asked.

"As a first reading," he said, "it appears that they're urging everyone who wasn't invited to leave the continent. They're cutting off the supply lines. Starving them out."

"There are a lot of experimental stations that went untouched," the Russian ambassador observed. "We have several on the opposite coast, for instance."

"So far, that's true, sir. Let's see Primavera, Pam."

He continued while she put up the photograph. "There are long distances involved, but they've proven that distance is not insurmountable with the attack on McMurdo. The signal we're getting is that they can attack any other base at any time they please. What we see at Primavera are twenty fighter aircraft and fourteen transports, though some of those are flying air cover. Some of our blowups show that the aircraft are finished in camouflage, and they're carrying an insignia we haven't seen before: a gold oval with the blue letters F-S-A-D. There are four heavy helicopters and one small helicopter now in operation. Off the coast are three naval ships, sixteen patrol boats, and four supply ships. They've got convoys moving equipment inland, and we've identified a number of surface-to-air missile sites as well as antiaircraft guns."

"Do we know about any group called FSAD?" the ambassador from China asked. "If this is, indeed, not the Argentineans?"

"We're searching for them now," McNichols said, "but so far, nothing's turned up."

Julia Highwater studied the photo, with its orange and green circles around aircraft and defensive installations. "This is not a force that couldn't be taken out in twelve hours by an American carrier battle group."

"Are they that optimistic, Mr. McNichols?" the French ambassador asked. "Do they think they can outfight a much larger force?"

"Perhaps, Mr. Ambassador. Or perhaps they believe that time is on their side. If they rely on history, such as that of the Falkland Islands clash, or the UN Assembly of Coalition Forces for the Persian Gulf crisis, it could be three weeks to three months before we could assemble a response. If they're counting on that, they may be bringing in more defensive capability than we now see. What they don't know about is the *U Thant*."

"Can the *U Thant* do it, Cameron?" Bentley asked.

"Well, you know, sir, that I've never seen her or met any of the people on board, and as far as I'm concerned, the people

are what count. All we have to do is go back and read the
mission objective for the *U Thant*. She was designed to quell
relatively minor insurrections or provide a rapid show of force
to encourage deterrence. This, of course, is more than a minor
insurrection, though we haven't seen heavy missiles or anything that might be construed as a nuclear threat. Their fighter
aircraft can maintain air superiority over the *U Thant*'s Harriers, if they've got well-trained pilots. On paper, with what
we see now in Antarctica, and giving an edge of capability to
our people, it looks like a fifty-fifty shot for the UN ship."

Julia Highwater said, "Or we can just ask the U.S. to fly
in a dozen B-52s or B-1s and bomb the hell out of them."

McNichols walked over to the easel, pulled the photos
loose, and found the first map. With his forefinger, he started
pointing out all of the stations located on the continent.

"There's just one thing, ma'am. They've got hostages."

She didn't like the sound of that. "Do you think they would
use them?"

"I suspect," McNichols said, "that nothing overt is going
to be said. We know, and they know, that if things don't go
their way, they can just drop a cluster bomb on any station
at random."

UNS U THANT
1250 HOURS LOCAL

Monmouth was on the bridge watching the recovery of two
Harriers that had been flying air patrol when the intercom
blared, "Bridge, Comm."

He stepped to the bulkhead and depressed the button.
"Comm, Bridge."

"You might want to come over here, sir. We have a message

from DIA that an extremely important broadcast is to be made at 1300 hours."

"Thank you," Monmouth said, releasing the button and hitting the keypad for the public address system. "Attention, this is the captain. The following people are to report to the communications compartment on the double: von Stein, Ernst, Cady, Baker, d'Argamon, Eames, George."

He repeated the announcement one more time, then turned the conn over to the third officer, Lieutenant Wilshire of the Netherlands, and left the bridge by the starboard corridor. The communications compartment was forward of the air controller's space, and he was the first to arrive.

The Japanese officer on duty told him it was to be a television broadcast which the National Security Agency would relay to them, and Monmouth asked him to turn the television so that those joining him in the cramped space would be able to view it easily.

Eames was the first to arrive.

"Hello, Captain," she said with question marks in her eyes.

"I don't know what it's going to be, exactly," he confessed, "but I'm told it's important."

All of the people he had called for but Baker had appeared a minute before the broadcast was to begin.

Cady told him, "Archie's on his way. He had to scrub some grease off his hands."

"I didn't say that this was supposed to be a formal gathering, Jim," Monmouth said.

The small compartment was not designed for a crowd, and they lined up two-deep against the bulkhead. George and d'Argamon settled cross-legged on the deck, and Monmouth envied them their agility. He could no longer imagine himself taking up such a position. Not without complaints from a variety of muscles, ligaments, and bones.

As the digital numerals of the bulkhead-mounted clock—set

for local time in the target area—went to 1300 hours, the snow on the television screen gave way to a few flickers, then a burnished gold banner with thirteen blue stars on it. A deep voice, off-camera and speaking in English, said, "Your attention, please. I present President Juan Silvera, speaking for the Front for South American Determination."

The camera drew back to reveal a distinguished man sitting in a gray leather, wing-backed chair. His eyes seemed to twinkle with good humor, and Monmouth was reminded of Ricardo Montalban. He smiled easily, comfortable with himself, and as if he knew just a little more than anyone else knew. He wore a conservative and expensive dark blue suit with a matching vest. The tie was muted, predominantly burgundy.

"Now we have a name to go with the acronym," Eames said.

Monmouth had seen the FSAD insignia in McNichols's pictures, too.

"Good morning, good afternoon, or good evening, ladies and gentlemen, depending upon the part of the world in which you reside. I am speaking to you from Primavera Base, Antarctica, the headquarters of the Front for South American Determination.

"It is a changing world in which we—you and I—live. Today, many societies on our earth are busily rewriting their histories, to bring them into conformance with the realities of the past, and I wish to speak to you briefly in regard to correcting yet another segment of international history.

"The Front for South American Determination, representing all nations of the South American continent, is intent upon correcting the injustices perpetrated in the Antarctic region. Until today, territorial claims on the continent have been a chart maker's nightmare. Though there have been many exploratory, charting, and scientific expeditions underwritten by many nations and organizations for nearly two centuries, the

Front for South American Determination recognizes only that the first permanent settlement—the basis of intent—was instigated by a nation represented by this consortium, in 1904. Under that legal claim, the Front now takes possession of the continent in the interest of its members."

"My God!" Eames said. "That was only a weather station, set up by Argentina on Laurie Island in the South Orkney Islands."

"It *is* Argentina behind all this," d'Argamon said as Archie Baker slipped into the compartment and stood next to Monmouth.

"Behind what?" Baker asked.

"Watch," Monmouth told him.

"The Front for South American Determination," Silvera went on, "will manage the continent for its consortium members. Toward that end, and until peaceful negotiations with interested parties have been completed, the Front is placing a moratorium on all scientific or other activities now taking place, or intended to take place in this summer.

"For nearly a century, Antarctica has been exploited scientifically and otherwise by nations which have failed to recognize the legal and historical territorial claims. From this point on, those claims *will* be recognized.

"When America ships wheat to another country, or when Brazil ships coffee, or Russia exports oil, they fully expect to be paid for their products. The same is true, and should have been true, for the product of Antarctica—which is primarily scientific knowledge. The Front recognizes the importance of endeavors in science and has no wish to hinder them. It will simply collect, for its consortium members, a licensing fee from those parties who wish to establish, or continue to maintain, a scientific outpost on the continent."

"Blackmail," Cady said.

"For justice to prevail, naturally, the negotiations will also consider fees for past usage of the continent by permanent and temporary expedition encampments."

"Naturally," David George said.

"Until agreements are in place, all scientific projects are to be halted. For those nations or organizations that no longer wish to conduct activities on the continent, arrangements can be made with the Front for the evacuation of their personnel."

"As soon as the back rent is paid," Cady said.

"There's a hell of a lot being left unsaid here," Baker added.

"Until further notice, or until negotiations are completed, all facilities, equipment, and scientific studies currently on the continent are hereby nationalized and become the property of the Front for South American Determination. Air and sea space is to be restricted for a hundred kilometers off the ice shelf.

"Yesterday, when the Front took rightful possession of its property, to emphasize its sovereignty, the activities of a number of illegal bases were curtailed. It should be noted that the Front took extreme care to protect lives, and that only communication and supply lines were affected. Supplies of fuel and food, as well as the establishment of a communications network, will be guided by the Front, and will commence as soon as the proper agreements are in place."

"If sixty dead and wounded is extreme care," Baker said, "I'm not sure I'd want to rely on their management of my food supply."

"The Front for South American Determination hereby applies to the world community, through the United Nations, for recognition of its historical right, and I, as spokesperson for the organization, thank you for your time and wish you all a good day."

President Juan Silvera smiled broadly and fatherly, and perhaps lovingly, then faded away.

"He didn't even respond to the UN resolution," Eames noted.

"Oh, I think he has," Cady said.

D'Argamon looked up at Monmouth from his seat on the floor. "Captain, can we make this ship go faster?"

UNS U THANT
1520 HOURS LOCAL

Cady had the full complement of the wing's flying personnel gathered in the wing briefing room. George, the SEAL commander, attended, also.

He let his exec, Commander Phillip Anderson, conduct the briefing on the FSAD declaration and show the videotape of the speech made by Silvera, then took his place at the head of the room and slapped his notebook down on the podium. Cady had an unlit cigar clamped in his teeth, and he pulled it free and dropped it in a pocket.

The aviators, who had been surviving, hoping, or dreading on the basis of rumor for several days, now appeared glum as the facts began to come out. They had all been training, as part of their air patrols, on the simulations developed by Terri Eames, and most of them had been subjected to critical reviews by the CAG and the squadron commanders. Morale was not at the highest, and Cady knew that condition wasn't desirable this close to entering into non-simulated combat.

He thought it was about time to start them on the upward curve of the morale cycle.

"Ladies"—for the benefit of the three female helicopter pilots—"and gentlemen, you've just watched an adequate performance by a relatively capable actor. Let's keep in mind, however, that it was just that: an act.

"I'm not an intelligence analyst, but Major Eames and I

spoke to one shortly after the broadcast. We don't yet know all of the details surrounding the FSAD, but the Argentines say they've been in existence for nearly two years, that they've been quiet, and that they haven't caused any trouble. The DIA has a list, which is getting longer, of the people who may be associated with the organization. Until today, the Argentine government says it was unaware of the aims of the FSAD.

"So far, there is not a South American country that admits to being part of any consortium headed by Silvera. Our analyst and his assistants think that might be open to change when they stop to think about the carrot Silvera is dangling for them. For the most part, those countries are extremely poor, and if the FSAD offers them a new source of income, they may well buy into it and give Silvera the recognition he's looking for."

Cady saw that Archie Baker, ensconced in a front row seat, was itching to ask a question.

"Major?"

"What kind of revenues are we talking about, Colonel?"

"I don't have any idea," Cady admitted, "though I asked the same question of Mr. McNichols. At this point, I understand that the Security Council staff has opened a line of communications with Primavera, through a FSAD office in Buenos Aires, and they're asking for details. McNichols, on a best-guess basis, thinks they might set a licensing fee of, say, a couple million dollars per year per base. That would be a hundred million dollar annual income for consortium members, after FSAD expenses, and DIA estimates they have at least a couple hundred million investment. What's more important, he thinks, is the reparations they'll require for past years of exploitation. Silvera is going after nations with what he thinks are deep pockets, and conceivably, the U.S., Russia, the United Kingdom, and others could be hit with a bill for several billion dollars."

"Won't happen," George said. "Oops, sorry for interrupting, Colonel."

"I don't think it will happen, either," Cady said. "But, if thirteen countries in South America recognize the FSAD as legitimate, we may have to work around a monkey wrench."

Cady saw some mystified looks in his audience. He constantly had to be on guard against using American idioms, even twisted ones, in front of his multinational collection of warriors.

"That is to say, those thirteen countries, if they get into a debate on the floor of the General Assembly, may urge the Security Council to back away from its resolution and our mission, or to delay it. We're under operational orders right now that I for one, thinking about those people killed or wounded, would not like to see changed. So, we're going to jump off earlier than planned."

He saw expectant faces in his audience now.

"We are now sixteen hundred miles from the Antarctic Peninsula, which is out of range of our aircraft. We are also damned short of intelligence sources other than the overhead stuff we're getting through DIA. We are going to get around one of those problems in order to correct the other. Major Baker?"

Archie Baker stood up and turned to face the sea of pilots. "Colonel Cady and I happened to remember, almost simultaneously as it were, that our supply room contains several rubberized fuel bladders. With the help of a Saudi mechanic, we think we've designed the absolutely perfect jury-rigged aerial refueling system. We're going to load three Seahawks to the maximum as tankers. As with all perfect systems, this is likely to be somewhat perilous, and rather than assign air crews, I will now ask for three volunteers."

Cady saw that the three female pilots were among the first of all the chopper pilots to get their hands in the air.

Baker selected one of them and two male pilots. "As soon as this briefing is concluded, the three of you and your aircrews will meet with Colonel Cady and myself for a mission briefing."

He nodded to Cady and sat down.

"I appreciate the unanimous support shown by the 11th and 12th Helicopter Squadrons," Cady said. "I've made a note to myself that Sea Apache pilots also consider themselves expert Seahawk pilots."

That drew a few laughs and a few hostile glares at the attack helicopter pilots from the Seahawk pilots.

"Now, let me say something about our overall strategy. We do not yet have specific missions finalized, but we are fully aware that our aircraft are not going to compete very well against Mirages and Tornados. Rather than test it, we are going to cede air superiority to the hostile forces, and our strategy will follow a probe and punch philosophy. We'll take little bites out of them, until there's nothing left to chew on."

That got some nods of agreement, too.

Cady glanced down at his notes. "Finally, I want to say something about the training we've been conducting in the last few days. Major Baker, Commander Anderson, Major Travers, and I have been riding you damned hard. We've pointed out some weaknesses to you. If you'll think about the criticism we've been handing out, as we have, you'll note that almost all of our comments relate to attitude. I haven't taken one note relative to flying ability. All of you are elite aviators in your respective services. You wouldn't be here if you were not. I commend you for your talents, and I'm happy as hell that you're flying for me.

"The only thing I'll ask of you is that you fly for each other, also. We're the best of the best, ladies and gentlemen. Let's not jeopardize that by forgetting that we're also serving our world, no matter its imperfections."

As they filed out of the room, Cady thought the faces reflected a bit of an upswing in the morale department.

UNS U THANT
1645 HOURS LOCAL

Archie Baker really wanted to go along on this jaunt, but he had assigned himself to the attack helicopters, and he wouldn't take a seat away from one of his transport pilots.

He and the six pilots and copilots who would fly the mission were on Hangar Deck 2, observing the installation of the fuel bladders in three Seahawks. The Saudi mechanic who was supervising the installation had taken their crew chiefs off into an alcove of the hangar deck to instruct them on aerial refueling procedures. It was going to be a new experience for everyone concerned.

The Sikorsky SH-60B Seahawk was the naval version of the U.S. Army's multipurpose Black Hawk. It had an elongated fuselage and rotors which, when they were unfolded for flight, were fifty-three-feet, eight-inches from tip to tip. It was a utility helicopter, designed to handle a large variety of chores, but it could be armed with two 7.62-millimeter M60 machine guns mounted in the opened side doors, and in the case of the Seahawk, a pair of homing torpedoes. Two of Baker's Seahawks were outfitted as LAMPS helicopters, utilized in antisubmarine warfare, and if he ran short of helos, he was prepared to take one of them out of LAMPS service. All of the helicopters were fitted with naval avionics, including radar and sonar. In comparison with the army's S-70 Black Hawk, the wheelbase was shorter and the rotor and tail pylon automatically folded for easier below-decks handling and storage.

These three had had their machine guns removed. All of the available weight allowance was going to be devoted to the fuel cells. With an empty weight of 10,900 pounds, the Sea-hawk's normal mission takeoff weight was 16,450 pounds. However, they could still get airborne with a gross weight of twenty-thousand pounds, and these birds were being prepped to lift off with four tons of fuel.

Senior Lieutenant Mikhail Makarov of the Russian Air Defense Force leaned in the side door of his Seahawk and examined the three fuel cells that were laying rumpled on the floor.

"They will take up a lot of space, Major," he said. "My crew chief will not have room to move about."

"I don't believe the brochures promised that this was to be a comfortable cruise," Baker said.

"That is funny. I did not even see the brochures."

"It was a joke, Mikhail."

"Oh. I see."

"All right, then," Baker said. "Let's go over some of the primary points again. No unnecessary radio chatter, even though we're operating with scrambled radios. People who hear garbage on the airways get worried. Everyone makes certain that their primary and secondary GPS systems are accurate and agreeing. Before you take off, I want each of you to verify with me the exact position where you're supposed to be, and for how long. Mikhail, you'll go first."

The Russian beamed.

"Don't forget that your own fuel is going to get critical at three points. At maximum takeoff weight, your range is three hundred and seventy miles, and that leaves you only a thirty-minute reserve. Over water, I don't want you getting deep into your reserves. The first two times, you refuel from your own on-board bladders. The last time, you tank up from Gail."

Gail Alhers, a blonde and statuesque Norwegian, nodded thoughtfully. Based on his experience with her, Baker knew she would be calculating distances, weights, and fuel consumption.

"The same with you, Gail. Don't let the Harrier drink it all."

"I will be certain, Major Baker."

He turned to Tex Hammond, who was actually a black man born to a U.S. airman and his Korean wife in Seoul. He flew choppers for the South Koreans in real life.

"Tex, you're the last off. You'll have to cover everybody. Mikhail, if he comes in light, Gail for sure, and the Harrier if necessary."

"I've got it down pat, Arch. No sweat."

Baker hoped he was right. His and Cady's perfect plan had a lot of ifs in it.

PUMA LEADER
1721 HOURS LOCAL

"Unidentified aircraft, respond."

The airplane was a twin-engined de Havilland Canada DHC-4 Caribou transport. It was older, and it carried no markings except for the tail number.

Tellez had been flying alongside it for five minutes, attempting to reach its pilot on several frequencies, including the international GUARD channel.

He had not gotten a response, and he did not think the pilot was particularly concerned about the heavily armed Tornado on his wing. He grinned happily and waved frequently.

The aircraft was probably a charter plane operated by some poverty-stricken company that couldn't afford better airplanes or even to maintain the ones they had. The radios were as likely to be missing as working. Either that, or the pilot was inexperienced at international flight.

Tellez tried for the tenth time. "This is a FSAD military aircraft calling the unidentified de Havilland Canada. You are flying in restricted airspace."

The two aircraft were at eight thousand meters, ninety kilometers north of the Shetland Islands, headed south.

Once again, Tellez did not receive a reply. The other pilot and his copilot could see him signalling them, but they only waved back at him.

President Juan Silvera's grand speech had had little effect, as far as Tellez could see. No one seemed afraid of the FSAD insignia on the side of his camouflaged fighter. No one, or at least these two pilots, was observing the boundary of exclusion for air travel.

Abruptly, Tellez dropped his left wing and banked quickly away from the transport.

"We are letting him go?" Jesus Ramirez asked anxiously from his seat in the rear cockpit.

"We are not. I will give him a warning shot across the nose." He armed the twenty-seven-millimeter Mauser cannons.

Tellez leveled off, reduced power, and fell behind the civilian airplane. As soon as he had clearance, he banked toward it again.

"Be careful, Roberto. They are civilians."

"Perhaps they are civilians."

He depressed the firing stud, and the airframe vibrated as the heavy shells thundered from the cannons.

The tracers walked ahead of him, curving toward the nose of the Caribou.

The airplane did not waver a bit, did not turn away.

He fired once again.

And the tracers walked right into the cockpit.

Tellez immediately released the firing button.

"My God!"

"Shut up, Jesus!"

"But. . . ."

As he watched, the Caribou slowly brought its left wing up and dropped its nose, spinning away and down. When it did not immediately recover from the spin, he knew the pilot were dead or hurt too badly to react.

Tellez whipped the Tornado inverted and watched through the canopy as the big transport spiraled lazily downward.

It seemed to take a long time before it slammed into the sea.

6 DECEMBER

Two of Archie Baker's Seahawks were sitting on the forward elevators, but the elevators were lowered below the main deck, to keep the helos out of harm's way, just in case Cady couldn't keep his Harrier on the flight deck. The first chopper, flown by the Russian Makarov, had taken off two hours before.

Cady made certain that the Martin-Baker ejection seat was armed, then cinched his harness a little tighter.

He pressed the transmit button and, on the flight deck control frequency, he said, "Any time you're ready, Shaker."

"Don't want me to finish my donut, CAG?"

"Have you noticed you're putting on weight?"

"Donut's gone. Wind her up."

Cady set the nozzle lever stop at twenty per cent, then ran the throttle forward, watching the tachometer readout climb to one hundred per cent. He held it there until he saw Adams salute, then snapped a return salute and came off the brakes. As soon as the fighter began to move, he slipped the nozzle lever down against the preset stop, aiming the nozzles down for the STOL run.

With the Pegasus engine creating its own thunder, the Harrier raced down the deck. The seven-degree upswept ramp on the bow looked like a barrier at first, then he was into it, the nose rising. A glance at the air speed indicator told him he had more momentum than he really needed, a result of taking off light loaded with only maximum fuel, two Sidewinders, an ammo load, and three aluminum canisters on the bomb pylons.

The Harrier leapt off the bow, and Cady slapped the gear button, but with the turbofan in full scream, didn't hear the gear clunk up into its wells. A few seconds later, and at three hundred feet above the blue sea, he retracted his flaps.

"Good shot, Shark. Go to air control."

"Gone, Shaker."

He punched the button for the air control frequency.

"Gypsy Moth One is with you, Beehive."

"Good morning, Shark," Giovanni Este said. "Let's have you at angels ten, heading one-one-five."

"Sounds good to me," Cady said.

"And turn off the IFF, please. We want you to come home so we won't advertise your presence."

"Roger that. One's out."

While he continued to climb to altitude, Cady dipped his wing and turned onto his heading. He shut off the IFF so as not to emit any signal that would warn anyone of his true identity if he was picked up on a radar.

He had been at ten thousand feet for ten minutes when the radio sounded off, "Gypsy Moth One, Jericho."

"Go, Jericho."

He thought Terri Eames's voice sounded a bit choked up. "I have a report I thought you might be interested in."

"I'm all ears, Jericho."

"A private charter airplane out of Christchurch, New Zealand, carrying six French scientists to Eights Station was shot down last night."

"Damn it! How did that happen? Weren't they warned off?"

"Apparently not, Gypsy Moth, at least not by friendly people. The pilot was using a satellite communications channel and notified his home base that he was under attack by a Panavia Tornado and had been hit. He then went off the air."

Cady didn't think much of fighter pilots who attacked unarmed civilian craft. He hoped he met up with this guy.

"Anything else?" he asked.

"Christchurch reports that they have a backlog of people and aircraft building up, all expeditions that were scheduled for a summer on the ice."

"They may miss this summer," Cady told her.

"Yes. Jericho out."

Cady loosened his harness and settled in for the long flight, holding his airspeed at six hundred knots. The skies were clear way out to the horizons, with just a gray line of clouds in the southwestern sector. The sea below was a deep blue, and so calm that it induced confidence. Eddie Purgatory had warned him, though, that he expected a late-morning front moving in on the continent. "Get in and get out," he had said.

An hour and twenty minutes later, Cady began his planned descent to two thousand feet, and six minutes after that, found Makarov's Seahawk exactly where it was supposed to be.

God bless Russian chopper pilots.

"Copperhead, Gypsy Moth."

"We have visual on you, Gypsy One."

"Let's see if this works, Mickey Moose," he said, using the nickname the American chopper pilots had given the Russian.

"At this point, I think we must make it work," the Russian said! "Otherwise, you will swim for a few minutes. I will hold at one-five-zero knots."

The Seahawk could make 184 miles per hour at maximum speed, but they had decided not to increase the stress levels of either machines or pilots by pushing the speed envelope during the intricate hookup, and Cady eased in some nozzle vector so he could maintain the slower speed. He swung in behind the Seahawk and saw that the crew chief, tethered by a nylon line attached to a wide leather belt while he worked at the open side door, had already deployed the hose. He was bundled up in a thick parka, but he looked pretty cold in the open doorway.

With the aerodynamic basket on its end, the hose trailed sixty feet behind and slightly below the helicopter. The rush of downdraft from the rotors tended to make the hose bounce erratically, but the basket, out of the downdraft, was relatively stable. Cady deployed the Harrier's refueling probe and nursed the throttle, closing in on the basket.

"Looking good, Shark," the crew chief told him. "Just a couple more feet. Attaway!"

The probe engaged the basket, and a red light on the basket glowed, confirming the connection. Cady nudged the throttle a tad, to keep pressure on the basket. He glanced upward and saw the silver disk of the helicopter's spinning rotors. He wanted to keep them up there, about thirty feet above him.

"I've got a good light, Copperhead."

"Here she comes." The crew chief ducked back inside the Seahawk to finagle the fabricated valves and pump.

Cady maintained his concentration on the helicopter's position, but took quick glances at his fuel readout. The fuel state improved nicely.

"Keep enough for yourself, Mickey Moose."

"We will do fine, CAG. Lieutenant Alhers will have plenty if we need it."

"Doesn't she have a nickname?" Cady asked.

"It is not one that we have mentioned directly to her," Makarov said.

If she were listening to the frequency, which she probably was, Gail Alhers now knew she had a covert nickname.

It didn't take as long as he had anticipated. When his readout told him he had full tanks, he notified the crew chief, then backed out of the basket.

"Scoot for home, Copperhead. With my thanks, by the way."

"At any time, Shark."

The Seahawk peeled away to the left, and Cady banked right and returned to his heading. From here on in, he would keep his altitude low, then lower as he neared the radars that the FSAD were likely to have emplaced.

A few minutes later, the sea changed colors on him, and he knew he had crossed the Antarctic Convergence. Everything suddenly seemed colder and grayer, and he nudged the cockpit heat up a notch. The line of clouds to his right rear were building, forming a gunmetal-gray wall to hide the other end of the world.

He changed course once in order to bypass a patrol boat cruising off the ice pack. He had picked it up with one of his infrequent active scans with his radar, which he was certain had a greater range than any radar on the boat.

Forty minutes passed before he saw the continent. At his low altitude, it came up slyly, a chain of pristine mountaintops first, then as he closed on it, the long white stretch of the coast. Or not the coast. It was the first time Cady had seen Antarctica, and he had to remind himself that coastal sightings were deceptive. The pack ice ringed the entire continent, and it could be miles wide. Behind it were various ice shelves, which might or might not be solidly linked to rock or lava below. The ice coming off the glaciers moved inexorably to the sea. He recalled Eames telling him that Admiral Richard Byrd's stations, Little America I through Little America V, established at the Bay of Whales on the Ross Sea between 1928 and 1956, had all disappeared, pushed off into the sea.

Cady kept losing altitude until he was holding the Harrier at five hundred feet above the sea. If he stayed low enough, he might evade any land-based radars. A look-down radar from a hostile aircraft was another matter. He was pretty certain that the C-130s McNichols had said were flying reconnaissance patterns did not have a look-down capability.

The sea had begun to fill with icebergs, some as large as, or larger than, aircraft carriers. Giant pinnacles of ice reared out of the sea, and though he was still above them, they seemed to be reaching for him. Despite their potential for treachery, they were eerily beautiful, serene, and majestic.

Twenty miles from the first of the pack ice, the vista widened and whitened. Here and there were pockets of dark gray, rock and cliffs exposed by the wind. Cady didn't know when he had last seen something that seemed so simultaneously magnificent, deadly, and alluring. He could understand how some people might become addicted to the desolation.

Below, and gone in a flash, were two whales sounding.

As he closed on the ice, he looked for penguins. Cady thought it would be good public relations to report back to his shipmates that he had seen penguins. He didn't see any, but he did spot several terns wheeling and soaring, searching for lunch, then a pack of around a dozen seals cavorting in the water.

The Harrier crossed over the edge of the pack ice—a nearly perfect vertical cliff almost seventy feet high—and his AGL, altitude above ground level, was suddenly 430 feet. Cady longed to switch on his radar for a quick look around, but the emanations could quickly draw unwanted company. Visually, he was alone in this world except for a few birds coasting along the seawall, probably petrels. He was going to have to get a new bird book.

He quickly brought up the readout for his secondary Global Positioning Satellite data receiver and verified that the second set of coordinates matched the first. It was nice when neither set was malfunctioning; it precluded guesswork or extrapolating a position. Checking the coordinates of his first target, jotted on his kneepad notebook, Cady adjusted his heading to 105 degrees.

He eased back on the throttle and let the craft sink a little lower.

"Anvers Island coming up," he said aloud to himself. "I hope."

Locked in a sea of ice like it was, Anvers wasn't going to look like the islands he had read about as a kid in Montana. He preferred the kinds of islands that Robinson Crusoe and Christian Fletcher had landed on.

He scanned the skies, looking for anything unfriendly, but found nothing, not even the birds now.

On the armaments panel, he selected the canister slung on his centerline hardpoint.

A few minutes later, he spied the collection of huts, sheds, and paraphernalia that was supposed to be Palmer Station. It was slightly to his right oblique, and he corrected his line of flight by two degrees.

The station came up fast. When he was almost upon it, he saw where debris from the FSAD attack had been stacked, and he saw that a few people were milling around outside one of the larger buildings. He aimed slightly to the left of them and watched his target—a circle of bare space—slowly come down the HUD and drift into the targeting rectangle. As soon as it was in place, he pressed the release button and "pickled" off the canister.

Out the right side of his canopy, he saw seven parka-clad people scrambling for cover, diving through doorways, sliding behind the corners of buildings. The sight of low-flying attack aircraft would probably frighten them for years to come.

And then he was past them, bringing the stick back a little so he could bring the tail down and check the rearview mirror.

He saw the small parachute on the canister blossom, then he drifted right into a heading for Faraday.

The destruction at Faraday Base seemed a little more extensive. Six structures had been leveled, and a tall antenna was laid flat on the ground, broken into a half-dozen pieces. Still, the sound of his approach brought a few people into the open for a few minutes, until they identified him as a warplane. Then, as at Palmer, they quickly scampered for protection.

He punched the second canister from its starboard pylon, then turned north toward Brandeis.

Checking his fuel state, Cady decided to seek a more economical cruise rate and backed off to 450 knots. His round-trip fuel allotment didn't allow for sight-seeing side trips.

The scene at Brandeis was more reassuring. The scattering of huts, some of which were connected by above-ground tunnels, were all intact, and when he went over at two hundred feet above the ground, he saw four people waving at him, as if they had expected him.

And they had expected him, or something like him. David George had warned his contact, Bandit.

And George had also convinced Cady, as long as he was headed that way, to drop the scrambled radios at Palmer and Faraday.

He banked left after dropping the canister, saw more arms waving from the ground, but he didn't hang around.

As soon as he saw a chute on the canister, he dropped the nose and turned west. The sea was about forty miles away, and he wanted to see it again real soon.

It was in sight when his threat receiver bleated in his ears.

UNS U THANT
1146 HOURS LOCAL

Lieutenant Commander David George had been loitering in the communications compartment for over an hour. Twice, he had called Eames in the adjacent Combat Information Center to see if she had a fix on Gypsy Moth One. She didn't have his exact position, but she had an estimated flight path provided by McNichols's visual contact, and she kept telling George to let time take care of it.

George was too eager for that. Time was getting in his way.

The communications supervisor, a Spaniard named Olivera, had let him commandeer one of the three consoles, and he had set it up to monitor the 361.5 frequency on which his portable scrambled radios operated.

By eleven-thirty, his level of expectation had risen so high that he was unprepared when the radio squawked, "Chestnut, this is Bandit."

He already had the headset in place, and he bounced his toe around on the deck until he found the transmit switch.

"Good morning, Bandit. Chestnut here. Hold on a second, will you? Have I got anyone from Palmer or Faraday listening in?"

After a second's hesitation, a female voice said, "This is Palmer. What's going on?"

"Faraday, here. Look, we've got a lot of very sick people, and we need. . . ."

"Please let me explain," George broke in. "The radios we air-dropped to you are scrambled, so we can speak in relative security. However, your transmissions could be triangulated, could be monitored so as to identify your positions, so please keep your transmitting time brief.

"For the time being, my call sign will be Chestnut. I represent the United Nations, and I assure you that help is on the way. Bandit is at Brandeis Base, and he was not aware that we were also dropping radios to Palmer and Faraday."

George provided them with a short update of the hostilities, along with a recap of FSAD's proclamation.

"Now, I would like to have a report—briefly, please—of the conditions at each of your stations. Palmer, please go first."

George made certain the tape recorder was running and pulled a notepad close to jot down the primary details.

After a minute to get herself organized, the woman at Palmer rattled off her primary concerns. "We have had two people die in the last three hours, another six are wounded, two of them critically. Our food supply is also in critical condition, and we are on half-rations. I estimate that we can last ten days. We need medical help immediately."

"We will get help to you as soon as possible," George said. "I can't tell you just when because I have to keep our current position secure. We are making plans to evacuate personnel as soon as conditions permit. Faraday, please report on your status."

The clipped British voice was prepared. "We had fourteen people in residence for the winter. There are six dead and six injured badly. We have ample food since they missed the storehouse and fuel storage. The bastards destroyed six residential structures."

George was about to respond when Bandit broke in.

"Harold, this is Bandit at Brandeis."

"Is that you, Zip?"

"Yeah, mate. Chris? How's Chris?"

"Ah, damn me, Zip. I'm sorry."

David George's brand-new radio net went silent, and George was reluctant to break the silence. He didn't know exactly what was going on, but he suddenly felt as if he had suffered a personal loss.

JAGUAR NINE
1150 HOURS LOCAL

Sancho Amador, a senior lieutenant pilot in the FSAD air force, did not know whether to be amazed or ecstatic.

He had been flying his patrol alone because his wingman, Jaguar Eight, had lost hydraulic pressure and returned to Primavera for repairs. He was sixty kilometers southwest of Primavera at eight thousand meters of altitude, lolling along, dipping his Mirage 2000 from side to side, completely enjoying his isolation and his freedom from superior eyes. He could fly as he wanted to fly, and as he loved to fly. It was a beautifully clear day, and in the warmth of his cockpit, this barren land was less intimidating, far less so than when he was forced to be on the ground, shivering in the cold.

Amador did not really know what he was looking for. His squadron mates all said it would be weeks or months, if ever, before the United States amassed support among the allies and sent a force to intimidate them. He supposed that some nation could be sending reconnaissance aircraft, but they would be high, at thirty thousand meters or so, out of his reach. Out at sea, he had found one of their own patrol boats, and he had nearly buzzed it, but decided at the last moment that a negative report might be filed by the commander with Colonel Suarez.

He was now some thirty kilometers inland and would soon turn for the coast. When he found the *Marguerite Bay,* he was to turn back.

In his dipping and swaying, as he toyed with the airplane, the nose came down and the radar picked up a speck. It barely caught his attention, but when it did, Amador leveled his wings, brought the nose down again, and found a solid blip on the scope. It was flying at 450 knots, very low to the ice, and toward the west. It was not transmitting an IFF signal.

It was not using radar, either.

Amador sat up as straight as his harness allowed.

This was a jet aircraft, and it was not one that belonged to his confederates.

He turned to the right by thirty degrees and began to follow it, quickly losing altitude.

When he finally saw it with his own eyes, he did not recognize the silhouette, except to know that it was not a FSAD airplane and that it should not be there. It was difficult to pick out against the ice, being a light gray in color. It was a fighter aircraft.

He only briefly considered making a radio report before fantasizing the reaction of his roommates when he showed them the gun camera film proving himself to be the first to be bloodied in battle against an armed adversary.

Amador selected an air-to-air Matra R.530 missile, then switched the radar mode to attack.

GYPSY MOTH ONE
1151 HOURS LOCAL

The Mirage leaped on him from high above, coming out of the sun.

Cady couldn't see it in the rearview mirror, but he knew it was there.

His threat receiver continued to chirp in his ears as he threw the Harrier into a tight right turn, then a left, and slammed the throttle forward. Now, he needed altitude badly.

The tone sounding in his headset changed pitch and urgency, and a glance at the HUD confirmed what he was hearing: "LOCK-ON."

The missile was infrared-homing, and Cady whipped the stick back to get his nose up and his hot exhaust aimed downward, away from the supercoolant of the infrared seeker head. He looked up through the canopy, and he saw the missile's propellent trail.

Half-mile away.

The Harrier was slowing to stall speed.

He kicked the rudder and brought the nose over to the right, falling out of his climb, and still struggling to keep the exhaust away from the missile.

The AGL readout on the lower right of the HUD read 968.

Airspeed 145 knots.

The data wasn't good.

He leveled the wings, got the nose down, and fought for speed.

The maneuver had thrown the pursuing missile off his track, though. It whistled past him, missing by several hundred feet, and impacted with a deceptively small detonation in the ice.

He didn't watch it. He had found his attacker and noted it was a delta-winged Mirage.

It was coming fast, still several thousand feet above, and nearing its cannon range.

Too close for its missiles, probably.

Cady rolled hard left, gaining airspeed, but losing altitude. AGL 420.

Swerving left and right, zigzagging.

The hard place was just below him, and the rock was coming down fast.

He had visual contact in the rearview mirror.

The Mirage's cannons began blinking, white and hot.

A thousand yards behind him.

The Harrier wasn't an ideal air superiority fighter.

But it could stop on a dime.

Cady slammed the nozzle lever full back, rotating the nozzles to their forward positions.

The Harrier abruptly cancelled her forward flight and stopped nearly dead in midair.

A startled and disoriented Mirage pilot jerked back on his control stick to avoid a midair collision and shot over the

Harrier, the turbulence of his passage rocking Cady's fighter violently.

Even as he slapped the nozzle lever forward again, Cady armed his AIM-9L Super Sidewinders, activating their infra-red-homing heads. The Mirage's exhaust was hot and close, and he heard an immediate lock-on tone.

He fired the first Sidewinder.

And knew at once that he wouldn't need the second.

The missile whisked off its launch rail, and its Rocketdyne solid-propellent motor accelerated it to Mach 3 in seconds.

The Mirage rolled right, climbing in afterburner.

Which excited the Sidewinder's infrared-homing eye.

The Sidewinder pursued, closing, curving upward, zipping right up the Mirage 2000's tail pipe.

A mini-nova erupted over the white wasteland. The bouquet of orange and yellow and red ballooned abruptly, and only debris barely resembling an airplane flew out of the fireball, spinning and tumbling toward the earth.

There was no parachute.

Cady only wished that it had been a Tornado, one that had shot down a civilian aircraft.

He rolled back onto his original heading, not looking back, but seeing Eddie Purgatory's predicted cloud front approaching the pack ice.

He did check his fuel state and said, "Shit."

DEFENSE INTELLIGENCE AGENCY
1202 HOURS LOCAL

Cameron McNichols didn't plan on it, but he got to watch the action in Antarctica live.

He had been forewarned of Colonel Cady's mission by Terri Eames, and he had been checking in occasionally over the course of the morning. His pictures were provided by a Teal Ruby, then a Rhyolite satellite which had been moved into an orbit which passed over the polar region by the Jet Propulsion Laboratory in Pasadena. The JPL was slowly bringing a number of satellites into position, and soon he would have much better coverage of the area, if not continual coverage. He had specifically requested an Aquacade, which had cloud-penetrating radar capability.

McNichols, Pam Akins, and half a dozen other analysts from his section had bailed out of what they should have been doing to watch the Harrier from the moment it crossed the coastline inbound. As soon as they saw the successful deployment of the third radio, McNichols said, "Pam, you want to get on the horn to Eames and see what they learn from those stations?"

"Right away, Cam," she said as she moved to another of the recently relocated consoles.

She was talking to Eames, with no hard data being reported from the scientific stations yet, when Jack Neihouse, another of his assistants, yelped, "He's under attack!"

"What? Where?"

"Right here, chief." Neihouse leaned forward and tapped a shape on the screen. "Mirage, I think."

The room full of analysts watched spellbound as the dog-fight took place, all in a matter of seconds. When it ended, there was a mixed reaction of sighs and victory yells.

"Son of a bitch!" Neihouse exclaimed. "I didn't know they could do that, stop like that."

McNichols was himself amazed at the way Cady, with apparent calmness, took care of business.

Akins, who had abandoned Eames and dashed over from her console, said, "He didn't see the Mirage coming. We could be doing something about that, Cam."

"You're right, Pam. I was thinking the same thing."

"Oh. I forgot about Major Eames."

"That's okay, I'll take it."

Without leaving his castered chair, but scooting it over to the next console, McNichols picked up the phone.

"Terri, Cam."

"What's going on, damn it!"

"Ah, your Colonel Cady got jumped by a Mirage."

"Oh, Jesus!"

"It's okay, Terri. He downed it and is back on track. In a few minutes, we're going to lose him in cloud cover."

He almost heard her relief over the telephone connection and he began to wonder if there was something going on between Eames and Cady. Unreasonably, he felt a little pang of jealousy. Hell, he hadn't even met her. She probably looked like the top sergeant he had had during his two-year stint in the army.

But she had a hell of a voice.

"Can you give me his position?" Eames asked. "He's stubborn and won't break radio silence, and he may be off-course for the refueling."

"Hold on, hon." McNichols turned toward the other console. "Jack, get the coordinates on the Harrier, will you?"

Neihouse nodded, tapped some commands into his keyboard, and overlaid the screen with a grid. "Yup, got him."

McNichols relayed the coordinates to Eames. "Any rewards yet from our radios?"

"Yes. Commander George just gave me the reports."

Eames read from what must have been inadequate hand writing, because she stumbled over a few of the details.

"Damn. I hate adding to the fatalities list," he told her.

"Don't forget the charter plane."

"I haven't. And it's thrown some of the UN reps into a frenzy. Sir Charles told me that some of the Latin American countries were leaning toward support for this FSAD bunch until that plane went down. The French ambassador, who happens to be on the Peacekeeper Committee, is yelling for nuclear retaliation, now, and the Latinos are backing off."

"Will they condemn the FSAD?"

"Well, I wouldn't go so far as to say that, hon. There are still dollar signs in their eyes."

7 DECEMBER

Paul Andover had left the warmth of his bunk, which was corralled by the stacks of his books, for an early morning walk. He was dressed for the fourteen degrees below zero chill, wearing his long silk thermal underwear, his vapor barrier boots, a woolen balaclava in bright blue that protected his face and beard, and a hooded parka.

He wasn't, however, paying much attention to either the cold or the light snowfall that had lingered through the night. The sky was not visible and the snow blanked out landmarks a quarter mile away, but by habit, he didn't walk far from the compound. No one left the station area to visit the outlying field experiments without checking out and without taking a buddy along. He paced back and forth through a two-inch-deep layer of fresh ground cover between the main hut and the garage that housed the Sno-Cats and snowmobiles. The wind was brisk, but he didn't notice that either.

Back and forth.

He hadn't slept at all.

He had not wanted to get out of bed, either, but when he heard others in the hut begin to move around, he felt like he wanted to stay away from them for a while longer.

On his twelfth lap, he stopped in front of the garage. It was a large affair, with a curved steel roof, and it was kept minimally heated so that the vehicles would start more readily. To the right of it was a stack of fifty-five gallon drums of oil and gasoline, and to the left was another stack of drums—the empties refilled—which were clearly marked "Used Motor Oil," or "Used Cooking Grease," or "Hydrogen Sulfate," or whatever. Like the Greenpeace people near McMurdo, they had decided early on that Brandeis Base would stay as environmentally pure as they could make it, and those drums would be airlifted to the ship on the next resupply mission. He assumed someone in charge knew where to find an approved toxic disposal site. Probably back in Europe which, as far as he was concerned, was polluted enough that they wouldn't mind a little more.

Andover stared at the drums and wondered if it was all worth the effort. The few people like him on the continent were about to be wiped out by some band of hot-blooded Latinos. Christine Amherst had been like him. She didn't like seeing smudges on her landscape, either.

He trudged forward to the pedestrian door, opened it, and stepped into the lukewarm heat of the garage.

The five Sno-Cats and the ten snowmobiles, all painted a bright, high-visibility orange, took up most of the space, and he wandered around them for a while, finally climbing up into one of the Sno-Cats and sitting in the driver's seat. It wasn't much more than a big box on caterpillar-like treads, and the seat, upholstered in a gray canvas stiff with cold, wasn't very comfortable. He sat and leaned on the control sticks and stared through the windshield at the garage door.

Christine's image was painted there, staring back at him with that half-smile he was so fond of. She wasn't a particularly beautiful woman, wasn't . . . wouldn't have won any awards, but she had been a beautiful person.

The small door opened, and Ruth Anne Oliver came in,

closed it behind her, then walked over to the other side of the Sno-Cat and pulled herself up into the passenger seat.

"Where are we going, Zip?"

"Ah, Ruthie, I don't think we're going anywhere."

She was silent for a long moment, sitting easily, resting her gloved hands in her lap.

"I'm very sorry about Christine," she said. "I know you were close to her."

"It was the beginning of a beautiful new age, maybe."

"The bloody bastards," she said.

"Yes."

"What are you going to do, Zip?"

"If I can figure out how to do it, I'm going to kill someone."

"I'll help you."

UNS U THANT
0845 HOURS LOCAL

Eames left the wardroom, went down the corridor, and stepped onto the elevator to find Cady already aboard.

"Good morning, Terri."

"Colonel."

"Jim, remember?"

"Not Shark?"

"You're in a bad mood, right?"

She wasn't, really, and she wasn't certain why she wanted to remain aloof from Cady, but something inside her told her it would be a good thing to do. It didn't bother her a bit that Cady had shot down the Mirage yesterday and likely killed its pilot. That man was probably responsible for the deaths of a number of noncombatants.

Cady, though, had come very close to losing his own life.

She had seen the replay of the imagery McNichols had captured. Then, Cady had nearly missed the rendezvous with Gail Alhers, joining up with her jury-rigged tanker Seahawk in a snowstorm when he had less than two minutes of fuel left.

Eames had grown up with the security of church and family, and though her family was partially estranged from her now, she still liked to go where the ground was firm. She suspected that Cady liked living on the edge, and consequently, he would not be someone she should get close to. It would lead to disappointment later, when he didn't come back from some mission.

"Sorry, Colonel, my mind is on something else," she said.

"Jim."

"Jim."

They got off the elevator on the bridge deck and headed aft to the captain's quarters. Baker was already there, pouring coffee, and he poured two additional mugs for them as they took seats at the table.

"There you go, darling. That will perk your day up."

"Thank you, Archie."

Baker, too, was a pilot who took a lot of risks, but somehow, she felt safer around him. First of all, he had a wife and two sons living outside of London—in Basingstoke she thought—whom she suspected, since he had told her all about them and showed her the pictures, he loved dearly. Secondly, and despite the fact that he had made no advances toward her, he made no secret of the fact that he considered Eames his girlfriend. He told everyone that, and he took particular umbrage at d'Argamon's attentions toward her. It may have been protective coloration on his part, in favor of her. She didn't mind.

All in all, it was a strange bunch she was living with.

Monmouth said, "Nice job yesterday, Jim."

"Thank you, sir, but if I'd been using radar, I'd have seen him earlier and not cut it so close."

"I've worked out an arrangement with McNichols," Eames broke in. "He's got a series of satellites on track now and will have regional coverage about twenty hours a day. On our sorties, if he's got a real-time view, he'll keep watch and let me know of potential threats. I can relay that information to the aircraft."

"That will help," Cady said. "If you'd get a schedule for his satellite coverage, we might be able to time our operations to coincide."

"I'll do that," she said.

After a knock on the door, David George came in. "Sorry I'm late, sir. I was on the radio to Brandeis."

"That's all right, Dave," Monmouth said. "Anything new, there?"

George pulled a chair over and sat down at the table as Eames made room for him. "Yes, sir, there is. I believe we have a point of departure, a guide, and ground transport."

"Very good," the captain said. "Timing?"

"That'll be up to Colonel Cady," George said. "We're ready to go as soon as he is."

"I wish we had Ospreys," Cady said, referring to the V-22 vertical takeoff aircraft capable of transporting troops, "but since we don't, we'll go with what we have. Archie was impressed enough with our brand-new refueling capability that he'll okay the same procedure for the Seahawks and Sea Apaches. That allows us to make our first move sooner."

"The sooner the better," Baker said. "If these arseholes think they've got a couple of months of freedom, they're going to get a bloody unwelcome surprise three days after their invasion."

"Let's keep in mind," Monmouth said, "that our first priority is protecting life. The people, the potential hostages, come first."

"They're first on our list, too," Cady said. "By 1000 hours, after we've been briefed by Eddie Purgatory on the weather, I'll have a mission plan for you."

"All right." Monmouth turned toward Eames. "Terri, have you got a track for us?"

"I do, sir. Given that we want to maintain our cover as long as possible and yet stay within a comfortable range of operations, I recommend that we reduce speed to sixteen knots very shortly. Then, DIA reports that two C-130s alternating out of Primavera appear to be acting as airborne early warning aircraft. McNichols doesn't believe that they have very sophisticated radar available, but recommends that we stay one hundred miles away from the perimeter of their flight paths."

"Have the C-130s been consistent in their flight patterns?" Cady asked her.

"They have, yes. They're flying a large oval coinciding with the peninsula, flying two hundred miles north and south of Primavera and one hundred and fifty miles east and west of it."

"What other traffic is DIA recording?" Cady asked.

"There have been several flights to Navarino Island and back by the transports and the tankers, apparently for additional supplies. The fighter aircraft have been flying random patrols or air cover for the transports."

Cady grinned at her, "Thanks."

"Back to the *U Thant*'s course," Eames said. "My recommendation will keep us out of radar coverage and at least a hundred miles off the continent, out of the supposed zone of exclusion established by FSAD. We'll pass four hundred miles south of Cape Horn."

Monmouth looked to Cady, who nodded, but said, "I'd like

to hold off on the speed reduction for four hours so as not to disrupt our flight plans."

The captain said, "That's what we'll go with then, Terri. Now, then, with the possible exception of a change in our orders coming from New York, I think we're ready to roll. When do we kick this off, CAG?"

"If Purgatory's predictions hold up," Cady said, "we'll launch aircraft at 1135 hours, Captain."

Eames looked around the table. Monmouth appeared to be his old, implacable self, but Cady, Baker, and George were all sitting a bit more rigidly than usual. Perhaps it was tension, but all of them also had new gleams in their eyes, and she sensed an aura of—if not gleeful—at least hopeful anticipation.

She hoped it wasn't blood lust.

THE SAN MATIAS
0921 HOURS LOCAL

The destroyer was making twenty-nine knots when the *Inga* was finally sighted by the bow lookout. Because of the low overcast and snowfall, the Russian ship was less than two kilometers away when she came into view. The *San Matias* had had her on radar for forty minutes, and apparently the Russians had noted their rapid approach on their own radar. The *Inga* had turned north and was making top speed away from them.

Not, however, before the Russian helicopter had returned once again to the *Inga*. The Mil helicopter's flight to Bellinghausen Station, despite the warnings from a patrolling C-130 which was looking for a Mirage fighter that had disappeared and was feared down, had prompted the C-130 pilot to ask Diego Enriquez to intervene.

He was planning on it, anyway.

Enriquez stood on his bridge with First Officer Dante Montez and watched the growing image of the Russian freighter off the starboard bow. The speed of the *San Matias* smoothed the seas to some extent, but they were taking wind and seas abeam, and the occasional roll was noticeable, perhaps five or six degrees. The thin sheet of brittle snowflakes seemed to come directly at them, splattering against the windscreens without melting upon contact.

"She is turning again," Montez said, "to the east, to run with the seas. They cannot possibly outrun us."

"No, they cannot," Enriquez agreed.

"Shall I order general quarters, Captain?"

"What is our position?"

"We are still thirty kilometers inside the one hundred kilometer limit."

Enriquez mulled over his options for only a second. "Order general quarters and turn to follow them. Continue to close."

The Klaxon sounded throughout the ship, and men ran for their stations, pulling on parkas, hats, and life vests as they ran.

The men on the C-130 patrol aircraft had not been able to see what the helicopter did in the few minutes it was down at Bellinghausen Station, but the consensus was that it had evacuated the last of the Russian personnel from the station. The flight, first of all, violated the rule prohibiting unauthorized flights inside the territorial limits. Secondly, and of concern to President Silvera, it allowed the Russians to escape. Diego Enriquez did not have to talk to Silvera to know that it concerned him. Enriquez had long before learned to read the minds of his superiors and to make his own decisions.

He grasped the railing that ran across the bulkhead below the windscreen and leaned forward to peer through the snowfall. They had closed to within a half-kilometer now, and he could more clearly see the freighter. It was small, perhaps fifteen thousand tons of displacement, not a very worthy prize. The hull was black and the superstructure was painted a dingy gray. Lashed to the stern deck was the offending orange helicopter.

Enriquez lifted the microphone from the communications panel below the railing and told the communications specialist to connect him with the international hailing channel.

When the technician told him that that had been accomplished, he depressed the transmit button and said in English, "This is the FSAD naval ship *San Matias* calling the cargo vessel *Inga.*"

He did not have to wait long for a reply.

"*San Matias,* this is the master of the *Inga.*" The voice spoke in stilted English, with a definite Slavic accent.

"*Inga,* you are trespassing in the territorial waters of the FSAD-administered continent of Antarctica. I am ordering your vessel and her personnel detained. You will come about and follow me."

The other captain's voice was agitated when it replied, "We are currently leaving the, uh, contested waters. Until I am informed of a legal definition regarding these limits, I cannot submit to your authority."

"I am informing you now," Enriquez said, angry at the rebuff. "You will come about immediately."

"Under international law, that would be submission to piracy," the Russian captain told him.

Enriquez turned to Commander Montez. "Use the five-inch gun."

"A shot over her bows, Captain?"

"No. Take out the helicopter."

Montez passed the order to the forward gun turret, but Enriquez had to wait nearly four minutes—intolerable—before the gun barked and a grayish-white plume erupted from the barrel. The round went wide to the right, creating a geyser twenty meters off the freighter's starboard side. He assumed he had given the freighter's captain ample warning, so he ordered a second shot fired.

The *Inga* immediately began to zigzag, and Enriquez could be assured she was broadcasting her perilous condition to the world. Well, the world had been warned already.

The second projectile also missed the helicopter, but slammed into the fantail, penetrating the thin skin of the freighter, and detonated below decks. The ensuing eruption of high explosive and shrapnel ripped out the stern deck, secondarily destroying the helicopter. It bounced high in the air, breaking its bonds to the decking, and fell back in several large pieces. The rotors were tilted drastically downward.

Within seconds, fire could be seen in the gaping hole in the fantail.

And the *Inga* began to make a 180-degree turn.

Enriquez smiled at his first mate.

GYPSY MOTH ONE
1135 HOURS LOCAL

Shark Cady slammed the throttle forward, and the Harrier leaped in response, racing down the catwalk into a flurry of snowflakes that blanked his vision. He couldn't see the bow. He did feel the craft becoming lighter, and when he hit the ramp, he was ready.

The Harrier sagged downward as it left the ramp, as it always did, and his adrenaline pulsed, as it always did. The airspeed came up slowly.

Looking down and back, he could see frigid water, more gray than blue, whitecapping from six- or seven-foot peaks.

The ship had already disappeared from view. Ahead was a wall of white.

Retracting his gear and flaps, Cady kept the nose up and started hunting for altitude. He checked the communications panel—the radios were preset for the command net, including the ship's CIC, the squadron net, and for air control. He was still with air control.

Keying the transmit button, Cady said, "Beehive, Gypsy Moth One is clear. Going to Jericho."

"Roger that, Gypsy One. Gypsy Two is on the deck."

Punching the Tactical One frequency button, he said, "Jericho, Gypsy Moth One."

Eames's steady voice came right back. "I've got you, One. You may cancel your IFF now."

Cady shut down the IFF transponder and checked the read-outs on his primary and secondary GPS receivers. They agreed that he was twelve miles south of sixty-degree south latitude. Behind him, the *U Thant* was plying the waters of the Drake Passage, and Cady was struck with the notion that, though their transport was different, he was seeing the same view that old Sir Francis had seen a few centuries before.

In his case, though, he could get above it, and he did, rising through the top of the storm clouds at seventeen thousand feet.

"Jericho, Gypsy One."

"Go, One."

"I've got clear skies at angels seventeen. Going to one-seven-oh."

"Roger, One."

"Gypsy One, Two's with you," Anderson said.

"Roger, Flip. Form on me. I'm holding at three-five-zero knots."

Twenty minutes later, the six Harriers of the 1st Squadron

were in formation, the five others in echelon off Cady's right wing, and he increased the speed to 450 knots.

On Tactical Two, David Stein, who had gained the nickname "Flaming Star," from the Star of David, said, "Landfall, four hundred and ninety miles."

Solomon Sifra told him, "You happen to spot any land, Star, let me know. I haven't seen any for a couple weeks."

"But is it land?" Miguel Olivera asked. "I think it is ice."

Cady thought that the squadron members were getting along better now that they had a known objective to focus on, rather than each other. Even Jasper "Tiger" Mikkelson, the New Zealander flying Gypsy Moth Six, who hadn't been speaking to Olivera for two days, was now congenial with everyone.

Mikkelson said, "It's ice, Miggy. Make a hell of a Singapore Sling."

Cady let them chat with each other for awhile. The transmissions were scrambled and at low power settings, and it wasn't likely that Primavera or her C-130 early warning craft would pinpoint them just yet.

On the command net, he checked in with the Seahawk converted to a tanker and now renamed.

"Jerry Can One, Gypsy Moth One."

"Go, Gypsy One," Makarov came back.

"Status, please."

"On course and on track," the Russian pilot said. "We will be in position when required."

"Roger that."

The three tankers would be making multiple trips, alternating with each other, in order to keep the appetite of the strike force quenched. The air tasking order he and Eames had assembled on the computer was a little tense in a couple spots where minutes would be crucial for tanker join-ups.

"How about you, Falcon One?"

Baker was leading a flight of three Seahawks and four Sea Apaches that had taken off forty minutes earlier.

"The weather is quite nice up here, old Gypsy. It will, however, change momentarily. We are five minutes from our descent phase."

"Break a leg," Cady told him. "Gypsy One out."

"Gypsy One, Jericho."

"Gypsy."

"We have a message from Pack Rat." The code name had been applied to McNichols's center at DIA.

"Good or bad?"

"Not good," Eames said. "The *Inga* has been fired on and is damaged. She has been taken into custody by a FSAD warship."

Damn.

"How bad, Jericho?"

"According to reports from the ship, her helicopter had evacuated the last of the scientists from Bellinghausen, and they were on a course away from the continent when she was attacked. She has extensive damage to the stern deck, has lost the helicopter, and has seven wounded, but is still operational. Fire below decks, but now under control. She has been ordered to stop transmitting, and Pack Rat says she's under escort toward the peninsula."

"We weren't going to be able to reach Bellinghausen on this trip, anyway," Cady told her.

"But this confirms that the FSAD wants to keep hostages."

"I suppose it does, Jericho. Has Gold Mine been contacted?" Cady was reluctantly prepared to abort the mission if Sir Charles had new reservations or was battling new reservations from the Security Council. It never changed; politics was at the heart of it all.

"Gold Mine says it is still a go."

"That's all we need to know, then. Gypsy One out."

Cady appreciated Bentley's decision. It had to have been a

tough one, especially if the Russian delegation was pressuring him.

With his harness loosened a fraction, he settled in for the boring part of the flight, watching the chronometer on the instrument panel and checking his fuel state frequently. Twice, he queried his aircraft for status reports. Once, they all joined on Jerry Can Three and took on fuel.

They were closing rapidly on Baker's group, which was now down in the stormy weather, skimming the sea surface, avoiding radar. Even the C-130s, unlikely to have look-down radar, would have a tough time interpreting radar returns among the clutter created by high seas and snow.

"Gypsy Moth One, Falcon One."

"Go, Falcon."

"Falcon Four has lost some oil pressure on her starboard turbine. I'm sending him back."

"Roger that. Copperhead now has three escorts. You have a met report, Falcon?"

"Snow."

"Beyond that, Arch?"

"Not too bad. Tailwinds, visibility a hundred yards."

"Thanks. You copy, Jericho?"

"Jericho copies."

"Jerry Can," Cady said, "you copy?"

"This is Jerry Can Two," Gail Alhers said. "I'll find the bent Falcon."

Six minutes later, Eames broke the now silent net.

"Gypsy Moth One, Jericho. My plot says you are forty miles behind Falcon and Copperhead and closing on a south-bound C-130."

"Roger, Jericho. All right, Gypsies, scatter time. Let's get 'em down on the deck."

Phil Anderson and Miguel Olivera, Two and Three, clicked their mikes in acknowledgement and dropped out of the formation, peeling away to the left. Gypsy Moths Five and Six, Sifra and Mikkelson, rolled away to the right, diving for the sea. David Stein pulled up on Cady's wing.

"Ready, Four?" Cady asked.

"Four."

Cady shoved the stick forward and dove for the mass of grayish white clouds two thousand feet below him.

As they entered the cloud, Cady heard Jericho feeding targeting information to the group. To preclude their having to use on-board radar until the last minute, she was using data taken directly from McNichols. She vectored Anderson and Olivera toward the C-130 on a northerly track and directed Sifra's element toward Baker and his helicopters, for whom they would fly air cover.

"All right, Gypsy Element One, come to one-two-two. Your target is at angels twenty, speed three-two-zero knots. Intercept in twelve minutes."

"Roger, Jericho," Cady said.

Cady made the turn to the left and locked in on the heading. A glance out the right side of the canopy showed that Stein was still with him, though he had taken a greater separation as soon as they entered the cloud cover. His Harrier was a shadowy silhouette two hundred feet away.

Vision to the left and right was far better than directly ahead. He was flying into a white wall. At 450 knots, the wispy cloud snaked past the canopy in a vaporous soup. By the time they leveled out at one thousand feet AGL, flaky snow was added to the flow. There was some turbulence, but since the winds had been estimated by Purgatory at less than ten knots, it wasn't extreme.

On the wing net, Cady heard a few short and crisp exchanges as pilots attempted to hold their positions. Baker reported that the helicopters had reached the pack ice and increased altitude to five hundred feet.

"Gypsy, Falcon, and Copperhead flights, Jericho. Pack Rat reports two fighter air patrols aloft, one on approach to Primavera from the north, and one cruising one-three-zero miles south of the base, heading one-eight-oh. Falcons and Copperheads, be alert."

"Falcon, roger."

Six miles from target, Cady called Stein on the squadron net, "Star, you've got the lead."

If his wingman was pleased at his sudden change in flight status, he didn't bother to demonstrate it vocally, which meant that Stein was getting better, Cady thought.

"Roger that, Shark. I've got the lead."

PRIMAVERA BASE
1252 HOURS LOCAL

Silvera and Suarez were staying close to the radio. The kitchen had delivered a platter of sandwiches to the operations hut, and Silvera had eaten only part of one. His stomach was upset.

Their communications with the outside world, conducted through the FSAD office in Buenos Aires, was on an open radio channel, though coded messages were being sent back and forth by telex. Pedro Indigo, the agent in Buenos Aires, who was Peruvian and had Indian blood in him, and therefore could be treacherous, had been silent for long hours. Their last communique from him had reported only the Security Council's condemnation resolution. Silvera was beginning to worry that Indigo had succumbed to the mounting pressure and simply packed his suitcase and gone home to Peru.

He wondered, too, what his four agents in New York, supposedly in contact with the representatives of South American nations, were doing. He had yet to hear from them.

When the telex machine began to chatter, Silvera expected yet more bad news. With the unexplained disappearance of one Mirage, presumed to have crashed for some obscure mechanical reason, and with the continuing absence of encouraging information from New York, he had begun to experience a depression that was rare in his life.

Suarez crossed to the machine, leaned over to read as it produced the message, then ripped it off and spent a few minutes decoding it. Finally, he brought it back to Silvera.

"Now, *Presidente,* the momentum continues to build on an international scale. We have achieved step one."

Silvera scanned the handwritten words. Argentina had announced to the United Nations, and the world, that she would henceforth recognize the legality of the Front for South American Determination as the representative of her interests on the continent of Antarctica.

"The rest will soon follow," Suarez assured him.

"I believe that is true, Colonel. We should now urge Calvera to accelerate the drilling program. It will be of utmost importance very soon, when we need to convince our patrons that they have made the correct decision."

"I will see to it."

"Colonel Suarez!" yelped a radar operator.

Suarez and Silvera both swung around to look at the man.

"Nightdog Two reports that he is under attack."

"What!" Suarez yelled. "That cannot be."

Silvera did not think it was possible, either.

UNS U THANT
1255 HOURS LOCAL

Sam Monmouth had turned the bridge over to Hermann von Stein, his first officer, and gone back to the Combat

Information Center which he thought was too damned crowded.

Besides himself, d'Argamon and the two tactical information officers who were off-watch were gathered at the back of the compartment. He assumed that Terri Eames had invited the TIOs, to give them a taste of live action, but he also assumed that the submarine commander had invited himself. As long as d'Argamon kept his mouth shut, Monmouth decided he would let him stay.

The secondary screen was tracking vessels near their position, including the *Dover*, which was fifteen miles ahead of them.

One of the two small screens contained a scrolling list of the air tasking order, so that Eames could keep track of where aircraft were supposed to be at any given moment.

The primary screen was filled with icons, most of them identified in the small boxes next to each symbol. Eames and Luigi Maroni, at the main console, and her assistant at the data input console were wearing headsets. An indicator on the console told him that Eames was using the powerful Searchwater radar, and the positions of aircraft on the plotting screen would have been established by data obtained from that radar, from the *Dover*'s radar, and from information supplied by Pack Rat. The sergeant at the input console was in direct contact with someone in McNichols's office.

Monmouth settled back in his chair and studied the screen, fixing the various players in his mind. The reality never looked like the clean, crisp plans laid out on paper.

The general outlines of the operational plans he had requested from Cady, d'Argamon, and George a couple days before were in the back of his mind, but the objectives of this sortie didn't fit into them very well. At the time, of course, they hadn't known the scope of the responsibilities with which the Peacekeeper Committee would charge them.

None of them were certain, either, what the weather and the environment of Antarctica would do to well-laid schemes, other than disrupt them substantially. Monmouth did know, based on Cady's first draft, that the Commander Air Group didn't plan to mount a massed air attack against Primavera at any time. His squadrons wouldn't survive against the Mirages and Tornados that were sure to meet them. Instead, he planned to use surprise and misdirection to whittle away at the FSAD defenses.

All of which could easily fall apart as soon as the Security Council or the Peacekeeper Committee wanted something different. Monmouth's job would be to keep the policy-making bodies dealing with policy and let the tactical people do what they did best.

Eames and Maroni talked continuously to one element or another, and there were a bunch of them up there on the screen.

There were two operations going simultaneously, code-named Spare Tire and Fifth Wheel, and Monmouth thought she was handling them well, though he wasn't sure which operation she was covering and which was under Maroni's control.

The symbols on the screen kept moving, but the pace seemed steady.

Until just now.

"Here we go, everyone," Eames said.

GYPSY MOTH ONE
1257 HOURS LOCAL

Cady approved of the way Stein had made his approach, dropping to five hundred feet AGL, keeping it flat and steady. As long as they were still over water, that was fine. His chart showed that, on the continent, there were some abrupt mountains. Cady had closed his distance on Stein's wing a little as the snow became thicker, lowering visibility. He hadn't seen the sea since leaving the *U Thant*.

He was worried about his other aviators. After his first sortie over the continent, he had briefed them fully on what they might expect of the terrain, but he hadn't been able to tell them adequately what a snowstorm would do to their sense of physical orientation. Technically, it didn't snow often in Antarctica. It was a desert as a result of a lack of precipitation. Snow on the fly was old snow, pushed to thousands of feet of altitude by hurricane-force winds. Still, when one was in it, the distinction between ground blizzard and snowstorm didn't matter much. At four hundred miles an hour in white pea soup, one wanted to be able to see *something*.

Jericho had confirmed that the C-130, now known as Target Alpha, was still on its course, but Jericho was no longer absolutely certain of the positions of the Harriers or helicopters since McNichols's satellite had lost sight of them in the cloud cover. He didn't have infrared available on this particular satellite. Eames's computer would be best-guessing their positions, based on their last reported coordinates, speed, and altitude.

"Gypsy One, Four. Climbing at full military power, going to radar at angels five."

"One."

Cady had shoved his throttle forward and hauled back on the stick to stay with the Israeli. There was some buffeting because of the wind, but he held the Harrier a hundred feet off Stein's left wing as they went to near-vertical.

If they hadn't been spotted by the C-130's radar by the time they reached five thousand feet, somebody would have become alarmed the second Stein went active with his Blue Vixen pulse-Doppler radar. Used first by the Royal Navy Sea

Harriers, the radar had all-weather look-down/shoot-down ability as well as track-while-scan and multiple target engagement capability.

They were each armed with two AIM-9L Super Sidewinder short-range missiles and two AMRAAMs (Advanced Medium-Range Air-to-Air Missile) which utilized an active radar seeker guidance system rather than the Sidewinder's infrared homing head. The active radar allowed a pilot to fire the AMRAAM and forget it while he engaged another target.

Cady checked his armament panel, selecting a Sidewinder just in case Stein missed.

"Got him, Shark. Coming left."

Cady clicked his mike twice in response.

"He's seen us, and he's panicking, diving to the east."

The wrong direction for him, and the right direction, as far as Cady was concerned, giving them his tail and hot exhausts as a target.

His altimeter reading on the HUD blinked through fifteen thousand feet and continued to rise, though the speed was draining off. The radar threat receiver activated a glow on the panel indicator and beeped a warning in his earphones as the C-130 painted them, but it was not an acquisition radar.

They popped out of the clouds into brilliant sunlight at 16,500 feet, and Cady kicked the nose down to follow Stein as he leveled out. He searched the sky ahead and found the four-engined silhouette of the transport two miles ahead just as it was about to disappear into the cloud bank. It seemed a particularly American silhouette, one that he had encountered all around the world for three decades, and Cady felt some distaste for shooting it down.

Come on, Stein. What are you waiting for?

"Got lock-on, Shark. Fox one!"

The AMRAAM dropped off Stein's starboard pylon, ignited, and arced away, streaming a white trail behind it.

The C-130's radar immediately quit emitting, and Cady saw the pilot whip a wing up as he rolled the big transport into a diving right turn.

He was allowed to try the maneuver for about two seconds, then the missile slammed into the fuselage and erupted.

A bright orange fireball spitting debris dove into the snowstorm.

"Good shot, Star," Cady said.

"Four."

"Gypsy Moth One has the lead."

"Roger. One has the lead." Stein eased off on his throttle and dropped back to a position off Cady's right wing.

"Jericho, Gypsy One."

"Jericho here. Go ahead, One."

"Target Alpha is down. Gypsy Element One going to HI-CAP."

"Roger Target Alpha down, confirmed by Pack Rat. Roger HICAP"

Cady and Stein had about fifteen minutes of loiter time, and they would serve as the High Combat Air Patrol while they waited for word from the others.

Cady tuned his secondary radio to the frequency Baker was using.

FALCON ONE
1302 HOURS LOCAL

Major Archie Baker had intended to manage his mission from a more-or-less central position, but with the loss of Falcon Four, he had assumed Four's escort role for Copperhead Two, a Seahawk flying empty.

All six of his helicopters were flying at 110 knots in a loose formation that barely kept each in sight of the others in a snowstorm that showed no promise of ever letting up. His whole future seemed to be white, and Baker had considered that his dreams would lack color from this point on.

"Falcon One, Jericho."

"Go ahead, darling."

"Falcon One, remember your protocol, please."

"My mistake," he said into his helmet mike. "I was thinking priorities, rather than protocols."

"Falcon One, Target Alpha has been destroyed. Your sector is clear of overhead surveillance except for a flight of two Tornados one hundred and seventy miles south of Palmer on a heading of one-eight-zero."

"Copied, Jericho. Thank you."

Baker punched in the frequency for the squadron net. His part of the mission had been given the code name Spare Tire.

"Falcon One, here. Listen up, now. Target Alpha is no longer with us, but remember that we are still in range of Primavera radars. Two hostile fighters are one-seven-zero south. Keep your heads down the rest of the way to the objectives, and be certain to exit on your assigned courses so that HICAP knows where you are. Copperhead Two, we will break off now."

"Copperhead Two, roger."

They were flying nap-of-the-earth, utilizing the Sea Apache's Singer-Kearfott AN/ASN-128 Doppler navigation system and Litton strapdown attitude and heading reference system. The three Apaches had their targets stored in computer memory, and Baker had no doubt about finding his objective, despite the fact that he couldn't see more than a couple hundred yards in any direction.

He called up his stored target information, and the objective appeared on his multifunction screen as a yellow circle off to his right. He banked to the right, and the yellow circle swung around until it was at the top of the screen. Checking to his right, he saw the Seahawk staying with him. It had had its ESSS (External Stores Support System) stub wings removed to increase its internal lift capacity, and it appeared a trifle naked.

Most of his attention was devoted to his multifunction screen which pictured upcoming obstacles for him in just enough time for him to jiggle the chopper up or around them. The ice shelf, a hundred feet below them, raced past with dizzying speed whenever he happened to catch a glimpse of it. At any moment, he was expecting to encounter a range of low mountains that had been pointed out to him on a briefing chart.

On the ICS, he said, "Henry, I believe you could make your call now."

"I'll chat 'em up, Major."

Lieutenant Henry Decker was his gunner/copilot, and had been for years. When Baker volunteered for special service, he always volunteered as a unit that included Decker. They knew each other.

Decker was a portly lad from the north, near the Scottish border, coming gladly off a sheep farm to raise a thick, healthy mustache and acclimate himself to the high-technology employed in the nose of a Sea Apache. He was only a passable pilot, but he relied on Baker totally for that aspect of their life together.

In the forward section of the tandem cockpit, which was already cramped, Decker had a copy of David George's scrambled radio resting on his lap, but plugged into the helicopter for its power and its antenna lead. It was not connected to Baker's system, but Decker left the ICS open so he could hear the conversation.

"Palmer Base, this is Chestnut Two."

He had to try three times before he got a response.

"Chestnut Two, are you any relation to Chestnut?"

"We're brothers under the sword," Decker said.

"We've been hoping to hear from Chestnut for some time now. Do you have any new information?"

"I have good news," Decker said. "In about . . ."

From habit, Baker twisted his left wrist and glanced at his wristwatch, then checked the chronometer on the instrument panel. He had long relied on his wristwatch, a nine-year-old, scratched, and battered Timex.

"Six minutes, Henry."

". . . six minutes, Palmer, you will see two helicopters land outside your house. We would appreciate it if you all dressed warmly and hopped into the nearest one."

"What?"

"It's evacuation time, Palmer."

"But . . . but, we've got important experiments under way here. We can't just leave them."

Baker heard Decker's exasperated sigh over the internal communications system.

"Palmer, the way I see it, you have two choices. In one instance, you come with us and enjoy a nice pot roast dinner. In the other, you starve to death if you're not shot first."

After a momentary hesitation, the voice at Palmer came back. "We'll be ready. What about the body?"

"I didn't know about a body."

"Dr. Norris died."

"I'm afraid we'll have to come back later for the body. A matter of weight, you know. Speaking of which, please don't bring your experiments with you. Don't bother with wardrobes, either."

"Very well, Chestnut Two, we'll be ready."

"Please be that way. Our fuel situation does not allow us time for tea."

"Chestnut Two, who are you?"

"Think of us as your friendly, neighborhood bus service."

The range of hills ahead appeared abruptly on Baker's screen, and he eased the stick back.

"Copperhead Two, you'll want two-two-hundred feet if you'd like to clear the hills."

The Seahawk pilot, who didn't have the sophisticated radar, responded with, "Appreciate the notice, Falcon."

As he climbed to clear the peaks, Baker noted that his yellow circle had moved down the screen and was now seven miles away.

"We're seven out, Copperhead."

"Roger."

The lee side of the low mountain chain did not provide any relief from the snow and wind. Baker slowed his forward speed as they neared the objective, but he was on top of it before he saw it appear through the snowfall, and he had to circle to the left and come back. The turbulence rocked the helicopter and kept him busy with the stick and collective, searching for stability.

Both helicopters made one circuit of the base, checking for any sign of hostile activity, before closing in on the cluster of huts.

Baker did not land. He hovered several hundred feet away as the Seahawk settled to the ice in a secondary storm of whipped snow and ice created by the downblast of its rotors. The pilot slowed the rotors, but did not shut down the turbine.

He had landed with his fuselage side toward the primary hut, so that those inside could see the UN logo attached to it.

Still, a couple minutes passed before a door opened tentatively and a couple of figures emerged. The Seahawk's cargo master finally got impatient, leaped to the ground, and ran toward the huts, gesturing frantically toward the chopper and waving the scientists forward.

They filtered out into the snowy light, a seemingly too-long line of them, Baker thought, worrying that their intelligence source had been misleading or was drawing them into captivity. The Seahawk was designed to carry a fourteen-man squad, but that included the squad's equipment. He counted fourteen people, seven of them being assisted in some way by their colleagues, and most of them dressed in bright orange or yellow parkas, and was relieved when the last man out of the hut slammed the door behind him.

The cargo master ran to the first of the injured, got an arm around his shoulder, and helped him toward the helicopter, then lifted him aboard. Baker assumed it was a "him." It was difficult to tell with the bulky clothing and parkas the scientists were wearing.

In less than three minutes, the evacuees were aboard the Seahawk, and the pilot reported, "We're topped off, Falcon One. There's a couple people here who are in real bad shape."

"Let's make all due haste for home, then, Copperhead."

The Seahawk lifted off, swung its nose to the west, and quickly picked up forward speed.

Baker fell in behind, regretting the fact that he was leaving his other four helicopters behind and wishing he could go active with the search radar and see where those Tornados were.

PUMA ONE
1305 HOURS LOCAL

At the southern limit of the preplanned patrol, 250 kilometers from Primavera Base, the intent was to turn to the west and return toward Primavera along the coastline.

Tellez and his wingman had been flying at six thousand

meters, above the storm, when he heard the first alarm sounded by the C-130 pilot.

"What unidentified aircraft could that be, Roberto?" Jesus Ramirez asked from the backseat.

"Very likely one of our own," Tellez told him.

"Perhaps it is the Mirage that went missing. Maybe Amador stopped somewhere to take a nap."

Minutes later, though, the C-130 pilot had screamed like a maniac, saying that he was under attack.

Tellez had broken in, "Under attack by what? What kind of aircraft? Identify it, damn it!"

There was no answer, and Tellez had rolled into a quick left turn, startling his wingman, Enrico Salazar, flying Puma Five. By the time Salazar made his 180-degree turn, he was four kilometers behind.

Tellez went to afterburners and checked the radar scope, which was already active.

Nothing.

He armed two Sky Flash missiles.

"Primavera, Puma One."

"Puma, this is Primavera. We have lost contact with Night-dog Two."

"I know that, idiot. Give me his last position."

"Uh, Puma, Nightdog Two went off our radar eighty kilometers southwest of Primavera, our bearing one-two-five."

Calculating rapidly, he estimated that he was over two hundred kilometers away, out of the range of his Texas Instruments radar. Tellez adjusted his course to the left while telling Ramirez on the ICS, "Jesus, be sharp!"

"The, uh, hostile may have dived to hide himself in the ground clutter, Roberto. Primavera should have seen him."

"Scan downward, Jesus, and do not trust the imbeciles at Primavera."

The HUD reported his speed had achieved Mach 1, and

Tellez eased the throttles back to military power to conserve fuel.

Seven minutes later, Ramirez exclaimed, "Hostile! No . . . hostiles! Roberto, they are all over."

Tellez glanced down at his radar screen and counted ten blips. Eight were not transmitting IFF data and would be automatically considered aliens. His Radar Homing and Warning Receiver (RHAW) indicated only friendlies. The unknown ships were not transmitting radar. Nightdog One was far to the north, at the very limit of the receiver, and Puma Five was a half-kilometer behind him.

"Pumas, Primavera. We are scrambling four Mirages."

Tellez ignored the warning from Primavera and keyed his transmit button. "Puma Five, are you painting targets?"

"Affirmative, One."

"Take the six flying low to the northeast. I will take the others."

"Five."

Tellez eased the nose down and went into a high-speed dive.

Ramirez said, "I estimate the two closest targets to be helicopters. One is using radar, probably terrain-following. The other two targets are fighter aircraft at two thousand meters altitude, no radar in use."

"We will destroy the helicopters first, Jesus."

COPPERHEAD FOUR
1312 HOURS LOCAL

Dave George stood in the open side door of the Seahawk, gripping the edge of the doorway tightly. When he stuck his head into the slipstream, all he got was a faceful of crisp snow particles and a frigid blast that threatened to rip the white balaclava from his head.

He pulled his head back.

Behind him, crouched on the floor of the compartment, with their backpacks in place and their weapons strapped across their chests, were twelve of his SEALs. The other twelve were in the second Seahawk. Through the door to his right, he could see one of the Sea Apaches flying escort. It was strange to see both the pilot and the copilot/gunner flying with their helmeted heads aimed down, not looking ahead, but concentrating on their electronic guides. George was more attuned to direct linkages; he wanted to see where he was going. Without really knowing, he suddenly felt as if his own Seahawk pilot was relying on those guys over there to get them where they were supposed to be. He was going to be damned glad to get off this thing and get his feet on solid ground.

George was wearing the cargo master's headset since the cargo master had been left behind simply because he weighed 215 pounds, and those pounds stretched the limits too far.

The pilot told him, "Commander, one minute."

"Gotcha."

"Also, Commander, we just splashed Target Bravo, the second C-130."

"Good for our side," George said.

George gave a thumbs-up signal to Lieutenant Bascom, his first squad leader, and Bascom rose off his knees in the doorway, grabbing the overhead coaming to steady himself, urging his men to get ready.

The chopper sat down in a hurricane of snow and hadn't even settled before George leaped out and hit the ground crouched and running. He looked back to see Bascom shoving the big equipment pack out of the door. SEALs were spilling out both sides of the helicopter and spreading out exactly as they had been trained. Three of them grabbed the equipment pack and slid it away from the chopper.

The Seahawk lifted off within a minute and disappeared to

the south, following a Sea Apache, headed for Faraday to retrieve the British scientists.

The second Seahawk put down right in front of him and immediately began to disgorge more SEALs. The racket created by the helo engines chuckled overhead, whipped away by the wind.

George turned toward the huts that appeared to be half-buried in the snow and saw the civilians approaching at a run. The first man in line picked him out and slid to a stop in front of him. Another guy, looking something like a Kodiak bear in his dark parka, came to a halt behind him.

"You wouldn't be Chestnut, would you?"

"Commander David George, United Nations," he identified himself after pulling his balaclava down to expose his mouth.

"Damned good to see you, mate." The man stuck his gloved hand out, and George shook it. "I'm Bandit, but most people call me Zip Andover."

"Zip, let's get your people on that helicopter. We don't have much time."

"Everybody's going except Gustav, here." Andover stuck a thumb at the bear behind him. "He's too big to say no to."

He *was* big, and that still left fourteen bodies to cram aboard, so George didn't complain about suddenly having another volunteer.

The SEALs began ushering the scientists aboard the Seahawk. One woman stopped and gave Andover a quick kiss.

"I'd rather stay with you, Zip."

"Go on, Ruth Anne. Save me a gingersnap."

"You've had too many gingersnaps," she said, then turned and ran for the helicopter and was pulled aboard by half-a-dozen helping hands.

The Seahawk lifted off sluggishly, joined the Sea Apache, and both soon disappeared.

When the rotor beats faded into the distance, the silence was almost total. The wind moaned.

"Come on, Commander, and I'll show you what I've got," Andover said.

Andover and his pal headed for a big building, and George followed them. He had the uneasy feeling that it had been too easy.

As soon as the Faraday people were picked up, Phase One of Mission Spare Tire would be complete.

Then came the hard part, Phase Two.

Getting out.

PUMA ONE
1315 HOURS LOCAL

From the backseat, Ramirez reported, "Somehow, they know we are coming, Roberto. They are scrambling."

On his own screen, Tellez saw that the two lowest targets, the helicopters, which had almost reached the coast, had split up. One continued to race for the sea, and one of them had turned back to face him. To the northeast, the two fighters had also turned in his direction. The fighters were emitting radar signals, showing up on the RHAW as "S" symbols.

Involuntarily, Tellez looked up through the canopy, but could not see the sky. There was something, a satellite, up there, watching him. The thought seemed particularly intrusive, but there was nothing he could do about it. All around him, the storm clouds boiled. He thought briefly that he should be hidden from the cameras overhead, but assumed that they would have infrared capability as well. There would be no hiding.

"Another search radar!" Ramirez exclaimed. "One of the helicopters has search radar! The one coming back at us."

"We will take him first." On the radio, Tellez ordered, "Puma Four, have you found the others?"

"Affirmative, One. There are six. We think they are four helicopters with a fighter escort."

Almost automatically, Tellez retarded his throttles as he leveled the airplane at six hundred meters of altitude. He did not want to overshoot his slower-flying target. The view outside the canopy was nonexistent—a white sheet of paper enveloped him. He felt himself becoming focused, as he always did in combat situations where his quarry could shoot back at him. His whole being became one with the airplane, the flight controls extensions of his nerves, the radar screen his eyes.

"Six-two kilometers to target," Ramirez intoned.

The Sky Flash missiles had a top effective range of forty-five kilometers. Tellez glanced at the armament panel to verify that he had armed two of his missiles. He reached over and rotated the switch to select one from the inboard left pylon for his first shot.

"Five-seven kilometers."

He was in level flight, headed directly for the helicopter, and some five hundred meters above it.

"Radar lock-on! They have found us, Roberto!"

Tellez ignored his navigator. The helicopter, though it was likely to be an attack type, would not have a missile with a range as great as that of his own Sky Flashes.

He admired the nerve of the helicopter pilot. The blip on his screen did not waver, but continued coming head-on toward him. As he watched, it changed attitude, climbing quickly now.

"Five-zero kilometers. It is almost time!"

Ramirez was too excitable.

They were closing at a combined rate of about seven hundred knots.

Milliseconds passed.

"Four-five kilometers! Shoot, Roberto!"

The semi-active radar head of the missile had increased its tone in his earphones, and the HUD displayed a solid, "LOCK-ON," but Tellez held off. He wanted to be certain of this kill, so he could go on to the next target. The helicopter which had now reached the ocean would be a sitting duck.

"Forty!"

And thirty-five.

And thirty.

Tellez squeezed the launch trigger gently, and the Sky Flash whistled off its pylon.

He only got to see a momentary glare of its rocket motor before it disappeared in the snow.

FALCON ONE
1316 HOURS LOCAL

"Missile launch," Decker said.

There was no anxiety in his voice; he was merely stating a fact.

Terri Eames's early warning, a result of Pack Rat's observations before the Tornados had disappeared from the satellite eye into the storm clouds, had been helpful, Baker thought. He was a little disappointed that they hadn't gotten clear of the coast before they were spotted, though.

"You've got a hot one, Falcon," Cady reported on the command net.

"We see it, Gypsy. You realize, of course, that my other elements have got a hostile going after them? And only two of your people in his way?"

"Flaming Star's on his way to help out, Falcon. Lead this guy to me, will you?"

"Soon as I dodge this bullet."

On his radar screen, Baker managed to filter out his worry about—and the blips representing—the four choppers and two Harriers inland which were under attack by a Tornado. He saw Cady's blip coming toward them at nearly Mach 1, but still eighty miles away, and he saw the green triangle of the FSAD aircraft at twenty-five miles. The missile it had launched, however, was about two miles away, probably doing over Mach 3, a streak on the screen.

"I believe it's a Sky Flash, Major. Might be time to dance."

"Very well, Henry."

Baker shoved the nose down into a high-speed dive, and the Sea Apache quickly accelerated to over 230 miles per hour, fifty miles per hour above its rated top speed. The altitude disappeared quickly, four hundred feet, 350, three hundred, 250. . . .

The missile dove to follow them.

The symbols on his screen—his own and the missile's—had almost merged when, at 150 feet AGL, Baker whipped the stick back and went vertical, nose up, climbing like no one expected a helicopter to do. The stresses on the airframe and rotors would probably have alarmed the engineering staff at McDonnell Douglas. If he had had insurance, it would have been cancelled. The G-forces shoved him back into his seat and made the skin on his face sag.

He never saw the missile come through the wall of snow, but it apparently missed since there was an orange flash in his rearview mirror where it probably impacted the ice.

"Missed," Decker said.

At 350 feet, the Sea Apache began to stall out, and Baker let it fall off to the left, dropping his nose, recovering his lift, but losing speed to about eighty knots. As he regained control and leveled off, the speed picked up. He started climbing again as he headed northeast.

"Hostile at sixteen miles, now, Major. Bearing one-six-seven, making four hundred knots. Still out of my range."

"I'll wager he's a surprised sucker, Henry."

"That may be. He's slowing now, turning to follow us. Probably mad at us, Major. Another lock-on. Launch."

GYPSY MOTH ONE
1320 HOURS LOCAL

Cady was impressed with Baker's tactics. His radar screen didn't reveal much of the detail, but he could tell that Baker had evaded the first missile launch while simultaneously drawing the Tornado away from a run at the fleeing Seahawk, Copperhead Two. Baker was now headed in the general direction of Cady, and the Tornado had slowed to turn after him. He could imagine the Tornado pilot as an angry man, incensed that he had missed such an easy target. His entire attention would now be devoted to the Sea Apache. He would be. . . .

Launching another missile.

Cady had gone hot mike, leaving his microphone open so he didn't have to push the transmit button.

"You might want to break right, Falcon."

"Doing that just now, Gypsy. How long are you going to hold off?"

"Until I'm in range."

"Very likely a wise choice," Baker told him.

The second missile also missed the Sea Apache. Cady saw its streak on the screen pass behind the helicopter, attempt to correct its course, then detonate as it lost its target.

He was forty-five miles away, but closing quickly. Arming an AMRAAM, he hoped its active radar would soon divert the Tornado.

Five seconds.

Six.

Seven.

"LOCK-ON."

Wrong target.

"You want to take a dive, Archie?"

"Going now."

The Sea Apache went into a dive to its left, and Cady brought the nose of the Harrier slightly to his own left.

The AMRAAM lost the helicopter and reacquired a new target, the right one this time.

And the Tornado pilot realized it. He corkscrewed a bit, then began climbing to the east.

Cady banked hard left, following him.

"Get out of here, Archie."

"For an Air Boss, you're being awfully damned bossy, Shark."

But the helicopter turned to the west, chasing after its Sea-hawk.

Cady launched his missile.

And two seconds later, it erupted.

Right on target.

PUMA ONE
1321 HOURS LOCAL

Tellez nearly evaded the missile.

Unlike other situations when he had been under missile attack—when he rented his talents out—he didn't see the missile trail in his rearview mirror. The snow prevented that. But the radar saw it, and he was at five thousand meters of altitude, approaching five hundred knots, when the telltale data on the screen yelled at him, "You're dead!"

He rolled the right wing down and kicked in rudder, forcing a high-speed spin, but the missile slammed into the left wing, shearing it off.

The concussion went unnoticed, but the airplane began vibrating, pitching, and rolling.

Ramirez punched out before being told to do so, and Tellez fought the Gs, reached up, grabbed the eject handle, and yanked it.

The rocket motor under his seat blasted him out of the cockpit, tumbling from the erratic action of the aircraft. In a flash, he was alone, the airplane gone, Ramirez gone. He had no horizons, and he was completely disoriented.

Then the seat automatically released him, the drogue chute deployed, drawing the parachute from its bag, and the canopy popped open.

He must have been horizontal to the earth, still doing around four hundred knots, because the opening of the chute nearly snapped his spine, and as he slowed, his body pendulumed downward, swinging back and forth.

He finally knew which way was up, but it didn't help much. No matter which way he looked, it didn't look good.

And he was cold.

So cold.

JAGUAR ONE
1330 HOURS LOCAL

Suarez saw the Tornado disappear from his radar screen and called the coordinates in to Primavera. "Get a helicopter out there."

"But, Colonel, the weather . . ."

"There are other helicopters flying. Get it up now."

His radar screen told him other things he could not quite

believe. To his southwest, two helicopters were forty kilometers off the coast, followed by a fighter aircraft. To his south, another four helicopters and two fighter aircraft were rushing toward the coast, pursued by Puma Four, according to the IFF data on his screen. Yet another alien fighter aircraft was closing on that group.

Puma Four did not even get close to the helicopters. He began evasive maneuvers as soon as the two escorts turned back on him.

Suarez was flying in albino chili. He could not see Jaguar Three or Four. Jaguar Two was a shadow so dim off his right wing it was almost a memory The HUD told him he was two thousand meters AGL, heading south at 480 knots, but in the snow, he felt almost stationary. It was almost like flying a simulator.

The targets on the screen were almost a hundred kilometers away, at the very top of the radar scope. As he watched, Puma Four reversed course, dodging the two fighters, and attempted another attack run, approaching the helicopter group from their rear. The helicopters scattered and the two alien fighters turned back on him yet again.

Puma Four abandoned the helicopters and turned into the fighters, reversed course again, and aimed himself for the helicopters.

A short streak.

One of the helicopter targets disappeared from the screen.

"Puma Four. One killed. Going after the. . . ."

Puma Four's symbol blinked out of existence.

The third unknown fighter had come from high above and shot him down with at least two missiles.

It was almost terrifying, it was so remote. In the storm, no one saw anyone else. Symbols on radar screens appeared and disappeared. He remembered talking to Diego Enriquez once about the expedition of Juan Diaz de Solis. At least de Solis had seen his Indian enemies before they killed him.

"Another helicopter, Primavera," he ordered, giving them the bearing toward the spot where Puma Four had disappeared.

He studied the blips on the screen, deciding that the three slow-flying helicopters were his best target. They still had three fighters for cover, but one aircraft had expended two of his missiles. He calculated an intercept point about thirty kilometers off the coast of Anvers Island.

"Jaguar Flight, this is Leader. We will come to heading one-nine-five."

The pilots of his flight acknowledged the change, and as he turned, the targets on the screen drifted off to the left.

Suarez could not understand where the alien aircraft had come from.

Their intelligence, gathered from friendly intelligence services which thought of themselves as excellent, he realized now, was insufficient in the extreme. An aircraft carrier of some kind was nearby, and they had not known of its existence. Some nation had mobilized its forces months earlier than expected.

It was disheartening, but Suarez had no doubt that they could prevail. As soon as he identified the ship and its position, he could mount attacks against it. His variegated, secondhand ordnance inventory included a large number of antiship missiles.

Switching to the naval frequency, Suarez called, *"San Matias,* Jaguar One."

"Go ahead, Jaguar One," Enriquez responded.

"We have had a massive attack against our forces."

"I have been monitoring it, Jaguar."

"There must be an aircraft carrier nearby."

"It is not on any of our radars," Enriquez said.

"Find it."

"I am massing my ships against attack. Protecting them is my first priority, Jaguar."

"Just find that carrier."

"You find it, and we will take it out."

It was not a boast that Enriquez could fulfill. If anyone were to attack an aircraft carrier, it would have to be Suarez.

The minutes went by, dragged by, and the targets on his screen, now heading west-northwest, began to crawl to the center of the radar screen, right into his clutches.

Fifty kilometers.

He was about to order missiles armed when the radio blurted, "Jaguar Leader, Three. Hostiles at two-five-five."

There they were, on the outer edge of his screen. Four more of the unidentified blips.

"They are flying an intercept course," Jaguar Three said.

"We will circle to the rear of our targets and see what they do," Suarez said. "Go to one-seven-five."

Three minutes later, he knew that the new aircraft were fighters and were reinforcements for the fleeing helicopters and fighters.

He judged the odds of meeting fresh pilots and fresh missiles. His four against ten unknowns—the three helicopters might well be armed.

He took Jaguar Flight into a circular holding pattern and watched as the four newcomers joined the escapees and then turned back.

"Jaguar Leader, Two. Should we not attack?"

"I have considered it, Two. It will be far better, when we learn the position of their aircraft carrier, to attack the carrier."

Suarez led his flight back to Primavera.

GYPSY MOTH ONE
1425 HOURS LOCAL

"Gypsy One, Four."

"I've got you, Flaming Star."

"Shark, we're clear of the coast, and we've met up with four Tiger Barbs. We had four hostiles tailing us, but they've turned back."

Cady had been out of radar contact with Gypsy Four and Baker's choppers for ten minutes.

"What's your status, Star?"

"We lost an Apache. Falcon Three. No survivors. I got a Tornado."

Damn it.

"Falcon One, you copy?" Cady asked.

"Copied," was the terse reply. Cady couldn't tell whether Baker's voice was showing grief or tension. He was currently trying to engage Jerry Can One for refueling.

The Seahawk helicopter Baker was escorting had already refueled and was on its way back to the ship.

Baker's contingent was now clear of the continent, and Cady's priority had to shift from FSAD intervention to getting his aircraft back to the *U Thant*. The Harriers could make it, some of them barely, but all of the helicopters had to meet up with the Jerry Can tankers and top off their tanks.

"Tiger One, Gypsy One."

"Got me, Gypsy," Jake Travers said.

"How's your fuel state?"

"High in the green."

"Good. You've got the escort. Gypsy Four, you're going to be shortest on fuel. Head for the Beehive."

"Will comply, One. Gypsy Four out."

"Five and Six, fuel states?"

Sifra and Mikkelson reported, and Cady ordered them to leave the formation and head for the ship. He wondered if Sifra's and Stein's feud would accelerate now that Stein had two kills, a C-130 and a Tornado. David Stein could be a little overbearing at times.

The four Harriers from the 2nd Squadron would cover the

retreat and refueling of the Sea Apaches and Seahawks. Cady would have to be one of the early ones back to the ship, also. He and Stein had lingered a bit too long over the continent and used excess fuel in their engagements.

"Jericho, Gypsy Moth One."

"Jericho. Go ahead, Gypsy One."

He reported the status of his mission, then asked, "Do you have a sitrep on Fifth Wheel?"

"All aircraft have cleared the mainland. Evac of Arctowski and Signy is complete and successful. Gypsies Two and Three are twenty-five minutes out from Beehive."

After shooting down the second C-130, Anderson and Olivera had joined with two 2nd Squadron Harriers to cover the helicopters evacuating the stations in the north. The mission in the northern section of the peninsula and islands had been designated Fifth Wheel.

"Copied, Jericho. Gypsy One out."

Well, they had the people in the most threatened stations out, except for the Russians who had been at Bellinghausen, and Cady didn't know what he could do about that.

Now, the games could begin in earnest.

Cady passed over one of the Jerry Can refueling helicopters—seen on his radar scope—and headed for his ship.

DEFENSE INTELLIGENCE AGENCY
1741 HOURS LOCAL

Most of Cam McNichols's people had given up on going home for any length of time in the near future. Cots and rollaway beds were set up in offices and cubicles throughout the floor. There were, in fact, more temporary beds than he actually had people who reported to him.

With the warming of the Cold War, McNichols had lost

staffing, but with the Antarctica crisis, analysts from other sections were volunteering their time—half-time, of course— so that he could man his consoles around the clock.

He had given up his own console to others and moved back inside his office to manage the data being developed by the crisis. The wall opposite his desk was forlorn. He was aware of the absence of both the console and his old, flowered couch, and the room seemed barren and somehow friendless. Outside his window, the seemingly endless rows of markers in Arlington Cemetery reminded him that new markers were being made for some of those coming back from Antarctica.

Some would make it, walking, and he was thankful for that. The *U Thant* had reported that all of the evacuees were now aboard, and the wounded were being cared for in the ship's sick bay. Sir Charles had asked the United States to send a hospital ship to rendezvous with the *U Thant,* but it would be ten or eleven days before a transfer could take place.

At three o'clock, McNichols had had his own crisis. The deputy director for analysis, who had given him the half-time assignment to the UN Peacekeeper Committee in the first place, had shown up unexpectedly. McNichols had known right away that the man smelled enormous potential for self-promotion in the Antarctica situation.

"I'm here to lend a hand, Cameron," Geoffrey Stewart had said.

"Need every hand I can find, that's for sure."

"Tell you what. Why don't I handle the phones in here and leave you free to manage the incoming information." Stewart didn't really pose the statement as a question.

McNichols hit the memory dialing button while saying, "I'll notify Bentley."

"No need to do that."

"It's already ringing." He switched on the speakerphone. Bentley's secretary put him right through.

"Cameron? Something new?"

"Yes, Sir Charles. Mr. Stewart, the deputy director, will be taking care of the liaison from here on out." McNichols watched Stewart's face.

"That, Cameron, is a very tall heap of bloody bullshit," Bentley said.

Stewart's face reddened.

"Well, Sir Charles, I. . . ."

"I will call your President immediately."

"Ah, no need for that," Stewart said.

But Bentley had already hung up.

McNichols didn't know what had taken place at levels higher than his, but Stewart had disappeared, and he hadn't seen him for almost three hours. He didn't mind, however, losing that helping hand.

He preferred the assistance he was getting from veterans in the department, rather than politicos.

On his desk were scattered stacks of photographs, reports from assets all over South America and a few other continents, eleven Coca-Cola cans, and two large, flat boxes still containing seven slices of pepperoni and/or Canadian bacon and pineapple pizza. Around his desk, in chairs drawn up so tight that their knees were pressed to the desk, were six people, three from his section and three borrowed from other sections.

Dahlgren, from the Southeast Asia desk, leafed through the papers on a clipboard in his lap. "It's here somewhere, Cam . . . yeah, right here. We had four reports from friendlies that were similar enough that we made note of it, though no one ever really followed up. It seemed like a crazy scheme, and nothing ever came of it. Over a span of four months last year—"

"Are these rumors or facts?" McNichols asked. It was always consoling to him when little bits of information picked up in odd corners of the world fit in with other little bits of data found in other attics of the world. It justified his job.

"Half and half. In three cases, our assets heard only about some agent of a South American consortium or group. In one case, the asset heard the Front for South American Determination mentioned specifically. Boiled down, this guy was pitching commerce or energy officials in Singapore, Ho Chi Minh City, Manila, and Taiwan. Said he could supply their crude oil needs at fifty cents per barrel less than the world spot market."

"Bet that pissed off the OPEC rowdies," McNichols said, looking at Dan Strang, who handled the Middle East analysis.

Strang said, "I haven't heard a damned thing about it."

"One catch," Dahlgren said. "They wanted earnest money up front against a guaranteed purchase of x number of barrels, but the barrels wouldn't be available for eighteen months."

"How many barrels?"

"I don't have anything solid. One source says five million on first order, but I think it's a guess."

"Any vows made or contracts consummated?"

"Not to my knowledge."

McNichols finished what he swore was going to be his last piece of pizza, sluiced it down with some Coke, and looked to Vern Gadsdale, who was their resident expert on world energy.

"What's your take on this, Vern?"

"I get to make some assumptions, Cam?"

"As many as you want."

"Okay, I assume the same bunch screwing around in the world's refrigerator is out and about in the world trying to sell oil. That's oil that they haven't yet got, which makes the potential customer nervous about putting up cash. They're dealing in promises, but I bet they've got proof of oil reserves in the form of lab tests, assays, core samples, or the like. I also bet, since the selling job occurred before the takeover, they didn't identify the exact source of their oil reserves, and that made the customer nervous, too. Not to mention, naturally, that the customer has never heard of the FSAD before. They were trying to raise up-front cash to underwrite their little venture."

"Are you going to come right out and say they've got an oil source in Antarctica?"

"You want me to?"

"It makes for a damned good motive, Vern. Better than historical precedence. I have a hard time buying their PR concept which says that, because they have an historical right to the continent, they're going to take over and charge eighty or a hundred million a year for others to use it. They go right down the tubes if the scientific people boycott them. However, if I'm a small country in South America, and I can see where I'm going to get myself a share of, say, sixty or seventy *billion* dollars a year in oil revenues, I'm damned sure going to recognize the FSAD as my agent."

"I hate to come right out and say it's there," Gadsdale said. "It's possible, I suppose, but no one has ever reported finding more than trace elements of precious minerals or other revenue-producing commodities. I take that back. There's large concentrations of coal, but the cost of getting it out doesn't leave a profit margin. Then, too, the previous treaty frowned on mining and other misadventures of the type."

"Okay," McNichols said, "just for the sake of argument, let's say they've got oil reserves—"

"Or think they have," Gadsdale said.

"Yeah, I like that even better. Unproven reserves. A hot Latin emotion, or a bunch of them in the same room, could overrule reason. They get some sample cores, see some traces of oil, and think they've got another Prudhomme Bay. First things first, they've got to establish a claim, say under some dreamed-up Homesteader's Act, which they're now trying to do. What next, Andy?"

McNichols had asked Andrew Casper to sit in with them since Casper was the South American analyst, and McNichols, on his other half-time, was supposed to be the European analyst.

Casper, a tiny black man with vivid eyes, said, "Hot Latin blood or not, they know an invasion of the continent is going to upset the Security Council, as well as a few other nations. They've got to gather votes to counter that. If I were in their shoes, I'd be sending my field salesmen around to all the ambassadors, whispering 'oil' in eager ears."

"They've got Argentina, already," McNichols said.

"But they also thought they'd have a couple months in which to accomplish the selling job," Casper said, tapping a small sheaf of photographs taken during the Spare Tire and Fifth Wheel operations with a delicate forefinger. "What they got instead was an immediate Security Council resolution and unexpected warplanes knocking off their aircraft in less than a week. I think we're going to see the results of a panic-selling campaign pretty soon. And some of these countries might actually want to see solid evidence in the form of black gold before they take a public stand in the General Assembly. I'd figure these guys at Primavera to be drilling through the ice pretty damned soon."

McNichols wrote himself a note and mulled that over. "All right. Let's say a few more South American nations, with oil bucks in their eyes, climb aboard the FSAD ship. The pressure starts building on the Security Council to nullify the resolution and study the issue for a year or two."

"I can see it going that way," Casper said.

"What do I tell Sir Charles?" McNichols asked.

Dahlgren said, "I'd tell him that time is the most important factor. He's got to get the FSAD off the continent, or eradicated, before the South American faction can sway enough minds on the Council."

McNichols picked up his phone and punched the memory button. "Don't go away, guys. I may get a question I can't answer. Not likely, of course, but possible. Have some more pizza."

Someone in the Peacekeeper Committee office had to go get Sir Charles off the floor of the Security Council chamber. It took a few minutes.

"Hello, Cameron."

"Good evening, Sir Charles, but I'm Pack Rat, now."

"What?"

"This cute major on the *U Thant* gave me the code name Pack Rat."

"I have never seen a cute major, Cameron."

"Well, I haven't seen her, either, but she sounds like she's cute."

Bentley forced a laugh, but he sounded harassed. "I assume we took care of your problem of several hours ago."

"I believe so, Sir Charles. It hasn't reoccurred."

"If it does, let me know."

"I'll do that, sir. Thank you. Now, I've got some experts gathered here, and we've posed some scenarios."

McNichols told him the gist of his group's hypotheses. "There's very little hard data on that, Sir Charles, except for some reports out of Southeast Asia. We're going to dig some more in that area, as well as some others, and see if we can't get corroborating stories."

"Where would these oil deposits be, Cameron?"

McNichols passed the question to Vern Gadsdale.

Gadsdale looked up at the map pinned to the wall. "Theoretically, Cam, near Primavera. It would explain why they chose that base as their headquarters."

"Could be near Primavera, Sir Charles," he said into the receiver.

"It's a very interesting theory," Bentley said. "It could explain some recent changes."

"Such as?"

"Chile has now recognized the FSAD as legitimate."

"I see."

"And talk in the halls says that Uruguay may soon alter its position on the resolution. Brazil's contingent is caucusing at the moment. A few of the old guard seemed to be holding their respective breaths."

"If the resolution is suspended," McNichols said, "we'll have to stand down the *U Thant.*"

"I don't know that the resolution is in trouble just yet, Cameron. The Europeans are standing behind France on the matter of the French scientists killed on that charter airplane. The Russians are raising holy hell about the *Inga*'s detention. There is some relief relative to the people we've just evacuated, but the switchboard and the mail room is jammed with angry opinions from scientists the world over. Everyone in the building is besieged by reporters. I don't believe the news tonight will focus on the triple-murder on Forty-second Street."

"Still, the possibility exists that we could be stopped in our tracks. Where do you want to go with this, Sir Charles?"

"Let me talk to Highwater and Albrecht."

When he hung up, Casper asked, "So?"

"They're going to talk about it."

"That's politics, right, Cam?"

*45 KILOMETERS NORTHWEST OF FARADAY STATION,
ANTARCTICA
1820 HOURS LOCAL*

Major Roberto Tellez had heard helicopters in a search pattern twice, tantalizingly close, but he had lost his survival radio when he ejected from the Tornado, and they passed by him unaware of his shouts.

Fortunately, he had not lost his parka, gloves, and balaclava in the survival pack, and he abandoned his G suit and helmet, then donned the arctic clothing and tromped through bitter cold and deep snow and windblown crystals for forty minutes, calling for Ramirez. He was cold to the bone, and his muscles ached deeply, but he thought he was otherwise unharmed by his ejection from the airplane. The movement, the constant shifting of one foot in front of the other, helped to warm him somewhat, but he worried about hypothermia.

He started his search by trying to walk in circles, using the compass from the survival kit, but in the snow, he wasn't too certain how well he was doing.

He found Ramirez still entangled in his parachute cords only a couple hundred meters away to the north of where Tellez had landed. The canopy had never opened. What was left of Jesus Ramirez was nearly frozen solid, but his survival pack had been shielded from the impact by the body and was intact. And wonder of wonders, the radio worked!

With dismal results, however.

The range was limited to five kilometers, and by the time Tellez found that it worked, the search aircraft were long gone.

Trying his best to recall what he had once learned in an arctic survival class, Tellez dug a snow cave, unrolled the thin, but thermally insulated sleeping bag, and crawled into both. He heated snow in a tin cup over a Sterno can flame for water, and he waited.

He waited nearly five hours, trying an SOS call on the radio every twenty minutes, before he finally contacted a C-130 pilot on patrol, who relayed his message to Primavera.

The helicopter used his radio beacon as a guide and landed within thirty meters of his position.

Trotting stiffly in the cold, Tellez hurried to it and climbed into the cabin. It was not a warm cabin, but it felt like a tropical heaven.

The pilot leaned back to shout above the roar of the engine, "Your navigator, Major?"

"He's dead. Leave him."

UNS U THANT
1900 HOURS LOCAL

Cady and Baker went together to the chapel on B Deck for the memorial service for Captain Emory Apstein of Israel and Second Lieutenant Gene Rigsby of the United States. The crew of Falcon Three had been confirmed dead by Copperhead Seven, killed instantly when their Sea Apache was blown out of the sky by a FSAD Sky Flash missile.

Cady had known them, though not well, and he was already struggling in his mind with the letters he would have to write to the next-of-kin. Apstein had been married, with three young children, and Rigsby, though single, had been engaged to be married. The ship's chapel was crowded, and Cady and Baker stood at the back while the Spanish Catholic chaplain presided over the mourning crowd, presenting a generalized service.

When it was over, Monmouth signalled them, and the three men went to the officers' wardroom on C Deck for coffee. The place was crowded, but they found a little privacy at a table in one corner. Cady saw Jean d'Argamon sitting with Terri Eames on the other side of the room.

"If he doesn't leave my girlfriend alone, I may boot his arse into the sea," Baker said.

Monmouth looked over at the Frenchman, then back at Baker.

"I don't think he means it literally, Captain," Cady said.

"Certainly, I do," the chopper pilot said.

"Wait until this is over, will you?" Monmouth asked.

"If you insist, sir."

"I insist."

Cady was pretty sure that Baker's interest in Eames was more brotherly, or perhaps even fatherly, than he allowed it to appear, but he wasn't at all certain that Baker wouldn't challenge the man to a duel of fists. Baker just didn't like the cocky Frenchman.

He didn't much care for the man, either, but he recognized d'Argamon's competence with sub-sea vehicles. And now, he found that he, too, was a little irked at seeing d'Argamon hanging around Terri Eames like a teenager. Throughout the mission today, hers had been a husky, steady, and soothing voice, even when the going got a little hairy.

"I know your official versions of the mission from the after-action briefing," Monmouth said. "Is there anything unofficial we should talk about?"

"Every man and woman under my command," Baker said, "did exactly what they were supposed to do. They followed the tactical plan to the letter, stayed on-course, and practically on time. If I hadn't lost Falcon Four to mechanical failure, I might have been able to assist Apstein."

"Don't start worrying about ifs, Archie," Cady told him.

Baker shook his head in resignation.

"How about you, Jim?" Monmouth asked.

"If this outfit had medals to give away, I'd give a few. As it is, I intend to write some letters of commendation to be put in personnel files."

"Who?"

"Stein, for one."

"Agreed."

"And Lieutenant Gail Alhers. She left her station on her own initiative to meet and escort Falcon Four when he had to turn back. And she still managed to rendezvous with and refuel all of her scheduled choppers."

Baker nodded his head in affirmation.

"I'll buy that," Monmouth agreed.

"And Archie."

Baker looked up from the circles he was drawing in spilled coffee on the Formica tabletop. "Forget it."

"His flying was worth a Navy Flying Cross, at minimum," Cady said. "Probably a DFC."

"You write the letters, I'll endorse them, and I'll have Sir Charles endorse them," Monmouth said.

"Thank you, Captain. You might even recommend that their respective services consider issuing citations to them when their cruises are completed."

"I'll do that. Any other evaluations? How about the other side?"

"The pilot of the Tornado I zapped was good," Cady said. "If Archie hadn't shunted him my way, I wouldn't have gotten him. David Stein feels the other Tornado pilot also knew what he was doing. On human competence, so far, it looks like we're going up against some capable people."

"And on the hardware side?" Monmouth asked.

"Henry Docker," Baker said, "identified the Tornado's missiles as Sky Flashes. That's an upgrade of the Sparrow, and pretty much state-of-the art. On missile range, they've got the helos whipped."

"We won't win any air superiority battles," Cady agreed. "But our edge is going to be with intelligence. They're lacking long-range surveillance and radar capability, and with what we're getting from McNichols, we'll be able to fox them a little. Our tactics are going to have to follow a probe-and-poke scenario. Get a little here, get a little there."

"That'll take time," Monmouth said. "The Committee might not have it."

"We can't afford a massive air strike, Captain. We wouldn't return from it," Cady said.

"On the other hand," the captain said, "we probably don't have time on our side. You probably don't want to know the politics behind this . . ."

"I probably don't."

". . . but Bentley thinks there's a small chance at the moment we might lose our resolution in the Security Council. That small chance is going to grow in the next few days or weeks, and he wants this wrapped up before that happens."

"How soon?"

"Who knows?"

Cady looked at Baker, who said, "Ah, hell, CAG, let's just do it."

TEN KILOMETERS NORTH OF BRANDEIS BASE, ANTARCTICA 2345 HOURS LOCAL

The going had been tough, despite the Sno-Cats.

All five of the Brandeis Sno-Cats were being used in order to accommodate the United Nations commandos and their equipment. Andover had had them prepared, the tanks topped off, the engine oil and filters changed, the engines run and checked, before the helicopters landed. The commando leader, David George, had expressed his approval, but had had his men hoist two full fifty-five-gallon drums of gasoline onto one of the roof racks and lash them in place with quarter-inch nylon rope, just in case they needed it.

He had also told Andover and Brelin to get rid of their fluorescent orange and dark-blue anoraks and find something in a lighter shade.

Andover was driving the lead Cat, with Gustav Brelin, George, and two of his men in the cab with him, one of them a Russian named Suslov. Andover had been surprised at the makeup of the commando unit.

The laboring of the diesel engine did not make casual conversation a pleasure, but Andover had learned that George's team was composed of men from all over the world: Russians, Asians, Europeans. It was truly an international effort, and one that Andover felt a part of, though not fully. He had asked, for instance, where they had come from, and George had replied, "Mr. Andover, let me make this graphic. They've got you spread-eagled on a table, naked, and the guy with the razor-edged knife asks, 'Where did they come from?' What are you going to say?"

Andover had decided he would just as soon not know. Not just yet.

It was not entirely dark, just dim, but they were traversing unfamiliar and dangerous territory, with snow-disguised crevasses apt to appear at any moment, and the vague light was made tricky by the snowfall.

"I think," Brelin said, "that the snow is letting up."

"I'm the meteorologist, Gustav. I'm the one who's supposed to say the snow is letting up."

George leaned forward from his seat in the rear and said loudly, to overcome the engine roar, "Is that right?"

"I believe so, Commander. Just a little."

"Damn. I had hoped to have the cover for longer."

"It should stop completely before dawn," Andover told him.

"We may have to hole up for the day, then. These bright orange vehicles can be spotted too easily from the air."

"I didn't have time to paint them," Andover said. "Besides, our intent was to have them easily spotted."

"Sorry, Zip. You have your objectives, and I have mine."

"I think they're the same, now," Andover said, thinking about Christine Amherst. She had been so beautiful to him.

"There!" Brelin warned.

Andover peered ahead and saw the depression in the snow that suggested there could be an air pocket below it. He pulled back on the right stick, braking the righthand set of tracks, and the Sno-Cat swerved quickly.

"Another!" Brelin said.

He jockeyed the left stick to avoid the potential trap on the right. In his rearview mirror, he saw the slitted lights of the four Sno-Cats following in his tracks, trusting to his judgment.

They had spent many hours climbing the plateau, following a ridgeline of rock and ice precipices that jutted ruggedly upward for two and three hundred feet on his right. He couldn't see it now, but he felt its presence. Five times, they had turned back to seek another route when they had encountered an impassable ravine or crevasse.

One of George's men, a sergeant from New Zealand, kept saying, "I can't get over it; there aren't any trees."

To get from one high mesa to a lower plateau, they had crawled west for three kilometers, then threaded their way back to the east and slithered down a rock-strewn slope.

Now, the surface ahead of him abruptly disappeared, and Andover yanked both levers back to stop the Sno-Cat. He moved the throttle to idle.

Gustav Brelin popped open his door and slid outside, letting in a blast of frigid air. Tentatively, he explored the drop-off ahead, slowly disappearing into the whiteness. The thin rays of light from the sun lit the snowflakes and reflected back at them.

Brelin reappeared a few minutes later, struggling through the deep snow, and climbed back into the cab.

"It'll be okay, Zip. Takes about a twenty-degree decline, then levels out. You want me to drive for a while?"

Andover considered the offer. He wouldn't be any good to himself or anyone else if he became completely fatigued.

"Yeah, Gus. For a little while, anyway."

They exchanged seats, and once he was settled, Andover turned back to the military people. "Down on the floor there, Commander, there's a canteen and a bag of gingersnaps."

George found them and passed them forward.

"I'm damned glad we connected with you, Zip," George said. "This would be a treacherous trip for a novice."

"It's treacherous for a vet," Andover admitted. "You guys want a cookie?"

8 DECEMBER

Emilio Suarez was still in shock. Yesterday afternoon seemed like a dream, one that he would surely wake up from soon.

He sat at the table in the operations hut, looking through the window at what was taking place on the field. It was a clear day, the sun bright enough that reflections off the snow hurt the eyes. Most of the men working around the runways and aircraft were wearing sunglasses. It looked like a bad scene from Hollywood, Suarez thought.

Despite the activity around the base—yet more snow removal, aircraft maintenance, the building of bomb, missile, and fuel storage areas—his work force seemed decimated, and it was. Silvera had diverted much of his manpower to the drilling sites. The ground forces, primarily designated for security details in addition to outright labor, had been culled from anyone capable of carrying pipe or mechanically inclined enough to work around diesel motors and other machinery. The seven drilling operations were being conducted by independent drillers recruited by Silvera, but they had brought with them crew enough to only support ten- or twelve-hour shifts. The president wanted them working around the clock.

Time, which they had thought they had in luxuriant quantities, was dribbling away.

On the far side of the runway, in one of the Tornado revetments, he could see the mercenary Major Roberto Tellez walking with several mechanics, inspecting an airplane. The man was amazing. He should have been dead, or at least in the makeshift dispensary, but he was up and preparing for an encounter that Suarez was positive he looked forward to. When he had spoken to Tellez earlier, Suarez had been able to sense the repressed fury in the man; he did not take well to being bested in battle. He seemed somewhat egocentric in that he showed absolutely no remorse for the death of his navigator, Jesus Ramirez.

Only Suarez seemed to mourn the loss of Ramirez or of Sancho Amador, whose Mirage had not yet been found.

He heard the door to the hut open behind him and felt the draft of cold air that rushed across the worn linoleum flooring. When he turned and saw that Silvera had entered, he glanced quickly at the status board that had been affixed to the wall next to the window. The president would want to know what was being done about the invaders.

The president was bundled up in a thick anorak and though he did not remove it, he tugged off his mittens and pulled the woolen cap from his head as he walked across the floor toward Suarez.

Suarez stood up. "Good morning, *Presidente.*"

"Well, Colonel?"

"There is no sign of the attackers," Suarez reported. "At the moment, I have the remaining C-130s picking up the last of the supplies at Navarino, which leaves only the fuel reserves. I have had to use fighter aircraft and the tankers for air cover. There are three tankers airborne in addition to six flights of two fighter aircraft. We are scouring the region."

"With what results?"

Suarez gestured with his hand toward the grease pencil scribblings covering the status board.

"Two hundred kilometers to the west, steaming away from us, are three Japanese whaling ships and their processing vessel. I think that we have cut their season short. In the Drake Passage, we have counted eleven vessels—six freighters, two Argentine warships, and three crude oil transports. Two of them are Very Large Crude Carriers and one is a ULCC. All of the ships are well outside the territorial limits."

"And there is no sign of this aircraft carrier you insist upon?"

"These aircraft had to come from a carrier, *Presidente.* No, there is no evidence of it yet, but it is there, somewhere. Our radars can be tricked, especially in a sea full of giant icebergs."

Silvera sighed and stared out the window. Suarez stood alongside him, waiting for directions, and unhappy with the slow progress of turning a scientific station into a military base. Two Mirages waited at the end of the runway, ready to take off and replace one of the air patrols. The air controller, Captain Arquez, standing behind Suarez, was wearing a headset and talking to them on the radio.

"Who do you think they belong to, Emilio?"

"The Americans, the British, the French? Who knows?" Suarez said. "According to the television and radio reports, the French are enraged about the de Havilland airplane Tellez shot down. Perhaps they had a task force in the southern Pacific that could have responded so quickly."

"We haven't even seen them."

"The weather, *Presidente,* is so—"

"I know about the weather. What is pressing me, Emilio, is the response I must take."

"Response?"

"Certainly. Our hostages at nearby stations have all been reclaimed."

"Tellez keeps two Tornados ready to make a long-distance dash," Suarez said. "We could attack McMurdo again, or Eights Station, or Russkaya, or Amundson-Scott at the South Pole with very little preparation time."

"And there is the Russian ship, the *Inga*," Silvera said, reaching into his pocket for a folded sheet of paper. He handed it to Suarez.

Unfolding it, Suarez read:

FRONT FOR SOUTH AMERICAN DETERMINATION MEMORANDUM

DATE: 7 DECEMBER
TO: UNITED NATIONS
RE: INCURSION WITHIN TERRITORIAL
   LIMITS OF ANTARCTICA

The unwarranted attack against aircraft of the Front for South American Determination and the illegal landings of alien helicopters at encampments owned by the Front for South American Determination on 6 December cannot be tolerated or allowed to pass unremarked.

As a consequence of the warlike actions perpetrated by entities unknown, the Russian freighter *Inga* will be sunk at 1300 hours, 7 December.

Let no nation underestimate the depth of our resolve to correct two centuries of inequity directed toward the rightful possessors of the continent.

Suarez thought it read like something Ricardo Fuentes would have written. There was no mention of the fact that hostages had been rescued from the encampments. And Fuentes did not say that Suarez had been caught unprepared for marauding helicopters and fighters, though Suarez felt as if the memo were an arrow pointing directly at himself. There was also no mention of the fate of those aboard the *Inga.*

"And the Russians aboard the freighter, *Presidente?*"

"We will let them wonder about that, Emilio."

UNS U THANT
0910 HOURS LOCAL

"When I was in it," Shark Cady said, "I didn't much care for the snowstorm. But it was damned good cover, and I wish we had it back, now."

"They will be fine, Colonel," Terri Eames told him.

The two of them were sitting in chairs behind the duty TIO, Luigi Maroni, in the Combat Information Center. In the soft light of the center, Cady had been watching Terri's hands. They rested on the chair arms; they moved to rest on her thighs; they went back to the arms; they gripped each other. Despite her calm voice and her reassurances, Cady thought she was nervous.

He was himself thinking rather longingly about one of the cigars in the breast pocket of his flight suit.

It was quiet in the CIC. The second officer, Jacob Ernst, had stopped in for a while, but Monmouth had charged him with taking care of the scientists evacuated from the stations on the peninsula—not an enviable task, and many were complaining about the cramped quarters they were having to share. They lived through a long winter in huts covered with snow, but they didn't get cabin fever until they were forced to share a ship. They ought to try a U.S. Navy or Russian vessel if they thought these quarters were confining. Ernst had just left to visit those who were ensconced in the ship's hospital. Fortunately, it was a well-equipped hospital, with highly competent personnel, and Captain Jan Gless and her staff of three doctors and six nurses had all of the wounded stabilized.

Eames had debriefed many of the evacuees as soon as they were aboard ship, but she hadn't learned anything new from them. Most of them hadn't even seen the aircraft that had attacked their stations.

Maroni had several ships identified on the screen, in addition to FSAD aircraft whose positions were relayed to him by the console operator at Pack Rat. To the east was the air patrol flight, two Gypsy Moths, and to their south were two Harriers from Tiger Barb Squadron. The Gypsy Moths were due to recover shortly, to be replaced by a pair of Sea Apaches.

Maroni keyed his microphone and spoke to the element from the 2nd Squadron. "Tiger Barb Five, I see you at Waypoint One."

"Roger, Jericho," the aviator responded immediately. "We're going to one-one-five."

Cady had set up their mission profiles so as to help protect the ship from identification. Flights from and to the carrier were doglegged so that UN aircraft approached or left hostile radar coverage in directions that didn't pinpoint the *U Thant*. At the moment, the two Tiger Barbs were conducting a radar probe. They would fly east, using their radar sporadically, until they drew the attention of FSAD patrols, then they would turn tail and head west.

The idea was to instill a mind-set in FSAD pilots and air controllers that their opponents were coming out of the west, on an approximate bearing of 240 degrees from Primavera. Cady wanted FSAD heads turned in that direction.

Jake Travers's flight, however, scheduled for takeoff at 1100 hours, might change the collective FSAD mind, and its head, once again. Cady fervently hoped that would be the case.

In his earlier briefing with Travers and his two wingmen, Travers had been a trifle incredulous.

"I'm looking for what?"

"Oil wells."

"That's what I thought you said, Shark. Why would we think they've got oil wells?"

"We don't know for sure that they do, Jake, but some people in New York and Washington think it's important information to have. They want to have positive evidence, yea or nay, and the satellites haven't seen a thing."

"Hell, CAG, if we have to do it, anyway, your country could save a bunch of cash on satellites."

Cady and the three mission aviators had pored closely over the enlarged and enhanced photographs of the Primavera region. McNichols had told Eames that these were the first clear shots they had gotten of the enlarged airfield. The aircraft parked around the perimeter of the airstrip were clearly visible, but McNichols had warned him that there were SAM and antiaircraft sites all around the field that were not visible. They were burrowed into the snow and covered with camouflage netting. There were also infrared photos, but the hot spots seemed to correspond to the heat sources seen in the clear pictures, and McNichols and his analysts thought the defensive positions might have been overlaid with a coating of snow in order to disguise their heat signatures.

"Even with the snow accumulation on the ground," Cady said, "you can pick out the places where there's been a high frequency of vehicle traffic. Some of these trails have been used for years and are well-packed; they lead out to field stations and various experiments. The road McNichols is most interested in runs along the ridge, here."

"That's a road?" Travers asked. "How does one tell?"

"According to the analysts, the shadows define it, and they're different from photos taken a year ago. Hell, Jake, look along here . . . see the line of shadow . . . a straight line."

"That's not straight."

"It's pretty straight," Cady said. "Anyway, it follows the ridge northward for about twelve miles, but it doesn't seem to go anywhere. What they want is for you to tell them why it's there."

"And they don't want me to make a wild guess?"

"Preferably not. Would you rather I take this one?"

"Get away, mate!" the Aussie said. "This one's mine."

"I will do the low-level pass," the Japanese pilot, Nikki Nakamura, flying as Tiger Barb Two, told him.

"Next time," Travers had responded. "The first time through, we need a hotshit aviator, like me."

"How did they make the movie, *Top Gun,* without you?" Nakamura asked.

"Wasn't easy, Nikki, for sure."

Now Cady watched as the two symbols identified as Tiger Barbs Four and Five on the screen turned onto a direct heading for the peninsula. He wasn't worried about Four and Five; they would skedaddle as soon as they were painted by hostile radar. He was worried about Travers's daylight reconnaissance mission, but he also knew that McNichols and Bentley were concerned about the timing. They had to have information quickly to counter what McNichols had described as a ground swell of enthusiasm building among South American nations. McNichols had also said, however, that politics being politics, the ground swell could ebb just as fast. All they needed was something with which to battle ground swells. Practically any half-substantiated rumor would do it.

While Bentley worried about the timing, Cady worried about the Russians, though not in a way that he had ever thought that he would worry about Russians. There was some talk, learned through McNichols, that the Russians were considering an evacuation mission on their own. When he checked the other screen on the bulkhead, which currently displayed a map of the entire continent, Cady was a little dismayed. There was no way he could mount defensive sorties for the stations on the main continent if the FSAD decided that a few more examples, like the one at McMurdo, needed to be set. And if the Russians, coming out of Christchurch, attempted a rescue mission of the people at their stations on the main continent, he was certain their transports would be shot down.

Then, less than fifteen minutes ago, McNichols had called Eames with the information that the *Inga* was going to be sunk. That gave him more Russians to worry about, and he knew that the Russian delegation to the UN must be raising holy hell. The power structure on the Security Council and the Peacekeeper Committee, however, had declined to recall the recon mission.

Eames looked over at him. "They're probably right."

"Who's right?"

"The Peacekeeper Committee. The FSAD will pull all of the people off the ship before they sink it."

"Let's both engage in wishful thinking," he said.

She gave him a dirty look.

She had her hand pressed against her stomach, and Cady had the probably inappropriate thought that he'd like to have his hand pressed there. He looked up at the plot. Though the ships weren't in radar range, the satellites had placed the *San Matias,* the *Inga,* the minesweeper *San Jorge,* and two patrol boats in a group seventy miles off the coast of the peninsula, 260 miles from the current position of the *U Thant.*

And forty-five miles away, the symbol that was the minisub *Calais* was going hell-bent for the coast. The *Dover,* just launched, was on the way to assume the patrolling station the *Calais* had recently abandoned.

"I hope they've taken them off the *Inga,*" he said. "D'Argamon won't give the FSAD boys the option of disembarking."

PRIMAVERA BASE
1050 HOURS LOCAL

Juan Silvera and his chief geologist, Armand Calvera, rode in one of the Primavera Sno-Cats. It and its seven brethren had been freshly repainted white in the prefabricated maintenance shed. Silvera was confident that overhead surveillance aircraft or satellites would not easily identify the machine as it traversed the rugged terrain east of the base.

Calvera was a squat and bulky man with hair as white as the landscape and the parka he wore. Silvera knew that he was close to seventy years of age and enjoyed a worldwide reputation in the society of geologists. His lively blue eyes had seen much of the world during his expeditions, and they had been active in Antarctica for six years. It was Calvera who had discovered the petroleum deposits while coring the earth underneath the lava layers below the ice in the attempt to map mineral layers.

Fortunately, he was a man of vision, and rather than discuss his findings with the station chief, he had gone to his cousin, Ricardo Fuentes, who was at that time the chief assistant for one of the deputies to the Argentine minister of energy. And over their dinner meeting was born the Front for South American Determination. Silvera was certain that many people would be shocked if they learned that Fuentes had been one of the architects of the organization.

Driving north along the icy ruts created by numerous vehicles, Calvera worked the track levers and evaded a large boulder, then pointed to the right and practically yelled to be heard above the roar of the diesel engine. "Over there, *Presidente*, is the first test site."

Even with the darkened lenses of his sunglasses, Silvera had to squint his eyes against the bright sun and snow in order to pick out the small derrick. It was barely a splotch against the ridge rising behind it, for the derrick had been draped in white plastic sheeting to hide it from prying eyes.

"Is it still operational?" he asked.

"Oh, it could be, but it is too much in the open, and besides, we won't find a major pool there," Calvera said. "It is abandoned."

Despite his age, Calvera handled the controls of the Sno-Cat adeptly, and they sped along the track, wavering up and down and sideways like a rattlesnake. For short stretches, the road was straight, and Calvera managed to increase his speed to fifty kilometers per hour. As they moved north, they crept closer and closer to the mammoth ridge that ran north and south, parallel to the coast some eighty kilometers to the west.

With the bucking and rocking vehicle creating so much noise, it was difficult to talk, and Silvera found himself rethinking the ultimatum that Ricardo Fuentes had drawn up. He wished he could rescind it, but unfortunately, he knew that Fuentes was correct. Without an overt action on his part to respond to the raid of yesterday, the unknown assailants would feel free to raid at their will. All morning long, he had felt that bombs would begin raining down on Primavera at any moment, and he had been less certain of Suarez's defensive preparations. The number of SAMs and antiaircraft guns had suddenly seemed insufficient, spread thinly over a wide area in order to protect the drilling sites as well as the air base. Already, they had lost five aircraft, and they had but one alien aircraft downed in retaliation.

And they could not even find that one.

Silvera had ordered a search for the attack helicopter shot down, in hopes of identifying his adversary, but in the confused heat of battle, no one had noted the coordinates, and Puma Four, who had had the victory, had died in the moment of his triumph.

Emilio Suarez, he knew, had been stunned by the immediacy of the response to their invasion. Silvera had, throughout his life, always attempted to prepare himself for the worst, and while the sudden appearance of hostile aircraft had surprised him, it was to a much lesser degree than that experienced by Suarez. His assumption, not yet shared with Suarez or Enriquez, was that one of the European nations had had a carrier in the region and was operating covertly under the auspices of the United Nations Security Council Resolution. The covert aspect would be required since the force was not large enough for a frontal assault. He suspected that Primavera would be harassed in small ways until the major force could be assembled.

The development erased some sixty days from his calendar, but he was not yet pessimistic. All it meant was that they must speed up Calvera's project and increase their efforts at persuading South American national representatives to support the cause of the Front for South American Determination.

And deflect the attacks of the unknown aggressor until the resolution was withdrawn.

It also meant, unfortunately, that some of his leverage was irretrievably lost, and that he would likely have to cede additional percentage points of the net revenues to member nations. Already, their greed was showing. Silvera's agents in New York called repeatedly, asking for permission to increase the offering. Brazil, as the largest nation, was demanding fifty percent. Argentina had finally agreed to 10.5 percent, causing Silvera to downgrade his own expectations to five hundred million American dollars.

He was fronting this enterprise, using his face and reputation, for a half-billion dollars. It was a small enough price, he thought, for assuming the risk of insulting the international community.

As soon as he had banked his share, Silvera was retiring. Someone else could be president.

"We are almost there," Calvera said.

They were right up against the ridge now, and when he leaned to the right and looked up at the top of it, Silvera almost became dizzy. Though they had gained some altitude since leaving the base, the peaks and rocky precipices still climbed thirty or forty meters above him.

"We are five kilometers from Primavera," Calvera said. "There! See?"

Silvera saw one of his surface-to-air missile batteries emplaced against the base of a cliff. The truck was covered with a white camouflage cover, on which snow had been sprinkled, and the crewmen were huddled over a small fire, trying to get warm. Later, perhaps tomorrow, the field engineers would reach them and erect a small shelter for them.

A few meters later, they reached a large vertical crevasse, and Calvera turned the Sno-Cat abruptly into it. Jagged ice and rock spires climbed upward on either side of them. Bereft of any foliage, any shrub at all, the cliffs seemed nearly extraterrestrial to Silvera. The road along the base of the ravine had been carved out of rock and ice with bulldozers and dynamite and was relatively smooth, though it climbed steeply for several hundred meters, until they reached the end of it in a small box canyon.

The drilling site was not allowed much space. Silvera estimated the width of the ravine at twenty meters, if that. It was surrounded on three sides by cliff face, but it was protected from the wind. As he got down from the Sno-Cat, he was struck by the absence of wind. It seemed warmer than it probably was.

More important, the site was protected from visual sighting from above. Thirty meters up the sides of the cliffs, drills had been used in the rock face to implant anchors, and a thin, but extremely strong, sheet of white Mylar had been stretched taut above the drilling rig. It covered the entire end of the canyon, but was placed with a pronounced forward slant so that most snow would slide off it. The structural engineer who had designed it guaranteed that it would hold a layer of ten centimeters of snow—to thwart infrared detectors seeking heat sources, but would allow a thicker layer of snow to slide off into the canyon.

Calvera and the engineers had prepared seven such sites all along the ridge north of Primavera. The geologist envisioned a future in which a hundred wells would be pumping high-grade crude, spilling their treasure into a one-meter pipeline to the coast. Silvera embraced the same dream for, at the end of its rainbow, was a very large pot with a half-billion U.S. dollars in it.

Here, at the first site, the derrick had already been erected on its prepared bed of concrete. Three shanties surrounded the base of the derrick, containing living quarters, stores, and power supplies. The derrick was enclosed with a plastic-and-fabric opaque sheeting, and two flatbed trailers parked near the base held tall stacks of drilling pipe. In tribute to Calvera's optimism, three more flatbed trailers, parked farther down the slope, were loaded with well casing.

"Sites Four and Six are also prepared to begin drilling, *Presidente,* but I wanted you to be here when we started the first hole. A ceremony of polite proportions, as it may be."

"I appreciate that, Armand. How about the other sites?"

"The equipment is all in place, and all seven will be drilling within two days."

"Wonderful. You will be richly rewarded."

"All I seek at my age, *Presidente,* is the legacy of discovery."

Silvera had been fairly certain that Calvera's predominant motivation was to have his name prominently displayed in geologic journals and histories. A world-class discovery of petroleum reserves would do that for him, whereas, if one followed the dictates of previous treaties which banned mineral mining and production, a suggestion that petroleum deposits *might* be present would probably not rate a very large footnote.

He followed the geologist around two huge tanks that were emanating heat. The snow on the ground near them was soft, beginning to puddle.

"The tanks hold the drilling mud," Calvera explained. "We have to heat it to keep it in a fluid state."

When they reached the derrick, Calvera pulled back a flap and waved Silvera inside. A dozen men—roughnecks, roustabouts, tool pushers, and military men conscripted for drilling duty—stood inside awaiting him. Huge propane heaters had raised the interior temperature somewhat. Silvera smiled and waved to the men waiting, and they smiled back. Everyone here was about to make history, and he thought that they were impressed with his presence.

"On this site," Calvera said, "we will drill quickly through one hundred and fifteen meters of ice. Then, there is a lava cap some seventy meters thick. That will be slower."

"How deep will it go?"

"My best guess is one thousand meters."

"Your best *guess?*"

"Drilling for oil is always a gamble, *Presidente.*"

UNS CALAIS
1235 HOURS LOCAL

The Belgian lieutenant, Oscar Moritz, was in the command seat, and Erik Magnuson sat behind d'Argamon at the electronics console. The submarine was trimmed to as sleek a profile as she could manage, and had been making twenty-six knots for over two hours. They were at a depth of sixty feet, and the high-speed revolutions of the propeller would be an easy target for any sonar.

Moritz asked, "Battery state, Magnuson?"

"Sixty-five percent, Lieutenant. We will have to complete our return to the ship on the diesel, but we are in good shape."

"Distance to target?" d'Argamon asked.

"One-five-nine statute miles," the technician told him. "We are not going to make it, are we, Commander?"

D'Argamon had no illusions about what the FSAD might be capable of perpetrating, and he said, "Not in time for the Russians, no."

THE SAN MATIAS
1255 HOURS LOCAL

The *Inga* was dead in the water some three hundred meters from the destroyer, and Commander Dante Montez, the first officer, could not seem to see enough of her. He stood forward on the bridge and scanned her with his binoculars.

Diego Enriquez could no longer feel the pulse of the engines under his feet; the *San Matias* was barely making headway, drifting on the same current with the freighter. A large ice floe was slowly passing behind the Russian ship, providing a magnificent backdrop for this production. It seemed almost as if the ship might be on stage, but Enriquez could see no movement of people on the decks or behind the bridge windows. The ruins of the orange helicopter were draped over the fantail, providing a bright spot of color in an otherwise drab scene.

The seas were choppy, but not strong. The *San Jorge* and the two patrol boats stood off by a kilometer. They seemed expectant to Enriquez, as if they were taking on human traits, but in reality, they appeared today exactly as they appeared on any day.

"Ready the starboard torpedo tube," he ordered.

Without lowering his binoculars, Montez repeated the order, and a few seconds later, the expected response came back on the interphone, "The starboard tube is ready."

Enriquez watched the clock on the bulkhead.

"Bridge! Bridge, radar."

Finally, Montez lowered his glasses and stepped to the intercom. "Radar, bridge."

"Bridge, we have two unidentified aircraft, bearing two-six-four, altitude four thousand meters, range six-three kilometers, speed five-nine-zero knots."

At that speed, and flying as a pair, they would be fighter aircraft, Enriquez knew.

"Is it an attack profile?" Montez asked.

"That is not apparent at this time, sir," the radar operator reported.

Montez looked to him, and Enriquez said, "Pass the report to Primavera Air Control, put the missile batteries on alert, and warn the *San Jorge.*"

"Right away, Captain."

Three minutes later, the aircraft were much closer, and they had changed neither their speed nor their direction. They had increased altitude to remain clear of the range of the destroyer's guns. The missiles were still capable of reaching them, however.

"I think," Montez said, "that they must be reconnaissance airplanes. They will witness what we do here, Captain."

Most of his deck officers were on the bridge now, prepared to become spectators. Carlos Estero and Umberto Mondragon stood to the port side of the bridge, speaking quietly to each other. Mondragon had tried to speak to him earlier, but Enriquez had brushed him aside.

"That is quite possible, Commander," Enriquez told Montez. The clock showed one minute to go.

"Perhaps," Montez said, "we should delay until they leave. Photographs could be damning."

"We always, always follow our orders, Commander."

Montez's face maintained its stoicism but for a small tic under his left eye. To hide it, he again raised the binoculars, turned to the windscreen, and scanned the skies.

Within seconds, he reported, "Two fighter aircraft. I cannot make out the type, but they are beginning to circle."

Enriquez moved to the starboard windows so he could watch the torpedo crew. He looked at the clock, then said, "Fire the torpedo."

Mondragon started to speak, then thought better of it.

Montez hesitated only momentarily before repeating the order, "Fire torpedo tube one."

The petty officer manning the fire control station repeated the order into his microphone, and the American-built Mk 48 torpedo leaped from the tube, entered the rough water with a minor splash, and left a curving wake behind as it arced toward the freighter.

The torpedo moved at a speed of forty knots, and it did not take long to reach the ship, guided by the torpedoman via its trailing wires.

It struck dead amidships, and there was a fraction of time lost while it penetrated the thin skin of the hull before erupting.

It exploded in blue-black rings of concussion waves that reached back to the ears on the destroyer.

Enriquez did not think that the exterior damage was all that impressive, just a sudden gaping wound in the side of the ship.

But then, hatchways all over the freighter burst open, and screaming people began to pour out of them, rushing madly about her decks.

TIGER BARB ONE
1302 HOURS LOCAL

The bright, clear day had made their aerial refueling from Jerry Can Three a breeze, and so Jake Travers was making himself be wary. It didn't seem right when everything went so smoothly.

As soon as the last Harrier had been topped off, outside the radar coverage from Primavera and its high-flying semi-Airborne Warning and Control Systems aircraft, Travers had taken his flight to the water, using his radar altimeter, which transmitted its signals straight down rather than forward, to maintain an altitude of one hundred feet above the gray granite sea. It was tricky flying, with little time for reaction, which kept a pilot constantly on alert and on edge, waiting for that unexpected turbulence which would plunge him straight into the ice-cold sea.

They had dodged icebergs on their way to the continent, going feet-dry, or as he thought of it, feet-frozen, south of Alexander Island. That put them in the area known as Palmer Land, two hundred miles north of the Americans' Eights Station, which was also known as Sky-Hi Station. Some 250 miles south of Eights was Vinson Massiff, the highest point in Antarctica at 16,067 feet.

Tiger Barb Flight had penetrated the continent close to the juncture of the peninsula with the main landmass, and as soon as they had, Travers turned his three aircraft north. They would approach Primavera from the southeast, popping over the ridge behind the station at the last minute.

They had three things going for them, Cady had explained. First, the FSAD people would be less likely to expect a raid in broad daylight—relatively speaking, since it was daylight around the clock. The first sortie, after all, had taken place in a snowstorm. Secondly, they would be looking to the west for potential incursions, and third, they might well have their minds focused on another event that was supposed to take place at 1300 hours.

Travers had tended to agree with Cady, but then he normally did. He liked the American Marine who was his boss, and more than that, respected his abilities and the way he thought.

And now, he thought, they would see if Cady was right.

They were forty miles south and thirty miles east of Primavera, flying nap-of-the-earth behind the protection of the tall ridge that ran down the peninsula. It possibly served as a radar shield.

If he could have distinguished them in the mass of ice below, Travers might have identified a series of small peninsulas, capes, bays, and inlets on his right. He had certainly memorized all of them from his map, but as it was, it looked like one solid ice cube to him. The supposed land formations with intriguing names like Cape Disappointment, Cabinet Inlet, and Whirlwind Inlet were hidden under a masquerade of snow and ice. Even the barren outback of his homeland had more going for it in the way of landmarks.

Since they had not yet been jumped by angry Mirages or Tornados, he was certain that they had not yet been picked up on radar. That would change quickly enough. Breaking radio silence for the first time in what seemed like days, Travers contacted Jericho and asked for an update on air coverage.

Jericho told him what he wanted to hear. FSAD attention appeared to be directed to the west. Three C-130s or KC-130s were orbiting, but their orbits had drifted westward, away from his approach. Two flights of fighters were airborne, a pair to the west of Primavera and a pair to the north. The western pair would be the ones to watch; they would intersect the exit route.

"All right, Tiger Barbs. Like the American beer drinkers say, it doesn't get any better than this. Let's execute, mates."

"Tiger Two," Nakamura said.

"Three."

They were lolling along at four hundred knots, almost too fast for the close-to-the-ground flight, using less fuel but more nerves. The concentration required for this kind of flying used up human energy at rapid rates.

Travers turned a few degrees to the left, and the ridge seemed to close on him faster. Tiger Barb Two, on his left wing, added power and pulled away, climbing steeply. Tiger Barb Three, on the right, also shoved his throttle to the stop, peeled off to the right, and began to climb.

Nikki Nakamura in Tiger Barb Two was armed with four Sidewinders and two five hundred-pound bombs. He was going to be the diversion factor.

Tiger Barb Three, flown by a German named Oberstein, carried only the Sidewinders for defense. He would climb to thirty thousand feet, and his powerful data receiver would be the receptor of the photographic imagery that Travers's sensors transmitted to him, a backup copy as it were. One or the other of them—or happily both—might get back to the ship with the information the Pack Rat people wanted to have.

Travers's aircraft sported two Sidewinders and a centerline-mounted reconnaissance pod containing video cameras capable of capturing both infrared and true images. The cameras were aimed downward and to either side. He reached out to the auxiliary control panel fixed to the right side of his cockpit and activated the cameras. Then he switched on the transmitter.

"I'm transmitting, Three."

"Hold on," Oberstein said. "There. I am receiving whatever it is you are sending, One. It looks a lot like everything else we are seeing."

"Copy."

Travers put his mind to watching the terrain, working the stick enough to keep the Harrier rising with the increasing altitude of the terrain and to jump a few towering outcrops of rock. Tiger Barb Three was already out of sight, but he could still catch glimpses of Nakamura, about five miles ahead of him and seven thousand feet above him, still climbing.

Nakamura wasn't required to perform any precision bombing. He would let go of his five hundred-pounders from sixteen thousand feet, above the accurate reach of the ZSU-23 Quads, and hope they hit something somewhere on or around the base, creating some confusion and perhaps a little panic. Then he would light out for the west. He would, in fact, be quite a ways into his exit route by the time the bombs struck. On the egress, Nakamura was flying as point aircraft, and he would take on any hostiles who threatened the recon planes.

As soon as the bombs went off, Oberstein would also head west, about fourteen thousand feet above Nakamura. If Tiger Barb Two were intercepted, Oberstein would try to help as long as his assistance didn't endanger the vital information he was receiving from Travers's sensors.

And the ridge passed under him.

Ahead, Travers could make out the oddly scattered shapes of Primavera Station twelve miles ahead. To the right of the main base, there seemed to be neat rows of tents or tent-like shelters. The military mind at work, he thought. Orderly rows and close-cropped hair.

He rolled slightly to the right and brought the nose down to lose a few feet of altitude. The crenelated ridge whisked by off his right wingtip, slowly rising as he brought the Harrier down.

Still holding four hundred knots.

Back on the stick to leap a hummock of ice and rock.

Primavera coming up.

And bang, he was hit by a dozen or more radars. The Radar Homing and Warning Receiver lit up with "A"s, "8"s, and

"9"s, indicating antiaircraft and SA-8 and SA-9 surface-to-air missile radars.

Half of them, he didn't worry about. He was too low and too close for the SAMs.

The others might be a problem.

Nakamura's bombs went off, one and two. He thought one had hit the far end of the runway. A black-and-gray-and-white geyser erupted from the earth, spewing chunks of debris that glinted almost silver in the sun.

Three white-hot streaks rose out of the snowy landscape on the far side of the runway.

"Two, you've got SAMs coming at you," Travers radioed.

"I see them, One. No sweat."

He was five miles out of Primavera when the antiaircraft guns found him and opened up.

They were having to fully depress their muzzles to find him that close to the ground. Bursts of high explosive and shrapnel appeared in smoky gray blossoms all around him, but mostly above the airplane.

Travers began zigzagging, which didn't help the cameras much, but which seemed to help his peace of mind. He kept his track to the east of the base, not passing over it.

He was traveling at almost six miles a minute, and the base was ahead, then there, then behind him. He thought about counting aircraft on the ground, but only got to six before they were gone.

The guns were closing on him.

Nine miles north of Primavera, they found him.

The shell must have exploded beneath him because he didn't see it. The Harrier bucked violently, and nearly went topsy-turvy, careening violently toward the ridge, before he caught it. Several seconds went by before he thought he might be stable.

He looked out the left side of the canopy and discovered

that his left wing was Swiss cheese. He couldn't count the holes in it. Jet fuel was flowing across the wing panels, vaporizing as it left the trailing edge.

"Well, damn it!"

He looked up just in time to see that an outcropping of rock wanted him, so he banked left.

But not much happened.

The airplane barely rolled. He had lost his ailerons.

Travers jerked the stick back, kicked the left rudder pedal, and slammed the throttle full forward.

He was doing 450 knots when the Harrier slammed into solid rock.

UNS U THANT
1307 HOURS LOCAL

"Son of a bitch!" Cady yelped.

"I am truly sorry," McNichols said. His voice issued from the overhead speakers in the CIC. He had just reported that the Harrier had crashed.

"Is there any chance of a survivor?" Eames asked from her position at the console.

"I shouldn't think so, no," McNichols said. "There was no parachute, and the wreckage is burning fiercely."

Everyone in the CIC—Monmouth, Baker, Cady, and Trish O'Hara on the data input console—had lapsed into silence. Cady came abruptly out of his chair, kicking it backwards. It rolled across the deck and slammed into the bulkhead.

"Son of a bitch," he said again.

"Easy up, Jim," Monmouth said.

Eames could feel his pain. It seemed strange. People named Shark didn't feel anguish. She had barely known Travers, but she remembered him as an amiable and laughing man.

Cady leaned over the desk top beside her. She thought he was on the verge of taking her headset from her.

"Pack Rat," she said, to discourage Cady, "do you see the others?"

"I do," McNichols said. "Tiger Barb Two is being pursued by two Mirages. Tiger Barb Three is behind them, but the Mirages are moving faster. To the northeast, Gypsy Moths Five and Six are still circling the ships."

Cady reached out for the desk microphone, which was shoved to one corner of her console.

"Jim," she said, "go chew on a cigar."

He looked at her.

Captain Monmouth touched Cady's shoulder, and he backed away.

"Jericho, Gypsy Five."

"Go, Gypsy."

"The *Inga*," Solomon Sifra reported, "is settling quickly. And now we can tell that there were people on board. We can see lifeboats being launched."

"Jesus!" Monmouth said.

"Are the other ships assisting, Gypsy Five?"

"Not so I would notice, Jericho. Wait. The destroyer has launched a missile at us. We will be busy for a few seconds."

Eames punched the keypad for the Tiger Barb squadron frequency and toed the transmit switch. "Tiger Barb Two, Jericho."

"Two."

"Sitrep, please."

"I am turning maximum revolutions, supersonic at eight-two-zero knots, heading two-six-oh, angels twenty-one, with two bogies seventeen miles behind. I will need to refuel, so please send Jerry Can. I am about to surprise these bastards. Two out."

Eames thought that Nakamura sounded surprisingly calm, given that he had just lost his squadron commander.

"Tiger Three, Jericho. Sitrep?"

"Three, here," Oberstein said. "I am at twenty-eight thousand, in pursuit, twenty-four miles from my target. The Mirages are outrunning me."

Cady started to say something.

Eames said, "Three, don't forget what your recorders have."

"I have not forgotten, Jericho. Three out."

Cady kept his mouth shut.

On the intercom, Eames said, "Beehive, Jericho."

"Beehive," the air controller, Giovanni Este, said.

"Launch Jerry Can One."

"Wilco."

"Allah Akbar!" Sifra shouted over the speakers. "The infidels are shooting at the lifeboats!"

"Goddamn!" Monmouth said.

Eames hit the keypad for the Gypsy squadron.

"What about your SAMs, Gypsy Five?"

"Two more have been launched; we can evade them. I am going to attack the destroyer."

Cady said, "Terri, they're not armed for that."

Eames pressed her toe on the transmit switch. "Gypsy Flight, RTB."

"But Jericho . . ."

"Right now, Gypsies. RTB."

"Gypsy Flight returning to base. Five out."

She went back to the Tiger Barb frequency just as McNichols's voice sounded in the overhead speaker. "Tiger Barb Two has just reversed course. He's taking the Mirages head-on. Four missiles fired."

Eames was about to break in when McNichols added, "By the Mirages."

She thought McNichols was trying very hard to keep his voice steady. There was an undercurrent of vitality that he was trying to suppress, and she supposed it was because he was normally an organizer of information after the fact. He had never before found himself in the middle of the action.

She tried to visualize the scene, the terror of it. One lone Harrier confronting the two faster airplanes and the four missiles.

"Tiger's slowing," McNichols said. "Damn, he's slowing fast!"

"Air brakes," Cady interjected.

"Now he's . . . he's hovering. Dropping. Now, picking up speed, diving. Missile missed. Another . . . all of them missed. Tiger's gone under them and the Mirages are splitting up, turning."

"Good move, Nakamura," Baker said.

"Have you been tutoring him, Archie?" Cady asked.

"No, but I might take lessons from him."

"Tiger Barb Two is climbing now," McNichols said, "gaining speed. He's headed right for Tiger Three. The Mirages have formed up again and are chasing him to the east."

On the squadron frequency, Oberstein said, "Tiger Three, tally-ho! I've got all of you visually, Two."

McNichols reported, "Tiger Two is looping back, taking them head-on again. Hostile missiles launched, two this time. I estimate separation at ten miles. Tiger Three is closing fast, twelve miles out."

"Arm 'em up," Cady said, almost as if he were talking to himself.

Eames glanced up and saw that both Cady and Baker had their eyes locked on the screen. Sergeant Trish O'Hara, her fingers flying over her keyboard, was manually updating the screen display as best she could from the information McNichols was furnishing, but she doubted that the configuration on the screen reflected the actual positions very accurately.

"I wish I had a better scale," McNichols complained. "I'm guessing at distances. They're closing fast, maybe five miles apart. Two dodged the missiles."

"Tiger Two, Fox two!"

"He's launched two." A few seconds later, McNichols added, "The Mirages are splitting up again. I think they just realized that Tiger Three is a threat."

"Tiger Barb Three. Fox two."

Then, from McNichols: "Three's launched two missiles."

Then: "A kill!"

"Damn it, Cam!" Eames said.

"Mirage blown to hell. Sorry, I'm new at this. Missile miss. Another miss."

"Tiger Three, Fox two."

"Three's launched two more."

"He's out of missiles," Cady said. "Bring him home, Terri."

"Tiger Three, Jericho. RTB."

"Wham!" McNichols yelled. "Second Mirage hit! He's . . . whatever . . . tumbling, I guess. I see a parachute."

Three minutes later, the Tiger Barb Harriers were formed up and making Mach 1, asking for rendezvous coordinates with Jerry Can. McNichols reported that two Tornados had turned south at nearly Mach 2, but they had slowed and joined with a tanker. They were out of the picture, as far as interception was concerned. No one seemed to be looking for the parachutist. Eames thought that was a sin in itself, abandoning their pilots to the brutal elements.

Monmouth and Baker left the CIC, and Cady moved to the back bulkhead and flopped in a chair. He was crunching a dead cigar with his teeth.

Eames felt as drained as Cady looked. She rolled her chair backwards and spun around to face him. Voices on the radio continued to chatter in her headset, but they were routine flight information calls to Beehive that she could push to the back of her listening mind.

In the dim red light of the Combat Information Center, Cady's face appeared a little garish.

"Are you all right?" she asked.

He was looking through her, but then focused his eyes and pulled the cigar out of his teeth. "Yeah, Terri, terrific."

"You made the right calls at the right times."

"This commander crap ain't all it's cracked up to be," he said. "Up there, I don't have to really think about it, just do it."

"You did fine."

"You're the cool one, Terri. Sorry I got in your way."

"If you were really bad, I'd have evicted you," she said.

"Next time, do it," Cady said.

"Somehow, I don't think there will be a next time."

His eyes drifted out of focus again, for a few seconds, then came back. "He was a damned good man, Terri. I liked him."

"Yes."

"And I sent him out there."

"And he went," she reminded him.

"Yeah."

"Why don't you go take a nap for an hour or so?" she suggested.

"In a minute."

She moved back to her console, but she was aware that Cady didn't leave.

Not until Giovanni Este and Shaker Adams had the Gypsy Moth and Tiger Barb flights back on the deck.

DEFENSE INTELLIGENCE AGENCY
1420 HOURS LOCAL

The captain of the *Inga* had issued an international distress call as soon as his ship had been torpedoed, reporting forty-seven souls on board and in peril, and a thousand screaming Russian diplomats from all over the world had gone right to the television and newspaper reporters.

The reporters were hungry for any tidbit, and legions of them had been roaming the corridors of the UN for days. Now, they were like rabid dogs, trying to find out what had happened after the *Inga* went off the air.

McNichols was glad he wasn't in New York.

It was a little strange to have the center of attention, in a crisis like this, focused on New York rather than Washington. Bentley, Highwater, Albrecht, and other members of the Peacekeeper Committee had had to barricade the hallway outside the elevator and stairway to their floor. Ambassadors from every nation, and especially from those on the Security Council, were besieged by Pulitzer-dreaming media personalities.

The Pentagon had gotten involved now, and McNichols was sending them copies of the information he was gathering for the PC. He wasn't certain, but he thought that the civilian side of the Department of Defense was hanging back, maybe hoping this thing could be taken care of by the UN. The generals and admirals, though, would be making contingency plans, ready to go when the civilians finally decided it was time to go.

McNichols, in an apparent loss of patriotic zeal, hoped that the U.S. civilians let the international civilians have their way with their brand-new ship.

The funny part was that the reporters didn't know what the Peacekeeper Committee really did, or that it had a resource like the *U Thant* at its disposal. So far, none of the actions of the carrier had made the news. Big Shot Silvera wasn't broadcasting his failures. And he wasn't such a big shot, either. The South American desk had gotten a bio on him. He was just another ex-army colonel on the lookout for himself. He had a few army buddies with him, too, according to best guesses. And a mediocre air force major named Suarez was likely to be involved.

McNichols was also not so glad he was in Washington. He

had never gone through such an adrenaline-producing, tension-raising, pulse-pounding episode before. He was certain he was damned nearly as fatigued as the pilots of those Harriers had to be. He was, in retrospect, quite happy that his eyesight hadn't been up to par when, at eighteen years of age, he'd thought he might like to fly fighter airplanes.

As a kid, he'd been a hell of a gunslinger, popping caps on every Billy the Kid or Jesse James in the neighborhood. As a fighter pilot, he knew he made a better dreamer than a doer.

McNichols was in his office, resting his head on his folded arms on the desk. Jack Neihouse was out in the improvised combat center, trying to get a closer view of the activity around the *San Matias*. At last report, however, the *Inga* and all of her boats had been sunk. Their eyes, several hundred miles in space, hadn't been able to detect any survivors.

Those facts had not yet been released to the newshounds. Bentley was going to use the information at the right time, he said. He hadn't yet told the Russian delegation, either.

He hadn't told McNichols what the right time was, but McNichols supposed it would come in the next hour or so. The zealous cry for new details from the media would push him into disclosure before it possibly came from another source.

He kept having flashbacks. He kept seeing the fiery impact of that Harrier as it smashed into the cliff. He kept wanting to know more about the pilot, and he knew he wouldn't ask.

Playing his personal games with satellites in space wasn't going to be fun anymore.

"Cam?" Pam Akins asked from his doorway.

McNichols raised his head and looked up at her. "It just looks like I was sleeping, Pam. Come on in."

"We just got the recon photos from the airplane."

She crossed the room and dropped the stack on his desk.

"Some of them are pretty bad," she said. "The airplane was jumping all over. But some of them are pretty good, too."

He rifled through the stack, finding both infrared and clear shots. The time and date of the aperture snapping was imprinted in the upper right corner of each photo. He had only to look halfway through the first bunch before he said, "Pam, see if Vern Gadsdale is around, will you?"

Gadsdale was already on the floor. He had been drawn to the UN support section, as had many others, when the action began.

He came into the office and pulled a chair up to the desk.

McNichols gave him the pictures. "They're in the order in which they were taken."

"By the pilot who went down?"

"Yeah."

"I hope to hell they were worth it."

"They were."

"Ah, damn," Gadsdale said. "They've got wells. Way back in the canyons, it looks like."

"Drilling rigs, anyway."

Gadsdale scooted McNichols's phone, Rolodex, and in-baskets aside and began laying out the photos on the desk top. After scrutinizing them carefully for several minutes, he said, "I count at least three. Maybe four, if this blurred shot isn't a duplicate . . . nah, it can't be. We'll have to compare the speed of the plane with the timing of the shots and match it up to the geography."

"It can't be a duplicate, Vern. He was flying too fast. What do you make of the infrared?"

Gadsdale compared two photographs taken at the same instant, one of them in infrared.

"The two tanks on the right are hot, the larger tanks to the left are not. I'm going to say the right tanks hold warmed drilling mud. The others are holding tanks, likely empty. There are lesser degrees of heat coming from within the derrick covering. That's probably space heaters, bodies, friction heat from the drill. Power supplies, too."

"So they're drilling for it, not pumping oil?"

"In these shots, Cam, they're drilling for damned sure. None of these wells are producing, or they'd have switched in pumps in place of the derricks."

"I'm not a petroleum engineer."

"I know," Gadsdale said.

"Which means that they don't yet have solid evidence of oil reserves to show their prospective consortium members."

"Not at these four sites, anyway," Gadsdale said.

McNichols slumped back in his chair. His eyes felt droopy. Pretty soon, he was going to have to take a nap, but he didn't think he could sleep.

Pam Akins stuck her head in the doorway, again.

"The UN Secretary General is on TV, Cam."

"What's he saying?"

"The Security Council just passed a resolution . . ."

"What's the gist of it?"

"They've issued a stern warning to the FSAD about the harsh treatment of civilians."

"Shit," McNichols said.

UNS CALAIS
1457 HOURS LOCAL

"Depth thirty feet, motors stopped," Erik Magnuson reported.

"Battery status?" d'Argamon asked. He was now in the left seat, commanding the submarine.

"Four-two percent, sir."

"Range to the first target?"

"One thousand, two hundred yards," Magnuson said while scanning his sonar scope.

"And that's the large one?"

"The closest, yes, sir. The *San Jorge.*"

That was the minesweeper. D'Argamon really wanted the destroyer, but she was on the far side of the grouping, and he did not believe he could get around to her without being detected. They had gotten this close by moving at less than five knots. If they generated any noise at all, they were certain to be picked up by even the most inept sonar operator on the destroyer.

"Let us have a look, Oscar, but quietly."

The mini-subs did not have periscopes. Instead, they had a tethered television camera on a remotely operated vehicle (ROV) which was controlled by the copilot. Moritz used the joystick and controls set into his right armrest to manipulate the robot, which was secured in a recess on the forward hull.

Watching through his port, d'Argamon saw the robot—three feet long by eighteen inches wide—rise out of the recess, trailing its Kevlar-shielded cable behind it. Slowly, with help from the small propellers mounted at angles on the aft end, the robot swam for the surface. Moritz, leaning forward to peer upward through his own porthole, kept an eye on it as his hand worked the joystick.

The picture appeared on the center multifunction screen as soon as Moritz deployed the camera eye on its stalk rising from the body of the robot. Water sluiced off the lens only to be replaced by droplets blown from the wavetops. The surface was choppy, and the robot rose and fell with the wave action.

Magnuson was leaning forward to watch the screen along with the two pilots.

"Come to the left, Oscar."

The robot rotated, and the vessels came into view. Whenever the robot fell into a trough, they disappeared behind the waves, but d'Argamon soon had them positioned in his mind. The minesweeper was closest, and two patrol boats were fore and aft of her. A half-mile beyond them was the destroyer. He did not see the *Inga* anywhere near.

The patrol boats seemed to be sweeping the area. Occasionally, one would stop and a crewman would scoop something from the water with a net on a long pole.

"I think they proceeded to sink the Russian ship, Commander," Moritz said.

"That appears to be the case," d'Argamon said.

From the time they left their station ahead of the *U Thant,* they had been out of communications contact. He considered a brief message on the low frequency radio, then decided against it. The risks were high enough without broadcasting their presence.

Magnuson, kneeling on the deck between the front seats, said, "Commander, do you see the life preservers?"

D'Argamon leaned forward and perused the screen carefully. Perhaps a dozen ring buoys were floating on the surface amid the jetsam and flotsam that had floated free of the freighter when she went down. As he watched, an elongated object rolled to the top of a wave.

"A body!" Magnuson yelled.

Except for the movement caused by the sea, the body was inanimate. Its head was dipped forward as it floated in a jacket preserver. The sailors on the patrol boat ignored it.

That vision would be impressed upon his mind for a long time, d'Argamon thought—men of the sea paying no heed to a human being, dead or not. The rage began to boil within him.

"Retrieve the robot. Magnuson, determine a firing solution for us—first the minesweeper, then the patrol boats. Arm the torpedoes."

"At once, Commander," Magnuson replied, sliding back to his seat and bending over his keyboard.

Within seconds, twelve green LEDs on the instrument panel confirmed that the torpedoes were on-line and armed, with the torpedo tube doors opened. The submarine's torpedoes were Mk 46s, weighing 568 pounds each, and normally used in an antisubmarine role. Larger, more sophisticated weapons were too unwieldy for the tiny sub. Still, with their active homing guidance system, they were accurate and would serve d'Argamon's purpose well.

The robot settled into her parking place, and the tiny whine of the cable winch died away.

"We want two for the minesweeper," he said.

"Yes, sir."

The only sound in the sub was that of the ordnance specialist's fingers tapping on his keyboard. After a short interval, he said, "I have solutions, Commander. Torpedoes One and Two for the minesweeper."

"Lock it in," he ordered.

Magnuson ordered the computer to maintain the firing solutions, and the computer would make any adjustments necessary by changes in their position. The minesweeper was easy; she was nearly dead in the water. The patrol boats were roving, but at slow speeds.

"Five knots forward," d'Argamon said.

"Aye, sir, five knots forward," Moritz told him, advancing the motor control.

The *Calais* eased into forward motion.

D'Argamon wanted to get as close as possible, to increase his chances for success.

"One thousand yards," Magnuson said.

He waited.

"Nine hundred yards."

Just a little more.

"Sir, the minesweeper is turning screws. They have spotted us."

An active and nearby sonar began pinging them.

"Fire all tubes."

"Aye, sir," Moritz said as he selected and fired each of the torpedoes.

The hull vibrated as, in sequence, the eight-foot-long torpedoes were ejected from the tubes by compressed air, then appeared ahead of them, their propellers churning the gray-green water and leaving a sparkling silver trail behind. The first two curved away to the right, and the second pair went left, quickly separating from each other.

"Close the torpedo doors, ahead full speed, take full ballast on the bow tanks. Full diving planes, coming left ninety degrees."

D'Argamon intoned the instructions aloud, as a warning for his crewmen, even though he controlled the diving planes and rudder. Moritz repeated the order as he advanced the power lever and started the pump on the ballast tank.

The submarine's bow settled steeply and she went to nearly forty-five degrees of angle in her rush for deep water.

"One hundred feet," Magnuson intoned. "The fish are running true."

Deeper. Safety depended on depth.

"Three hundred feet. Active sonars pinging us. The destroyer has us now. She's starting to move."

The torpedoes began to detonate, the concussions coming in staggered gasps and ringing against the hull.

"Two hits on the minesweeper!"

D'Argamon had returned the diving planes to neutral, but he kept the rudder hard left, corkscrewing toward the bottom.

"Another hit, one patrol boat. The last fish missed the target. Five hundred feet."

Down and down. The light coming through the ports deepened.

"The destroyer is on the move. She's still coming our way. Six hundred feet of depth."

"Let us have half speed now, Oscar. We want to start losing our cavitation noise."

When he was aimed eastward,·intending to pass under the destroyer, d'Argamon centered the rudder and began to ease the rate of descent.

"Take on ballast in the stern tanks."

"Aye, Commander," Moritz said.

"Eleven hundred feet."

A little more depth, and he would find the layer of colder water he had noted earlier. The line of temperature change would help to disguise them.

"They have a solid sonar lock," Magnuson said.

"Four knots, Oscar."

"Aye, four knots."

The submarine slowed and continued to sink.

"Torpedoes!" Magnuson called out. "One . . . two . . . three of them."

THE SAN MATIAS
1514 HOURS LOCAL

A damnable submarine!

Diego Enriquez could not believe it.

His sonar operators had to have been sleeping.

It should never have gotten this close.

The general quarters Klaxon was still squalling, and men were racing about the ship, attempting to reach their duty stations. The only fortune in his day was that the portside torpedo tube crew had been drilling at the time of the attack and were immediately to hand.

"Bridge, sonar."

Enriquez punched the button. "Bridge."

"The target has gone under us. Depth four-five-seven meters, bearing zero-eight-five, range three hundred meters."

"Helm, hard to starboard," Enriquez ordered.

"Sir! Hard to starboard."

The destroyer heeled ten degrees to the starboard side as she began to come about.

The torpedoes went off, spewing columns of water high in the air.

"Bridge, Sonar."

"Sonar, Bridge," Enriquez said.

"All misses."

"Goddamn it!"

"Bridge, Comm."

"Bridge," he answered as Commander Montez rushed onto the bridge, sliding to a stop before the engineroom telegraph.

"Sir, the *San Jorge* is requesting assistance to take off survivors. Captain Mellendez says he cannot save her."

Enriquez glanced out the port window. The minesweeper was listing badly to port, and black smoke spumed from her ventilators. Soon, he knew, raw red flames would reach the deck from her lower spaces. The railings were lined with men screaming and waving. It was too reminiscent of a scene he had just witnessed, and in fact, had initiated.

Four hundred meters to the north of the minesweeper, the burning remnants of Patrol Boat Seven were beginning to sag beneath the surface. The boat had taken its torpedo in the magazine and erupted like a miniature atomic blast. Patrol Boat Four was circling the debris, searching for survivors, but without apparent luck.

He looked back to the *San Jorge*. She, too, had had sonar operators who slept at their posts. It was difficult to feel remorse for her; had she protected herself, he would not now have lost a third of his capital ships.

"Sir, the *San Jorge*—" the communications technician said.

"Send Patrol Boat Four to her assistance," the captain ordered.

"But, sir, there are a hundred and forty men aboard."

"They will have to do as best they can. We are busy; we have a submarine to catch"

JAGUAR LEADER
1545 HOURS LOCAL

Emilio Suarez had been on the ground on *Isla Navarino* when the hostile aircraft attacked Primavera. He had taken off as soon as he could, escorting the last two C-130s which were heavily laden with supplies and ordnance.

When Primavera Control notified him of the submarine attack, he called on two patrolling Tornados to assume the escort and turned his Mirage westward, cursing all the way.

The gray sea was littered with icebergs, and it took him a few minutes to find the ships when he reached the area.

He was forced to correct himself.

Ship.

And one patrol boat.

The *San Matias* was ten kilometers northeast of the patrol boat, and he could tell by her wake that she was making wide-ranging search sweeps. That alone told him she was unsuccessful in her attempt to find the submarine.

He flew on past her and made a low pass over the patrol boat, which was escorting six lifeboats, all tied in a train behind her. Each of them was loaded with men, many of them swathed in white bandages. The frigid wind and sea seemed to be taking its toll. Greenish water splashed high on the boats and cascaded over the sides. Most of the men were crouched into tiny balls, hiding below the gunwales.

He banked to the left and circled the boats, wagging his wings at them. Heading back toward the destroyer, he dialed the naval frequency on his primary radio.

"San Matias, this is Jaguar Leader."

A minute later, by the time he was orbiting the destroyer, he had Enriquez on the other end.

"Captain," he said, "you must go pick up your survivors."

"I have, Colonel, a submarine at bay. I will not leave it now to escape and then return to sink more of my ships."

"But you must," Suarez insisted. "Men are dying."

"More will die if this submarine is let loose."

"Captain, I order you to return to the lifeboats."

"I do not accept your orders," Enriquez told him.

"Diego," Juan Silvera's voice broke into the channel, "it would be best if you did as Emilio suggests."

"But *Presidente.* . . ."

"Our men are a valuable asset, Diego, and we will need all of them that we can muster. Let us not squander them."

Suarez rolled out of his orbit and took up a heading for Primavera.

With all the difficulties suddenly appearing before them, he thought that Captain Diego Enriquez might also pose a problem.

UNS U THANT
2210 HOURS LOCAL

Captain Samuel Monmouth left his stateroom and used the cross-corridor to take himself to the starboard side of the ship. He walked up the carpeted hallway to the communications compartment and let himself in.

Eames was there, and she and the duty officer came to attention.

"As you were. Am I late?"

"No, sir," Eames said. "It'll be a couple more minutes."

"Any word from d'Argamon?" he asked.

"I just checked with Luigi, Captain. Nothing yet."

McNichols's office had reported the sinking of the *San Jorge* and one patrol boat, so Monmouth had already determined that the Frenchman's mission was to be rated a success. The satellite had also recorded the destroyer *San Matias* engaged in a search pattern, though she had finally given that up. They didn't know whether she had given up because d'Argamon had eluded them or fallen prey to one of the many torpedoes she had launched.

Monmouth was getting a little anxious. He wanted to know whether or not he could call the mission a complete success.

"Here we go," the duty officer said.

"Put it on the overhead," Monmouth told him.

"Aye, aye, sir."

There was a lot of static in the transmission coming from the overhead speaker, but he could hear, "Jericho, Raccoon."

Eames settled at the console and took the microphone.

"Raccoon, this is Jericho."

David George's voice didn't sound as gung ho as it had a couple days before, Monmouth thought.

"You're breaking up a little, Jericho, but here's the status. We spent the whole day under cover because of the clear skies. We're underway now, approximately twenty-five miles from the target. Personnel condition is excellent."

Monmouth wondered if George was embroidering the status of his people a little. They had spent a long time in the cold.

"Raccoon, per order of Flagstaff"—Monmouth's code name—"you have a change in objective."

There was a long pause, then George said, "I will need an authorization code for any changes."

"Foxtrot Tango," she said.

"All right. The change?"

Eames had a map with her, updated from the photos shot by Travers, to give her approximate locations for the drilling sites east of Primavera. Monmouth thought she described their locations and hidden conditions to George very well.

"We're to capture drilling rigs?"

Eames looked up to him.

"Blow the hell out of them."

"Raccoon, Flagstaff says to blow the hell out of them."

"Copy, destroy the rigs. Secondary objective?"

"You then go back to your original orders."

"How soon can he make it?" Monmouth asked.

Eames repeated the question.

"Let me talk to my guide." A minute later, George continued, "Maybe by early morning, but that's doubtful. Depends on the terrain. The next morning is more likely."

"Copied. Hold on."

Eames looked up to Monmouth.

"Make it 0230 hours, 10 December," he decided. That would be close to the sleepiest part of the night for any defenders, and they wouldn't have to push as hard, risking the chance of being spotted en route to the targets."

Eames repeated the information, then added, "The met report is for high winds and more snow."

"I know. My guide already predicted it."

She signed off, "Jericho out."

"Raccoon out."

Eames got up from the console, and Monmouth opened the door for her.

As they walked down the corridor toward the bridge together, Monmouth told her, "Sir Charles is going to hold a press conference in the morning."

"On the ship sinkings?"

"Yes. He suggested that we probably don't want to miss his stellar performance."

"Very well, sir."

Monmouth stopped with her as she pushed the button for the elevator.

"Captain?"

"Yes?"

"Have you talked to Cady?"

"About?"

"Ah, well, he seemed pretty disturbed this afternoon."

"He'll be fine, Terri."

The doors quietly slid open behind her, and she stepped in. "Yes, I'm sure he will be."

The doors whispered closed, leaving Monmouth alone. He stood there, staring at the door.

She's in love with him, he thought, but also remembered that he was frequently in error about romantic relationships.

He didn't need love getting in the way of the operational orders he was expected to carry out.

Heading for the bridge, he thought pleasant thoughts about a Maine coastline.

9 DECEMBER

Cady hadn't enjoyed his breakfast, leaving his sausage and scrambled eggs unfinished. He blamed his lack of appetite on d'Argamon's and Moritz's high spirits. They were holding court in one corner of the wardroom, rehashing with supposed accuracy their attack run on the *San Jorge* and their subsequent narrow escape from the torpedoes of the *San Matias*.

The *Calais* had in fact suffered some minor damage. Concussion from a torpedo, depleted of fuel and automatically detonating nearby, had disabled an electric motor control module, and the three crewmen had suffered an agonizingly long couple of hours suspended lopsided at 1800 feet of depth while Erik Magnuson crawled around in the aft engineering spaces and eventually bypassed the control board manually. They had not returned to the *U Thant* until well after midnight with their batteries exhausted, running on the auxiliary diesel engine.

When he couldn't take any more of the ego presentations, Cady refilled his coffee mug and carried it up a deck to his stateroom.

Monmouth was waiting in the corridor for him, leaning against the bulkhead outside his door.

"Did I miss a summons, Captain?"

"Nope. I came down to watch your TV, if that's all right?"

"Sure," Cady said, opening his door. "I don't suppose we want the 'Today Show'?"

"Bentley's holding a press conference at eight. We'll get it live on Channel Three."

With the compartment door closed, Cady was free to be more personal with Monmouth. He set his coffee on the desk top and said, "I can offer you orange juice, Sam."

"That'll do it," Monmouth said, taking the single easy chair.

Cady found his juice supply in the refrigerator, poured a tall glass, and passed it to the captain. Then he used the remote control to turn on the television set, mounted on the bulkhead above the end of the bed, and keyed in Channel Three. The screen was blank, and he turned down the volume to eliminate the hissing white noise.

Cady retrieved his coffee cup and sat on the edge of the bed. He looked expectantly to his commander.

"I think this is planned so we've got fifteen minutes," he said. "Is this where we have a heart-to-heart?"

"Eames is worried about you."

That surprised Cady, first that she'd worry, and second that she'd go to Monmouth to express it.

"She doesn't even like me, Sam."

Monmouth's face didn't show a reaction to that statement. He said, "And I'm a little concerned, myself."

"I've got it under control, Sam."

"Do you? Did you play football, Jim?"

"Football? Yeah, in high school. Halfback."

"I'll bet you didn't care who called the shots—the coach or the quarterback, as long as you got to carry the ball."

Cady reflected on that. Probably true. Hell, it *was* true.

"Much as we'd like to be," Monmouth continued, "we can't always be where the action is, making the snap decisions to go left or right or over. Some of us end up as coaches, and we send the right kid in with the right play, but we can't control the defense or the turf. If the kid trips up, we send in the next kid with the next right play."

"I hear what you're saying, Sam," Cady said, not that he liked it.

"Guilt goes with the job, Jim. I don't want to see you assigning yourself to every mission because you know you're the best aviator and you think you should be taking the highest risks."

"I don't . . ."

"Who's going to replace Travers as squadron commander?"

"Phil's got the 1st Squadron pretty well in hand," Cady said. "I thought I'd take the 2nd."

"No. You'll tie yourself up in routine, and you need to roam a little. Give me a name."

Cady sipped his coffee. It was getting cold. He looked up at the TV just as the screen flickered and Connie Chung appeared.

"There's Connie," he said, reaching for the remote.

"A name, Jim."

"Stein's proven himself. He should probably have it."

"But?"

"But, he's a bit headstrong, a little mercurial."

"I've never met anyone remotely like that," Monmouth said, letting the sarcasm drip.

Cady let it slide off. "He needs more time. Nikki Nakamura is solid, though, both as an aviator and decision maker. I'll name him."

"Fine by me," Monmouth said. "Anything else we need to talk about?"

Cady grinned at him. "Eames was worried about me?"

"You want to turn up Connie?"

Cady got the volume adjusted just as Chung finished her introduction and the picture changed to that of Sir Charles Bentley. He was standing just outside the UN Building before a bouquet of microphones in a breeze that ruffled his gray hair and made his ears appear to stand out more than they actually did. A few flakes of snow drifted in the air.

"I'm glad to know it snows in New York, too," Cady said.

"Try Maine sometime. It's better there."

Compared to the conditions in the Antarctic, the path through the Drake Passage that the *U Thant* was following, now at twelve knots, was positively balmy. Still, not many of her crew took leisurely walks on the deck. The skies were overcast, the wind kicked waves into twelve- and fifteen-foot monsters, and when it snowed, the brittle flakes clung to the steel decks and transformed themselves into sheet ice. Cady had decided that he'd just as soon avoid snow in the future, no matter where it was.

Because of the ice on the deck, Cady had not scheduled any Harrier flights for the morning. Two helos from the 11th Squadron were flying patrol chores at the moment.

The snow he saw on the TV screen didn't make him feel much better about the weather. Some of it began to stick to the shoulders of the chairman's coat. The lapels of Bentley's topcoat were made of mink or something similar, Cady thought. He hoped to hell it wasn't seal fur. Bentley looked very solid, standing there, all alone, and Cady supposed he was taking a lot of political heat that wasn't showing in his face just yet.

Looking at the committee chairman on the small screen, and then glancing over at Monmouth, he was happy that he was working for people like Bentley and Monmouth.

Bentley cleared his throat and said, "Good morning to you all, and thank you for coming, ladies and gentlemen. I have a short statement, and then I'll take questions.

"First, I will confirm the rumors that have been making circles among you. Unfortunately, the Front for South American Determination did, in fact, carry out its threat and sink the Russian vessel *Inga* on December 7th at one o'clock in the afternoon. Our intelligence estimates at this time suggest that all persons on board perished. . . ."

"How many, Sir Charles?" some reporter yelled.

"According to the captain of the vessel, there were forty-seven people on board. Please wait with your questions. We are currently trying to verify that number. We do know, and we do have photographic evidence, that many died while in lifeboats launched from the *Inga*. The boats were sunk by gunfire from the FSAD destroyer *San Matias*."

A barrage of questions erupted from the reporters, and Bentley waved them away.

"At the time, FSAD patrol boats and a minesweeper were on the scene, but none of them went to the assistance of the victims.

"As a consequence, the Peacekeeper Committee of the United Nations Security Council ordered a retaliatory strike, and the minesweeper *San Jorge* and one patrol boat were attacked by United Nations forces at two-thirty in the afternoon of the same day and sunk. Hostile casualties are unknown at this time, though the attacking force suffered no losses."

Cady noted that this was the first public announcement that the UN had a military presence in the area.

"The United Nations Security Council wishes to make clear to the Front for South American Determination, and to President Juan Silvera, that it will not tolerate terrorism or barbarism. All such future acts will meet with immediate retaliation as long as we proceed to carry out the mandates of United Nations Security Council Resolution 233.

"Now, if you please, your questions."

"What United Nations forces?" was the first question, posed by a hawk-faced lady in the front ranks of the reporters, waving her hand wildly for the camera panning the media gathering.

"In the interest of security," Bentley said, "we will not discuss either the type or the size of the military resources available to the Security Council. As far as I know, the Council is not declaring a war, but it will use the appropriate amount of force necessary to compel the Front for South American Determination to comply with the dictates of the resolution."

Bentley recognized a British correspondent, whom he apparently knew. "Yes, Geoffrey?"

"I have heard from several sources, Sir Charles, that the Russians are considering a separate action, in response to the sinking of the *Inga*. Can you respond to that?"

"The appropriate forum for complaints is the Security Council, in my view," Bentley told him. "We who are members have listened carefully to the comments from the Russian delegation, and I am certain that their concerns have been addressed by the Council."

Monmouth told Cady, "He didn't come right out and tell the whole world that the Russians are mobilizing a few hundred air transports and escort fighters out of Cam Ranh Bay."

That forced Cady to switch his attention from the screen to his boss. "They're doing that?"

"According to McNichols. New Zealand has given them permission to land at Christchurch, ostensibly in preparation for a relief and evacuation effort of their other bases in Antarctica."

"And what do you think, Sam?"

"If that's all they're doing, fine. If it's cover for an independent air strike, then we'd better get our job completed, first. And the Russians aren't alone in this migration, Jim. Reporters are gathering by the hundreds in Christchurch and Buenos Aires, asking the FSAD for permission to fly to Primavera in order to cover the story live. So far, and fortunately, they've been denied access."

The rest of the press conference was predictable. Bentley professed to be unaware of a concerted effort by some South American nations to overturn the resolution. The key word there was "concerted." It allowed Bentley to dance around the question.

He did not mention, and no reporter thought to ask about, other kinds of military action that might be taking place. The concept of scientists as hostages and the evacuation of the stations did not arise, either. Cady thought that Bentley operated on the principle of not volunteering information.

He was patient with those reporters who seemed to be hard-of-hearing and asked the same questions over and over. Cady had often thought that press conferences could be half as long as they were, if the reporters bothered to listen to the answers given to other reporters.

When Connie Chung came back with a stable of political, academic, and retired military experts from Los Angeles, Philadelphia, Washington, and Boston, who would determine what Bentley was *really* saying, Cady shut off the set.

Monmouth stood up. "Are we clear on the game of football, Jim?"

"I won't take myself entirely out of the action, Sam."

"I wouldn't expect that, but you don't have to carry the whole load."

"I'll spread it out," he promised, though he didn't know if he could live up to the resolution.

"You don't want to be a d'Argamon, after all," the captain told him.

Irritating as it might be, though, Cady had to admit that Jean d'Argamon had accomplished his mission rather thoroughly.

PRIMAVERA BASE
0915 HOURS LOCAL

President Juan Silvera met with his commanders in the small living room of the station manager's hut. Enriquez had fought a stiffening wind to fly in by helicopter from the *San Matias* half an hour earlier. Fuentes, who was not a commander, stayed near the kitchen door and the coffeepot.

Silvera stood with his back to the oil-fired stove, his hands clasped behind his back. He was having difficulty staying warm. His spine seemed to be permanently chilled. The view through the small window of swirling, wind-driven snow did not warm him.

Enriquez, sitting in one of the straight-backed chairs by the table, nursing a mug of coffee, was irritated about being called away from his ship. He was also, no doubt, blaming Silvera and Suarez for his failure to locate and destroy the submarine that had sunk the minesweeper and one of his patrol boats. He seemed to have no remorse whatsoever for those who had died—twenty-two—when his two vessels went down.

Enriquez's motivations were almost too simplistic, Silvera thought. He liked to be in command, and he probably liked to kill people. Silvera had often thought that greed was a much loftier goal.

Suarez, on the sofa, just looked worried.

"Gentlemen," Silvera said, "we obviously have a major problem. In our preinvasion planning, everyone—and I mean everyone"—looking at Ricardo Fuentes who leaned against the kitchen doorway—"assured me that we would have forty-five to ninety days of unencumbered activity before the United Nations could assemble a reaction force.

"We barely have our toes dug in. Our supplies and materiel are disorganized. We still have fuel reserves on Navarino. Our defenses are not yet in permanent sites. The missions of our aircraft have been altered. Our shield of hostages at adjacent stations has evaporated. Unless we use the Chileans and Argentineans at Esperanza, Marambio, O'Higgins, Tenient Rodolfo, or Captain Arturo Prat as hostages, they are no longer a protective factor. And we cannot use them, of course, without losing the support of Chile and Argentina."

"There are still many foreign bases within reach of our fighters, *Presidente,*" Suarez said.

"Yes. Perhaps there are. Unless the opposing forces are in a position to intercept our strikes. Can anyone here tell me where the United Nations has based its aircraft?"

None of his subordinates could answer the question, naturally. The press conference of Sir Charles Bentley this morning had provided the first confirmation that his unseen adversaries were indeed United Nations aviators and sailors.

"It is most fortunate that we have television, is it not, gentlemen? Otherwise, I would have no intelligence at all. And is it not a shame that Sir Charles Bentley did not provide us with details?"

No one wanted to respond to that, either.

"Despite the assurances I was given, within days we are under attack by fighter aircraft, helicopters, and unbelievably a submarine. We have lost seven aircraft and two vessels. Thirty-nine men are dead, and twenty-one men are taxing the ability of the field hospital to treat them.

"On the scorecard, in our column, we can count one helicopter and one airplane as trophies. Does anyone here disagree with this assessment?"

Suarez said, "I examined the site of the wreckage personally. The fighter was a Harrier, which suggests two things, *Presidente.*"

"Enlighten me."

"First of all, the aircraft carrier may be much smaller than we thought at first, which is why we are having difficulty locating it. Secondly, our fighters are superior in capability."

"Yes. The score sheet tells me of our superiority. These airplanes come at us from the west and from the southeast. They appear to surprise you every time, Colonel Suarez."

"Our ground-based defenses performed very well," Suarez insisted. "One bomb hit the end of the runway, already repaired. The second bomb missed anything of significance. The antiaircraft fire and missiles drove them off."

"I reviewed the radar tapes, Colonel," Silvera told him. "The bomber stayed well above the range of the guns. It was not precision bombing. I suspect it was merely a diversion for the aircraft we shot down. That one flew a straight line alongside the ridge, staying away from the base, and I have no doubt but that it was on a reconnaissance mission, taking pictures of the wells. Do not forget that I was at drilling site number two when the attack occurred. I *saw* the damnable intruder as he went by."

Enriquez placed his mug carefully on the table. "Do you think then, *Presidente,* that the wells have been discovered?"

Silvera had been pondering that very question throughout the long night. "I believe we may have contained the damage by shooting down the airplane. Still, someone somewhere has a suspicion, or the UN would not have flown the mission. They knew specifically where to look."

"It has to be the tracks in the snow," Suarez said. "They are discernible from the air."

"We must protect the drilling sites at all costs, or our support from the member nations will evaporate. And we must protect our remaining military resources. We have lost too much already."

The three men in the room nodded their concurrence of what Silvera thought was all too obvious.

"And we have made major mistakes," Silvera said, looking directly at Enriquez. "Shooting down the French airplane was a mistake. Killing the Russians was a terrible mistake."

Enriquez looked back at him, apparently unperturbed.

"We have public relations problems, on top of our military problems."

No one disagreed with his assessment.

"Tell me what we are to do."

They all looked at each other, and finally, Fuentes straightened up from his slouch in the doorway. "We must, first of all," he said, "intensify our efforts at the United Nations. We have Argentina and Chile in our corner—"

"Those two were a given, from the beginning," Silvera reminded him.

"But, *Presidente,* with another five or six votes—"

"The other eleven nations all know of our proposal, Ricardo. Some are to the point of negotiating percentages, yet all want to see evidence of the first barrels of crude oil before they will commit." Silvera waved his arm in the general direction of the ridge. "If we do not protect those drilling sites, and the men working them, we will not achieve the negotiated settlement that you planned on. Your problem, Ricardo, is that you always foresaw a political solution, and you cannot adapt to the reality.

"The reality is that we are faced with a military problem long before we anticipated the possibility, and we must overcome the military obstacle in order to make the political moves that will be our salvation."

Silvera surveyed his subordinates and could not resist shaking his head in wonder. It never changed. The reservations he had harbored silently from the initiation of this scheme were being fulfilled. It seemed to him that most of the men he had met in his life, whether in the military or in political circles, had had elevated perceptions of their own beings. They saw themselves as grand strategists when in fact their shortcomings should have been apparent, if not to themselves, then to their colleagues.

Ricardo Fuentes imagined himself as a superb politician, a manipulator of people from the background, a weaver of intrigues, the successor in fame to Juan Perón. Diego Enriquez was but a bully who would never have seen command if it were not for friends who saw profit in utilizing his ruthlessness. And Emilio Suarez was perhaps competent, but the ideals that drove him were less nationalistic than personal. Worse, while he might have been an able mechanic, he was not the craftsman he thought himself. He could deal with the science, but the art escaped him.

Not that Silvera would place himself much above them. He had some vision, yes, but his disillusionment with the progress of his own life and its unfulfilled expectations had led him to this enterprise as the means to achieve a final few years of comfort.

He turned slightly to face the navy man.

"Diego?"

The naval commander leaned forward and handed his mug to Fuentes. "Fill that for me."

Fuentes frowned, but took the mug into the kitchen.

"We must," Enriquez said, "show our resolve by enforcing the one-hundred-kilometer territorial limit."

"You would thin out your resources that much, knowing now that you are stalked by submarines?"

"I will not be caught unaware the next time. The captain of that submarine is a dead man."

Silvera shook his head again. "No, Diego. You do not have the assets with which to promote that design. The successful completion of a well is our single and only goal at this time, and in view of that, you must bring all your vessels back to the coast."

"That is stupidity," Enriquez said.

"Remember that we answer to a higher body. Recall the patrol boats from the Shetlands. Order the *Marguerite Bay* to return from the south."

"And how am I to locate the United Nations carrier if I do that?"

"You will not worry about the carrier. Or the submarine, unless either come into range of your guns or missiles."

Silvera shifted his attention to his air commander. "Emilio, we will be needing more jet fuel. Send three of the tankers for it. We will tighten the air defense, stop flying such extended patterns."

"But we will lose our long-distance radar coverage, *Presidente*."

"So be it. As it is, we allow large gaps in our defenses, through which the hostile aircraft easily penetrate. And the C-130s are defenseless. Tighten it up. Keep six or eight aircraft on the ground on alert."

"That is wearing on the aircrews," Suarez said.

"It is wearing on all of us. The runway is, however, vulnerable, and we must protect it. If we lose it, your aircrews will have many hours in which to rest. While we are at it, move the base radar antenna to the top of the ridge. We have a blind spot to the east and southeast, and we must eliminate that."

"We may not have enough cable to accomplish that."

"Then get the cable. Or should I run and get it?"

"No, *Presidente*."

"Now, go and accomplish this before more UN Harriers harass us."

They stood up, but Suarez said, "If we do not keep our extended radar coverage, a massed attack by sixty or seventy aircraft will wipe us out, *Presidente*."

"There will not be a massed attack."

"You are certain of this?" Suarez asked.

"It is partly instinctual, Emilio, and partly based on the facts. I have reviewed the past encounters, and I believe we are dealing with a small force. Armand Calvera says he needs less than a week to bring in the first two wells. If we are diligent and alert, we can hold them off for that long. And I also believe we will not see reinforcements for the United Nations ship for the forty-five to ninety days that we first envisioned. By then, they will be too late."

As the two men donned their parkas and left, Silvera looked to Fuentes who had emerged from the kitchen with Enriquez's mug.

"I may have surprised myself, Ricardo. I actually believe what I just said. This is still winnable, and it is but a few days away."

FALCON ONE
1540 HOURS LOCAL

The Sea Apache was pitching and yawing the closer she came to her intended targets.

Baker had often told his gunner, Henry Decker, that the helicopter talked to him in little ways: body language, the particular changing nuances in the whine of the turbines, the feel of the stick and the collective in his hands.

"What's she saying to you now, Major?" Decker asked on the ICS.

"She objects to her current flight level, Henry."

"I do, too, Major. Can she and I vote on this?"

"We are not being overly democratic at this time, I'm afraid. I get to be dictator."

"You could at least be a benevolent one," Decker said.

Baker was skimming the sea at sixty feet of altitude, with Falcon Four on his right, trying to match both his altitude and speed. The Apaches were armed with 2.75-inch rocket pods and a Royal Navy Sea Skua antiship missile on each stub wing. The two helicopters had four missiles between them, which Baker felt was sufficient for the three patrol boats they were seeking.

The boats were reported by Pack Rat to be en route from the Shetland Islands to the peninsula, holding a steady course that Baker and his wingman could easily intercept.

If they could even see the Shetland Islands or the peninsula. Thirty miles ahead, a low line of white against the gray sea was not landfall, but a building storm. The precursor of the storm, angry winds, had already reached them, and the turbulence made sea-surfing flight a gambling situation. At any moment, a sudden downdraft could smash them into the sea.

Just as he thought that less comforting thought, the nose of the Sea Apache dipped, the rotors lost lift for a second, and he was suddenly at thirty feet above sea level.

"All right, Henry, I acknowledge your vote," Baker said.

He eased back on the stick and climbed to 150 feet, with Falcon Four trailing him in apparent glee.

"Falcon One, Jericho," Luigi Maroni said.

"Jericho, Falcon."

"Squawk me once, please."

Baker activated the Identification Friend or Foe transponder briefly. The *U Thant* was in a position now where the ship's radar could keep them in view for most of their flight toward the peninsula.

"Thank you, Falcon. You are so low that I receive only sporadic return from the ground clutter. Your targets are now at your heading one-six-eight, range four-six miles. There is an overflight of two Mirages at two-one-four miles, your heading one-four-three."

"Copy, Jericho. Falcon out."

Baker corrected his heading by four degrees to the right. He was battling a quartering wind off his right rear.

"I just did a little navigating job, Major."

"And what did you discover, Henry?"

"That we have an eighty mile per hour tail wind."

"I thought we were covering the distance rather rapidly."

"In this direction, yes. The return might be another matter."

Baker checked his fuel state, which was all right at the moment. He also checked the horizon, which was not all right. The storm seemed to be zooming in on them, and this was not a ground-level blizzard. The cloud formation, now an ugly concrete color, climbed to almost thirty thousand feet.

"Have you got a plan, Henry?"

"I did have, yes. Now, however, after considering our environment, I believe we don't need to be as close as I planned. We can light off the Skuas at eight-and-a-half miles, cross our fingers in regard to a hit, turn our tail south, and run like foxes before the hounds."

"Sounds good to me," Baker told him.

On the squadron frequency, Baker told his wingman, "Four, take greater separation, go to one thousand feet, release missiles at your earliest opportunity, and RTB."

"Four."

The two helicopters spread apart to avoid a collision as the sky darkened and visibility dropped. Brittle snowflakes began to click against the windscreen. The wind velocity ebbed and flowed, bouncing Baker against his harness when the chopper bucked. After a few minutes of being tossed around, Baker was certain his body would be showing bruises from the harness for weeks.

"Going active," Decker said.

"Go."

Decker switched his radar from the passive mode, then soon reported, "Targets, three of them, two-nine miles. Come right two degrees."

The Apache was yawing, forced by the inconstant wind on her flanks, over an arc greater than two degrees. Combined with the ten- and fifteen-foot drops and rises as the lift changed on her, she wasn't responding well to fine-tuning.

"If you'd give me a plus or minus ten degrees tolerance, Henry, we'd be just fine."

"Two-six miles."

Decker's clipped response suggested the man wasn't happy with their situation, an attitude he rarely took no matter how bad the conditions were.

They were in the thick of the snowstorm now, but it was an eerie and strange place to be. The dark clouds above filtered out the sun, and though it was four o'clock in the afternoon, it felt like twilight.

The snow particles were frozen so hard, they were nearly the same as miniature hailstones. They clattered against the windscreen so hard they could almost be heard above the roar of the turbines and the deafening effect of his helmet earphones. Baker *thought* he could hear them, anyway.

He was glad the windscreen was armored.

And he began to worry about ice forming on the rotors. It was not an unheard-of phenomenon.

The Apache was talking to him more urgently. The collective felt stiff and unresponsive.

"Two-four out," Decker reported.

Abruptly, the helicopter whipped into a left bank. Instinctively, Baker reversed it and found level flight again, watching the turn-and-bank symbol on his multifunction screen.

"Falcon One, Four."

"One."

"This is getting pretty rough, One."

Baker was about to send him back when Decker said on the ICS, "You remember a line about, 'the better part of valor'?"

"You're absolutely right, Henry. There is another day." On the tactical channel, he said, "Four, abort and RTB."

"Roger that, One, with pleasure."

The Sea Apache fought her way into a left turn—away from

the area where Falcon Four might be flying—and assaulted the head winds.

"You do realize, Major, that I am extremely disappointed by this turn . . . of events."

"I know you are, Henry."

PRIMAVERA BASE
2300 HOURS LOCAL

The weather was absolutely abominable, and Tellez remembered with some longing one of his profitable sojourns in Angola, where he had spent the better part of his days damning the heat, the humidity, the flies, and the mosquitoes.

He had pulled a parka over his flight suit and crammed a fur-flapped hat on his head, and he took refuge beneath the wing of the new Tornado, which he had unceremoniously commandeered from one of his junior pilots. With his hands jammed in his armpits, Tellez danced a quick jig to keep warm as the blizzard whipped at him. Every few minutes, he yelled at the two men trying to refuel the fighter from a tanker truck, urging them to greater speed.

They were performing a hot refueling, with the turbofans still turning. Miguel Umbrago, his new navigator, was still in the rear cockpit, monitoring the instruments and trying to keep his cockpit warm.

A Sno-Cat pulled up alongside the airplane, behind the tanker, and stopped. Emilio Suarez jumped down from the driver's seat, and ducking his head into the wind, which was difficult for it seemed to swirl from a thousand directions, trudged over to stand next to Tellez.

The colonel's lips were quivering from the cold.

"Hello, Emilio."

"The air controller tells me you intend to take off again. You have already flown twice today."

"There is a Harrier pilot up there somewhere," Tellez said. "We are destined to meet again. With drastically different results, this time."

"There is nothing flying today, Roberto. I barely got the KC-130s off for Navarino this morning, and they will be staying there for awhile. You do not have to do this."

"These are precisely the conditions in which an attack against us would succeed wonderfully, Emilio. Four Harriers could devastate this base if we have no defenders up."

"I appreciate your dedication. . . ."

"You are paying for it."

". . . but the risks are far too great. Plus, we do not have the airplanes to squander."

"With me at the controls, Colonel Suarez, there is no risk. And I am not ordering others into the air."

"President Silvera—"

"Will let me do my job, or write me my last check. In fact," Tellez said, "with the way everything is proceeding, I suggest he pay me in gold."

Emilio Suarez de Suruca shook his head in resignation, then turned back to the Sno-Cat.

Tellez shook his own head in wonder. He had never before had a commander who would not enforce his own orders.

When the refueling was complete, he scrambled back into his cockpit and closed the canopy to trap what little heat was left before he strapped himself in. A ground crewman in an orange parka led him out to the runway and turned him into what was supposed to be the center of it.

He checked his compass, which was the only way he could tell that he was staying on the runway.

"Are you ready, Miguel?" he asked on the intercom.

"I cannot see the runway, much less the end of the runway,"

Umbrago said. The tremor in his voice indicated that he did not think highly of this endeavor.

"You must have faith, in that case. What is the state of the INS?"

"The Inertial Navigation System is aligned correctly, Major."

"That's all we need to find our way back."

Tellez rammed the throttles into afterburner and the Tornado lurched ahead, fighting the deep snow on the steel planking. He concentrated only on his compass and his airspeed. His arms and hands moved of their own accord, correcting drift and babying the aircraft as it slowly picked up speed. He did not think about the rapidly approaching end of the runway.

At 165 knots indicated airspeed, the nosewheel broke loose of the surface on its own, and he rotated. Tellez kept the afterburners engaged, pulled in the flaps and landing gear, and accelerated nearly straight up, heading for the calm at the top of the storm.

GYPSY MOTH ONE
2335 HOURS LOCAL

Cady thought that Sam Monmouth would probably like to have another little chat with him when he returned from this mission.

The captain hadn't said anything when Cady brought his Harrier to the flight deck and took off, but he wouldn't be as speechless around dawn, when Cady returned to his roost.

At thirty-five thousand feet, he was out of the turbulence of the storm that raged below, and he was extremely alone. Cady had elected to not bring a wingman along. This was his crusade.

It was nearly midnight, but the rim of the sun was still

above the horizon. A thin glow of light reflected off the dark clouds, creating little glints that sparkled like small diamonds. It was like viewing an entirely new, and roiling, gray landscape. It could have been relaxing, but Cady was far from relaxed. He was on oxygen, which tasted dry, and he frequently wet his mouth with water from the pair of baby bottles he had brought along.

He had been actively emitting with his search radar for the last twenty minutes, daring anyone with guts enough to come meet him. So far, he had seen nothing to alarm him. Only fools were out flying in conditions like this.

He was approaching Primavera from the north, and according to his readouts, using the Global Positioning System for navigation, was seventy-five miles away from the base.

He continued to be alone. The radar had revealed that even the FSAD's C-130s weren't flying tonight, though the clutter on the screen created by the storm could be deceiving.

"Gypsy Moth One, Jericho."

"Hello, Jericho," he said, recognizing the female voice. "You're supposed to be off-duty."

"I just put myself on duty, Gypsy. This mission was a last-minute decision, was it?"

"It looks to me as if all their aircraft are grounded, which makes the timing perfect."

"You're carrying only Mk 82s according to your flight plan."

And four more of them than he was supposed to have. He had taken off with twelve of the five hundred-pound bombs, four less than the Harrier could handle, but four more than Cady's compromise with the flight deck of the *U Thant* dictated. The takeoff had been dicey, and he wasn't that certain that he hadn't dragged the tail pipe through a few wavetops before he got the speed up to acceptable standards. If his crew chief had seen the takeoff, Cady would be banned from the pilot's seat. Shaker Adams had seen it, but had refrained from comment.

"I intend only to leave them behind, not engage in any aerial magic, Jericho."

"This is your payoff, right?" she said.

Her voice carried a tinge of anger, and Cady didn't bother responding, partly because he wasn't going to admit to a revenge motive, and partly because he now had a blip on the upper right edge of his radar screen.

It came halfway as a surprise. He had been certain the storm would keep FSAD aircraft grounded.

After a few seconds studying the screen, he knew it wasn't an errant airliner. It was doing at least Mach 2, it had an active search radar, and it was on a heading for an intercept. He was holding 650 knots, and he made some rapid mental calculations. The results weren't exactly encouraging.

"Gypsy?" she asked.

"Still here. I'm going to be busy. Got a bogey coming on strong."

She didn't give him any "I told you so's," but asked, "How far to contact, Gypsy?"

"He's at one-twenty miles, coming from the southwest."

"Turn around, Gypsy. You're not armed for air-to-air."

"I can beat him," Cady said, shoving the nose down and heading for the rolling gray cloudscape.

DEFENSE INTELLIGENCE AGENCY
2337 HOURS LOCAL

McNichols had gotten well into the first forty minutes of the best sleep of his life, stretched out on the cot in his office, when Andy Casper woke him up at ten-thirty.

"Oh, Jesus. What's up, Andy?"

"You might want to be. A single aircraft took off from the *U Thant*. It's not on any schedule they've shared with us."

So he had groaned loudly to demonstrate his displeasure, but rolled out of the cot, tipping it over, and crashing to the floor. He looked dumbly at his shoes, tossed under the desk, then decided they were too far away. Rolling onto his knees, he climbed to his feet. He then walked barefoot out to the control area and sat in a chair for an hour and watched the infrared spots moving on the screen.

At eleven-thirty, just to be watching something different, Casper switched the screen display to the satellite's direct visual sensors. The satellite was relatively far to the north, and they were seeing a slanted version of the underside of the world. On full telescopic view, they had a nice shot of the Harrier. It looked like a fine scale model, though its coloring blended with the clouds below it and made it difficult to track. If he looked away, it took awhile to find it again.

"You want to paint that thing or something, Andy?"

Casper designated it on the screen by encircling it with a blue circle. The computer would keep the target and the circle together.

Casper also put a yellow computer-generated circle over the single Tornado flying orbits to the southwest of Primavera.

"That's all they have up, Andy?"

"That's it, Cam. One plane for most of the day. They moved three tankers to Navarino Island, but the rest are on the ground at Primavera."

"You talked to the *U Thant?*"

"About an hour ago. To Maroni in the Combat Information Center. He said Cady's flying this one solo."

"If he can find the damned ground," McNichols said, "he picked a good time. Uh, oh!"

"Yeah. The Tornado spotted him. He's flat moving out."

McNichols scooted his castered chair across the floor to a desk and picked up a phone. He punched the button for the direct line to the CIC on the *U Thant*.

"Jericho."

"Pack Rat. You see Ca . . . what the hell . . . Gypsy Moth One?"

"No. He's been out of coverage for quite a while."

"He's under attack by a Tornado."

"Thanks, Cam," she said.

McNichols watched the two airplanes converging. Despite the broad vista created by the placement of their eye in space, the fighters seemed to be closing on each other very rapidly.

"There!" Casper yelled. "I think that was a missile launch."

The two of them sat in awe in front of the screen. "Shoot back, damn it, Cady!" McNichols said.

But then Cady's airplane disappeared from the screen.

UNS U THANT
2339 HOURS LOCAL

Eames was a little disgusted with herself.

She had infringed all kinds of protocols when she questioned Cady about his motives on the air. As a combat air controller, she was supposed to remain objective and somewhat aloof. She was supposed to be supportive as long as she protected the ship, then the aircrews. As a tactical information officer, when the ship was in a threat situation, she was supposed to provide the decision-makers with the data on her screens and at her fingertips.

Judgments about motivation—hers or anyone else's—in combat situations were for someone else to make.

Monmouth had told her that he'd spoken to Cady, and that all was well. Right now, it didn't look to her like all was well.

She glanced at the right screen. Willem Wiecker, a captain from the Netherlands, was manning that console and tracking shipping and civilian aircraft movements in the area on the ship's standard radar.

The data on her own screen was obtained via the Thorn EMI Searchwater radar set developed by the British. The narrow beam-width of the antenna and the pulse-compression methodology used in the radar kept the search area to a minimum and assisted in distinguishing between a target and ground clutter. The original Searchwater utilized a PPI (Plan-Position Indicator) screen which, on the A-scope for amplitude and range, could even provide a target's silhouette. Her set was modified so that signals produced by the radar were processed by the computer and displayed on her screen, at her discretion, as either a symbol or the true radar image. While she still had him in range, and in the radar image mode, Cady and his Harrier had almost looked like a Harrier.

But he had passed beyond her 250-mile limit, disappearing into an increasing number of false returns created by the snowstorm. Now her screen only displayed the dotted line of his computer-projected course and the manually-input purple line of the Tornado's projected intercept track.

Either aircraft could have made course and altitude changes which she didn't know about.

She felt blind.

"Terri," Wiecker said, "look at this."

She looked over at Wiecker's screen. The *Calais* which was back on point patrol, was shown along with several freighters and one passenger liner now plying the Passage. On the upper left edge of the screen, near the 220-mile limit, were four aircraft, and their IFF transponders had identified them as airplanes of the *Fuerza Aérea Argentina*. The ship's computer further identified them, with a probability factor of eighty-two per cent, as locally-built Pucaras.

"They are flying almost three hundred miles off the Argentine coast," Wiecker said. "That is not, or should not be, a normal pattern for aircraft of the Argentine Air Force."

"If anything, we'd see naval aircraft," Eames agreed.

"They have turned our way."

"They've probably detected my search radar and gotten curious." She switched off the Searchwater radar. It wasn't doing her any good at the moment, anyway.

"Keep an eye on them, Willem. If they get within a hundred miles, I want to know about it."

She wondered if the Argentines were going to get involved. And then she wondered what had happened to Cady.

"Gypsy Moth One, Jericho."

"Hold on," Cady said, "I'm dancing with a missile."

PRIMAVERA BASE
2340 HOURS LOCAL

Primavera's radar operator had alerted Suarez to the incoming solo fighter some time before; the aircraft was plainly visible, emitting search radar.

Suarez had immediately contacted Tellez in Puma One and vectored him toward the intruder.

Suarez had also ordered his alert aircraft to take off, over pilot objections about the weather, but one Tornado was bogged down in deep snow on the taxiway and had blocked access to the end of the runway. A dozen soldiers were frantically trying to dig it out.

He stood behind the radar operator and watched the screen and knew that the alert aircraft wouldn't get off the ground in time to intercept the intruder. Tellez controlled Suarez's immediate future.

"He evaded the missile," the operator said. "He is forty-four kilometers away now."

Tellez had fired way too soon, far beyond the Matra's thirty-five-kilometer range, and Suarez guessed that Tellez had wasted a very expensive missile in order to divert the hostile aircraft from its target.

The diversion had worked to some extent. In eluding the missile, the UN fighter had been delayed by several seconds

"Puma One is fifty-two kilometers from intercept," the radar technician said.

Tellez would not be soon enough.

"All antiaircraft and SAM batteries are to fire as soon as they acquire a target," Suarez ordered.

The radio operator repeated the instruction on the defensive battery command net.

The door burst open and Silvera swept in, bringing a blast of chill air with him. Ice particles were caked on the front of his hat and on his shoulders.

"What is it, Colonel?"

"We are under attack, *Presidente.*"

"In this weather?"

"The pilot is alone, and he is suicidal," Suarez said, "and we shall assist him."

GYPSY MOTH ONE
2341 HOURS LOCAL

Cady had lost speed to 350 knots as he dodged the missile, which hadn't been difficult. Its rocket motor had burned out and its momentum had all but evaporated by the time it neared him. He guessed it to be a Matra Super 530, with a normal range of twenty-two miles.

The early release suggested to him that his adversary was desperate, as well he might be. Cady's radar screen was a mess, but he could still pick out the base at Primavera and only the one defensive aircraft. The Tornado had slowed a great deal once it followed him down into the storm, and Cady thought he could beat it to the target.

Maybe.

The Harrier was all over the place, being tossed sideways, up, down. Once, he nearly went inverted. Archie Baker had told him it wasn't the best weather for Sunday flying, but Cady had forgotten that Baker was given to understatement. Or, rather than forgotten, had chosen to ignore it. Eddie Purgatory and Archie Baker had not been able to make him shy away from this mission.

Cady kept his eyes on the HUD, following the symbol of his airplane as it rose and fell or leaned left and right, countering the movements with pressure on the stick and rudders. Beyond the HUD, he couldn't see a thing. He was in the middle of a complete whiteout.

He was at two thousand feet AGL according to the radar altimeter, and he feared he was getting some ice buildup on the wings. It was difficult to tell, though, if the controls were sluggish. The air was so unstable, nearly all of his attention was devoted to keeping the Harrier level. His calf muscles felt bunched up and his forearms were on the edge of cramping.

A brief look at the radar screen showed him off course to the right and twenty miles from the target. He put the target on the HUD, then tried to make the left turn onto his heading, but the wind forced him to overshoot, and he had to turn back to the right again.

Another glance at the screen.

The Tornado was going to be in effective range in seconds, if he was carrying Matra Super 530s.

Cady decided he wasn't going to see the base. There was no way he would break out of this.

Visibility zero, ceiling zero.

Speed down to three hundred knots, perhaps a result of ice. He tapped the throttle forward.

The Harrier went sideways, shoving him violently toward the right side of the cockpit.

Then straightened herself out. She was trying her best.

Cady switched hands on the stick and used his right to quickly select his bombs, choosing "Ripple." He would spread them out. He used the joystick on the right side of his armrest to center the target reticule on his radar return for Primavera, then locked it in place.

At fifteen miles out, he was down to 1500 feet, but was still holding three hundred knots. He ran in a little more throttle to hold the speed and altitude as he brought the nose up.

When he looked again at the screen, the Tornado was about twenty-five miles away, still coming at him almost broadside from the west, and with dogged determination.

If the Tornado did indeed have the Matra missile, the pilot would illuminate him with the Tornado's radar, and the Matra would home on the reflected radiation. Cady cut in his Zeus active countermeasures. The radar jamming might give him a few more seconds.

Ten miles to target.

Eames was probably wondering about his dance with the missile. *She worried about him?* Pack Rat, if he was using infrared, would already have told her he was still airborne.

Eight miles.

Cady triggered the pickle button and saw the "COMMIT-TED" characters appear on the HUD.

Drifting way off to the left. He corrected, fighting the wind into a right bank.

Seven miles.

The Tornado launched a missile. Cady's warning receiver chirped in his earphones.

And Jesus! A SAM launch.

Black spots in the snow ahead.

Antiaircraft bursts.

Six miles. He punched off two bursts of chaff.

He couldn't give it up now.

Cady jigged the airplane to the right, then back again.

He didn't know where the Matra went. Elsewhere, though, confused by the jamming.

The surface-to-air missile shot past him on the right, and an orange pulse flashed in the whiteness as it exploded above him.

Another launch from the Tornado, the threat warning receiver sounding off excitedly.

Four miles.

The Harrier leapt upward as an antiaircraft shell went off below her. Cady quickly scanned the instruments but didn't see any indication of damage.

Shoved the throttle to the stop. More chaff.

Two flares, in case he had infrared-seekers coming at him from somewhere.

SAM launch.

Slammed the Harrier into a hard right bank, counted to three, then countered with a hard left bank.

Back on course, but a different course.

One mile.

Another Matra missed. The warning receiver quit yelping at him.

Looked at the screen.

The Tornado had turned to follow him and was on his tail, twelve miles back, gaining on him.

Felt the bombs release, and counted as all twelve dropped away.

One tactical nuclear warhead would have been enough.

Cady kicked the left rudder, slapped the stick over, skidded into a tight left turn, then centered the controls for a few seconds, gathering speed, then started a steep climb.

White, white, white.

Almost midnight. A white night.

He thought about the ridge below. He should just be passing over it.

Couldn't see a thing, though.

But the SAMs and triple-A should be shutting down, to let the Tornado pass through.

That might help.

PUMA ONE
2343 HOURS LOCAL

"Another miss, Major! The jamming prevents acquisition," Miguel Umbrago yelled on the ICS.

Tellez ignored his navigator. They were fifteen kilometers from the base, at five hundred meters of altitude, and he called on the radio, "Primavera! Shut down the defenses. I am coming through!"

The Primavera air controller did not answer. His radios were probably jammed by the Harrier's—Tellez was certain it was a Harrier—electronic countermeasures. Or, if the airplane had dropped bombs, the base might be in confusion.

"SAMs are still launching!" Umbrago called out.

Tellez could see them on his radar screen because he was so close. All along the ridge, the surface-to-air missiles were leaping into the sky, chasing the plane that had turned to the east.

An airburst of shrapnel exploded off his left wing, a gray puff in the whiteness that surrounded him.

"Mother Mary of God!" Umbrago exclaimed.

"God damn them!" Tellez shouted and countered the anti-aircraft fire by hauling the Tornado into a right turn.

He would have to avoid overflying Primavera and the ridge to his left which was a mine-field of surface-to-air missiles and antiaircraft batteries. If the Harrier was escaping to the east, Tellez would lose ground.

The attacker had come from the north. Every time, they came from a different direction. Tellez wondered how many ships were out there, sprouting Harrier aircraft at will. They might well be United States Marine expeditionary forces, like their amphibious assault ship, the *Wasp*. According to Silvera, though, the Americans had announced no unilateral action; they were supposedly cooperating with the United Nations.

He came around in a tight circle for 270 degrees, climbing as fast as he could. The Tornado had achieved 2500 meters of altitude by the time he rolled out of the turn, heading east.

The Harrier appeared on his radar screen again, and now it was headed north, parallel to the ridge, and twenty kilometers to the east of it. It had increased speed to over six hundred knots and was no longer emitting radar energy. Tellez was fifty kilometers behind, but the defensive batteries had apparently begun to shut down, now that their quarry was lost to them. He could now pass over them in relative safety.

Glancing at his armaments panel, Tellez saw that he had one Matra left, but he also had four Sidewinder missiles for use at closer range. And if that were not enough, he had the guns.

He pushed the throttles forward and sought the magic number: Mach 1.

FIVE KILOMETERS NORTHEAST OF BRANDEIS BASE,
ANTARCTICA
2345 HOURS LOCAL

When they heard—rather than saw—the disturbance to the west, most of the SEALs had deserted the warmth of the Sno-Cats and stuck their heads out from under the protective white shrouds that covered the snow crawlers.

Paul Andover went to look, also, lifting the edge of the parachute canopy, saw nothing of interest, and climbed back into his seat behind the controls. The diesel engine was idling, providing a source of energy for the cabin heaters.

They had been parked here, in this depression, slowly accumulating a layer of snow, for over two hours, since making their last twelve-kilometer dash from the site where they had hidden out for the day. Since arriving, David George's men had devoted their time to inspecting and preparing their equipment under the watchful eyes of their superior officers.

When the explosions and gunfire, muffled by the curtain of snow, began to die away, George came back and crawled inside with Andover. He opened a Thermos and poured them both coffee.

"I don't know that I should drink any more of this, Commander. If I have to pee again, I'll freeze the thing off."

"You mean you can find it?" George grinned at him. "I'm so damned cold, I won't even look."

"What do you make of that commotion, mate?" Andover asked.

"Gregori thinks, and I agree," George said, "that there were some five-hundred-pounders going off, in addition to triple-A. Probably some SAMs, too. We heard aircraft, but I don't know how many."

"Friends of yours, I hope?"

"I imagine so, Zip. And damned good friends, to be out in

this crap. I suspect it's a bit of a diversion for our activities. We'll have to see if we can't get some idea of the damage, so I can report back to them."

George dug into his pack and began examining its contents, coming up with a pair of woolen socks. He started unlacing his boots.

Andover had decided he kind of liked the blond-haired semi-American. He wasn't given to gossiping much, and Andover hadn't learned a great deal about the organization behind him and his troops, but the variety of nationalities among the commandos said a lot. Even the Russian, Suslov, though quiet, was relatively personable and obviously competent. Andover had never thought that he'd think that way about a Russian.

"About time to jump off?" Andover said.

"That it is, my friend. I can't tell you how much I've appreciated your—"

"Save that for later, Commander. You aren't losing Gus and me, yet."

"Look, Zip—"

"We're only a couple kilometers from the ridge, but there's still some rugged terrain," Andover told him. "I've been thinking about this, about these wells that are supposed to be hidden along there. If they're spread out, it's going to take awhile to find them."

"According to Jericho, they're spread out," George said.

"Then, I'm recommending you split this party up after we reach the ridge. Gus will lead one group, and I'll take the other. We go north and south and take out whatever we find."

"I can't subject a civilian—"

"I've got a personal stake in my continent, mate. I'll do it on my own, if I have to, and the odds are ten-to-one that I beat you there."

George thought it over, sighed, and said, "I hope I don't regret this."

Andover didn't care if he regretted it or not. He turned off the ignition, and the two of them climbed down from the Sno-Cat. A pair of ski poles were holding the parachute canopy away from the side of the vehicle, and five men were squatting in a circle, field stripping their assault weapons. Their skis and poles leaned against the tracks of the Sno-Cat.

The man named Bascom, ranked as a lieutenant Andover had gathered, stood up.

"Commander?"

"Just as soon as I tell Jericho."

George opened the pack containing his radio, extended the antenna, and turned on the power. He waited a few seconds for it to warm up, then transmitted, "Jericho, Raccoon."

There were more damned code names running around than Andover could keep track of. During the long trip, he had heard Beehive, Copperhead, Gypsy, Tiger Barb.

The response was rapid, and surprising to Andover, a woman's voice. "Go, Raccoon."

"Jericho, may I have a sitrep on Primavera?"

"Single bombing flight. Pack Rat reports bombs on or near target, but no other BDR at this time."

"Copied. Raccoon's launching now."

"Flagstaff wishes you Godspeed. Do you have a time to target?"

"A couple hours, at least. We're not absolutely sure what we'll run into. Raccoon out."

As George stowed his radio again, Andover said, "Can I at least ask what a BDR is?"

"Bomb Damage Report, Zip. They don't have one."

"So we'll provide one?"

"Maybe, if we can see that far. We'll hope that Harrier hit something."

Andover wasn't exactly sure what a Harrier was, but he hoped it hit something, too.

And he hoped the pilot got away.

UNS U THANT
2347 HOURS LOCAL

"We've got an infrared shot on a bird that just now came over the horizon," McNichols said, his voice now channeled to the overhead speakers.

"Well, tell us, damn it!" Eames said.

Monmouth knew she was getting pretty agitated. From his seat at the back of the compartment, he had noted the rigidity in her back and the way her hands, normally on the move, were motionless over the keyboard, waiting to do something. She had responded confidently and calmly to Dave George's call, but as soon as she was refocused on the screen, which in the area of Primavera was now blank, she had tensed up.

Jean d'Argamon leaned forward and put a hand on her forearm, saying, "Easy, *ma chérie.*"

She shrugged his hand away.

"Commander," Monmouth said quietly.

D'Argamon looked across the compartment at him, then scooted his chair away from the console.

"My bird's still on an extreme angle," McNichols said, "but we're showing a number of intensely hot spots around the Primavera area—something's on fire. I've got a reading for an aircraft seven-seven miles northeast of Primavera, heading zero-one-zero, making, ah, call it Mach 1. Got to be the Harrier."

Eames's fingers fluttered over the keyboard, and a blue square appeared on the plotting screen.

"The bandit's on intercept at Mach one-point-one, two-eight

miles back of the Harrier, bearing one-nine-one from the Harrier."

The green triangle blossomed on the screen, and after Eames entered several commands, dotted lines appeared, projecting the courses of both aircraft.

"Gypsy Moth One, Jericho."

"Go, Jericho."

"You have a bogey at your one-nine-one, two-eight miles."

"Copy one-nine-one, two-eight. Thanks."

Now they waited.

Monmouth thought he might enjoy court-martialing Shark Cady, if he made it back.

PUMA LEADER
2349 HOURS LOCAL

"He is still jamming," Umbrago said. "Still climbing. Going through nine thousand meters. He will be out of the storm level soon."

The better to see him, Tellez thought. He eased back on the throttle as he went through eight thousand meters. He remembered reading about the ability of the Harrier to suddenly come to a near-stop, using its vectoring nozzles. He did not want his own excess speed to hamper his acquisition of the raider.

A glance at his radar screen revealed only a cloud of white dots in the approximate region of his quarry. The radar jamming effectively prevented his use of his remaining Matra Super 530. Umbrago was tracking him by estimation from the most dense part of the radar return on the screen.

His fuel state was good. He had time to run this bastard to ground, and he could only hope that it was the same pilot who had shot him down before.

And killed Jesus Ramirez.

In quickly thinning wisps of vapor, they popped out of the cloud cover into daylight. The top rim of the sun was on his left and behind him. A few stars were on the verge of visibility. Scanning the skies around, he saw only the bouncing shadow of the Tornado racing across the cloud tops ahead and to the right of them.

"I think he must be twenty-two kilometers ahead," Umbrago said.

Tellez leveled off and, ignoring his self-generated cautions about speed, shoved his throttles past the detents into afterburner. As the Tornado accelerated, he selected two Sidewinder missiles. The radar jamming would not affect their heat-seeking heads.

"Eighteen kilometers to target. He is turning east."

Tellez rolled the Tornado into a shallow right turn.

The Harrier was not using his radar, but the pilot was aware of them, either by way of his threat receiver or by some other means. Tellez looked up through the canopy toward the stars, thinking once again of those hidden eyes. Surely, the American or Russian satellites were watching. It was an eerie sensation, and he did not feel entirely alone.

Miguel Umbrago saw him looking and said, "Do you think they are up there, Major?"

"They are up there, Miguel. The target?"

"Eleven kilometers."

The storm clouds boiled under them, rolling, always moving, five hundred meters below.

At eight kilometers of distance, Tellez spotted the alien aircraft. He had held off with the Sidewinders in order to do so. It was the first time he had seen his enemy with his own eyes, and even then, it was just a small object scooting over the clouds, its color almost indiscernible from the background.

The fact that it moved in a straight line was what had distinguished it for him.

"Do you see him, Miguel?"

"What? Where?"

"Just about at your eleven o'clock. He is turning north again."

"There! Yes, I see him."

"Say goodbye to him."

Tellez released his two missiles.

GYPSY MOTH ONE
2351 HOURS LOCAL

Cady knew he had a problem as soon as Eames verified that the Tornado was still after him. He wasn't going to outrun it.

When the infrared threat receiver sounded off, he knew his problems had doubled or tripled.

Flying at 31,000 feet, he hadn't exactly been trying to hide from his pursuit. He had been looking for smoother air and top speed. With the Harrier so light—half a fuel load and only the canisters of ammo for the guns, he was topping Mach 1.2, but it wasn't enough. He could get it up to Mach 1.3 in a dive, but that wouldn't be enough, either.

The Tornado was playing with him to some extent. Cady had expected the attack run much earlier.

As soon as the "MISSILE LOCK-ON" indicator flashed, Cady rolled inverted, cut the throttle to idle to reduce his heat emission, and tugged the stick back. The Harrier put her nose down and dove into the maelstrom.

At that speed, the Harrier wasn't up to violent maneuvering, and she protested a little—creaks in the airframe, but decided to go along with him. As soon as they were hidden in the clouds, the stick centered, the dive straight down, the buffeting started.

Cady dumped the air brakes.

Killed the radar jamming. These were heat-seekers, and if they were as good as the AIM-9Ls, they could home on the heated skin of the aircraft, where air friction raised the temperature. The snow and the cold wouldn't help him in that regard; they only made the warmer surfaces stand out better.

He switched his own radar to active and found the missiles right away. Two of them.

Two, three seconds out?

Airspeed 640 knots.

Altitude 26,500 feet.

Punched off four flares.

Sucked oxygen. His mouth was dry.

And pulled the stick toward his belly, counted to four, and centered it.

The Harrier leveled out, headed south.

Both missiles found his countermeasures flares and detonated behind him, disappearing from his screen.

Again, Cady pulled back on the control stick, this time shoving the throttle full forward. He was making 620 knots by the time the fighter went vertical.

On his radar screen, the Tornado was clearly outlined, just now passing over him, but five thousand feet higher. Cady brought the nose back some more, to follow the FSAD aircraft, and performed a half-roll, getting his head back on top.

If he had had a missile, now was the time.

He fired a few thirty-millimeter rounds from the Aden gun, but he knew they would be ineffective. He rationalized the burst by telling himself he was checking the gun. The damned thing might have frozen up.

The Tornado was losing speed, turning right, coming down.

Cady turned with it, hoping the pilot would turn back toward him for another attack run.

He did.

Continuing to climb, he watched the blip on the screen as it completed its circle and lined up for a head-on pass at him. Cady had almost reached the top of the storm. There was no snow here, the clouds thinned out, and he passed through open valleys, disappearing into upthrust towers of vapor.

The Tornado pilot probably had more radar and infrared missiles, but Cady hoped he was taking Cady's flight profile as a challenge. "Hey, asshole! Guns at twenty paces?"

The seconds ticked off, the planes closing at a combined rate of over 1200 knots. Cady waited for a missile launch.

Not yet.

Not yet.

The guy thought he was macho.

Guns it was.

He watched the blip closing on him.

Zooming in.

Shot out of a cloud bank and into an open clearing.

And there he was.

The distinctive face-on silhouette of the Tornado was backlit by the cloud bank behind him.

The twin twenty-seven-millimeter Mauser cannons began winking the second the other pilot saw him. The tracers leapt out at him, curving downward, diving below, then starting to rise.

This was a game of chicken, and back in Montana, Cady would never have given in.

Which is what the other pilot expected of him now. Hold the line, walk into the wall of deadly hail.

Cady surprised him and chickened out.

He rolled right, going inverted, but rising up out of the stream of twenty-seven-millimeter shells.

Squeezed the trigger on the Aden gun at the same time.

Didn't really expect to hit anything.

And then they were past each other, the Tornado's wing a

flash below his head as it went by. Cady got a glimpse of the faces of the two crewmen looking up at him, but he wouldn't recognize them on any street corner in the world. Their faces were hidden behind their helmet visors.

Cady rolled out and into a left turn, ready to come back on the Tornado for one last pass. He didn't think he would be as successful this time.

The guy would use his missiles.

But, on the screen, the Tornado was going down.

In big, slow circles.

He wasn't in dire straits, Cady didn't think, but he wasn't coming back.

Cady abandoned his left turn, rolled back to a northerly heading, and made certain he had all of the throttle arc he was entitled to.

PRIMAVERA BASE
2355 HOURS LOCAL

Silvera had forgotten the coffee someone had passed to him. He held it in his hand, but it was cold.

He and Suarez were shoulder-to-shoulder, leaning over the head of the radar operator in the curtained-off area at the back of the operations hut. Silvera was not as adept at following the radar images as Suarez, and the air force chief had been explaining what he thought was happening. When the radar returns showed one airplane again heading north and one aircraft losing altitude in large circles, Silvera's heart began to sink.

Behind them, on the other side of the curtain, a dozen voices fought for supremacy as airmen and soldiers on telephones and radios sought to learn the extent of the damages to the base.

"What is happening?" Silvera asked.

"Try to reach Puma One, again," Suarez told the radar operator.

"He is not answering his calls, Colonel."

"There, see!" Suarez said, stabbing his forefinger at the radar screen. "He is leveling off at one thousand meters, headed this way. He must have some degree of damage."

"Yes, sir," said the operator.

Suarez spun around and pushed his way through the curtain into the outer operations room.

"Arquez! Captain Arquez! Clear the runway immediately for an emergency landing!"

The harried captain in charge of radar and air control bolted out of the chair where he had been listening to radio reports.

"Colonel, there isn't time—"

"Just send a bulldozer down the center of the strip. Get the lights on. Do it, now!"

"Sir." Arquez switched frequencies on his radio and started talking to his ground units.

Silvera had followed Suarez out of the radar alcove, and he stood in the middle of the hut watching the people taking reports. He forced himself to wander from desk to desk, reading the notes jotted on scraps of paper:

Bomb in residential area—four dead, twelve injured . . . station manager's hut destroyed . . . ZSU-23-4 AA gun—destroyed, two dead . . . Two Mirages—destroyed . . . 1 KC-130 tanker—damaged . . . Taxiway 2-West— cratered . . . Supply Hut 4—destroyed . . . Maintenance Revetment—destroyed, six wounded . . . SA-9 missile vehicle—destroyed, one dead, four wounded . . . Sno-Cat— destroyed . . . secondary radio antennas—heavily damaged . . . southeast of runway—one crater, eleven wounded . . . SA-8 missile vehicle—badly damaged . . . ordnance stack four—destroyed.

He thought idly that he would have to find another place to sleep. Crossing to the window, Silvera peered outside. In several places, fires still raged. Men ran back and forth. A Sno-Cat raced across the runway, heading toward the dispensary, no doubt loaded with wounded men. The engine of a Caterpillar bulldozer roared, and the big tractor headed toward the runway.

Suarez came to stand beside him.

"It is not too bad, *Presidente*."

"What happens, Emilio, when they send more than one airplane?"

10 DECEMBER

Roberto Tellez had been cursing a blue streak for five minutes. He was so angry that he was barely aware of the abominable conditions he was flying under, and in.

He felt as if he had been conned.

The Harrier pilot—he had seen him clearly—had led him into. . . .

"Major, we are down to two hundred twenty knots," Umbrago said.

"I know what we are down to, Lieutenant!" he snapped back.

"The sweep. . . ."

Tellez did not bother answering. He was about to adjust the wing sweep forward, anyway. He found the lever behind the throttles, eased it ahead, and looked outside the canopy to verify that the wings came forward to their slow speed twenty-five-degree position. He felt as if he could not trust the airplane and was required to visually confirm every operation. He was half afraid that he had lost a gear box or hydraulic pressure for the wing sweep actuator.

The left turbofan was shut down. He did not know what was wrong with it, but he suspected that one round—one round!—from the Harrier's guns had found the engine or the air intake. He was certain that there was no further damage to the aircraft.

One round.

As soon as the two airplanes had passed each other, the yellow master alert indicator on the HUD had begun to flash incessantly, in syncopation with a sudden vibration in the airframe. When he glanced down at the instrument panel, he found every red light for the left turbofan glaring at him, and he had immediately pulled the left throttle back to cutoff, shut off ignition and fuel flow for the engine, then pressed the engine fire extinguisher button.

The loss of power effectively ended his engagement, and Tellez had watched in fury as the radar showed the attacker sailing merrily away.

"Major, we are losing fuel from the fin tank."

So. There was another accidental hit, in the integral tank within the vertical stabilizer.

"The fuel available will be sufficient for our needs, Miguel," Tellez said, reining in his anger.

He went to the radio. Primavera had been calling him, but he had ignored them. "Primavera Control, Puma One."

"This is Primavera. What is your status, Puma?"

"Two-two-zero knots, five hundred meters. We have lost an engine, and I am coming straight in."

"Ah, Puma, we have a bulldozer on the runway, clearing a path for you. You will have to go around."

Tellez evaluated that course. He was losing speed quickly. Checking the wings, he saw that a thin coating of ice was forming. It was a struggle to keep the nose up and maintain altitude. If he lost the radar, he would never find the airstrip, and he still had vivid memories of being down in that ice- and snow-locked terrain, with the imbeciles flying search and rescue unable to find him.

"Negative, Primavera. We are coming in directly. Order the bulldozer off the runway."

"Puma, you had better attempt a belly landing parallel to the runway."

"Get the bulldozer out of the way," Tellez ordered.

"Six kilometers," Umbrago reported.

Tellez could see nothing through the windscreen. Blowing snow swirling past the canopy did not allow him to see even the pitot head on the nose of the airplane. Only his radar picked out the base for him, and his radio compass told him he had a perfect alignment.

"Four hundred AGL, Major."

Tellez deployed the flaps and the leading edge slats for increased lift. The right turbofan was churning out one hundred percent power.

"Three kilometers."

He lowered the gear, relieved to see positive indicators for down-and-locked. The Tornado employed anti-skid brakes and powerful nosewheel steering for short landings in wet and icy conditions, but their capability was stretched to the limits at Primavera. The PSP landing mat provided a firm foundation, but it also became quickly caked with ice. And on top of that, the loose snow built up and formed a crust.

"Two-zero-zero AGL, two kilometers."

Tellez was fighting the left-side drag, correcting with rudder, and attempting to keep the wings level as the airspeed deteriorated. They were now flying at 170 knots, barely enough to keep the airplane airborne.

The ice was building further on the wings.

The tail wanted to drop, and he shoved the throttle to military power, not willing to risk using the afterburner on the right side only.

"One kilometer," Umbrago said. The tenor note in his voice revealed his heightened tension.

Suddenly, and vaguely, Tellez saw bright spots in the snow ahead. There were several, spread across his horizon. Not runway lights.

"Fires," Umbrago said. "The intruder found some targets."

That made Tellez even angrier, and he had to force himself to concentrate on the landing.

The flares along the runway finally appeared, and he had to jink the Tornado to the right by fifty meters to achieve alignment.

"Fifty meters AGL."

Then he had reached the flares, but he could not distinguish the runway between them. Far ahead, the headlights of something—the bulldozer probably—were off to the side of the airstrip. The surface looked soft.

No second thoughts now—they only involved ejection, anyway.

He retarded his single throttle and flared the aircraft.

It settled.

Touched.

The wheels began to rumble.

The crust of the snow broke, and the landing gear sagged into the deep snow, dragging the nose down. For a few seconds, he was afraid they would flip end-over-end.

He hoped the bulldozer had carved its trail down the center of the runway, and he hoped he was centered on it. If one of the main gears found cleared area and the other did not, the anti-skid brakes would not matter a bit.

The Tornado slowed rapidly, and halfway down the runway, the wheels broke into a flattened, but icy, surface. Tellez reversed thrust on his right engine and applied brakes gingerly.

Seconds later, the airplane came to a full stop, thirty meters short of the end of the runway.

"Major, you are a magnificent pilot," Umbrago said on the ICS. "I am happy to fly with you."

Tellez also thought he was a magnificent pilot, but he said, "If I were, Miguel, there would now be a dead Harrier pilot for my trophy case."

"I am sure that will come, Major."

GYPSY MOTH ONE
0117 HOURS LOCAL

The conditions surrounding the *U Thant* were mild compared to what was taking place on the continent. The seas were running at perhaps ten or twelve feet, and the skies were clear. A few billion stars were the only ice crystals Cady could see. There was some gusting wind, but Shaker Adams brought Cady on board without a problem.

His crew chief was on the flight deck to meet him, his grin expressing his delight that Cady hadn't damaged the chief's airplane in any visible form. A tractor towed him onto the elevator as he unbuckled and disconnected, then raised the canopy.

The chief slapped a ladder against the fuselage, and Cady crawled over the coaming and worked his way to the deck of the elevator. He stretched tired muscles and drank in the salty air. He guessed that the temperature was just about at the freezing level, but it felt damned good.

His crew chief was an East Indian with twenty-four years service in the Royal Air Force. He was trying to eyeball the skin of the Harrier without being too obvious about it.

"Nothing more than ice there, Chief. I hope so, anyway."

"There had better not be, Colonel. Ah, I am to tell you to report to the captain as soon as you're aboard."

"He's probably asleep."

"Not ten minutes ago, sir."

"Well, I was afraid of that."

As soon as the elevator clunked into position on the hangar deck and the false tank hatch unfolded and closed above them, Cady stepped off the elevator and scanned the deck. Besides his ground crew, only the fire watch was on the deck. The absence of activity and one Harrier that was supposed to be there made the hangar seem particularly cavernous.

He spent a few minutes with the chief, assuring him that all systems had worked beautifully, then left the hangar and walked to the aviators' dressing room to strip out of his gear and don a clean flight suit. The dressing room and the ready room were also devoid of life. It was a quiet ship.

Cady dropped a quarter in the vending machine in the ready room, selected a Coke, and drank it down quickly. So much time on oxygen dried out his mouth and throat.

He sauntered down to the elevator and pushed the call button.

He was in no hurry.

He remembered times like this. Laying strips of rubber off the Ford pickup's big tires on Broadwater Avenue, getting stopped by the cops, but not getting a ticket. Instead they called his folks, and left him to dread going home. The penalty was never a simple matter of paying a few bucks in a fine. Instead, he had to face his parents, stand quietly through the dressing-down, and hope his sentence was only life after school stocking shelves in the drug store and not a three-week loss of his transportation. At the time, three weeks was about as close to infinity as one could get. One time, after his team in a car-based water balloon fight took out the windshield of a car belonging to the other team with a five-gallon water balloon, he not only had to pay for the windshield, but also got life in the drugstore, lost the truck for two weeks, and was kept out of one Friday night football game. That had been pure hell.

On the bridge deck, he went forward and requested permission to enter the bridge. Lieutenant Alferd Wilshire, the third officer, was on duty, and he said, "The captain's in his quarters, CAG. You're supposed to report to him there."

"Thanks, Lieutenant."

He had known Monmouth would be in his stateroom. Avoidance behavior and delaying tactics.

Cady went back down the corridor, turned into the cross hallway, and found Monmouth's door. He rapped on it lightly.

Monmouth pulled it open. "Come on in, Jim."

Cady stepped in. Monmouth had a glass of something-or-other in his hand, but he didn't offer any of it to Cady.

"Sit down and brief me."

Cady took one of the chairs at the table, and Monmouth sat opposite him. He quickly detailed the important aspects of his flight.

"You have any idea of bomb damage?"

"No, Sam. The snow was so thick I couldn't pick up a target with the laser range finder. I barely saw the field, but I got the bombs off on an angle across the runway and into some of the buildings. I'm hoping I got a few of the aircraft."

"And the Tornado? Tell me about that."

Cady hadn't intended to be specific about his head-on clash with the defender—and wouldn't be in his written report, but Monmouth's eyes had him pinned down. He provided the details of his narrow escape.

"So you played psychological games with this guy?"

"Don't get me wrong, Sam. He's a hell of a pilot, to be up in that weather in the first place, then to chase me down in it. But I think he also has a high opinion of himself as a pilot. I used it against him."

"Once, you did. The second time might have been different."

"Yeah," Cady admitted. "It would have been. I got in a lucky strike. I don't know how badly damaged he was."

"Not too badly. McNichols reported that he got back to the Primavera airfield safely."

Monmouth sat back in his chair and studied him for a long minute.

"Tell me, Jim, about your rationale for this mission. I was under the impression you had grounded all flights over the continent because of the weather."

"I did."

"The rules don't apply to you, of course? You and the FSAD pilot are above them?"

Cady avoided a response by saying, "I had two objectives in mind, Sam. One, because of the weather, I didn't expect to run into any heavy opposition. That was a plus. Two, I wanted to divert their attention to themselves, give them some problems to deal with prior to Dave George's operation kicking off."

"Admirable," the captain said. "On the first concept, if you'd taken in six or eight planes, you'd have still met little opposition and caused a hell of a lot more damage. But, naturally, you're the only aviator qualified to fight the weather as well as the FSAD."

Cady wisely decided to keep his mouth shut. Monmouth was just getting heated up.

Monmouth held up a clinched fist and began to graphically enumerate his points, ticking off a finger for each statement:

"One, you violated your own ban on bad-weather flying.

"Two, you took off from this ship with four more Mk 84 bombs than allowed in the aircraft standard operating procedure. I'm not sure how you got off with two thousand pounds more than approved, but you did."

Monmouth had already investigated his takeoff weight.

"Three, you flew a solo mission against hostile targets when your operations profile states specifically that such a mission will be comprised of at least two aircraft. You wrote the profile, Shark.

"Four. You didn't bother briefing, or even notifying, the

commanding officer and the Combat Information Center of your mission."

"I suspect it would have been turned down," Cady defended lamely.

"You're also a clairvoyant?"

"No, sir."

Monmouth stuck out his thumb and turned it straight up. "And five, you flew while mentally disabled."

"What!"

"Don't fuck around with me, Jim. This whole damned event was staged as a response for Jake Travers. You're bent on revenge, aren't you?"

Cady let his head sag a little and pursed his lips while he considered the statement. Finally, he said, "It's out of my system now, Sam."

"Let's hope so. Let's also hope that Anderson and Naka-mura are as good as you are, when you're at your worst."

Cady looked up. "What does that mean?"

"It means your squadron commanders are going to have to shoulder the load. As of now, you're off flight status."

"Sam."

"That's it."

Cady had just had his hot rod taken away from him.

DEFENSE INTELLIGENCE AGENCY
0145 HOURS LOCAL

"Hello, darlin'. Hope I didn't wake you."

"I'm awake, Cam," Eames told him.

"I don't know what a bed looks like, anymore," McNichols said. "What I did, though, I waited a courteous amount of time to call and find out what kind of damage Cady thinks he inflicted at Primavera. We watched him land on the ship half an hour ago."

"I haven't had a post-mission briefing with him yet, Cam. He's in with the captain right now."

"I hope he's getting a medal. That was some hellacious flying."

"I don't think he's getting a medal," Eames said.

"Well, I'd be interested in a BDR, soon as you get one."

"He wasn't carrying recon pods, Cam. And I don't know how much he saw, with the weather as bad as it was."

"Tell you what we got," McNichols said. "One of my sensor satellites—I say, 'my,' but they're really on lend-lease from NSA and I know I can't afford them—picked up the concussions of twelve bombs. . . ."

"Twelve? They're not supposed to leave the ship with more than eight."

"That, I don't know about, Terri. We recorded twelve heavy impacts. Then, I've finally gotten tied into an Aquacade that was moved from its geo-stationary orbit over India to a spot where we can see a lot more of what we want to see, especially using its radar sensors. This honey can see through clouds, though the snow in this case hampers it a bit."

"Such as?"

"My people are still going over the images, but we're pretty damned sure he got two fighters and maybe one of the transports. There were several buildings on fire. There were some perimeter hits we're not certain about, but which suggest hits on antiair sites. SAMs or triple-A."

"Let me update my scoreboard," she said. "That leaves them with six Tornados and seven Mirages."

"Reads the same as my scoreboard."

"They're losing their ability to punch."

"Slow, but sure," he agreed. "We've been watching closely, to make sure they don't attempt another long-distance attack on one of the other stations. When the weather clears up, we'll be even more alert. They might well retaliate with a few missiles aimed at Eights Station. That's not too far away."

"We're not really in a position to protect them."

"I know. We've already sent warnings to the station."

"What's the political climate right now?"

"Well, now, my dear, it's iffy, at best. I talked to Sir Charles around eight, and at that time, it was still two against everyone else, though the sinking of the *Inga* has bunches of people in a dither. Argentina and Chile are still hanging in the FSAD Camp, though, and talk around the halls seems to suggest that another half-dozen are ready to jump ship in favor of FSAD. I don't know what they're waiting on. The other thing, the U.S. has diverted a carrier battle group, led by the *Enterprise,* out of the Caribbean, apparently headed your way."

"What! Why?"

"Somebody's getting impatient, I imagine. I suppose the French and maybe the Russians are pressuring the President to intervene and get this thing wrapped up. The Russians are still assembling a fleet of aircraft at Cam Ranh Bay, also."

"That defeats the purpose of the *U Thant,* Cam."

"True. And Sir Charles would like to prove her viability. You'll probably be getting some hints relative to speed."

"I suppose. All right, thank you, Cam. I'll get back to you after I've talked to Colonel Cady."

"Night-night."

"No sleep, here. Operation Yellow Jacket is set to go in fifteen minutes."

"Oh, damn! I'd forgotten," McNichols said, then hung up.

He levered himself out of his chair, looked longingly at the cot, then went out to the rows of desks behind the consoles. Jack Neihouse had relieved Andy Casper and was sitting at the head desk. Pam Akins was on one of the NSA consoles, and a volunteer from the African analysis section was sitting at the other. Akins was monitoring Aquacade data acquisition, and the other console was tuned into a Keyhole (KH-12).

The Aquacade was telescoped in on Primavera in real time, but the screen showed only a dirty white array, with a few blue and red spots.

Behind them, six people were scrunched over three desks, painstakingly poring over the photos and imagery captured by the Aquacade.

McNichols sat on the corner of Neihouse's desk. "Anything new?"

"Nothing new, Cam. We're waiting for Yellow Jacket, but don't know that we're going to see much. A bunch of little guys in white parkas don't show up well."

"I think these are a bunch of big guys, Jack."

"Big balls, for sure," Neihouse said, pointing at the screen. "I wouldn't go out in that crap for anything."

FOUR MILES NORTHEAST OF PRIMAVERA BASE
0217 HOURS LOCAL

Commander David George had taken the first squad and the Dane, Gustav Brelin. The second squad, under the command of Gregori Suslov, had pushed off to the north, following Zip Andover.

George thought he had acclimated to the temperature fairly well, as long as they kept moving. Every fifteen minutes, he had stepped his skis out of Brelin's tracks and stood beside the trail to examine his twelve men, urging them frequently to drink more water. Brelin, he didn't worry about. The Danish scientist appeared to know exactly what he was about.

The fourteen of them were moving on their wide cross-country skis, everyone carrying an eighty-pound pack. Except for Brelin, each man also carried a weapon, and a few had elongated missile pods strapped to the sides of their packs Brelin and Anderson had both begged for something to shoot but George was adamant in denying civilians, especially un trained civilians, access to lethal hardware.

The terrain was rough, forcing them into detours severa times. It was all uphill, too, climbing toward the peak of th ridge from the east side, though the grades weren't too steep The surface underfoot was tricky, with hidden potholes an snow-disguised chasms. The fourteen of them were linked to gether with a long nylon rope, so that if one man went int a hole, the others could haul him out. It had happened twice

David George was concentrating on the ground when Breli abruptly came to a halt, and George ran into the back of him

Without saying a word, Brelin pointed to the southwest.

In the whiteout, it was difficult to see much.

Except there. And there. And over there.

Spots out in the snow with just a little more brightness.

The wind whipped around them, howling.

He put his lips close to Brelin's ear and said, "What d you think they are, Gus?"

"Fires, maybe, Commander. They're still a long way of but they're in the direction of Primavera."

"How close are we to the ridge?"

"We're standing on it."

George looked down and searched the area. A dozen yard away, darker shadows bespoke an abyss.

"The cliff edge goes in and out, Commander. We want t be careful, and we want to go south, I think?"

George said, "Let's go with your recommendation, Gus."

"All right, then. Let me go ahead a little ways and recon noiter. Soon as I find one of these wells, if they're there, I' come and get you."

George was beginning to wonder if they were there or no himself. It was an unlikely damned place to find an oil wel

PRIMAVERA DRILLING SITE #2
0229 HOURS LOCAL

Private Santiago Romero was numb with the cold. He could not feel his toes, no matter how hard he wiggled them. His hands felt like disembodied hams, barely able to clutch his AK-74 assault rifle.

He looked back at the shroud-covered oil derrick, glowing with the light of its interior incandescent bulbs and its big propane-fired heater. The lucky ones were in there, the drillers and roustabouts, the soldiers who had been detailed to work on drilling shifts around the clock.

The unlucky ones, like himself, were out in the cold, walking the slippery and treacherous canyon floor between the drilling rig and the antiaircraft battery at the mouth of the canyon. It took him sixteen long minutes to go from the well to the shanty erected next to the ZSU-23-4 gun, where he was allowed to stay for five minutes to warm himself. Then, because it was up a steep trail, barely marked by the vehicles that had crossed over it, it took him twenty-two minutes to walk back to the rig where his reward was ten minutes near the heater.

Occasionally, Romero would look up to the tops of the high cliff, but he could only see snow. There were no stars, no cliff tops. He thought it ridiculous to walk a route so immune to prying eyes. For five days now, twice-a-day, for six-hour stints, Romero had made the same series of walks, and he had never seen anything but what he was supposed to see.

He had come to view his life as one devoted to securing warmth. He looked forward to each rest stop with increasing fervor and anxiety. What if he reached one of his journey's ends and found the heater inoperative? How would he ever get warm enough to make the return journey?

He did not know where his home was. Was it supposed to be at the drilling rig or at the ZSU?

Would he ever get back to his real home? His brothers and sisters would welcome him with open arms, he knew. His father would demand his share of Romero's paycheck, which was why his father had induced him to join this movement, anyway.

Romero cursed the luck with which his twenty years of life had been blessed and trudged ahead through the snow. It was coming down so fast, he could only dimly make out the crooked line of footprints he had himself made on his way up the road.

He was concentrating on those older, disappearing footsteps, trying to step into them, when a huge paw clamped itself over his mouth. Another huge arm wrapped itself around his neck and jerked him off-balance. He was so startled and numb, he dropped his rifle.

"Sorry, my friend, you're running around with the wrong gang," a deep voice said in his ear.

He forgot about the intense cold for long enough to realize he was very frightened.

Panicked, Romero tried to struggle free of the grip that threatened his very breath.

And then he saw the blade, from the lower corner of his right eye.

It was clutched in the paw, and it was massive, elongated stainless steel shining in the white of the snow. It must have been warm for he saw snow droplets melted on it.

It rose high.

It came quickly down, drawn beneath his chin.

And then he felt the warmth.

His own blood, seeping down his collar.

FSAD Private Santiago Romero collapsed in the snow when the big man let go of him.

The last thing he heard was the deep voice saying, "Sorry, Commander. Now I've got myself an AK-74."

PRIMAVERA DRILLING SITE #2
0233 HOURS LOCAL

David George watched him wipe the blade of the K-Bar on the body's clothing, then resheath it beneath his parka. He shrugged his shoulders. "Okay, Gus. You earned it."

The two of them had just rappelled down the side of the cliff, about a hundred-foot drop. He could tell that Brelin had rappelled before, though not in a long time. He knew the routine, though he looked a little clumsy accomplishing it. And it was Brelin who had been the first to see the sentry coming down the trail, and he had acted smoothly and without warning.

George had been surprised as hell. Brelin and Andover were serious about their anger.

He put it behind him, lifted his set of night goggles from around his neck to his eyes, and signalled to Lieutenant Bascom at the top of the cliff with an infrared flashlight whose beam would only be seen by someone wearing night goggles, which Bascom was.

He got a double flash in return, then turned his flashlight toward the top of the cliff on the other side of the trail and clicked it three times.

Sergeant Tu flashed the return signal twice, and three minutes later, all of George's squad had slithered down the ropes to the bottom of the ravine and spread out on either side of the road.

He was about to signal them forward, up the road toward the well, when Tu bounced up, crossed the road, and slid to a prone position beside him.

"Hey, Commander, while I was waiting up there, I went out to the edge of the cliff and took a look down the hill."

"And found something?"

"ZSU-23-4 Quad. There's a shed with an active smokestack there, too, but I don't know how many hostiles are present. There's two on the gun."

George thought he could take an oil derrick with only seven people, so he checked his watch, then said, "Take it out, Tu, but not before 0250 hours, then back to the top."

"Thank you, sir."

The sergeant recrossed the road, grouped his six SEALs and started down the hill.

George sent three of his SEALs across the road to replace them, then using hand signals to coordinate the advance, they began moving up the slope toward the rig. Where the road hadn't been bulldozed, there was lots of cover—gigantic boulders fallen from the cliffs were topped with snow. He darted from one to the next, checking that the men on the other side were matching his pace. The surface was irregular with scrabble and stones, but they were frozen in place and tended to trip him up rather than slide out from under his boots. Brelin and his two SEALs on this side stayed with him. As he ran, he kept flexing his fingers within his mittens, trying to warm them toward the time he would have to extend his forefinger through the trigger slit in the mitten. When they were closer forty yards away, George stopped the group and surveyed the site.

There were no guards that he could see. Brelin's victim had been the only one. There were several flatbed truck trailer parked around, along with a single utility Sno-Cat. The overhead sheeting that protected the site from surveillance was quite an achievement, George thought. Silence wouldn't be factor. The diesel engines driving the rotary table and the winches were straining and bellowing.

The fact, however, that they were trapped at the end of a box canyon, with a hundred-foot rope climb to safety, encouraged his decision not to tarry.

The rig itself was also wrapped in some kind of fabric; it allowed the interior lights to glow through. It looked damned warm inside, and it made him think about how cold he was. He shrugged out of his pack, watching the others do the same. Struggling with the stiff nylon of the pack cover, he ripped open the Velcro closure. Near the top of the pack, where they were handy, were the quarter-pound blocks of C-4 plastic explosive. The timer-detonators were wrapped in foam and kept in a pocket of his parka. He prepared three of the blocks, inserting a detonator into each.

Petty Officer Alan Mosler, a New Zealander of French extraction, and the other demolitions man on this squad, moved up beside him. He had left his assault rifle with his pack and was juggling his three blocks of C-4 in his mittened hands.

George surveyed the distance they had to cover, then looked at his watch. They would go for 0251.

"Put three minutes on them, Alan."

"Three minutes, Commander."

The two of them set the timers, then as the rest of the squad covered them, leapt up and ran as quickly as they could on the ice and snow for the derrick, slowing as they came within ten yards of it. George took the left side, slapping one package against the leg of the derrick, charging to his left to place another charge near the big fuel tank feeding the diesel engines, then on his way back down the slope, lodging the last one on the back end of the Sno-Cat. Mosler sited his charges on a derrick leg, next to a large fuel bladder, and under the flatbed of one of the trailers loaded with drilling pipe.

Brelin handed George his pack and rifle as he reached the group, and everyone rose and retreated down the slope.

George had been counting to himself, and when he reached 150, he slid to a stop and bellied up to a boulder. The rest of the team followed his example.

Without warning, a staccato rumble of explosions from behind them sent concussion waves rolling up the canyon. George felt the pulsations massage the back of his arms. He turned to look, but a bend in the canyon prevented his seeing anything significant.

Those inside the derrick were alarmed by the detonations, and a flap popped wide, spilling direct light on the snowy ground, and four heads poked through, looking down the slope. The front door of one of the living huts also slammed open, two men running outside.

And with snap-cracking suddenness that carried crisply in the frigid air, the six blocks of *plastique* went off. The shock wave went lateral across the end of the box canyon, slapped the hard rock walls, and rolled in waves down the slope. The secondary explosions of fuel went upward in red and yellow neon that climbed all the way to the camouflage cover high above.

Shrapnel from the Sno-Cat and spinning pieces of shattered drill pipe sliced wood, tin, and flesh. The screams of the men caught in the center of the firestorm were fortunately drowned in the cacophony.

And the near legs of the derrick buckled, and the sixty-foot tower leaned out toward them, teetered, then came crashing down, hitting the ground with enough force to send tremors racing under George's feet.

The diesel engines groaned into silence.

Fire raced through the wooden buildings.

Now, he could hear screams.

George turned to Brelin and said, "Ready for the next one, Gus?"

"I'm not looking forward to climbing that damned rope."

PRIMAVERA DRILLING SITE #4
0327 HOURS LOCAL

Franco Novarro was team captain of the rig, and he was damned proud of the fact that they were through the ice and ninety-five meters into the lava cap, moving faster and deeper than the other six teams.

Novarro's contract with the Front for South American Determination was a rewarding one due to the conditions under which they had to drill, but it also contained incentive clauses for speed, for discovery, and for well-completion. He intended to collect his bonuses, which he would share with his crew, on each one of those clauses. He had spent most of his time training the raw recruits sent to him from the military ranks, urging them to levels of competency which would help him collect his bonuses.

Which is to say that he *had* intended to collect.

Fifteen minutes before, he had received a radio call from someone at Primavera saying that the drilling sites were under attack. Sites Two and Three had been destroyed. He was urged to take all precaution available to him. He was told that armed help was on the way and would reach him within twenty minutes, which Novarro interpreted as an hour or so.

Novarro did not shut down his drill. He would not lose a meter of progress, if he could help it. The big diesels continued to roar, the rotary table continued to turn, and the diamond-toothed drill bit slowly chewed at the ultra-hard lava rock. The men manning the deck had trouble concentrating on their tasks, though. They kept turning anxious faces to the west, even though they could not see beyond the plastic-impregnated fabric covering the derrick.

He did turn the off-duty shifts out of their bunks and issue weapons to them. The weapons were an odd sort, an armory composed of cast-offs since it was assumed by someone in command that they wouldn't be needed. There were old Springfield .303s, Winchester saddle rifles, two World War II vintage M-1s. The ammunition supply was just as jumbled, and it took some time to sort out the correct ammunition for the correct rifles.

He spread his men out in a defensive line down the slope from the rig, covering the approach from the canyon opening, and then he called the commander of the surface-to-air missile launcher parked at the end of the canyon. The commander had already been alerted, but he refused to send any of his men to help. He needed to defend his own equipment.

Novarro cursed him solidly on the telephone, then hung up.

He would protect his rig and his bonuses, himself, at any cost.

Standing outside the protection of the derrick, he scanned the canyon in which he was trapped and looked up at the continuing snowfall.

And had a thought.

He walked down to find the foreman of the first shift.

"You tell these people to watch the canyon top. I know it is difficult to see, but if there is any movement at all up there, shoot first."

PRIMAVERA DRILLING SITE #4
0334 HOURS LOCAL

That old Dave George was pretty smart, Zip Andover thought. The tactics for the attacks on the second targets were going to be different.

George had known that, once the first drilling sites were hit, the word would go out fast and the FSAD people would be alert and waiting for them at the next pair of targets.

They hadn't known how many sites they would find, but

George figured at least four. He thought there might be more, but on this morning's raid, four was the magic number, if they found that many.

And after the initial attack, George had allowed for limited use of the squad radios, to update each attack team in regard to the situations they found. Gregori Suslov's team which Andover was guiding, had blasted the bloody hell out of the rig they found with plastic explosive. Only after they were back on the rim of the ridge—Andover had one hell of a time with the 110-foot rope climb—and headed north again had they learned from George that there might be an antiaircraft installation at the other end of the canyon. Suslov said he would check on the next one.

Andover had ranged ahead of the others, seeking another well, now knowing better what he was looking for. He found it two-and-a-half kilometers north of the one they had destroyed.

Now, Suslov's team was gathered at the edge of the canyon rim, looking down on the camouflage curtain. Andover couldn't see any movement down there, but the roar of diesel engines clearly announced a presence. On his stomach, he backed away from the edge. Extreme heights made him dizzy. The video he had seen of Stallone's *Cliffhanger* had nearly made him sick.

He found Suslov well back from the edge, talking on the radio, and Andover moved in close to hear the low-pitched voices. He wished he had brought his bag of gingersnaps with him.

". . . found another rig, too," George was saying.

Suslov looked out to the west, but Andover didn't think he could see much in the snow.

"Raccoon, it'll take us maybe twenty minutes to get in position. And I want to see if we can find one of those triple-A units."

"We'll make it twenty minutes, then," George said over the radio. "Then head for Chatterfield."

Chatterfield was the code name for the ravine in which they'd left the Sno-Cats. On their way back, they were supposed to set mines and booby traps of some sort, using Claymore mines, because George figured that there would be pursuit, and he wanted to slow it down considerably.

"Be advised," George added, "that we're about two miles from Brandeis, and we hear Sno-Cats and trucks coming. It won't be long before we've got troops all over us."

"Acknowledged," Gregori Suslov said and stuck the radio back in his parka pocket.

"I'll go look for that antiaircraft whatever-it-is," Andover told him.

If his role was to be confined to that of guidedog, Andover wanted to do as much of it as he could. He owed that much to Christine Amherst.

These bastards must pay dearly for the peaceful and productive lives they had taken.

"All right," Suslov said. "You and Maldone will go together. If you do not find anything within ten minutes, you will come back. Otherwise, we will leave here without you."

"I understand that, Gregori."

"Go."

Andover used his right hand and pushed back his parka sleeve to check his watch, which was strapped on over his shirt and underwear sleeves, then looked for Maldone.

The Italian smiled at him, and the two of them hoisted their backpacks and headed out, following the rim of the canyon around to the west side. Andover's pack wasn't too heavy; he carried medical supplies and climbing gear. A 250-foot rope was coiled and taped to the side of the pack.

The terrain was uneven, and they scooted on their backsides down into small depressions, then scrambled, fingers and toes flailing and grabbing, up the opposite sides. They moved as fast as they could, and the diesel engine sounds dimmed behind them.

Seven minutes later, and a quarter-mile from Suslov's group, they reached the western edge of the ridge. The two of them went onto their bellies and crawled up to the drop-off.

Andover didn't see a thing down there, but the cliff was probably around two hundred feet high at this point, and the snow hampered his vision.

Maldone wriggled around to get out of his backpack, and Andover reached over to help him. After digging around in it, he came up with some gadget.

"Infrared imager," he said.

"Still doesn't mean anything, mate," Andover said, and watched while the SEAL fiddled with some switches, then held it to his eyes.

He scanned for a few minutes, then said, "Mr. Andover, we have us an SA-9 Gaskin."

"That means even less," Andover admitted.

"It is a surface-to-air missile launcher. There are four missile tubes on top of a BRDM scout car chassis. Gun Dish radar, probably. I cannot make out details, but that is my best guess. We must be careful because they probably have infrared sensors and may detect our heat."

They backed away from the rim, and Maldone unstrapped the LAW from the side of his pack. The second targets were to be attacked from the ridge, without conducting a ropefall to the canyon bed, with M72A2 Light Anti-tank Weapons. Each squad carried three of the six-pound weapons. Lieutenant Bascom had told Andover that the two-pound rocket fired by the weapon could pierce over eleven inches of armor plate.

Maldone pulled the LAW from its canvas cover, removed the safety pins which released the end covers, and pulled the telescoping smaller section of the launch tube from the outer section. That action cocked the firing mechanism. He raised the sight on the end of the tube, then rested the whole contraption on his shoulder.

"All right, Mr. Andover. Now we will—"

He was interrupted by the sudden chatter of small arms fire from behind them.

"Damn it. Now they will be alerted," Maldone said. "Please stay clear of the end of the weapon, Mr. Andover. There will be a backflash."

Andover skirted to the side by five feet, and Maldone walked on his knees toward the rim of the cliff, with the LAW held firmly to his shoulder. After checking with the infrared sight and finding his target again, Maldone spent some time aiming the LAW.

The tempo of gunfire behind them intensified. Andover heard a couple powerful whooshes and subsequent and muffled explosions and supposed that Suslov's men had fired their own LAWs.

Maldone was straining to see into the snowfall.

And the edge of the cliff erupted, chunks of rock and ice spraying upward. The bullets whistled as they went by, and Andover felt the compression of the air caused by their passage. The sound of the firing followed the arrival of the heavy slugs. Some kind of machine gun, he guessed, as he went down and dug his face in the snow.

"What the hell's that, Maldone?"

There was no answer, and Andover looked up to see the Italian sprawled on his back. Alarmed, he slid across the snow to find that the SEAL no longer had a face. A heavy-caliber slug had hit him in the left eye and exploded his skull.

"You bloody bastards!" Andover screamed.

He grabbed the LAW from where it had landed beyond the body and squirmed his way to the brim of the cliff. Seconds after he peered over it, the machine gun rattled again. Rock chips smashed into his face, and he rolled away.

He heard a truck engine starting, a diesel.

They were moving the SAM launcher.

Rolling six feet to his right, he found the bulky infrared nightsight. He kept his chin in the snow as he eased up and used the nightsight to look for his quarry.

The SA-9 had all but disappeared, but Andover found the greenish image of its missiles peeking from behind a rocky outcropping. Twenty feet away, he saw a green man, standing on the front seat of a utility vehicle, obviously using an infrared device, looking back at him. He was directing another man with a heavy machine gun mounted in a traversing ring above the passenger seat.

Andover pulled his head down and scooted backward just as the machine gun opened up again.

Without thinking too much about it, Andover crawled to his pack, ripped the Velcro open, and pulled off the rappelling rope. Working quickly, he wrapped one end of it around a ten-ton boulder, then crawled along the rim until he found the indentation of a vertical crevice. He tossed the rope over, then went back and got the LAW.

He forgot to bring the infrared sight.

Slipping up to the edge feetfirst, Andover wrapped the rope around his calf and under the instep of his left foot and used his right foot to hold it in place.

He counted to three and went over the edge.

Dropped six feet before the slack went out of the rope.

It dragged through the lock of his foot and the grip of his left hand for another four feet before he got himself stopped. His right arm held the LAW firmly against his chest.

The machine gunners found his heat signature, and the gun rattled again.

The shoulder of the shallow crevice he was in protected

him to some degree, but rock particles splattered against his face, drawing blood, and ripped at his clothing.

Andover relaxed the grip of his hand and his foot, and he began sliding down the rope. Projections of rock banged into his back, spun him on the rope, and threatened his grip.

The machine gun followed him down, pausing once, probably to reload.

He had nearly reached the bottom, the rock-strewn slope becoming visible, when his crevice disappeared. He was suddenly fully exposed.

The machine gun roared.

The slugs banged and ricocheted off the cliff face, the stream of amber tracers working toward him.

He let go of the rope.

Too late.

He was slammed into the face of the cliff as three or four heavy rounds caught him in the leg, arm, and chest.

Then tumbled ten feet, losing the LAW, hitting the angled slope, and sliding thirty feet down it.

The pain was incredible.

He couldn't move his leg, and he looked up—he was head-down on the slope—to see the red stain spreading over his thigh.

His breathing was shallow and labored. He couldn't catch his breath. He thought the round had gone through his lung.

He could move his left arm, though its sleeve also was turning red.

Andover saw the LAW resting five feet away, and he pulled himself over onto his stomach and slid his way to it, using his hand to claw at the rocks that were frozen into the surface of the slope. Every inch gained was agony.

He reached the LAW, got his hands on it.

He didn't know how to use the damned thing.

Waves of blackness rushed up to him, then receded.

He was losing too much blood. He would pass out soon.

He heard men yelling, heard their feet scraping on the rocks and gravel as they attempted to climb the slope toward him.

Pulling the LAW over his shoulder, he aimed it in the direction of the missile launcher.

He was closer, and he could see it without the infrared nightsight.

Sixty feet away.

But it wasn't there.

Yes, it was. His hands were so shaky, the sight on the barrel kept bouncing up and down.

The body of the launcher vehicle was hidden by boulders, but the missile tips stood high.

He found them in the sight.

For you, Christine.

Started to squeeze the trigger.

The missile noses wavered and fell away.

Re-aimed.

Rifle fire cracking in the coming dawn.

Slugs bouncing around him.

Squeezed the trigger.

The rocket left the launch tube with a shooshing sound and, half a second later, found the second of the four raised missiles.

Andover's view turned white.

Finally.

And at last.

PRIMAVERA DRILLING SITE #4
0356 HOURS LOCAL

Franco Novarro dragged himself across the frozen ground with his elbows, grunting with every centimeter he gained. He could feel the broken ends of his leg bone grating together, and the pain made him want to yell his outrage. There was no blood, but an air cleaner from one of the diesel engines, projected at fantastic speed, had smashed into his thigh, dropping him where he stood.

The rig's diesel engines no longer sang their bass song. Instead, he heard the screams of men down the slope crying for help. The sizzle and crackle of fire was a predominant melody. One of the fuel tanks had caught fire, leaking diesel fuel along the ground, and a river of flame was moving quickly downhill, melting the snow under it.

He remembered those thirty seconds as if they were a nightmare. One of his men had started firing upward at the canyon rim, the target real or imagined, followed by everyone else. Then a withering return fire from automatic weapons erupted, scattering his ragged troops like drunken field mice. Ricocheting bullets and ice flew everywhere. Then came the two flashes—rockets?—and small detonations in the confines of the derrick and the fuel storage. He had stood terrified and stupefied until the machinery shed blew up and knocked him flat.

The derrick was still standing, but the canvas and plastic covering it was on fire, the flames building and leaping and climbing, reaching high. Soon, they would lap at the camouflage sheeting covering the end of the canyon.

The door to the hut was open, blown off its hinges, but dragging himself over the wooden step made from a pallet and across the threshold was murder. His leg bones bent and scraped, sending pure hell along his raw nerve endings.

He found the portable radio on the floor, pulled it close to his mouth, and keyed the transmit button.

"Primavera!"

"This is Primavera. Who is this?"

"Site Four, you idiot! We need help." He was gritting his teeth so hard against the pain that it was difficult to talk.

"What help? We are sending you help."

"We have been attacked, goddamn it! This is not in my contract!"

"Please list your damages. Did you see the attackers?"

Novarro was lying on his side, trying to ease the tension on his leg, looking up through the doorway at the fire climbing the derrick. As he watched, the tips of blue flames reached the camouflage sheeting.

He did not think he would get his bonuses.

"I do not know the damages, you bastard! I have dead and wounded. The derrick is on fire."

The fabric of the camouflage, stretched taut by its load of snow, ignited.

"There are people on the way to you," the Primavera radio operator said. "You will just have to wait."

Novarro dropped the radio and watched horrified, as the tiny rent in the camouflage sheet began to spread and tear, a great rent racing toward one corner.

And the snow began to come down, tons of it, in great cascading waterfalls, as the sheeting split wide open.

It would suffocate the fires, he knew.

A huge mass of packed snow slammed into the ground outside the door, shattering the doorstep, and spraying him with snow and ice.

Novarro looked up in time to hear a solid thump, and then the tin roof of the shed caved in on him

PRIMAVERA BASE
0401 HOURS LOCAL

Juan Silvera had gone with the rescue convoy to the drilling sites, and Emilio Suarez stayed close to the radio, as he had for most of the night.

For the first time, Suarez had begun to doubt the outcome

of Silvera's venture. In a matter of hours, they had sustained heavy damage from a single bomber they could not stop. And then, in the aftermath of that attack, just as they were extinguishing the fires and assessing the damages, Drilling Site #3 radioed that they were under attack, then went off the air.

Now, Sites 1, 2, and 4 were also out of contact.

"Colonel," the radio operator said, "I cannot raise SAM Unit Eleven or two of the ZSU-23s, three and nine."

Suarez had to think a minute before he recalled where they had been emplaced, near three of the drilling sites.

"Call the convoy and tell them to check on the batteries."

Roberto Tellez, who had spent the last few hours sitting in a straight chair at the side of the room, nursing one cup of coffee after another, got up and walked over to him.

"We are getting very damned close to the attrition ratio I predicted, are we not, Colonel?"

Suarez hated to admit it—he remembered how he and Silvera had scoffed at Tellez's forecast of thirty percent losses, but he nodded.

"And about two months before you, or I, expected it."

"But a ground attack, Major!"

"Commandos, I expect, dropped when they evacuated the station personnel with helicopters. We should have been alert to the possibility, but you and the president seemed to think the only threat would come from the air." Tellez sipped his coffee. "I haven't heard you order anyone to look for them."

Tellez seemed to be constantly and irritatingly suggesting to Suarez what he should be doing.

"We do not even know where they are."

"Up on the ridge, I should imagine. Their tracks will soon be obliterated."

"I can't get helicopters launched in this storm."

"Then send your men on foot, Colonel. Otherwise, plan for additional raids against us."

"They would have to scale the cliff. They are not trained for that."

"Then they must learn on the job," Tellez said. "And I myself should prepare to make a full-scale, full-load bomb run against Eights Station. If we do not respond to this, they will walk all over us."

"We will need all of our aircraft to defend Primavera. Three of the tankers are at Navarino."

"If I were you," Tellez said, "I would abandon the concept of defense and try to think in terms of attack. Find that aircraft carrier, Emilio. If we can stop it, we can hold this godforsaken place for the weeks we need before the UN sends another force."

Tellez turned and walked back to his chair.

Ten minutes later, Silvera called in on the radio.

"The first drilling site is completely destroyed, Emilio, as is the antiaircraft gun. There are seven dead and six wounded. I have sent most of the convoy on to check the other wells."

"Is the drilling rig repairable, *Presidente?*"

"Not without parts from the mainland. And I suspect the others will be the same. You will immediately assemble three infantry platoons to protect the rest of the rigs. Get them up on the ridge. Move antiaircraft units into closer proximity, also."

"Immediately," Suarez agreed, then glanced over at Tellez. "I will also send a ground party to search for the raiders."

"Do it. If we lose the last three wells, the cause is lost."

Suarez called to Captain Arquez, and the two of them decided on which SAM and antiaircraft gun units to move.

"And I want three platoons deployed around the wells," Suarez said.

"We are short of ground transport," the captain told him.

"Then march them out there, but get them there as soon as possible."

"Of course, Colonel."

Arquez left the operations hut, and Suarez wandered around, got himself coffee, ate a sandwich, and worried.

He passed the telex machine and saw that a message had printed off during the frantic activity surrounding the attacks on the wells. He ripped it out of the machine and sat down at a desk to decode it.

DATE: 10 DEC
TIME: 0311
TO: PRESIDENT, FSAD, PRIMAVERA
FROM: FSAD LIAISON, BUENOS AIRES

CONTACT ARGENTINE AIR FORCE INTELLIGENCE REPORTS SUSPICIOUS SHIP SAILING DRAKE PASSAGE. ULCC CORNUCOPIA UTILIZING POWERFUL MILITARY TYPE SEARCH RADAR, SAILING AT TWELVE KNOTS, WELL BELOW CAPABILITY.

ECUADOR, GUYANA, SURINAME, PARAGUAY AMBASSADORS HAVE MADE THIRD DEMAND FOR EVIDENCE OF PETROLEUM PRODUCTION.

Suarez motioned to Tellez. "Come, Roberto, take a look at this."

Tellez crossed to the desk and took the decoded message from him.

"The first paragraph, Roberto. What do you make of that?"

"An Ultra Large Crude Carrier?" Tellez mused for a few moments. "And Harrier jump jets. They might well go together, Emilio."

"Do you think so?"

Tellez smiled. "Colonel of air forces, I think that we will now turn your war around."

DEFENSE INTELLIGENCE AGENCY
0455 HOURS LOCAL

McNichols called Sir Charles at his apartment.

"Don't you ever sleep, Cameron?"

"Sorry to wake you, Sir Charles."

"Oh, I wasn't asleep, either. You are the third to ring me up in the last fifteen minutes. Do you have something new?"

"Yes, sir, I do. We have radio reports from the SEALs. They've confirmed the existence of at least four drilling operations near Primavera."

"Four?"

"That's correct, though all four were destroyed. The SEAL commander thinks there may be more, and he hopes to verify that tomorrow night."

"He has to wait, does he?"

"It's stopped snowing, Sir Charles, and he has to hide out for the day."

"Isn't there some way he could . . . ?"

"He lost three people," McNichols said. "Two SEALs and a civilian guide are all MIA."

"Ah, damn! I hate this, Cameron."

"Yes."

"But the word I just got is that Argentina will seek a cease-fire in the General Assembly in the morning. This morning. They want everyone to put aside their weapons until some peaceful resolution can be achieved. You and I both know that the representatives will vote in favor of peace, every time."

McNichols thought that over. "It would play right into the hands of the FSAD, giving them all the time they need to complete a well, if that's what they're trying to do."

"That is the strategy I read behind this maneuver. You see why I want to know about any other wells, Cameron? If there are no more, and if a cease-fire means everyone stays in place. with no shipment of additional equipment into Antarctica, it does them no good."

McNichols sighed. "Let me talk to Monmouth. If the weather clears enough, maybe they can get some aircraft in there. If not, we'll send the SEALs."

THE SAN MATIAS
0600 HOURS LOCAL

"A supertanker? You must be crazy, Emilio."

Diego Enriquez tried to imagine Harrier jets taking off from a supertanker. He supposed it was possible, but it stretched credibility.

Enriquez was in his cabin, and he stood near the porthole and gazed out at the swollen seas. Heavy waves rolled toward him, unstoppable, ponderous. A patrol boat struggled to hold its position a kilometer away. Just beyond it, the *Marguerite Bay* was taking on fuel oil from the tanker. It was no longer snowing, but the skies were overcast, a grayish white that suggested the whole world was monotone.

A herd of giant icebergs was massed to the north; he could see them if he leaned against the bulkhead and pressed his head to the porthole.

"I am not crazy, Diego. You must position your ships farther to the north, between us and the supertanker. Otherwise, we may lose more of the drilling operations."

"The president is certain that this crude oil carrier poses a threat?"

"I have not yet spoken to the president," Suarez said.

"Then do so, Colonel. He is the one who ordered me where I am."

Enriquez replaced the telephone in its bulkhead cradle and

stood for a moment in the middle of his cabin, thinking. The fact that Suarez had failed to defend the drilling sites could not concern him, except for the potential loss of the support they expected from South American nations. And, in any event, he was powerless to do anything about it.

Except.

That ULCC.

If that ship did indeed carry a military threat. . . .

He charged out of his cabin, down the narrow corridor, and up the companionway to the bridge.

Carlos Estero had the watch, and he saluted as Enriquez entered.

"Find Lieutenant Mondragon."

"At once, Captain."

The navigator, who had been up most of the night, arrived panting on the bridge still buttoning his shirt. He saw Enriquez at the plot, and crossed the deck to join him.

"Captain?"

"We are going to sink an oil carrier, a supertanker, Lieutenant. All we must do is find it."

SIX MILES NORTHEAST OF PRIMAVERA BASE
0625 HOURS LOCAL

Defying David George's prayers for godly intervention in Mother Nature's affairs, the snowstorm had dissipated, leaving gray clouds that were luminous with the sunlight. They didn't cast any shadows, but they were entirely too obvious on this unsullied plain east of the ridge.

Both of George's SEAL squads had reached the Sno-Cats forty minutes before, but it had taken a while to get two of the balky engines started. His men were fatigued by the trek and by the cold, and when they finally got all five of the vehicles underway, most of them climbed in and collapsed on top of their gear in the cramped cabins. They waited patiently, with few voiced complaints, for the heaters to raise the interior temperatures.

In George's Sno-Cat, Sergeant Tu was driving, and Gus Brelin, still holding his captured AK-74, was sitting beside him, giving directions. They had headed east immediately.

George leaned forward between the front seats.

"How are you doing, Gus?"

"I wish I knew about Zip."

"I'm sorry we couldn't wait."

"No, we knew that's the way it would be."

George had reported to Jericho as soon as the two squads had rejoined after the raids, but he had only listed three people as missing. He knew damned well that Christopher Belau, from the Netherlands, was dead, but he didn't know yet about Andover or the Italian, Maldone. Suslov hadn't been able to locate them after the attack.

"Gus, with the weather the way it is, we're going to have choppers on our ass soon. We're pretty exposed here."

They had left the white parachutes taped to the Sno-Cats, with strategically placed rips over the windows, but a single dog moving on this plain would draw eyes, much less five Sno-Cats speeding in trail.

And leaving their tracks clearly behind them.

Brelin shook his head, throwing off ghosts, no doubt, and leaned forward to look through the windshield.

"Yeah, Commander, I know. Tu, you want to take a left here? We'll go north for awhile."

"Right on, Gus," Tu said, and turned left.

George figured they were making twenty miles per hour. It wasn't fast enough, but he couldn't do anything about it.

Suslov had been digging in the stash behind the rear seat.

and he came up with a canvas bag full of food. He passed out MREs.

Brelin opened Tu's for him, and doled it out to him while the driver concentrated on finding the smoothest path. The Sno-Cat was bucking and grinding its way over hillocks and into dips. It seemed as if they should be flying along at a hundred miles an hour, the plain ahead was so featureless and even, but Brelin's trained eye spotted the treacherous footing when he found it, and he told Tu when to turn left or right.

Suslov got on the squad radio and told the men in the other Sno-Cats, who were carrying Stinger surface-to-air missiles, to get the weapons out and ready, just in case a helicopter spotted them.

Twenty minutes later, they rolled onto a broad, smooth stretch of ice that Brelin called a lake. After a few minutes, Brelin told Tu to turn west.

"Back toward the ridge?" George asked.

"There isn't anyone I know about who looks for stray dogs in their own backyard, Commander."

FIVE KILOMETERS NORTHEAST OF PRIMAVERA BASE
0611 HOURS LOCAL

Paco Sacramento was a sergeant in the FSAD Ground Forces Unit. He had once served in the Colombian army, and he knew jungles and mountains and stifling heat and buzzing insects.

He did not know snow and cold and snowshoes.

He did not like them.

The other thing he knew was obvious trails, and the ruts in the snow ahead, where dozens of skis had plied, was obvious enough.

He and his eight men had been plodding their way through

the snow for almost two hours, following the ski tracks on their unwieldy and unfamiliar snowshoes. It was hard work, and he felt they must be falling far behind their quarry. No one had expected to find ski tracks once they had made the climb up the face of the cliff. But at Site #1, Sacramento had counted at least six separate pairs of tracks. Perhaps there were one or two more, but he could not tell for certain.

Six men, they could handle with ease, and they had set out immediately, confident they would overtake and kill the intruders.

But within a couple kilometers, the tracks they were following intersected with and joined another set of multiple tracks. He did not know now how many rabbits his wolves were chasing.

Once, when he felt they were losing distance, he had called Primavera on the radio and asked for a helicopter. The control officer, named Arquez, had told him that helicopters were not then available. He wished he knew what was going on back at the base. He had heard from one of his men that his good friend, Sergeant Jalisco, from his home village, had been killed. He would like to know if that rumor were true or not.

He stopped them for their fourth five-minute break, and sipped from his canteen. It was a standard-issue canteen, not of the Thermos variety, and he found that his water was nearly frozen solid. It came as something of a surprise since the forced march was keeping them fairly warm.

After the five minutes elapsed, he said, "All right, let us go on. Wences, you will take the point."

"Ah, Sergeant. My legs are so short, they will slow us down."

"Go."

Grumbling to himself, Wences shook the snow from his snowshoes, then started out, staying in the tracks made by the skis.

And five minutes later, Wences came to a stop and looked back at him.

"What is it?"

"I hit something, Sergeant. Stepped on something."

Trip wire?

Delayed action?

"Down! Everybody down!"

Six of the nine of them were flat on the ground when the Claymore mines went off.

The concussions were loud in Sacramento's ears, and he could hear the sizzle of antipersonnel shrapnel zinging about at knee-high level.

Wences screamed the loudest when he was hit, the shrapnel shredding the legs of his pants and his flesh.

Contrarez had almost completed his dive to the ground, and he took the shrapnel in the face. He was rolling about in the snow, whimpering, flinging drops of blood everywhere. His face appeared as if it had gone through a meat chopper.

Calles was closest to one of the Claymores, and he lost his left leg. He was also unconscious.

Sacramento whipped the radio out of his pocket.

"Primavera!"

"This is Primavera. Who is this?"

"Sacramento, damn you! I need a helicopter fast. I have wounded."

"Sacramento, at this time. . . ."

Another voice took over. "This is Colonel Suarez. What happened, Sacramento?"

He described the booby trap.

"You haven't seen them?"

"No, damn it! Colonel, these men will die!"

"I am sending a helicopter for them now. You move ahead quickly, and you catch the bastards."

"There are over a dozen of them," Sacramento complained.

"I will send reinforcements for you. Go now!"

Sacramento sighed. He should be back in the jungles.

He detailed one man to apply field dressings to the wounded and to watch over them, and he and his remaining four soldiers again took to the trail.

UNS U THANT
0720 HOURS LOCAL

Captain Samuel Monmouth had called the conference in the wing briefing room in order to have some space, though only he, von Stein, Cady, Baker, d'Argamon, Eames, and Purgatory were in attendance.

He leaned on the podium and studied the faces. Cady's was inscrutable; he was hiding his feelings well. None of the others knew that he wasn't flying. It was to be his and Monmouth's little secret until Monmouth thought the time was ripe to reverse his decision.

He pushed the public address system microphone on its flexible conduit out of the way. "Major Eames."

"Sir?"

"What is the current situation in our theater of operations?"

Eames stood up, and Monmouth watched the eyes of those who followed her.

"As of 0700 hours, the FSAD naval forces were moving to the north at flank speed. A C-130 and two Mirages were flying air patrol in the vicinity of Primavera, and another Mirage made a pass over us, though it stayed well away. Three KC-130s are still on the ground at Navarino, though it appears that they've completed refilling from fuel bladders. Commander George reports that his group is burrowed in for the day, though he has heard a helicopter in the area."

"Do you think, Major, that our cover is blown?"

"I think that it is likely, sir, yes."

"Commander von Stein, after this meeting, I want you to inspect our defensive systems. Test fire all guns, run simulations on the fire control radars."

"Aye, sir."

Eames sat down.

"Let me tell you, then, about the conditions outside our theater of operations," Monmouth said. "The first of the Russian transports and a squadron of MiG29s has landed at Christchurch, coming out of Cam Ranh Bay. Some little bird whispering in someone's ear says they'll make a dash for the continent on the fourteenth of the month.

"The *Enterprise* task force, commanded by Admiral Conway, and including a Marine Expeditionary Force, will arrive in our zone by the seventeenth. I'm told that they're only coming to assist us."

"For about five minutes," Cady said. "Then they'll take over."

Monmouth knew Conway, too. And being an American commander, Monmouth also knew that Americans liked to control the command structure. When he had thought about it, he'd found himself highly resentful. He didn't want any Americans taking over his battle for him.

It was difficult to recall his military heritage.

"More pressing," he went on, "is the political forum. In talking to Sir Charles this morning, I've learned that Argentina will introduce a cease-fire resolution on the floor of the General Assembly, probably within the next few hours. There will be support from several representatives, and it is likely to pass. The issue will then be passed to the National Security Council, which will receive it on the eleventh. They could well take action on the same day, but Sir Charles believes the vote will be held off until the twelfth."

"And then we all stand down?" Baker asked.

"More than likely, Major."

"And let the FSAD complete whatever it is they set out to do. The drilling, I mean."

"That worries Sir Charles," Monmouth told him. "And he has a broader worry, dealing with broader perspectives, as he does. He is concerned, as am I, that the *U Thant* will have fallen short of her mission, in the worldview. There has always been a debate over whether or not the United Nations can enforce a peacekeeping role, and if we fail here, the expenditures made for the ship and its complement of personnel and equipment are going to come under intense criticism and review, possibly resulting in abandonment of the concept."

He paused to allow anyone to dissent, but didn't find any takers.

"To date, we've been following, as much as the weather and developing circumstance would allow, the probe and punch battle plans we formulated several days ago. We can continue to do that, and perhaps achieve our objective in another five or six days.

"I don't believe, however, that we have the luxury of time or of delaying tactics by the Peacekeeper Committee available to us any longer."

The nodding heads told him they understood.

"Sir Charles wants this operation completed no later than noon on the twelfth in order to forestall the Russians, the American task force, and the Argentine resolution. Can we accommodate him?"

Cady sat up and looked at Baker and d'Argamon, who both nodded, then said, "If Purgatory will cooperate, I don't see a major problem. I've been thrashing a few ideas around."

"Just tell me what kind of weather you want," Eddie Purgatory said.

"I do not worry about weather," d'Argamon said. "I wil

take *Calais* and *Dover* together, and there will be no more FSAD naval force."

"Which is only part of the problem," Baker said, "but there's nothing that we can't overcome."

"Well," Cady added, "there is one little problem."

"You and I will have to deal with that one privately," Monmouth told him. "I want you to put your heads together and come up with something that doesn't involve a massed assault. I don't think we could survive that."

"Speaking of survival," Cady said, "I'm worried about our SEALs. I want to send a couple choppers in to either extract them or provide some cover. I think I've figured out a way to do that."

"It's about time Henry and I got a spot of fresh air, anyway," Baker said.

FALCON ONE
0950 HOURS LOCAL

The overcast had burned off, and it was a beautiful flying day—if one were flying the verdant Virginia countryside or chasing along the spring-flowered coast from Dungeness to Brighton, as Baker enjoyed doing.

Racing along the western coast of the Antarctic Peninsula, however, there were other distractions.

"Look!" Decker said. "Ten o'clock. On the ground."

Baker found Decker's target easily. A large colony of penguins. As a quick guess, he estimated there were over two hundred of them, most of them standing stately along a sea-splashed inlet in the ice. A few were attempting sprints, tripping up, and landing on their bellies, sliding along the ice. They seemed unperturbed as the three helicopters flashed by them, two hundred yards off the coast, and fifty feet above the sea.

"Any hostiles there, you think?" he asked.

"Not a one, Major. They're on our side."

"Not that I'm not happy that you saw the penguins, Henry, but keep your eyes aimed upward, will you?"

"One eye is *always* aimed upward," Decker insisted.

They had lost radar coverage from Jericho a half-hour before, and so far, Pack Rat hadn't passed on any juicy tidbits concerning the FSAD deployments.

While they had approximate coordinates for the hideout selected by George and his SEALs, and were about sixty miles away at the moment, they were going to have to ask George to broadcast a homing signal soon.

And that could excite a couple of Mirages flying figure-eight orbits over Primavera.

Baker checked outside his canopy to his right and found Copperhead Three and Jerry Can Two right where they were supposed to be, on his level, spread about forty yards apart.

"We're about twenty minutes out," Decker said. "Should I try and reach George now?"

"Let's give it another five minutes, Henry. The later, the better."

But it wouldn't wait until later.

On the chopper's ICS, Baker heard the portable radio Decker was tending crackle and snap, then, issue, "Falcon One, Raccoon."

Decker responded, "Go, Raccoon."

Baker was aware that, when George was talking to British or Australian nationals, more of his Aussie accent came out. He suspected George did it deliberately.

"How far out are you, mate?"

"Maybe twenty minutes," Decker told him.

"I wonder if you could cut that in half? I have an idea these blokes have located us."

NINETEEN KILOMETERS NORTHEAST OF PRIMAVERA BASE
0952 HOURS LOCAL

Sergeant Sacramento's replacement troops turned out to be seven sailors, once deckhands on the minesweeper *San Jorge*. They carried Kalashnikov AK-74 assault rifles with which they were unfamiliar and uneasy, and they were dressed in an odd assortment of secondhand arctic clothing. All seven were most unhappy to find themselves in a frozen wasteland with very little prospect of either hot food or a hot stove.

Their attitudes were quite similar to those of the five men in Sacramento's squad who had survived the Claymore mines. Their minds were not on the job at hand, and their conversations consisted almost entirely of complaints.

Sacramento could not help thinking that a man who was dreaming of food or heat would be less effective in a firefight. He wished that he was back in the jungles of Colombia.

The helicopter, one of the Aérospatiale Super Frelon cargo carriers, was unarmed, and it had not reached them for a long time. It had first retrieved the injured men and returned them to Primavera before picking up Sacramento's pursuit party. He had not complained, thankful that Colonel Suarez had been compassionate enough to overrule Captain Arquez.

When at last they had been picked up, Sacramento knelt near the pilots and directed the course of their flight by pointing his finger. He could barely hear himself think with the roar of the three turboshaft engines. They had followed the tracks of the Sno-Cats east, then north, then onto what might have been considered a lake of ice in the middle of a flat plain. Swept clear of snow by thirty-kilometer-per-hour winds, the solid, hard ice had refused to accept the evidence of passage. The spoor of the Sno-Cats had disappeared.

Sacramento's first impulse was that the raiders had continued northward, and so he had instructed the pilots to continue across the lake to the north. When they reached the far shore—a jumble of upthrust rock and blue ice—there was no sign of vehicle tracks.

And so they had begun a crisscrossing search pattern, following the edge of the ice farther to the northeast, then east, then south again. Finally, they had made the circuit back to where the tracks had first disappeared onto the ice. With nowhere else to go, Sacramento told the pilot to follow the western edge of the ice. He did not think, however, that the raiders would have turned to the west, heading back toward the ridge overlooking the drilling sites.

But that was where they found the exit tracks.

The helicopter stayed low, the copilot now assisting the pilot in following the churned snow, and Sacramento slipped back to the cargo compartment and warned his twelve men to prepare themselves.

Soon, they would find the icemen who had decimated his squad, and soon, he would return the favor.

UNS U THANT
1000 HOURS LOCAL

Commander Hermann von Stein, first officer of the *U Thant,* had grown up militarily in the navy of West Germany. In the unified German state, the military was as yet a chaotic structure, and he had been relieved to receive his assignment to the United Nations. He would stand to one side and wait while the lines of command and promotion tracks in his native land sorted themselves out.

Von Stein, a muscular, broad man with blue eyes and fair, short-cropped hair, had begun his duty with the *U Thant* with some degree of incredulity and a larger degree of distrust as part of his mind-set. He had not thought highly of the concept, nor of the ship's ability to fulfill her mission. He had been disdainful of her commander, a man who spent more time listening than leading.

And within six weeks, he had begun to change his mind about a ULCC-turned-aircraft carrier and an American named Monmouth.

He was reluctant to admit that he was learning, but the people aboard the ship had taught him many things about human relationships, and he had learned from the technology available, much of which was far superior to what he had had available in German service.

The weapons control system of the *U Thant* was an adaptation of that utilized by American Aegis class cruisers. Designated the Mk 10, the system could track multiple targets— over a hundred hostile ships and aircraft as well as inbound missiles—and under battle conditions was directed by the tactical information officer in the Combat Information Center in conjunction with a ship's officer serving as the tactical action officer and designated by the Captain—currently Monmouth himself, von Stein, or Jacob Ernst. Major Theresa Eames occasionally served in both capacities. When data-linked with satellite or airborne radars and infrared sensors, the Aegis system provided a five hundred mile range of coverage. Since the United Nations did not have its own satellites, however, that data-link technology had not been incorporated. On its own, the SPY phased-array radar, working in conjunction with the Searchwater narrowbeam radar, could pick up incoming aircraft at over two hundred miles and low-flying missiles at nearly fifty miles.

The weapons controlled by the Aegis computers were powerful and, in the slang of von Stein's two teenage sons—admirers of American rock and roll—awesome. Forward, the two tank hatches just aft of the bow aircraft elevators opened partially to expose the twin Mk 46—upgrade of earlier versions—Vertical Launch Systems (VLS). The canisters of the carousel-type launchers contained sixty-four missiles each and were currently loaded with SM-2 Aegis antiaircraft missiles and Tomahawk surface attack missiles. Since the FSAD forces apparently did not include submarines, von Stein had ordered the antisubmarine rocket torpedoes (ASROC) downloaded from the launcher, except for two ASROCs. Being a cautious and conservative man, von Stein did not want to entirely discount the possibility of a FSAD submarine. The Pack Rat intelligence sources, while evidently reliable, might well have missed seeing a submarine.

Both fore and aft, from beneath the third set of false tank hatches and from behind panels that opened on the lower superstructure of the stern, were four computer-controlled, radar-guided seventy-six-millimeter guns. The Italian Otto Melara 76/62 guns were fed by a revolving magazine containing seventy antiaircraft rounds, and the firing rate ranged from single rounds to 120 rounds per minute. In the unlikely event that an inbound antiship missile evaded the *U Thant*'s defensive missiles, the guns had a high probability prospect of blowing the hostile missile out of the sky.

Von Stein, working from the CIC with Luigi Maroni as the TIO and Sergeant Trish O'Hara as the data entry technician, had already tested the guns, firing ten rounds from each. The forward guns, when ordered into operation, rose hydraulically from below decks to give them an optimum field of fire. The stern guns, after the panels on the superstructure slid aside, rolled outboard on telescoping rails and provided a nearly 180-degree field of protection to the rear of the ship.

The Mk 10 Aegis system was fully operational, and the SPY radar was currently displaying seven vessels and nine aircraft on the left multifunction screen. All of the vessels had been identified as commercial, plying the Drake Passage en route to one destination or another. Two of the aircraft were Gypsy Moth Squadron Harriers flying combat air patrol. The remaining seven aircraft, all to the north beyond the one hundred mile "bubble" of airspace designated by Monmouth as the *U Thant*'s safety zone, had been identified as Chilean and Argentinean air force and naval aircraft. They appeared to be monitoring the ULCC's voyage, and if they had not been suspicious before, they would be since the big and powerful radars had been activated.

"Lieutenant Maroni," von Stein said to the TIO, "we will want to watch those aircraft closely."

"I have already entered them in the computer, Commander. The alarm will sound if they enter the bubble."

"Very good. Now, let us tell the Gypsy Moth airplanes that they have become enemies."

Maroni toed his transmit button and spoke into the cantilevered microphone of his headset. "Gypsy Flight One, Jericho."

"Jericho, Gypsy Three," Olivera replied.

"Three, you are now Hostile One. Take an attack profile on Beehive at your discretion and reset IFF modes and codes." Maroni provided them with new identification codes to simulate enemy aircraft.

The two Harriers were 120 miles southeast of the ship, and von Stein watched as their symbols on the screen changed to green triangles. The data box next to each symbol began to change rapidly as the two aircraft dove to an altitude of three thousand feet and circled back toward the ship.

When they entered the bubble, a chirping alarm sounded

and Maroni said, "Commander, two hostiles inbound, range nine-eight miles, altitude angels three, heading one-three-nine, speed five-four-zero."

At his section of the console, von Stein ran the palm of his right hand over a trackball, and a circular cursor zipped across the screen and wrapped itself around the first target. He locked it in, then homed another cursor on the second target.

"Sergeant O'Hara, trial engage," von Stein ordered.

"Trial engage, aye," she replied.

The antiship tracking data display, shown on a separate monitor just below the big multifunction screen, started to blink, and a list of the missiles selected by the computer appeared.

"Sir," O'Hara said, "six SM-2 missiles selected."

"We will take three from each launcher," von Stein told her.

"Aye, aye, sir."

In front of von Stein and Luigi Maroni, two amber buttons were blinking. They were identified in large block letters as HOLD FIRE buttons. Either of the officers could stop the launch process at nearly any time after the commit order had been given.

On this test, von Stein did not intend to go to the commit stage. They needed every Harrier they had.

On the large multifunction screen, the computer had added the intercept tracks projected for the SM-2 missiles against the incoming targets.

"What do you think, Lieutenant Maroni?"

"I think we could splash two Harriers in about forty seconds, Commander."

"I do, too. Stand down the test."

"Disengaging trial," O'Hara said.

They secured the system, and von Stein ordered the VLS doors closed.

He was not worried about any ship, airplane, or missile that the FSAD might aim in his direction. And he hoped that some-day, when he returned to German service, he might have as sophisticated a system at his disposal.

Hermann von Stein, in his sixteen years of military service, had never been engaged in a military action. He had per-formed countless simulations, war games, and trial tests, but the threats had all been remote, shoved to the back of his mind. And while he had attended the memorial services for the helicopter and Harrier pilots, he still found it difficult to believe that the *U Thant* was actually involved in a shooting war.

ELEVEN MILES NORTHEAST OF PRIMAVERA BASE
1007 HOURS LOCAL

The five Sno-Cats were parked in a semicircle, backed up against the twenty-foot rock cliff they had encountered after turning north again, and covered with parachute camouflage. In the bright light of a cloudless day, though, David George knew they were no longer assets. An aircraft at five thousand feet might miss seeing them, but ground troops or low-flying helicopters would see them as the bull's-eye at the end of an arrow-straight track in the snow.

Which is why the vehicles were not occupied. Using the hard scrabble at the base of the cliff to mask their footprints, the two SEAL squads had worked their way two hundred yards to the west, until they ran into an intersecting rock face that ran north and south. They used grappling hooks to secure ropes on top of the thirty-foot cliff, then climbed the precipice to find another few thousand acres of snow field. George had split them up into eight groups, and each group had dug a snow cave and backed themselves and their equipment into it.

From his own cave, shared with Gus Brelin and Gregori Suslov, George had a commanding view of the Sno-Cats and the blinding landscape to the east. He felt somewhat vulnerable because he couldn't see behind him.

But the threat was coming from the east. He had heard the helicopter a number of times without seeing it, and he knew that sound would travel for long distances in the frigid air over flat ground.

The sound was growing in intensity and volume now, though.

"They've got our track," Brelin said.

"Yes."

"I wish Zip were here. He'd have something flippant to say."

"This will not be an assault ship," Suslov said. "Not if our intelligence is correct."

"What is that? What do you mean?" Brelin asked.

"The intelligence people have told us that the FSAD has a Kamov chopper at sea and four transports and a Gazelle inland," George said. "The Gazelle might carry some light weapons, but this is likely to be one of the Super Frelons. It'll be carrying troops. We can handle the troops."

He didn't bother telling the Dane that the problem wasn't the soldiers or the helicopter; the problem was the fighter-bombers they could call in.

It was one of the big Aérospatiale choppers. It came in low from the east, its silhouette increasing in size and its thunder growing in intensity. It was almost on top of the cliff before someone spotted the Sno-Cats, and then it abruptly peeled off to the north. When it wasn't fired on, it came back tentatively, circling the area, flying directly over the snow caves. The downblast of its rotors kicked up a storm of loose snow as it passed over, bringing a mini-avalanche down over George's peephole. He used his mittened hand to open it up again.

The Super Frelon circled back to the east, then settled to the snowpack a hundred yards beyond the Sno-Cats and south of the cliff. A dozen men spilled out of it, spreading out, dropping into the snow. The chopper took off immediately and backed away, getting out of range of small-arms fire.

George detected the squad leader immediately. With arm signals, he began moving his soldiers toward the Sno-Cats.

"It is an easy shot," Suslov said. "I could take him out, and the rest would scatter like ground squirrels."

"It's a tempting thought, Gregori, but let's give Falcon a few more minutes before we risk having them make radio calls."

The FSAD soldiers took all of five minutes reaching the Sno-Cats, and when they did, they quickly discovered their abandoned state. There was a flurry of activity as the troops began searching the ground for the SEALs' escape route. It wasn't long before one man yelled to his leader and pointed to the earth near the cliff.

The squad leader crossed the ground to examine the evidence, looked up to the higher plane, then west toward the intersecting cliff. His eyes scanned intently, finally rising until George felt as if they were staring each other down.

He said something to his men, and all of them fanned out away from the base of the rocks and started moving toward George's hideouts.

In a loud whisper, George called to the next snow cave, "Tu."

"Yes, Commander."

"Hold fire until my signal. Pass that on."

George looked out through the slit of his snow cave entrance at the antenna wire laying on the top of the snow. He pulled his radio close and poised his finger over the transmit button.

Suslov and Brelin poised their fingers over the triggers of their assault rifles.

FALCON ONE
1009 HOURS LOCAL

"Falcon One, Jericho."

"Go, Jericho," Baker said.

"Pack Rat says you turned inland seventeen minutes ago," Maroni said.

"Pack Rat's pretty close to being right."

"Pack Rat also says that you are apparently undetected so far. There has been no change in the status of FSAD aircraft."

"Thank you, Jericho, I appreciate that." Baker signed off.

"It's nice to know that Big Mother is watching over us," Decker said on the intercom.

"Isn't it? I think it's about time we had a homing signal, Henry."

"Very well." Decker went to the portable radio and transmitted, "Raccoon, Falcon."

The response was immediate.

"Falcon, we've got thirteen armed troops on the ground and a Super Frelon a half-mile away. Anything you can do about that?"

"Hold your transmit button down," Decker told him, "and we'll see what happens."

Fifteen seconds later, Decker said, "Major, come left six degrees."

"Six degrees."

Baker eased into the turn, checking to see that Copperhead Three and Jerry Can Two followed.

They were bobbing and weaving with the terrain, which was almost opaque with its sameness. The shadows of hills and crevices and a few outcroppings of rock provided some definition.

He checked his fuel state, which wasn't encouraging.

"We're going to have a bit of a timing problem, Henry."

"I've been thinking about it, Major."

"And?"

"And nothing. No solution other than that we have to kill everyone first."

"That's probably right."

They had intended to land, then refuel Falcon and Copperhead from the tanker helicopter before proceeding with the rest of the mission. They needed an empty tanker in order to transport the second half of George's SEALs. With enemy troops in contact, though, they were running short of time. And as soon as the UN choppers appeared on the scene, there was going to be an alert at Primavera, less than twenty miles away.

"That bloody damned Purgatory could at least have given us some snow," Baker said.

"Not until tomorrow, and that's only a maybe. You know the met guys," Decker said. "Four miles to go."

Baker keyed his transmit button on the squadron net. "Copperhead and Jerry Can, Falcon."

"Three."

"Two."

"Put down right here and refuel. Take on as much as you can, Copperhead, then go in for the extraction. Overload the troops. Jerry Can, you take the rest of them."

"We'll be in overload, too," Gail Alhers said.

"But not for long. You can refuel me in flight, after we're out of here."

"Roger that," Alhers said.

The two transport helicopters dropped out of formation and disappeared behind them.

Decker passed the information on to George that he was to put eighteen of his people on the first Seahawk and six on the second.

"One mile, Major."

There was very little change in the terrain. At a mean level of fifteen hundred feet above sea level, it undulated some, but the predominant features were less than fifty feet in height or depth. Baker kept the Sea Apache skimming the ground and his eyes searching for any sign of his objective.

He cut his forward speed to eighty knots, but they still shot over the edge of a cliff into clear view of the enemy before Baker was quite ready for them. The meeting surprised them all, he was sure.

Directly below, figures advancing across the snow scattered, diving for cover. Two men took shots at them. Ahead, the Super Frelon was idling on the ground.

"Sidewinder, Henry."

"Lock-on. Gone."

The missile screamed off the pylon, and Baker banked hard to the right.

The Frelon was struggling to get airborne, her engines not yet at full power, when the missile plowed into the cockpit. Orange sheets of flame followed the eruption, spewing outward in a ragged ball, followed by a junkyard of debris and a clinic of body parts. One rotor flew off and sailed toward the cliff, impacting end-on like a giant, flat arrow.

Baker continued to make his turn.

Decker spoke on the portable radio. "Raccoon, where are you?"

"Top of the cliff. Anything in the valley is yours."

Coming from the south, Baker lined up on the soldiers who were all prone in the snow, aiming their pitifully small rifles toward them.

One man appeared to be using a heavy portable radio,

and Baker was afraid that stealth was now a thing of the past.

Decker selected the thirty-millimeter Chain Gun, linked to his helmet for aiming, and the gun began to chatter. Ahead, fountains began to erupt in the snow, a steady stream of them working back and forth, closing in on the ground troops. Baker saw one man blown apart before the Sea Apache screamed by.

When he circled back this time, he brought the helicopter to a hover so Decker could finish the job.

There didn't seem to be anything to finish. None of the bodies splattered over the snow moved. Bright splotches of red stained the morning.

"Copperhead, Falcon," he called on the squadron net. "How are you coming?"

"Another couple minutes, and we'll be on the way, Falcon."

"Snap it up. I think we'll have company from Primavera damned soon."

As he watched, men began to emerge from the snow atop the ridge ahead, several of them waving at the helicopter.

And as he watched, one of the figures laying on the ground struggled to sit up, to raise its rifle, and to squeeze off a burst of automatic fire.

Two men on the ridge went down.

"Shit!" Baker yelled.

Decker opened up with the Chain Gun and cut the man in half.

PRIMAVERA BASE
1014 HOURS LOCAL

Emilio Suarez was not above assuming his share of the duties, especially since their aircraft losses had increased the workload on the remaining aircrews. He had taken his place in the alert revetment at 1000 hours, prepared to sit in his airplane for a four-hour stint.

The canopy was partially open, and a four-inch flexible rubber hose piped warm air from a portable propane heater into the cockpit, not only for his benefit, but also to keep the instruments ready for instant action. The pilot of Jaguar Seven sat in the Mirage parked next to him, and the ground crewmen shared the seat in a four-wheel-drive pickup parked just behind and between the aircraft.

Despite the heat duct and an outside temperature that had risen to four degrees above zero Fahrenheit, it was cold in the cockpit. A wind gusting to twenty knots brought chilled air and floating snowflakes inside. He supposed the wind chill index was close to -15 degrees. Suarez used a terry cloth towel to wipe the instrument panel and HUD down frequently. He had his parka draped over his shoulders and wore his gloves.

With the radio on and tuned to the channel used by the Frelon helicopter, Suarez monitored the activity taking place to the north. He had not heard anything from them in almost ten minutes.

Arquez had just reported to the alert craft and to the two Tornados flying patrol to the west that there was no indication of alien aircraft in the area. Nightdog Two had recorded a radar contact with two aircraft to the north, but they had turned back toward the mainland of South America.

He was about to check in with the Super Frelon when Sergeant Sacramento's excited voice ran over the static on the channel.

"Primavera! Primavera! We have been attacked!"

"What!" Arquez yelped. "By whom? Give me details, Sacramento!"

"Assault helicopter. I've never seen one like it. The Frelon is down. Most of my men are down. I need. . . ."

Suarez heard the thunder of a big gun drown out the sergeant's voice on the radio, then the transmission was lost, replaced by carrier wave.

He raised the canopy and threw out the heat duct, waving frantically at the ground crewmen in the truck. They spilled out of it and raced for the auxiliary power unit.

Nine minutes went by before his Mirage was started, the inertial navigation system was spooled up, and the engine was warmed enough for takeoff. Jaguar Seven's jet engine would not start. Suarez left the runway a minute later, retracting his flaps and gear, climbing steeply toward the north, fighting the crosswinds.

"Primavera, Jaguar One."

"This is Primavera."

"Give me a vector for the Frelon's last position."

"Go to zero-three-one degrees."

Suarez found the heading and kept the afterburner engaged. At three hundred meters, he leveled out.

He was over the site of the downed helicopter in less than a minute, reducing throttle and banking to the right to circle the flames and smoke still rising from the charred wreckage. To the west of the dead helicopter, Suarez saw bodies sprawled in the snow. One of them pushed upward to a sitting position and waved weakly at him. The snow and ice was churned into craters and rubble from the impact of dozens of rounds of large-caliber shells.

"Primavera, this is Jaguar. What are your radar contacts?"

"Jaguar, we show only friendly contacts," Arquez said.

"Bring Nightdog Two south. We have a hostile helicopter somewhere near. Get another Frelon out here to retrieve the wounded."

Suarez scanned the horizons, but he could not find what

he was looking for. It had had at least ten minutes in which to get away, but still it could not be over twenty or twenty-five kilometers from him.

He chose north and pulled out of his circle, climbing again to enhance his visibility. The wind on the ground was kicking up some snow, but it was nothing that should hamper his vision.

He was seventy kilometers north of Primavera when he spotted it.

Them.

There were three helicopters, flying so low that their shadows seemed almost a part of the aircraft. They were not emitting radar, and he slowed the Mirage as he approached from the rear. When he was within eight kilometers, he identified them as an Apache attack helicopter and two Black Hawks. They were finished in low-visibility gray, but they stood out clearly against the snow.

He armed two of his Super Matra missiles.

FALCON ONE
1028 HOURS LOCAL

"Falcon One, Jericho. Pack Rat reports that you have company."

"Copied," Baker said just as his threat receiver activated.

"And bloody damned close," Decker said.

"Copperhead and Jerry Can," Baker said, "break left and under me. Now."

He pulled the stick back, bringing the chopper up abruptly, then banked right crossing over the top of the two Seahawks. Whipping the tail around, he aimed the Sea Apache directly at the attacker.

"Henry."

"Launching one, Major. Also countermeasures."

The Sidewinder shrieked off its rail, climbing upward toward the oncoming Mirage.

Not, however, before the Mirage had launched two of its own missiles.

"Hasn't got a lock on us anymore," Decker said.

The Mirage rolled right, avoiding the Sidewinder.

"Break south!" Baker yelled to the other pilots as he banked hard to the left, chasing the Mirage, which he wouldn't catch in a million and one years.

"He's got me!" somebody screamed.

Both missiles whistled by the Sea Apache, curving toward the Seahawks.

A second later, they both smashed into one Seahawk, and it disappeared in a cloud of debris and fuel-fed flames.

"Son of a bitch!" Baker yelled to himself.

The Mirage was circling back for another pass.

"Jerry Can, scoot for the sea," Baker ordered.

"Not just yet, Major," Alhers replied. "I still haven't fueled you."

"Go, damn it!"

But he was too busy to watch what she was doing. He had the Sea Apache up to 160 knots, climbing through two thousand feet, rolling again to the right, toward the approaching Mirage.

The pilot elected to engage Baker.

He came, head-on, cannons blazing.

The red tracers sailed high above the canopy, and Baker dove, turning left, looking for the ground.

The Mirage flashed by above them.

"You might have shot him down, just then, Henry."

"Bloody fucking gun's jammed, Major."

"Ah. That's a suitable excuse."

Baker would really have liked having a forest below, some

place he could dive into and find a hiding place. Lacking a forest, he would have to use what was available, and his first priority was to draw the defender away from Jerry Can, who was unarmed.

He was flying sixty feet above the rugged terrain at 180 knots, aimed more or less to the east.

"You see him, Henry?"

"Got him. He's coming around after us."

"Leaving Gail alone, is he?"

"For now. Probably thinks we're the greater threat."

"And we are," Baker said.

Decker didn't say anything.

"Aren't we?"

"Of course. What is it we're looking for, Major?"

"How about a deep hole in the ground?"

"One that we don't make ourselves?"

"Preferably."

"I see a shadow over to the left. Come left five."

"Left five." Baker banked into the new heading. The back of his mind was counting seconds until the Mirage caught up with them.

"I think that's what we want," Decker said.

The elongated blackness against the snow came up fast, and Baker bled off speed as they neared it. It was a large crevice; at least it was long. In width, he judged it at about ninety feet. If he was careful, he wouldn't lose any rotor tips.

The alternative, a pair of gray mountains to the east, was too far away.

He zoomed in above the crevasse, brought the helicopter to a hover, and spun the nose to the south. Looking out the right side of the canopy, he saw the Mirage coming at him broadside. Just as the cannons opened up, he cut pitch.

And dropped straight down, leaving his stomach forty feet above.

He couldn't see the bottom, but he wasn't looking for it. The rotors cleared each edge, and he stopped his descent some twenty feet from the top.

The Mirage shot over the top of them.

"Cussing us, I bet," Decker said.

"He'll come at us from the south."

"Think so?"

"He likes to turn right, I think, Henry, and he won't get a shot at us broadside, so he'll try it along the length of the crevice."

"Or he could wait us out."

"Which would not be a long wait, I'm afraid," Baker said after glancing at the fuel state.

"I'll use both Sidewinders, Major."

"Good idea," Baker told him, though he wasn't so sure. They were the last of their armament, with the Chain Gun locked up.

The part of his mind that was counting seconds told him that time was up, and he brought the Apache straight up, rising out of the crevasse. Gusts of wind whipping across the top of the hole had to be countered.

The Mirage was coming down at them.

Decker locked on and fired the Sidewinders.

The Mirage fired two missiles, then swerved to evade the Sidewinders.

Baker dropped back into his hole, going lower this time, the chopper steadier as the wind died away.

Watching the ice-coated sides of the crevasse, which were narrowing as he went down.

Forty feet down, he judged.

Ten-foot clearance on each side of the rotors.

Fifty feet.

Sixty feet.

Three, maybe four feet of clearance on the rotors.

He stopped his descent.

The enemy missiles went over them, beyond, impacting far down in the crevice, detonating, shaking the earth. Ice chunks spilled down the sides, some pieces striking the rotors.

The Apache vibrated.

The shadow of the Mirage whisked over them.

The vibration disappeared.

The earth settled down.

Baker waited.

Almost two minutes, then brought his lady up out of the pit. Which cleared the antennas for line-of-sight transmissions.

". . . Falcon One?"

"You calling me, Jerry Can?"

"He split for the south," Alhers said. "Let's get out of here."

"Bet he was out of ammo," Decker said.

"Comin' your way, darling," Baker said. "I do need a spot of petrol."

UNS U THANT
1120 HOURS LOCAL

As soon as Baker and Alhers were clear of the peninsula—feet wet, Eames told Cady that she felt as if she could leave the CIC.

"You're becoming a real mother to us all," Cady said.

She wrinkled her nose at him. "Don't you believe it."

He held the door for her, and they slipped through the light trap and into the corridor.

"Nikki and Phil are waiting in the wing briefing room for us."

"I want something to eat first. I'm starved," she said.

They stopped by the wardroom on C Deck and talked the steward into making up eight roast beef sandwiches.

"And chips," Eames said. "A couple bags of potato chips."

Cady carried the paper sack, and they took the elevator down to the first hangar deck level. Nakamura, the new 2nd Squadron commander, and Anderson were waiting for them.

"Damn," Anderson said, "food. You think of everything, CAG."

"Terri thinks of everything," he corrected.

"Anything from Baker?" Nakamura asked.

Cady grimaced. "He and Gail are on the way back."

"Cornwell?" Anderson asked.

"No."

"Shit."

Eames passed out sandwiches and opened the bags of potato chips while Cady dropped quarters in the vending machine and came up with root beer and cola. They settled into seats in the front row, and Anderson produced a clipboard on which he had listed a timetable. All they had to do was fill in the blanks.

"Where's d'Argamon?" Cady asked.

"Outfitting the subs," Anderson said. "He told me that we could just plug him in anywhere we want to. He's going to do his own thing, anyway."

"No doubt. What did Purgatory say?"

"He hates to predict as far away as the twelfth of December, but he gives us a good shot at having some high winds. Lots of ground-level snow blowing around."

"But not enough to keep us out of the air?" Cady asked, then took a bite out of his sandwich.

"Fifty-fifty. He won't guarantee anything."

"Fifty-fifty?" Nakamura said. "I think that I will become a meteorological officer in my next life. I can say it is going to snow or it is not going to snow, and I can get paid for it."

"When did you get into reincarnation, Nikki?" Cady asked.

"Since reading Shirley MacLaine."

Cady watched as Eames drew a thick line across the bottom of the timetable, under twelve noon on the twelfth of December. There was no sense in thinking beyond their deadline. What they would do here is brainstorm, outlining the defenses they had to go up against, and pencil in the time requirements of round-trips to the targets by submarines, Harriers, and helicopters. The fuel and ordnance requirements and the wear and tear on aviators and submariners had to be considered. When they had a general outline, Eames would enter the scenario into the computer and let the software point out the deficiencies in the plan.

Cady thought that one of the things they had going for them was that this plan wouldn't have to be submitted through forty levels of bureaucracy clear up to the Pentagon. Monmouth could sign off on it as soon as he had an okay from Bentley, and Bentley, being a good politician, wasn't interested in the details. He only wanted results, and he expected them to deliver.

Or the *U Thant* would go out of existence.

Shark Cady didn't want that to happen. In the last few days, his faith in what they could accomplish had increased in quantum jumps. He was realist enough to understand that total peace in the world was a nice ideal, but it was not one that was likely to be achieved in several lifetimes, much less his own. The *U Thant* represented an approach to the containment of brushfire warfare that precluded involving individual nations in massive preparations for war. Rapid and appropriate response could do much to maintain peace. He wanted to make it work, and he was proud of the fact that he was a part of it.

Almost a part. He was going to have to have another long and contrite, discussion with Sam Monmouth.

He suddenly realized that he had drifted off. Eames wa

looking at him, studying his eyes, as her writing hand idly sketched doodles on the bottom margin of her schedule.

Her own eyes appeared fatigued. There were dark smudges under them that she had failed to disguise with her makeup. The dark irises still had fire in them, though. He thought that, given the chance, he might like to study them for several hours.

She worried about him? She worried about everyone.

"All right," he said. "First objective: Primavera Base."

"The entire base?" Anderson asked. "Or just the runway?"

"Aircraft, wells, runway, vehicles, in that order, I think, Phil."

"What about the destroyer and frigate?" Nakamura asked.

"Let's give those to d'Argamon as his first priority. We'll back him up with some Skua antiship missiles."

"Delivered by helicopter?" Eames asked as she wrote notes at the top of the page.

"Let's try it that way with the computer, first, and see how fast our resources are used up."

"Speaking of resources," she said, "our count on FSAD aircraft is now at thirteen fighters and five helicopters, only two of which are armed. They've got four C-130s left and seven KC-130 tankers. If we're not going to count the training jet, we're down to eleven Harriers, nine Apaches, and five Seahawks. How are we going to deploy them?"

"Actually," Cady admitted, "we're down to ten Harriers."

"Uh, CAG," Anderson said, "last time I counted. . . ."

"I'm grounded."

While the three of them wanted to get into the reasons for that, he was sure, they prudently said nothing. He thought Eames's prim smile suggested that he had just verified her suspicions.

"But let's plan on having me available," Cady said. "That condition will change."

FALCON ONE
1241 HOURS LOCAL

The ship was steady as a British Gibraltar, the winds were light, and Shaker Adams put Baker and Alhers down on the two forward elevator pads with his characteristic charm.

Baker shut down the turbines, and the elevator took them two decks down while he and Decker unhooked themselves. As soon as the elevator came to rest, he clambered out of his cockpit, found the deck, and spent two minutes stretching tired muscles.

Crewmen swarmed around the choppers, moving them toward their maintenance areas, and Baker said, "Henry, go get some sleep."

"May I eat first, Major?"

"If you hurry."

He crossed the hangar deck to intercept Gail Alhers. Two medical corpsmen in white jackets were setting up a gurney next to her helicopter, preparing to transfer a wounded soldier.

She was statuesque, nearly six feet tall, and proportioned to match her height. The flight suit tried, but did not succeed in hiding most of those proportions. She was also a mathematics genius—she automatically remembered formulas and equations that he had forgotten years before.

"Those were nice tactics, Major," she said, smiling.

"I wanted to tell you how much I appreciated your hanging around for us, Gail."

"Well, I knew you were low on fuel."

"And I wanted to tell you to never do it again."

"Sir?" She lost the smile.

"When I give you an order, I expect it to be obeyed. When I say you are to go, you go."

She came to attention. "Yes, sir."

"This is between you and me."

"Yes, sir."

Baker turned and walked aft, pulling off his helmet, studying the work being performed on his helicopters as he went.

When he reached the end of the hangar deck, he passed through a hatch, then climbed the stairs one flight, headed for the dressing room.

But he heard voices in the wing briefing room, and stuck his head inside.

"Hi, Archie," Cady said. "Come on in."

"I'm sorry about Captain Cornwell," Eames said.

Baker sighed. "And Lieutenant Allouete and Airman Deacon."

He tossed his helmet on a chair. "Is that an available sandwich?"

Nakamura passed it to him. "Roast beef. It's good, but probably a little dry by now."

"Dry doesn't hurt."

He flopped in a chair. "It could have been worse. We could have still had sixteen SEALs on board Copperhead when she was hit."

"You got them redeployed all right?" Cady asked.

"Yes, except for one fellow Gail brought back. He took a hit that broke his leg. The rest of them, we dumped out a mile-and-a-half west of where they were. With no tracks behind them, the guys in the black hats should figure that we've extracted them."

"That was the idea," Cady said.

PRIMAVERA BASE
1315 HOURS LOCAL

The Buenos Aires liaison of the Front for South American Determination sent a telex to Silvera, notifying him that Argentina and Chile had sponsored a resolution in the General Assembly of the United Nations calling for a cease-fire in Antarctica. It was currently being debated on the floor, but already one proviso had been added that Silvera did not care to see. It called for all forces to remain in place; no flights or sea traffic was to be allowed.

That was not good. They could be starved out if the cease-fire lasted over ninety days. And they could not obtain replacement equipment for the drilling rigs. Silvera had Fuentes send a message rejecting the clause to the Chilean and Argentinean representatives, via his liaison office in Argentina.

Other than that, he was happy to see that Fuentes's efforts were paying off. They had a strong voice in the General Assembly through Argentina. And with Chile also offering support, perhaps others among the remaining eleven nations would follow along.

It was going to work out.

Silvera sat down at one of the unoccupied desks and looked across the room toward the window. The wind was still blowing, raising a minor flurry of snow. One of the articulated vehicles—two boxes on treads linked together in the middle, called a Naudwell—creeped across the tarmac outside. It was carrying the dead retrieved from the wells, including two unidentified bodies assumed to be from the raiding party. The wounded, and there were many, had been brought in earlier. The two doctors available—one from the station and one brought in with the invasion troops—had declared their facility overloaded. Silvera had commandeered one of the Quonset hut dormitories for them, but the doctors were also complaining that Silvera and Suarez had underestimated the casualty expectations. They were running short of medical supplies.

Even if the resolution went through with the "in-place" proviso, surely medical needs would be met, he thought. And then again, maybe not. Some of the UN ambassadors would have the sinking of the *Inga* fresh in their minds.

That damned Enriquez! He was supposed to have taken the passengers and crew off the Russian ship.

He turned halfway in his chair and told the technician at the switchboard, "Find Calvera for me."

It took a few minutes, but the telephone on the desk in front of him rang, and he picked it up.

"This is Calvera."

"Where are you, Armand?"

"Ah, *Presidente*. I am at rig number six. It has made the most progress."

"Why is that, Armand?"

"Five is slowed by an exceptionally thick layer of lava, and seven has broken a drilling bit. They are pulling pipe now to replace it."

"So. Number six. Tell me of the progress."

"We should know something in the next twelve to eighteen hours, *Presidente*."

"It had better be a positive sign," Silvera told him.

"I am confident. As long as we do not suffer another attack."

"We have quadrupled the guard, and each well has a surface-to-air missile unit, as well as two antiaircraft guns in place. You will not suffer."

"Let us hope so, *Presidente*."

"Besides, the raiders were extracted by helicopter this morning. If we have a worry, it is from the air."

"I will let you do that worrying, *Presidente*. I must concentrate on what is coming out of the ground."

"Very well, I suppose that is a suitable division of labor." Silvera hung up as Tellez came into the operations hut.

He didn't even look at Silvera, but crossed the floor and pushed through the curtain into the radar area.

He was back in two minutes.

"Silvera."

Silvera studied him for a moment. He could be an abrasive man, but Suarez swore that his skills were worth the price of enduring him.

"Yes, Major?"

"Who ordered the ships moved?"

"Moved?"

"The whole damned fleet is moving north. Nightdog has them on radar, but no one notified me."

Silvera got up and went to look at the radar screen. It was a secondary screen, just installed, and it repeated the signals captured by the C-130s. He did not know why he had to see for himself. Tellez was rarely wrong.

He backed out of the curtained-off alcove.

Tellez said, "We need those ships where they can help defend the station."

Ignoring him, Silvera walked to the front of the hut and told the radio operator to switch to the naval frequency. He picked up the desk microphone, depressed the transmit button, and spoke into it. "Primavera calling *San Matias*."

Enriquez was asleep, but someone went to rouse him.

When he finally came on the air, Silvera asked him, "Diego, where do you think you are going?"

"I am going to rid the seas of a crude oil carrier. That will solve your problems, will it not, *Presidente?*"

Silvera detected a bit of disdain in Enriquez's use of his title.

"That problem will be solved by other methods, Diego. You are to return to your assigned station immediately."

After a long moment, Enriquez said, "It is too bad that you do not understand naval strategy or tactics, Silvera."

He went off the air, leaving Silvera unsure of whether he was going to follow the order or not.

"I would, I think," Tellez said, "keep my eyes on that man. He will either get himself or us killed. I prefer that he kill himself, however."

THE SAN MATIAS
2240 HOURS LOCAL

Umberto Mondragon, the navigator, had been monitoring the radio calls of Nightdog One and Nightdog Two, made to Primavera and to the orbiting patrol aircraft, and he thought he had pinpointed the position of the ULCC fairly well.

Enriquez stood near the plot as Mondragon explained.

"She is still making only twelve knots, Captain, but she has turned slightly south. I put our interception point right here."

Mondragon had drawn lines for the projected courses of the *Cornucopia* and the task force, and they crossed at a point sixty kilometers north of King George Island.

"Well within our declared limits," Enriquez said.

"Absolutely, Captain."

Enriquez turned to the windows and looked out at his fleet. They were all sailing in good formation, but for one patrol boat which had stopped thirty kilometers back to repair a fuel pump.

The visibility was good, perhaps too good for a surprise attack. Still, he did not expect to spring a surprise, anyway. The UN forces had access to satellite surveillance, and according to Suarez, had powerful radar aboard the ULCC.

He had been formulating his attack plan for some time, now, and he had underestimated nothing. If the crude carrier were indeed a homing spot for fighter pigeons, and if she indeed had sophisticated radar, then she undoubtedly also had effective defensive systems.

He was not daunted by the possibilities. Tactics would take the day, and he was an expert in that regard.

Watching one of the patrol boats fighting the heavy seas a kilometer off the destroyer's bows, Enriquez wished her well. She and her sisters would play a dominant role in his plans.

Patrol boats were expendable.

"Sir?" Mondragon said from behind him.

Enriquez turned to face him. "Yes, Lieutenant?"

"About the radio calls. Should we not respond to Primavera?"

"We are observing radio silence, Lieutenant, are we not?"

"Yes, sir. Of course."

11 DECEMBER

UNS CALAIS
0500 HOURS LOCAL

Jean d'Argamon was disappointed.

Both Cady and Baker joined Captain Monmouth in seeing him off, but Theresa Eames did not appear. Monmouth gave him a hearty handshake, but Cady and Baker refrained. They did wish him well, though he could have gotten along without their felicitations.

He was not the only one disappointed, of course. Since d'Argamon insisted on leading the mission, they had flipped coins, and Rolf Arnstadt, the captain of the *Dover,* had lost. And since d'Argamon was most comfortable in *Calais,* he had moved Oscar Moritz to the *Dover.*

No one was happy, except the commander of the 21st Submarine Detachment. He was going to sink another ship. Perhaps he would get four.

He stood in the hatchway of the submarine and gave Monmouth a proper salute. After it was returned, he signaled to Moritz, standing in the hatchway of the *Dover,* and the two of them dropped into the cockpits, secured the hatches, then took their seats.

Ivan Suretsev was in the right seat, and Erik Magnuson had already powered up his console in the back of the compartment.

"Contact Beehive, Lieutenant, and signal our departure."

"At once, Commander."

The deployment went smoothly, with *Calais* submerging first, followed by her sister submarine. They leveled off at six hundred feet of depth and proceeded south, side by side, holding twenty-four knots of speed. They could signal each other with flashlights if need be.

D'Argamon settled himself into his seat, rearranging his bulky clothing for comfort.

"You may extend the VLF antenna, Magnuson."

"Aye, sir."

The long antenna would trail behind them in the water, just in case the *U Thant* might have to signal them in regard to a change in the course of the task force led by the *San Matias*. D'Argamon preferred to be isolated from those who might change his orders, but Monmouth had told him that things were coming to a head in the UN meetings, and there was always the chance that Monmouth might have to abort the mission.

He briefly considered having a lapse of memory and forgetting to deploy the antenna, but he had heard rumors on the ship that Monmouth had forbidden Cady to fly as a result of some infraction. He thought it best to not cross the captain, not if he wanted to return to the French navy with commendations enough to insure his next promotion.

"Lieutenant Suretsev, use the light and signal the *Dover*. See if they wish to place a small wager on who sinks the most tonnage."

Suretsev grinned at him. "They will not bet, Commander. We are the veterans, after all."

DEFENSE INTELLIGENCE AGENCY
0615 HOURS LOCAL

Sir Charles called.

McNichols took it in his office, sitting on his cot, leaning forward against his desk so he could reach the phone. He was afraid if he tried to stand up, the cot would tip over again, leave him on the floor, and leave Sir Charles hanging by the coiled cord.

"Good morning, Sir Charles."

"Good morning, Cameron. I called to tell you that I approved a plan of action for Captain Monmouth just a few moments ago."

"Do you have details, sir?"

"No. I approved the general outline. Monmouth will send you the schedule for the submarines right away, and as soon as it is finalized, the order of battle for the aircraft. Is that all right?"

"That's fine. What's the tone of things on the floor?"

"There will be more debate on the Argentinean resolution this morning, and there is a vote scheduled for eleven o'clock."

"It will pass?"

"Oh, I should think so, Cameron. The NSC will get it sometime this afternoon, I imagine."

"Is Monmouth going to be in time?"

"His plan says so, but you know about plans, Cameron."

"Yes, Sir Charles, I do. I'd better call the ship."

He managed to get off the cot without destroying it or himself, then went out to the information center and got the latest data from Jack Neihouse before he called Eames. Neihouse also had the plan of attack for the subs, faxed to them by Eames.

On the screen of the left monitor was a real-time view provided by the Aquacade. The image was of the northern region of the peninsula and most of the Drake Passage, and he could pick out ships in the Passage. After he studied it for a minute, he found the *U Thant*.

McNichols leaned against a desk and picked up a phone.

He watched the ship and tried to imagine where Eames was located on it.

She was already on duty when he called, so he suspected that something had started. He had learned that Terri Eames was very—perhaps too—conscientious, much like himself.

"Good morning, Cam."

"How are you doing, Terri?"

"I'm fine. The subs just took off."

"Yes, I got your message. Are you married?"

"What?"

"Something I had to ask."

"To my job," she said.

"That's great," he told her, amazed at himself for asking. "Look, here's the latest on the FSAD toy boats."

He gave her the coordinates and heading. "They're managing to hold eighteen knots."

"I'll be able to paint them on radar in a few hours."

"Yes, but there's still the wells."

"The SEALs will hit them again in the morning."

"That's good. However, they might like to know that the security's been beefed up."

"You've seen the rest of the wells?" she asked.

"Not directly. We're interpreting, as we usually do. What happened is that three SAMs and six ZSU-23 Quads have been moved north of Primavera. Also north of the four wells that your SEALs took out. We watched the transfer and emplacement. From the way they've been spotted, near the ridge and on top of it, we're figuring there's another three drilling sites. They brought in a few loads of ground troops, too. I'll send you our pictures."

"Thank you, Cam."

He wanted to ask her how old she was, but thought that his better course was to see if he could get into the Peacekeeper Committee's files and find her dossier. He was supposed to be kind of a spy, after all.

"Look there, Cam," Neihouse said.

McNichols looked over at the screen.

"By the way, Terri, you have two Tornados headed your way at Mach 2."

PUMA ONE
0706 HOURS LOCAL

"One, Puma Six. We have been acquired by a search radar."

"Copy, Six. Ignore it, unless I tell you otherwise."

Tellez was happy to have personally verified the information Suarez had obtained through his informants in the Argentine Air Force. Like that of his wingman, Tellez's Homing Radar and Warning Receiver had also noted the probe, but he was not worried about it.

The two Tornados were at ten thousand meters, well out of range of antiaircraft guns and most missiles, and he did not think that the ship would fire missiles at them, even if they had them. If they still thought they were covert, they would not reveal themselves by launching missiles.

From his altitude, he could still pick it out visually, steaming through the gray sea. It was a huge ship, and once he had seen it, he had no doubt but that the Harriers were flying off it. He could not see any airplanes on the deck, nor could he determine that it carried any defensive systems. There were no escort vessels, either.

Looking at it and thinking of it as a threat seemed preposterous, but the power of the radar signal emanating from it was clear enough.

He considered forwarding his verification to Diego Enriquez, then decided against it. The man would meet his own fate, and if Silvera could not control him, then he would meet it sooner than planned.

He continued scanning his own radar scope. There were two unidentified aircraft sixty kilometers to the southwest, and they had turned in his direction, probably directed toward him by the ship. They, too, were of no concern. They could not catch him, and he was not going to attack the ship, anyway.

Not this time.

His mission on this sortie was to spot the ship if he could, but of higher priority, to escort the tankers returning from Navarino Island to Primavera. He did not even carry antiship weapons.

His pylons were loaded with Super Matra antiaircraft missiles, however, and he would be happy to meet up with the Harrier pilot he had encountered yesterday.

If the two aircraft shown on his radar were still there on the return leg, they were dead airplanes.

Forty minutes later, Tellez slowed his flight to sub-sonic flight and Umbrago rendezvoused them with the three KC-130 tankers, code-named Esso One, Two, and Three, circling in behind them to top off their tanks. Then, at eight thousand meters of altitude, they all headed southeast, on a course intended to skirt the position of the *Cornucopia.*

Tellez did not think that the UN forces would interfere with them.

TIGER BARB TWO
0810 HOURS LOCAL

The two Tornados had gone on to the north, at speeds far above the ability of Nakamura and Oberstein to intercept. It was nice to think of the pilots as rats deserting their sinking ship in Primavera, but Nakamura couldn't forget them. He and his wingman set up a figure-eight orbit to the northeast of the *U Thant,* just in case they returned.

They were at twelve thousand feet, conserving fuel, when Nakamura heard the call from the ship.

"Tiger Barb Two, Jericho."

"Two," he responded. Out of deference to Jake Travers, a man he had admired, Nakamura had refused to take the Tiger Barb One code when Cady named him squadron commander.

Eames said, "Pack Rat reports three transports—probably tankers—and two Tornados on a southerly heading. We will have them on radar shortly, but we're estimating them at your heading of zero-six-zero, angels two-five, range three-zero-five miles."

"Copy, Jericho. We will look them over."

Nakamura rolled out of the orbit to his right and found his heading. He advanced the throttle to military power and began to climb. A brilliant sun made the skies bright, but it was also in his eyes. Despite the lowered sun visor on his helmet, he had to squint his eyes when looking to the east. Behind him, he could see the scattering of islands that defined the tip of the Antarctic Peninsula. The *U Thant* was clearly visible, also, appearing serene and defenseless, and he would protect her at any cost.

If the FSAD fighters were escorting the tankers, they would all be flying at or near the tankers' maximum cruise of 386 miles per hour. That would make the Tornados attractive targets.

Or bait.

At twenty thousand feet, Nakamura snapped his oxygen mask in place, then started and adjusted the flow of oxygen. When they reached 28,000 feet of altitude, Jericho gave them a course correction.

At ninety miles of separation, the five targets were clearly identified on his radar. They were not transmitting IFF signals.

"Jericho, Tiger Barb Two."

"Jericho. Go, Two."

"We have acquisition. Five targets, nine-zero miles."

"We show targets, also, Two. Message from Gypsy Moth One: scatter the fighters and ignore them. Take the tankers, then run. Gypsy Moths Three and Four are being launched to back you up."

Nakamura understood Cady's thinking. Without fuel, the Tornados and Mirages would be useless. Perhaps not today, but maybe tomorrow or the next day.

"Tiger Barb Three?" he asked.

"Copied," Oberstein said.

"Let us go, then."

KC-130 AIRBORNE TANKER
0832 HOURS LOCAL

Delbert Ketchum was from Little Rock, Arkansas. He had grown up with visions of himself as a dashing fighter pilot, and he had spent six years in the United States Air Force after graduating from the University of Alabama. He had not achieved his dream, however; he had been disqualified for fighter training, and he had spent four years flying transports for the Military Airlift Command.

He had then spent sixteen years flying transports for anyone who would pay him, and frequently, he had found the higher pay in regions south of the American border. If it was multiengined, he could fly it. Often, it was overloaded, and he flew it with prop tips barely clearing the water in order to avoid Coast Guard and Customs radars.

The Front for South American Determination didn't offer

the same monetary incentives as some of his contacts in Bogotá, but Ketchum had felt he needed the break. It was supposed to be a cakewalk, running supplies and JP-4 into the Antarctic.

But the two hard-charging blips on the radar screen weren't part of a cakewalk. Ketchum had never been caught before because he knew when radar returns suggested that tomorrow was a better day.

"Hey, Puma, we got company."

"I see them, Esso Two. Maintain your course."

Ketchum looked over at his copilot, a Mexican national named Ric who had once been a *Federale* working the Texas border. He shrugged.

Above and to the left, Ketchum could see the other two KC-130s. The Tornado pilots were hanging around on his right, one above him, and one a thousand feet below. He didn't know the jokers who were flying them, and despite the impressive firepower hanging under their wings, Ketchum didn't have much faith in them. He had flown with Latinos before.

He looked again at the radar screen. The bogies were about thirty miles out, now.

"Hey, Puma, I'm turning this hummer back. We'll try again, tomorrow."

"You will continue as you are," the Puma guy said.

"Bullshit! You ain't carrying forty tons of flammables."

"You will do as I tell you, Esso Two, or I will shoot you down, myself."

That was *machisimo* talking. Ketchum's cargo was far too valuable to be expended by the guys who needed it.

He dropped the left wing and rolled out of the formation into a left turn.

He was a half-mile away from the flight, diving, when Ric said, "He's coming after us, *compadre.*"

TIGER BARB TWO
0836 HOURS LOCAL

Nakamura hit the toggle and went hot mike.

"What's going on, Three?"

"Mein Gott! He has launched on his own transport!"

"This is crazy. You take the higher plane, Three. Launch on lock."

"Roger, Two."

Each of the Harriers was armed with two Sidewinders and two AMRAAMs. The latter missile gave them an increased launch distance plus an active radar-homing capability. They could fire the missiles and then forget them, moving on to other targets, or in this instance, getting the hell away.

The first Tornado was just turning away from his pursuit of the tanker he had just fired on, and the second Tornado was turning to engage them when Nakamura heard the lock-on tone in his headset. He pressed the release stud twice.

Two AMRAAMs dropped from the pylons and ignited.

The KC-130 headed north erupted.

The tons of jet fuel created a splendid orange-red fireball that all but consumed the four-engined tanker shot down by its own escort plane.

Oberstein released his missiles, and Nakamura led the way in a diving right-hand turn, headed south at maximum revolutions.

He tried to reacquire his missiles visually in the rearview mirror, but couldn't find them.

Going down through 25,000 feet, the airplane vibrated as it stretched the limits of its speed capability.

His radar antenna was unable to view the action behind him.

In the rearview mirror, he saw the Tornado in pursuit, accelerating rapidly. The other Tornado had probably taken himself out of the action when he diverted to chase the escaping tanker.

Oberstein was on his wing, back a half-mile.

Then twenty thousand feet.

The sea was coming up fast.

The Tornado would be launching in seconds.

"Hot damn, Tiger Two, Three! You got them. Splash two 130s."

Nakamura thought the comment came from David Stein.

"Where are you, Gypsy Four?"

"Seventy miles on your left oblique. Come left ten. Go under us."

"Roger."

"Tornado's launched two!" Stein called. "Tiger Three, break, break!"

Nakamura craned his neck backward and to the right to look for Oberstein, and saw him just as he broke into a right turn, away from Nakamura.

Two missiles followed him, arcing hard.

And streaked into the fuselage.

The Harrier broke in two, the pieces of the fuselage tumbling. A wing came off and spiraled away.

And a split second later, Nakamura saw the seat eject through the canopy.

"Jericho! Tiger Barb Three has ejected!"

"Roger that, Tiger Two. I have the coordinates, and we're launching Copperhead."

He rolled inverted going through thirteen thousand feet, pulling the stick toward him, diving back toward the north.

Then rolled again, and eased the stick back, slowly pulling into level flight toward the south.

He saw the two approaching Harriers, still below him, but climbing. Twenty miles away.

Nakamura couldn't find the Tornado in his mirror, but knew the fighter-bomber was back there.

"Tiger Two, Gypsy Four. Put your nose down some more."

"Roger."

He eased back into a shallow dive and watched as the Gypsy planes climbed above him.

His spine itched.

He waited.

"He's turned off," Stein said.

"Waiting for his buddy," Gypsy Three, Miguel Olivera, said.

Nakamura dumped his speed breaks, and as Gypsy Two and Gypsy Three went over him, pulled back into a climb, then rolled out on top to fall in behind them.

With three Harriers coming at them, the Tornado pilots, perhaps thinking of their fuel states and the distance to Primavera, veered away and climbed for altitude. At supersonic speed, they were soon out of sight.

"Scared them off!" Stein shouted exuberantly.

Nakamura did not think so. If they had had more fuel, they would certainly have engaged.

"Let us look for Oberstein," he said.

PRIMAVERA BASE
0845 HOURS LOCAL

"Primavera Control, Puma One."

Suarez took the microphone from Arquez. "Primavera. Go ahead, Puma One."

"Delgado shot down a Harrier."

Suarez was elated. Every victory counted. "That is wonderful! Congratulations, Puma Six."

"Thank you," Delgado said, but he did not sound very enthused.

"The bad news," Tellez said, "is that we lost the KC-130s."

"Lost them! How did you lose them?"

"In three very big bangs."

Mary, Mother of God!

Suarez dropped the microphone on the desk and turned away.

Silvera was standing there watching him.

He took three steps to stand in front of the president.

"You had better hope that Fuentes's friends come through for us, *Presidente*. At the rate we are going, we do not have much time left."

UNS U THANT
0935 HOURS LOCAL

Since the FSAD Tornados had been reported, Monmouth had been on his bridge. The ship was on full alert, with every man and woman at their battle stations, but he had not yet sounded General Quarters, which would deploy the guns and missile batteries to their operational configuration.

Lieutenant Alferd Wilshire had the watch, but Hermann von Stein was also on the bridge, ready to assume duties as the tactical action officer if they should be attacked. Lieutenant Maroni, in the CIC, had been providing him with continual updates of the action taking place as he assisted Eamos.

Sir Charles Bentley had called him, but only to relate that the debate on the floor of the General Assembly was heated. No action had been taken, and Monmouth thought that typical.

The intercom sounded off. "Bridge, CIC."

Monmouth was standing near it, and he slapped the button down. "Bridge."

"Sir," Maroni said, "the chopper is closing on the life raft."

"Put the squadron net on my speakers."

"Aye, aye, sir."

The dialogue between Copperhead One and the two 1st Squadron Harriers clicked on, channeled to the overhead speakers on the bridge. He listened as he watched Shaker Adams bringing Nakamura aboard. The Japanese aviator hadn't wanted to leave his orbit of Oberstein, but his fuel state had prompted Cady to order him back to the ship. Two more Harriers were on the aft elevators, prepared to take off in relief of the two 1st Squadron planes.

Monmouth recognized Miguel Olivera's accent. "Do you have a visual, Copperhead?"

"Not yet."

"Come on, damn it! Move that thing," David Stein said.

"The pedal's on the floor, Gypsy Four."

Cady had told him that Stein hadn't taken the news of Nakamura's promotion to squadron leader well. He had been short-tempered and ill-humored since, but the target of his sarcastic remarks had shifted from Sifra Solomon to Nakamura. Monmouth thought Cady's evaluation of both men had been correct, and he was relieved that Stein wasn't in command of the 2nd Squadron.

"All right, Four, we see it," Copperhead One said.

"Hurry! We haven't seen a move for awhile."

Monmouth looked out at the ten-foot seas running alongside the ship and pictured the bright yellow one-man life raft bobbing over the crests of waves. It was enclosed, with a tent-like canopy raised over it, but Nakamura had reported that Oberstein was in the water for nearly two minutes before he got it inflated and climbed into it. His survival radio wasn't working, or had been lost, and Nakamura's report had noted that Oberstein wasn't using his left arm. He thought the German was badly injured.

"That's it," Stein said, "easy now, don't tip it over with rotor blast."

"Four, we've done this before."

"Gypsy Moth Four, Jericho." Eames's voice.

"Four."

"Back off."

"Roger that, Jericho."

The Seahawk would lower a man—probably the medical technician riding with them—on the winch to retrieve Oberstein.

The bridge became super-silent as all of the occupants waited in anticipation for the report.

"Jericho, Copperhead One."

"Copperhead One, Jericho."

"The pilot is dead, Jericho."

Long pause. "Copied. RTB Copperhead One."

"Shit," von Stein said. He and Oberstein had known each other in the German military.

"I'm sorry, Hermann," Monmouth told him.

The first officer smiled grimly and shook his head sadly. "Let us get these bastards, Captain."

"We will, Hermann, very soon."

Monmouth crossed to the starboard side of the bridge and looked south. He couldn't see it, yet, but Purgatory had promised bad weather.

That was good.

THE SAN MATIAS
1021 HOURS LOCAL

The destroyer's speed was hampered by the frigate *Marguerite Bay*. She could only make twenty-one knots, and Enriquez did not want to leave her behind.

Mondragon had calculated that they would intercept the *Cornucopia* within eight hours, but that would be too soon, anyway, for what Enriquez had in mind. And then again, it was not soon enough. Certainly, Suarez and his exalted airplanes were doing nothing to counter the threat.

As they had been for the past five hours, and would be for the next six hours, every sailor on every vessel in Enriquez's fleet was occupied with training. He had been disappointed twice in the past days with their performance, and he would not tolerate slow reaction or inaccuracy in the future. His only concession to his subordinate commanders had been to allow the men a four-hour rest before the battle ensued.

When he saw that the last patrol boat captain had clambered from his boat to the landing stage lowered alongside the port hull, Enriquez went below to the wardroom. The patrol boat commander arrived two minutes after he had entered the room and stifled the conversations taking place.

He surveyed his audience of ship and boat captains. They were a varied lot, ranging from hired mercenaries to true patriots. Some of them looked ill-at-ease in the uniform of the Front for South American Determination; they would be more suited to a pirate's leggings and rough cotton shirt.

He managed to address them as gentlemen, then said, "For the last hour, we have been blessed with overcast skies, which precipitates a change in our plans. In one half hour, the main body of the fleet will reduce speed to eighteen knots. The freighter *Paloma*"—which, empty, was the fastest of the support ships—"will increase speed to twenty-three knots and continue to the interception point."

The captain of the twenty-year-old freighter raised his hand, and Enriquez nodded to him.

"We are to make this journey unescorted?"

"You will serve as a radar and visual shield for Boats Two, Five, and Thirteen, Captain. Additionally, with the overcast conditions, American or Russian satellites will be unable to view your passage. If the patrol boats stay close enough to you, as they will, your heat signature should appear as one to their infrared detectors." Enriquez had thought this out very thoroughly.

The patrol boat commanders just mentioned appeared as unenthused as the master of the freighter.

"By the time you reach the crude oil carrier, you will have some cover of darkness from the storm, and the main body of the fleet will be some fifty kilometers behind you. The *Cornucopia* will be watching us closely with her radars, and as a lone freighter plying the passage, you will go almost unremarked. At my signal, the boats will break from cover and attack the supertanker with all available weapons."

The captain of Patrol Boat Two said, "Are we certain this ship is truly what we believe it to be?"

"We are." His communications section had monitored a report by Puma One to the effect that Harrier aircraft had taken off from the tanker.

"And what weapons does she possess?"

"That is unknown," Enriquez said.

"What of the submarine, Captain Enriquez? I had a very good friend on board the *San Jorge.*"

"The submarine will not bother what appears to be a single, unarmed ship. And the ships and boats of the fleet are maintaining vigilance against submarine attack. If she comes near, we will catch her this time."

"And what if we are unsuccessful?"

"If the patrol boats cannot sink a converted oil carrier, even a double-hulled one, then the *Paloma* will ram her at full speed."

The freighter captain blew out his cheeks and pursed his lips. He let his breath go with an audible whoosh. "Sir, I have a crew of twenty-two men."

"And you have lifeboats, Captain. If you must resort to ramming, remember that we will have boats to pick you up within a couple hours."

"I am not certain, Captain Enriquez, that this is the wisest—"

"The alternative is court-martial," Enriquez told him. He would know that the sentence was predetermined.

"I am sure the patrol boats will accomplish the mission," the captain of the *Paloma* announced.

UNS CALAIS
1150 HOURS LOCAL

With his flashlight, Oscar Moritz signaled the *Dover,* and both boats slowed to eight knots.

Jean d'Argamon clambered out of his seat, and since he did not wish to fight his way into the tiny head, unceremoniously stood in the cabin and urinated through the open doorway into the toilet.

As he returned to the cushions of his seat, he told his crewmen, "Now would be the time to relieve yourselves, if you are so inclined. We will be running under extreme silence conditions for the next few hours."

Both Moritz and Magnuson followed his example, though they both chose to squeeze themselves into the tiny compartment one after the other.

An hour before, d'Argamon had taken the *Calais* to the surface for long enough to deploy a UHF antenna and get an update from Jericho on the position of the FSAD fleet. The information provided by Pack Rat was that the FSAD vessels were hidden by overcast, but that the infrared sensors still placed them on the previously predicted track, still maintaining twenty-two knots average speed.

According to Magnuson's computer plot, the submarines were currently eighty-five nautical miles from the targets. At a speed of eight knots, then five knots as they got closer, combined with the fleet's forward progress, they would close with the targets in about three hours.

"In one hour, Magnuson, we will want to send our message."

"Yes, sir. I'll remember."

They were to send a coded, single-word message on the VLF radio when they were two hours away from their attack point, to alert the *U Thant* to the coming action.

Erik Magnuson passed out the box lunches the ship's steward had prepared for them, and after d'Argamon traded his ham sandwich on rye bread to Moritz for a chicken salad sandwich, he noted the flashing light in *Dover*'s porthole.

"What are they saying, Oscar?"

Moritz turned in his seat to read the Morse-coded message. "They say, 'we'll take that bet.' "

PRIMAVERA BASE
1219 HOURS LOCAL

Suarez, with Roberto Tellez in tow, had come to Silvera's new quarters—a first-floor room on the end of a dormitory building—to join him and Fuentes for lunch. Ricardo Fuentes had ordered the meal, and it was served by a steward from the station mess hall.

Both Suarez and Tellez appeared fatigued, Suarez because he worried too much, and Tellez because he never slept. It seemed to Silvera, he was always in the air, obsessed.

"The worst part," Silvera said, "is the waiting. Take heart, though. Ricardo thinks the cease-fire will take effect in forty-eight to seventy-two hours. Then, we will have all of the time we need."

Suarez seemed to take heart in the statement, but Roberto Tellez appeared skeptical.

"You do not think so, Major?"

"I think," the pilot said, "that Diego Enriquez will unravel the fabric. If he attacks the UN ship, there will be no cease-fire."

"And I think," Fuentes told him, "that that is a reversal of your own position. You were very hot to sink that ship, your-self."

"Yes. I have changed my mind since. If I had had antiship missiles with me this morning, there would be no carrier."

"No carrier!" Fuentes exclaimed. "You could not even pro-tect the aerial tankers."

"Tankers piloted by cowards. If they followed orders, they would be on the ground here, now. You cannot even get your naval arm to follow orders."

"Gentlemen, please," Silvera said. "Squabbling among our-selves does not improve the situation. We cannot undo that which is done. I agree, however, that Enriquez is a problem. What do we do to turn him back?"

"I will place a missile down his stack," Suarez offered.

"That does not help, either, Colonel."

"Tell me, *Presidente*," Suarez said, "where does Calvera now stand?"

"He will bring in well number six within twenty-four hours. He assures me of this," Silvera said. "He is already seeing signs of oil."

"That is encouraging," Suarez said.

Fuentes smiled. He did not often smile, but when he did, he reminded Silvera of a small child who had just won at marbles. There was a great deal of self-satisfaction revealed in his face, as if all accomplishments were a direct result of his actions.

Tellez's face was just the opposite.

"You are less optimistic, Major?"

"I am just an employee, Silvera."

"Tell me what you are thinking."

Tellez took a sip from his wine glass. He was not a drinker, Silvera thought, the antithesis of most of the pilots.

"This whole enterprise," Tellez said, "has been driven on wishful thinking. *If* the well comes in. *If* the General Assembly passes the resolution. *If* the Security Council follows through. *If* we get another day, or another two days. You went on international television, *Presidente,* and crowed about our resolve, and yet, we have failed to demonstrate it. If it were up to me, I would not hope that the diplomats did what I wished for. I would level Eights Station. I would take advantage of Enriquez before I put him in front of a firing squad."

Suarez and Fuentes both appeared a trifle alarmed.

Silvera said, "Enriquez sank our last closely held hostages. If we attack Eights Station, we eliminate the next closest group of hostages."

"All right, then," Tellez said, "but use Enriquez. He is going to attack the carrier, anyway. And fail, I suspect, based on his past history. Let him do it, and I will use him as the diversion I need for an aerial attack. I will sink that ship, and then you will have all the time you need. Do not rely on Calvera's hopes. Do not rely on the Security Council."

Silvera sighed and looked to Suarez.

"Roberto is probably correct," Suarez said.

"I disagree," Fuentes said. "We will turn public opinion even more away from us, as happened when Enriquez sank the *Inga* and Tellez shot down the French airplane. The nations are coming into alignment behind us. It just doesn't show yet, but it will."

"A dream," Tellez said, "and a forlorn one. We need decisive action. We need to go beyond the defense of this station, which is precarious at best."

Silvera looked at the earnest Tellez. He was, after all, the man with the broadest experience of armed conflict.

"Formulate a plan for me, Major."

"Before you make a rash decision, Juan," Fuentes said, "we should talk to the people who put up the two-hundred-and-twenty-five million dollars to back this venture."

"What they think or what they say," Tellez countered, "will not make a difference at this point in time. If we cannot stop Enriquez, I doubt that they can. Use him."

Silvera knew Tellez was correct. Still, everyone had a boss, and he thought it would be prudent to check in with his bosses.

"Make your plans, Major, but I will make the final decision."

UNS U THANT
1320 HOURS LOCAL

Cady had missed his breakfast and he was hungry. He picked up a plate of spaghetti swamped with meatballs and sauce, a cup of Parmesan cheese, and two big chunks of garlic bread from the serving window. Eames took a chef's salad and a cellophane packet of wheat crackers.

They carried their plates and cups of coffee to a corner table in the wardroom and sat opposite each other. Eames gave him the computer printout copy of the air tasking order.

"That's what it looks like after I recalculated aircraft speeds and deleted Tiger Barb Three, Colonel."

"Thanks, Terri."

"I hate saying that."

"What?"

"Deleting Tiger Three."

"I know. It's tough."

Cady spread the printout on the table next to his plate while he spread Parmesan cheese over his sauce.

Cady and Phil Anderson had decided to provide more leeway in time-to-target after talking to Eddie Purgatory, who was willing to assure them now that they would have the dirty weather they were hoping to have. The air tasking order provided by the computer program listed every aircraft, its location at scheduled times during the strike, its armament and fuel load, and its turn-around time if it was coming back for refueling and rearming. The program took into account the movement of the *U Thant*. Since something—aircraft readiness, mission diversions, the positions of the opposing forces—always changed, it served primarily as an ideal against which he, the tactical information officer, or the tactical action officer could judge progress. It helped the TAO keep track of where aircraft were supposed to be during the confusion which normally arose out of a major air operation, and it assisted the ordnance and fuel techs in their preparations for the mission.

Cady spun spaghetti onto his fork, shoved it in his mouth, and scanned the listing to make certain that the remaining ten Harriers, nine Sea Apaches, and five Seahawks were all included.

"That won't fly with the captain, of course, Colonel," she said.

He looked up. He had figured out that she only called him by his rank when she was upset with him.

"It won't?"

"No. He'll want more than two Harriers covering the ship. And you've placed yourself on the roster."

"I didn't plan on losing Oberstein."

If one planned these things too far in advance, all of the variables changed. No one had known that the Tornados would interfere in his air tasking order.

"No one did, Colonel."

"Jesus. Won't you call me Jim?"

Her dark eyes were hard to read. They held his own, but

did not reveal what she was thinking. She toyed with her salad, moving the fork back and forth, but not really eating.

"You don't like military women, do you?"

"What!" He dropped a meatball, but fortunately it dropped back on his plate.

She put her fork down, her elbows on the table, and rested her chin on her folded hands.

"You try very hard to be so correct with me. Practically every other man on the ship, outside of Major Baker or Captain Monmouth, of course, expects me to react enthusiastically to casual passes or sexual innuendos. I get a pat on the behind at least once a week, but I've come to expect that kind of behavior from men in the military."

Cady didn't know what to say. As an alternative, he stuck a piece of garlic bread in his mouth.

"It's not that I don't appreciate your treating me as a professional, but I don't understand why you try to observe the rules regarding sexual harassment when you don't bother much with other regulations."

Cady grinned at her. "Maybe I'm scared of you."

"I think you are. You certainly weren't frightened of Monmouth."

Her reference to his unauthorized flight irked him a little but he said, "I wasn't thinking clearly at the time."

"And you are now?" Eames tapped the printout.

"I am."

"He's going to ask me, you know?"

"Sam? Ask you what?"

"Whether you should be flying."

"When did you become flight physician?"

Instead of answering the question, she said, "It makes me very angry when I acknowledge the regulations because I'm trying to get ahead in my profession, but people like you don't have to."

"I got caught," he pointed out.

"But it won't go in your file, I'll bet. If it were me, there would be a big black mark on the outside of my personnel file."

She was probably right, Cady thought.

"Is that why you don't like me?"

"I'm ambivalent about you," she said, but a flicker of light crossed her eyes. "I think you're like the other aviators. You live to fly, and you don't want to have very much get in the way of that."

Cady started to make some retort he hadn't thought through, then caught himself. "You're right, Terri. What else do you want me to say?"

"Nothing."

They finished their meals in silence. Cady didn't know when he'd had a less satisfactory conversation. Nothing seemed resolved.

On their way out of the wardroom, she said, "One thing, Jim. If you want to chew on a damned cigar, chew on the damned cigar."

She turned left after passing through the doorway, and Cady looked after her and waved the printout. "Thanks, again."

He was having a few dozen second thoughts about the air operation he'd come up with by the time he arrived on the bridge to meet with Monmouth.

The captain was sitting in his chair, and he took the printout and read through it slowly.

"That'll be fine, CAG, with a few changes."

With Eames's warning, Cady was ready for the objections. "I need all of the Harriers."

"We won't leave the ship unprotected. And I've already reluctantly let go of both subs."

"Would you settle for two Sea Apaches?"

"They're too slow," Monmouth pointed out.

"Everything we've got is slower than a Tornado or a Mirage."

"Three Apaches."

"Done."

"Then. . . ." Monmouth started to say.

"I lost Oberstein. That's the only reason I put myself on the roster, Captain."

Jacob Ernst, who had the watch, moved to the far side of the bridge, motioning a petty officer to follow him.

Monmouth held up the air tasking order and rattled it. "Can I be sure you're going to follow what you laid out here?"

"Absolutely, sir."

"Let me think about it."

Shit. He was going to ask Eames, and I've just pissed her off royally.

And Cady wasn't even sure how he'd done it.

UNS DOVER
1455 HOURS LOCAL

Oscar Moritz was still ticked off that the Frenchman had taken his boat away from him—typical decisioning for a Frenchman, and even more so for d'Argamon. The only tempering factor was that Arnstadt had been left behind and Moritz had made the mission. That, however, had been the result of luck.

He watched the instrument panel closely and monitored Sagretti, the Italian lieutenant who was his second officer. On the weapons and electronics console was Sean McAllister, a Scot who seemed competent enough. He had the sonar in passive mode, and he'd been excited when he found a herd of at least a dozen whales. This was the first time the *Dover* had been more than forty miles away from the mother ship.

Moritz's boat, the *Calais,* was still off the port side, and both subs were at their cruise depth of six hundred feet, when McAl lister said, "Lieutenant, I'm reading screws. Seven thousand yards."

"ID?"

"Hold on, sir." McAllister donned a cushioned headset, which allowed him to concentrate more fully on the sounds he was picking up.

"Overlapping sounds, Lieutenant. There is a medium-size screw and several smaller ones."

"That will be one of the warships and several patrol boats," Sagretti said.

Moritz unclipped his flashlight from its holder on the bulkhead next to him and tapped out a message to the *Calais*.

"They've also picked up the track," he said after reading the reply. "We get to deploy the robot and check it out."

"Goodie," Sagretti said.

Moritz didn't think the Italian cared much for d'Argamon, either.

It took them six minutes to get the robot to the surface, and in the light of the shadowy day, the picture on the screen was one small freighter with three patrol boats dogging her. Sagretti spun the robot slowly on the surface, waiting as it rose and fell with the waves, but no other ships appeared.

Moritz signaled the other sub with the information and read the reply.

"D'Argamon thinks they're decoys for the main fleet. We are to let them go by. He will watch them for a little while."

"He just wants the targets for himself," Sagretti complained.

Moritz did not doubt it. Without informing his crew, he eased the throttle ahead a few notches and increased speed from five knots to eight. He wanted to reach the hostile ships ahead of d'Argamon.

After ten miles, Moritz pulled the throttle back, and let the speed bleed off to four knots, reducing velocity for silent running. They encountered the rest of the fleet forty minutes after they had expected to do so, and forty minutes after they had signaled the *U Thant* that they would do so.

"Multiple screws," McAllister said. "Over a dozen of them. Eight thousand yards to the closest. I read it as a patrol boat."

"Sonars operative?" Moritz asked.

"Yes, sir. We've been pinged a couple times, but I think they missed the significance. There have been no course changes."

"Only patrol boats?" Sagretti asked.

"They're using the patrol boats as a screen," McAllister said. "There are four sets of heavy propellers behind them."

"I believe we will take a break," Moritz said and killed the throttle. "A very quiet one."

"Shall I arm the torpedoes?" Sagretti asked.

"Please do."

THE SAN MATIAS
1541 HOURS LOCAL

Enriquez happened to be leaning against the brass rail behind the windshield on the bridge, looking forward, and he saw a flash of white just over the horizon.

A second after the flash, the intercom sounded off, "Bridge Comm."

He pressed the pad. "Bridge."

"The *Paloma* is under attack by a submarine! Patrol Boat Two has been hit by a torpedo."

Enriquez let up on the button. "Sound General Quarters Commander Montez. Full speed ahead. Signal Patrol Boats Eight and Four to accompany us."

"At once, Captain."

The Klaxon began yelping.

Diego Enriquez let loose a long string of profanities under his breath. The goddamned submarine was going to upset his plan. He cursed the sonar operator aboard Patrol Boat Thirteen. He had specifically assigned Thirteen to the *Paloma*'s task force because she had a decent sonar. They should have detected the sub long before it had a chance to fire on them.

The destroyer's stern heeled down as full power came on the propellers. She leapt ahead.

"How far?" he asked Montez.

The first officer checked with the radar compartment, then said, "They are nineteen kilometers away, Captain."

"You make sure we are getting full turns, Commander. I don't want that sub to get away from me again."

"Ah, sir?"

"Commander?"

"Are we diverting from our mission to chase the sub?"

"We will do both."

"Ah, yes, sir."

The gun and missile stations all checked in, confirming their availability. Enriquez checked his watch. Much better. He was going to make navy men out of them yet.

Four minutes after they had gone to full speed, with the *Marguerite Bay,* the two freighters, and the remaining patrol boats beginning to fall behind, the intercom bleated, "Bridge! Sonar. Torpedo in the water, homing on us, range six hundred meters, bearing one-nine-five."

"Behind us!" yelped Montez.

Lieutenant Mondragon, who had just reached the bridge, said, *"Another* submarine?"

"Come full to port," Enriquez ordered.

"Sir, there—"

"Full helm to port, goddamn it!"

The helmsman, his eyes showing his fright, didn't wait for a repeated order. He spun the helm hard to the left.

The destroyer heeled over by ten degrees, and Enriquez glanced out the port window.

And saw the patrol boat they were bearing down on.

"Helm to starboard!" he yelled.

The helmsman tried to respond.

But too late.

The destroyer's bow sliced through the fifty-foot patrol boat amidships, scattering crewmen and debris to either side of her hull.

Then the torpedo slammed into her stern and erupted.

A bright spray of red flame spewed over the fantail, and the destroyer immediately began to lose headway. The intercom became a confused array of voices calling out damages, crying for help, and summoning medical assistance. The propellers had been damaged; a propeller shaft was vibrating, shaking out of her bearings; watertight compartment doors had slammed shut, but were warped and distorted. The engineer shut down the drive train.

Enriquez leaned against the window and looked aft. Missile crews were abandoning their stations. Torpedomen on the port torpedo tube deserted their positions and ran aft. Some were throwing life preservers to men from the patrol boat, the pieces of which were being left far behind.

Absolutely no discipline at all.

Farther aft, the flames were beginning to mount and injured sailors were screaming—soundlessly to Enriquez—and writhing around on the deck.

Enriquez turned back to a white-faced Montez.

"Call the *Marguerite Bay* and tell her to pick me up. I am transferring my flag."

"You are not even a damned admiral," a voice said from behind him.

Enriquez spun around, ready to denounce the clown, and found Mondragon aiming his Army Colt .45 sidearm directly between Enriquez's eyes.

"You son of a bitch! Put that away."

The last thing Enriquez saw was a bright flash from the muzzle of the automatic.

It was much like a duck shoot in an amusement park, Moritz thought. The FSAD fleet steamed above them, scattering in all directions, and without having to move his boat or betray her position, he would pick them off. If they were not to panicked, they might track his torpedoes backwards to their origins.

Perhaps someone would.

"I have a freighter," McAllister said.

"Let it go. Next target."

"Patrol boat."

"Range?"

"Nine hundred yards, two-eight-six, I have a solution."

"Fire the number two torpedo tube."

"Aye, aye," Sagretti said and pressed the firing button.

They heard the compressed air eject the torpedo from the tube.

"Torpedo away," Sagretti reported.

"Running true," McAllister echoed.

"Oscar," Sagretti said, "let us not forget about tonnage. We have a five hundred U.S. dollar wager on the line."

"Sean, find the *Marguerite Bay.*"

Emilio Suarez and Roberto Tellez were in the operations ut, planning their attack on the *Cornucopia,* when the radio

operator got the first call. He immediately turned up the vol
ume on the speaker.

"Primavera, this is the *San Matias!*"

"*San Matias,* Primavera. You have not been answering ou
calls."

"Primavera, the ship is going down! We need assistance
Send helicopters quickly!"

Suarez rolled out of his chair, crossed to the radio table
and grabbed the microphone from the operator.

"Let me speak to Enriquez."

"Sir, the captain is . . . dead. He . . . died . . . in the firs
explosion."

"The other ships?"

"We are still under attack. Two patrol boats are . . . hi
All are now taking evasive action."

Suarez shook his head in disbelief. He turned to Captai
Arquez. "Send the helicopters. All of them."

"Sir."

Suarez completed his turn and looked at Tellez.

The pilot picked up the notes they had made, rolled the
into a ball, and tossed them in the wastebasket.

"That solves one problem," he said.

UNS CALAIS
1559 HOURS LOCAL

"They jumped the gun, Commander," Magnuson said.

"What?" d'Argamon said.

"The *Dover* did not wait for us. I am hearing detonation
The fleet is dispersing."

"Cancel the firing solution," he called to Magnuson as h
turned the submarine south. "Full speed, Suretsev."

Suretsev advanced the throttle, asking, "We're letting the other two boats off the hook, Commander?"

"The warships are more important."

Suretsev called to Magnuson, "Secure the remaining two torpedoes."

"Torpedoes secured, sir."

D'Argamon silently cursed his luck and his battle plan. His luck had allowed one of his precious torpedoes to go wide of its target, a second patrol boat. His battle plan—engage all targets of opportunity—in the priority of warships, patrol boats, then support vessels—had allowed Moritz to fire torpedoes without waiting for the *Calais* to catch up.

Twenty minutes later, he reduced speed when Magnuson began picking up high speed propellers.

"Can you find the *Dover*, Magnuson?" he asked.

"No, sir. I'm tracking fifteen sonar returns, all on the surface. They're all over the place. There's another . . . no, that's a vessel going down. A couple slow screws, probably support ships."

If they had had a large enough computer capacity, they might have stored in memory the propeller signatures of some of these ships and been able to identify them. D'Argamon knew that many ships in the U.S. Navy could recognize almost any ship of the Russian Navy, particularly submarines, by the distinctive characteristics of their propellers. No two propellers were ever cast alike.

Magnuson's screen was showing the waterfall display of the sonar, and he had many targets to choose from, but what d'Argamon wanted was a heavy warship.

"Can you find the destroyer?"

"No, sir. I think that may be what I hear going down."

"Damn it!"

"The pattern suggests they're searching for the *Dover*, Commander."

"While they're looking for her, let us find the *Marguerite Bay.*"

FALCON ONE
1622 HOURS LOCAL

As soon as the subs had reported they were two hours away from attack, Archie Baker had assembled his aircrews, lifted the choppers to deck level, and taken off from the *U Thant* with three Sea Apaches and two Seahawks, Copperhead One and Jerry Can Three.

Their mission was in support of the submarine attack on the FSAD fleet, with the primary objective one of search and rescue, should one of the small subs run into trouble. All of the helicopters were armed with two Sidewinders each for air defense, and the Sea Apaches and Copperhead each carried a pair of Royal Navy Sea Skua antiship missiles.

Just in case.

The timing was off, somewhere. Somebody was delaying. Baker had ordered an aerial refueling, then sent Jerry Can Three back to the ship. Jerry Can One was on the way as a replacement tanker.

Under the concrete clouds, reflected in a cement-colored ocean, it was a dismal day, though the winds were light.

They had not seen much. Earlier, they had passed a single freighter, some six miles to the left of the helicopter flight. Baker had checked through Jericho with Pack Rat, who identified it as a ship that had left the fleet on its own nearly an hour before. Jericho seemed relieved to have the ship identified as a sole freighter.

When Pack Rat had relayed to Baker that they were within a hundred miles of the fleet, to its northwest, he set up an orbit and waited.

And when Pack Rat reported a large explosion within the fleet, Baker had broken off his orbit and headed in the direction of the vessels. Falcon Six and Falcon Seven were stepped off his right side, and Copperhead One trailed the formation.

"Let me know when they acquire us, Henry."

"You're at the top of my calling list, Major. In fact, now that you mention it. . . ."

"The ships have found us?"

"No. It's one of those bloody damned C-130s."

THE MARGUERITE BAY
1624 HOURS LOCAL

Captain Jorge Encinas was feeling very much on the defensive, but his training with the Argentine navy prevailed. As soon as the *San Matias* was torpedoed, and as soon as he learned that Captain Enriquez was dead, he had assumed command of the fleet.

He had immediately ordered the tanker and the two freighters to the rescue of survivors from the destroyer and Patrol Boat Eight, and he had ordered the rest of the boats to assume a crisscrossing search pattern, looking for the submarine.

The frigate he commanded was nearly fifty years old, seemingly consumed by rust, but some of her weapons had been replaced, and he controlled decent surface-to-air missiles batteries and a first-class ASROC antisubmarine emplacement.

The ship was steaming north at three-quarter speed, toward the screen of patrol boats and the spot from which the *San Matias* had just disappeared. It had taken very little time for her to go under, and the sight of her bow rising almost vertically from the water before she slipped beneath the surface was a disturbing one. Encinas had hoped one day to command her. Enriquez had promised him that it was coming, as soon as Silvera named Enriquez Admiral of the Fleet.

To the port stern quarter was the *Crimean Native,* a ten-thousand-ton freighter, struggling mightily to achieve top speed, which was not great, even though she was empty, heading toward the gaggle of lifeboats and patrol boats near the site of the sunken ship.

Encinas liked to manage his battles with a communications technician standing nearby to handle the duties he did not need to distract him.

Right then, the technician said, "Captain, the *Paloma* has requested instructions."

"What is her condition?"

After a moment's interrogation, the specialist said, "She was not struck. The submarine appears to have departed. They have taken aboard three survivors of Patrol Boat Two, and the other two boats are undamaged."

Encinas saw no reason to bring the three vessels back into the area of danger. He said, "Tell her to return to her course."

They were within three kilometers of the destroyer's last position.

"Sir, message from Primavera."

"Tell me."

"Nightdog Two has identified four inbound helicopters. Two-nine-six, range one-one-zero kilometers, with a speed of one-eight-zero knots. Primavera is launching its alert aircraft."

"We seem to have stepped in the dogshit, have we not, Specialist?" Encinas turned to his fire control officer. "You heard that, Lieutenant?"

"Yes, sir."

"Alert the antiaircraft batteries. Pass the word to the boat captains."

"At once, sir."

The technician blurted, "Captain! Boat Eleven reports a torpedo in the water, tracking on Nine . . . Nine's reporting evasive tactics."

Encinas stepped forward to the windshield and peered ahead in the gloom of the day. He could see the boats darting and zigzagging, but he was not certain which boat was which.

Until a white explosion identified Boat Nine for him.

"Nine's been hit!" the communications man yelled.

"Ask Eleven if they've got a sonar target."

A second later, "Eleven has a target. His bearing zero-three-five. Information passed to our sonar."

"Helmsman," Encinas said, "three degrees to starboard."

"Aye, Captain, three degrees to starboard."

Four minutes later, the technician said, "Sir, sonar's got a target. ASROC is ready."

"Lieutenant, fire two of the rocket torpedoes."

"Aye, sir," the fire control officer said.

Two tubes of the ASROC launcher spit fire, and the missiles arced high and ahead of the frigate. Seconds later, the missiles crashed into the surface and released their torpedoes.

Encinas waited.

"The target has been acquired, sir. Both torpedoes are homing."

The fire control officer reported, "Both SA-N-4 surface-to-air missile launchers are prepared, sir. Eighteen missiles are available. Both fifty-seven-millimeter guns are ready."

"Thank you, Lieutenant."

Encinas had a great deal of faith in the Soviet-built missiles and antiaircraft guns.

"One torpedo has detonated, sir, probably on countermeasures. The other is still homing."

Encinas counted seconds.

"A hit, sir!"

FALCON ONE
1634 HOURS LOCAL

"Thirty miles to target, Major. We're getting hit by a Strut Curve surveillance radar."

"They've got Soviet radars, huh, Henry?"

"That they have. And here's a Pop Group fire control radar. We're likely to meet up with SA-N-4 missiles."

"And how do you feel about that, Henry?"

"Your group therapy sessions are getting to you, Major."

Baker went to the squadron net, "Falcons, Copperhead, take combat spread. Copperhead, you hang back unless you see a clear shot."

"Copperhead One, roger."

"So what are you seeing, Henry?" Baker asked on the ICS.

"It's a bloody mess. Fourteen targets, most of them bunched together. Come right three points, Major."

"Three." Baker eased to the new heading and checked that the other choppers followed him onto the new course.

On the radio, he said, "Copperhead, when I said hang back, I meant more than fifteen feet."

"Roger."

The Seahawk slowed its forward speed.

At twenty miles out, Decker had better definition and suggested that the patrol boats were ringing the freighters and warships.

"We're missing one of the big vessels, Major."

"That's the explosion Pack Rat detected, then. D'Argamon got one of them."

"Maybe a small boat or two, also."

"Good. We'll meet less unfriendly fire."

Baker defined areas of fire for the other two Sea Apaches, then told Copperhead he could clean up what was left.

"Appreciate that, Falcon One."

"Any time. And remember, people, the SA-N-4 has a range

of six nautical miles. We will launch the Skuas at eight nautical miles. The poor bastards won't have a chance to try their luck."

Baker lost some altitude, dropping to a thousand feet over the sea.

"What about height, Major?"

The British Aerospace Dynamics Sea Skua could be programmed to fly at any of four altitudes.

"Let's try fifty feet, Henry. We've got some heavy seas running, and we don't want to slap a wave."

"Good by me. Switching to tracking and illumination."

"Go."

The Sea Skua's semi-active radar seeking head required that the launch vehicle select the target and illuminate it for the missile. The Skua was a comparative lightweight when it came to antiship missiles. It was designed to disable, rather than destroy its target. Once hostile radars and antiaircraft missiles were out of action, the attacker could move in with other weapons.

Except that they had no other antiship weapons.

"Coming up on release point."

"Whenever you're ready, Henry."

Decker fired the two missiles, and milliseconds later, four more launched from the other two Sea Apaches.

The slim missiles dropped from the helicopters, found their sea-skimming altitude, and whished away.

Baker increased his altitude by five hundred feet, giving Copperhead One a clear field of fire if he detected ships that still wanted to, or could, engage them after they were introduced to the Skua.

Two minutes later, Decker said, "We're making hits. Three . . . four . . . five. I don't know what happened to the last one."

"Any idea *what* we hit, Henry?"

"Two of them got the major vessel."

"Good. Distance to target?"

"Six miles."

"Copperhead," Baker said on the radio, "you might as well unload."

Two more Sea Skuas raced across the sea.

"Two more hits," Decker said. "I think we can hope the SAMs are out of the picture. May see some AA."

"Let's go."

Baker increased his forward speed and gained more altitude. Within a minute, they found the ships visually, assisted by several climbing spires of smoke.

He counted four vessels on fire. No SAMs were launched, but as they got closer, several varieties of antiaircraft gun opened up on them.

The largest ship, he noted was the frigate, *Marguerite Bay.* She had two fires raging, one forward and one amidships. One of her fifty-seven-millimeter guns appeared to be still operable, but manually and not under radar control.

"Let's ostracize the frigate," he told his other aircraft. "We'll take out the gunboats."

The four helicopters dove to sea level and raced toward the boats, chasing down isolated craft and opening up with the Chain Guns. In six minutes, every boat was holed, burning, or otherwise in dire straits.

"Falcons, Copperhead, let's find Jerry Can," Baker said, as he pulled off a patrol boat that Decker had just raked with the M230.

As he swung left, passing behind the frigate by four miles, the radio blurted, "Falcon One!"

"Go, Copperhead."

"I just spotted one of our subs."

"What! On the surface?"

"Roger that, Falcon. Someone's waving at us."

"Pick them up. We'll cover for you."

Baker scanned to his left and found the Seahawk a couple miles away, north of the frigate, which seemed almost impotent. Its single fifty-seven-millimeter gun kept firing at them, but never came close.

He banked hard to the left and picked up speed. Falcon Six rejoined with him as they closed on the Seahawk.

"Falcon Seven, where are you?"

"A mile behind you, on your six. I've got some damage."

"How bad?"

"We'll manage, One, but we lost landing gear and a bunch of skin to an AA round. No vitals."

"Stick close," Baker told him.

"Look at this, Major."

Baker had already seen it. The sub was on the surface, but low in the water, canted to her right side. One dark-suited figure was halfway out of the hatch, and the waves swamping across the hull appeared to be pouring into the hatch. As he watched, and as the Seahawk came to a hover above it, the man pulled himself out of the hatchway. Right after him came two more figures.

"Which one is it, Henry?"

"They don't advertise, Major."

"Falcon One, Jericho."

"Jericho, Falcon One."

"Pack Rat shows two fighters headed your way. Call it one-eight-zero miles, coming out of Primavera."

"We needed a little excitement, Jericho."

"Can I have a sitrep?"

"We just made a mail stop, but we'll get right back on the track for home."

DEFENSE INTELLIGENCE AGENCY
1651 HOURS LOCAL

Cameron McNichols figured it was maybe fifteen degrees outside. A cold front had swept through the area during the morning and was doing its best to hang on. Inside, the temperature was at the regulated sixty-five degrees.

He was sweating.

His palms were moist.

"Jesus, Andy. I'm going to have to get out of this business. Get back to paper-shuffling intrigue."

"After you go, can I have your cot?" Casper asked.

"If I make it as far as my cot, that's all the further I'm going."

He picked up his notepad, got up from the desk where he'd been sitting all afternoon—though it seemed like all week— and walked back to his office. He was wearing a pair of slacks from one of his suits and an open-collared dress shirt. He'd begun to feel so grungy in his standard casual clothes that he'd gone down the hall to the men's room, taken a paper towel bath, and changed clothes.

His hair and beard felt stiff. In about ten minutes, he'd send out for shampoo.

Plopping in his chair, he punched the direct-dial button for Bentley, who answered immediately.

"I almost called you, Cameron, but I didn't want to interrupt anything important."

"You're too courteous, Sir Charles."

"I am, am I not? Do you have news for me? Good news? If it's bad, just hang up."

"We finally got the Aquacade into a decent position," McNichols said, "so we've been getting some pretty decent radar imagery. We get to see right through the cloud cover."

"Spare me the technology, just now, would you, Cameron?"

"Yes, sir," McNichols said, leafing back through his notes, which covered what he had watched and what he had heard from the *U Thant.* "On our side, we lost a submarine."

"Oh, shit!"

"We did get the crew off, two of whom were injured, but the sub was badly bent. We sank it."

"On purpose? Cameron, that is a lot of dollars."

"It wasn't going to be repairable, and our people on the scene didn't want the bad guys to get any of the high-tech stuff."

Bentley sighed. "I suppose it was necessary. What else did we lose?"

"That's it. On their side, they lost the *San Matias* and six patrol boats. The *Marguerite Bay* is badly damaged, four patrol boats are damaged or out of action, and one freighter was on fire. We're going to say very positively, Sir Charles, that the Front for South American Determination no longer has an effective navy."

"But that's excellent, Cameron!"

"It was rough-and-tumble for a while. We had a couple of their fighters chasing our choppers for a little bit, but after they exchanged a few missiles, with no hits, they gave it up."

"Do you realize, Cameron, that you are now speaking in the first person, plural?"

McNichols grinned to himself. "I guess we're kind of a family now."

"This will be extremely helpful, I think. The cease-fire resolution passed the General Assembly, but now I may have some ammunition to use in the Security Council."

"I hope you can hold them off, Sir Charles."

"I do, too, otherwise, our family may be broken up."

UNS U THANT
1730 HOURS LOCAL

"The Sea Skuas performed as advertised," Cady said. "Baker took out their SAM and fire-controlled radar capability while he was still out of range, then went in and mopped up."

"You're keeping a close eye on both our human and technological performance, aren't you, Jim?" Monmouth asked.

"I'm keeping notes, yes."

The two of them were sitting at the table in Monmouth's quarters, working on a bowl of potato chips and tall, iced glasses of orange juice. Monmouth glanced at his paintings of Maine from time to time and thought about a roaring fire and a hot toddy.

"You'd make some changes?"

"I will make changes," Cady said. "This is pretty much a shakedown cruise for us, and after it's over, I'll write you an after-action report, with recommendations for the future. For example, we need better aerial refueling capacity, and I'd like to explore the possibility of converting V-22 Ospreys to tankers. Our weapons inventory needs some refinement also. . . ."

Monmouth had an urge to interrupt, to say he'd be happy to look at the report after it was all over, but he sipped his juice and listened. The success of Baker's and d'Argamon's missions against the FSAD marine forces had given everyone on board the ship a glow of satisfaction. There was a positive charge in the air and quite a few more smiles on faces than he'd seen in a while. Cady was talking about the future as if he didn't think tomorrow was going to be much more difficult than a short game of billiards.

"What about people, Jim? Any changes you'd make there?"

"Archie Baker is a tremendous asset, Sam. We have to hang onto him at any cost. His helo pilots all make the grade in my book, too, but he'd have the last word on that. I don't think I'd change any of my people, either, though there's a few, like Stein, who need some seasoning."

"Shipboard personnel?"

Cady took a moment to think about it. "There's a few in

my support detachments who aren't fitting in. I wouldn't have any recommendations about your crew except to say that Dave George, Shaker Adams, and Terri Eames all get pluses. Hang on to them, if you can."

"You're not mentioning d'Argamon?"

"Maybe he'll have learned something after this sortie, Sam. Humility, he's never going to learn."

Baker's choppers had reported picking up d'Argamon, Suretsev, and Magnuson from the stricken *Calais*. She'd barely made it to the surface after a torpedo had holed the hull and flooded the motor compartments. D'Argamon and Suretsev had cuts and bruises from being slammed around in the cabin, and Magnuson had a black eye. Monmouth thought, however, that Cady was probably right.

Monmouth had worried about the *Dover* for half-an-hour after the battle, until Moritz checked in on the VLF and said they were en route to the *U Thant,* claiming the destroyer and a patrol boat as prizes.

"And yourself, Jim?"

Cady slumped back in his chair and looked Monmouth straight in the eyes. "My evaluations of my own performance always seem to differ with that of my superiors, and I don't deserve any plus-marks this go-around, I guess. If you want to fire me, fire away. The only thing I'd ask is that you put me back on flight status for tomorrow's sorties. I'm needed."

Monmouth thought that he was always pretty aware of what was taking place among members of his command, but he had been surprised more than once in his career. He made it a point to ask people about other people, as well as to rely on his own observations.

He asked, "Have you been playing footsie with Eames?"

"What! Of course not. Where did that come from, Sam?"

"She's pretty high on you. She thinks you're needed, too."

Monmouth could see the confusion cross Cady's dark eyes.

"All she told me was that I could chew my cigars in her CIC."

"That's all?"

"And that I'm anti-women in the military."

"Are you?"

"I'm still a little uncomfortable with it," Cady admitted. "But I recognize competence when I see it, and competence is what I'm looking for."

"Me, too," Monmouth said.

He thought that Eames was doing a good job of keeping Cady off-balance, and that was probably all right.

"From my conversations with them, I think the guys flying for you would drive their Harriers right into the sea, if you asked them to, Jim."

"I'm not trying to be buddy-buddy with them, Sam, and I'm not trying to get them killed."

"They know that, too," Monmouth told him. "In the future, if you want to bend the regs, you ask me, and I'll tell you whether or not you can do it."

Cady hesitated, but said, "That's a promise."

"Those, I know you don't break. Okay, you get your joyride."

UNS U THANT
2115 HOURS LOCAL

Terri Eames had napped for four hours after the *Dover* called in, then got up and showered before going to the wardroom for a baked potato sprinkled with everything the steward could find. Then she went to the CIC and found Maroni and Trish O'Hara on duty.

She checked the status board. "How are we doing, Luigi?"

"The helos are back all right, Terri. Falcon Seven had to be landed on a dolly since it no longer has an undercarriage.

Baker swears it will be airworthy when needed again, though. He's down on the hangar deck, bullwhipping the guys trying to repair it."

"The *Dover?*"

"In the moon pool. Jan Gless is holding the *Calais* crew overnight for observation."

"The grapevine," O'Hara said, "says d'Argamon put a move on one of the civilian scientists in the dispensary and got his face slapped."

"Female scientist?"

O'Hara grinned. "I assumed so, but I didn't ask."

"Okay, you two take a break for a couple hours. I'll hold down the fort."

"We've still got a few hours on our tour to go," Maroni said.

"I'll want you fresh for tomorrow, but if I need you, I'll yell."

After they left the CIC, Eames took her place at the console and checked the status of all the sensors. Since they weren't attempting to remain covert any longer, the big Searchwater radar was operating. No aircraft were showing on the screen, however, and only two ships were identified, a container carrier moving east in the Passage and the freighter that had escaped the FSAD fleet earlier in the day. It was 120 miles south and was tagged for close monitoring. No one knew what its intentions were, but it wasn't armed and wasn't much of a threat. Most of her staff seemed to think its captain was deserting the cause.

She was just settled in when the intercom buzzed.

"CIC, Eames."

"Major, this is communications. Sir Charles Bentley would like to speak with you. I'll put it on your line four."

She was surprised and sat up in her chair as she picked up the phone. She'd never talked with the top boss before.

"Major Eames, sir."

"Good evening, Major. I'm sorry to bother you, but I didn't want to wake Captain Monmouth, and Cameron McNichols has spoken highly of you."

"It's no bother, Sir Charles."

"When Captain Monmouth wakes, would you tell him that the Security Council has tabled the cease-fire resolution?"

"I'll be happy to," she said.

"Tell him also, that the respite is only for twenty-four hours. The Peacekeeper Committee managed to convince the Council that we'd have the problem resolved within that time."

Eames tried to be upbeat. "I'm sure we will, Sir Charles."

"Thank you. By the way, Major, I now understand Cameron's dilemma."

"Dilemma, sir?"

"You have a beautiful voice."

PRIMAVERA BASE
2225 HOURS LOCAL

Captain Arquez knocked on the door to Silvera's sleeping room in the dormitory, and pushed it open, letting the light from the hallway flood in. The heavy drapes were drawn over the window.

"Sorry to disturb you, *Presidente*. An urgent message from Buenos Aires."

"I was not asleep, Captain. Thank you."

He took the message, and the captain departed.

Silvera had been trying to sleep, but unsuccessfully.

He sat up in the bed and turned on the bedside light.

It was a short telex, two sentences.

The first sentence said that the ceasefire resolution had been tabled in the Security Council.

The second said that the contact with the Argentine government had hinted that Argentina would withdraw their support within twenty-four hours if they did not see substantial progress.

12 DECEMBER

The body heat of Sergeant Tu, Gregori Suslov, Gus Brelin, and David George had kept the interior of their snow cave almost tolerable. George had slept for nearly seven hours, wrapped in his thin-skinned arctic mummy bag. He awoke feeling refreshed.

It was dark inside the cave, which was just forty inches high—no one was going to stand up—and he checked his watch, then slipped out of the bag and rummaged in his backpack, leaning against the wall of the cave. He found packets of cocoa and some chicken noodle soup mix and set them aside. With his butane lighter, he lit a sterno can and placed it on the snowpacked floor next to his sleeping bag. He sat back on the bag, unfolded the tripod legs of a cooking rack, and placed it over the can.

With water from his canteen, he started a cup of water heating. The tiny source of heat felt good, and he warmed his hands over it, watching the shadows dance on the walls of the cave. The bulgy forms of his sleeping cave-mates took up most of the space. Brelin snored like a locomotive pulling out of Penn Station.

He found his razor and a stick of shaving soap, and he was halfway through the ritual when Tu woke up.

He sat up and looked at George.

"You can't be serious, Commander."

"You'd be surprised, Tu, how much better you'll feel. Does wonders for the morale."

"My morale is <u>high enough</u>, sir. I'm freezing my ass off, ten thousand miles from anywhere civilized, in a house of snow, with three guys with B.O. Who could be happier?"

"Want to borrow my deodorant?"

"No, thanks, sir. I'm not sure it works."

Within fifteen minutes, their activity had awakened Suslov and Brelin, and they soon had four flames burning under four different preferences for breakfast. Tu had awakened the inhabitants of the other snow caves by way of the portable squad radio, and the SEALs were pulling themselves together, working on breakfast, and cleaning weapons.

Brelin said, "I'm damned close to high tide. I've got to piss something awful, but I don't want to open the door because it's so hard to close again."

"If you can hold on a little bit, Gus, we'll be pulling out at 0300."

"I can wait."

"Think it's snowing out there, yet?" George asked him.

"This is Antarctica. Flip a coin," he said, then added, "Zip would have known."

"Yeah."

George felt deep remorse about Andover. The guy was—had been—likable, but more than that, he had been a civilian. He shouldn't have had to pay the price that assholes like the FSAD had forced on him.

Suslov got out the map, and they all leaned over it as George took them through the planned march once again. He wasn't quite sure how far they would have to go since the short helicopter hop had disoriented Brelin—his idea of their location was a best guess. George had left behind on the ship his Position Location Reporting System (PLRS) because of its weight, and while it might have been nice to have the Global Positioning System give him his precise position on the face of the earth, he decided it didn't really matter. A mile in any direction was still snow.

"Now," he said, "Pack Rat is pretty positive that we've got three wells to hit, and from what Jericho told us last night, they're going to be well-defended this time."

"Three teams?" Suslov asked.

"I think so. And we want to be fairly precise in hitting them all at the same time. I'll take one, you the second, and Bascom the third."

"I go with the first group?" Brelin asked.

"Gus. . . ."

"Don't give me any shit, Commander. Zip was my buddy, and I've got scores to settle. Plus, I've got my own gun." Brelin patted the butt of the AK-74 resting next to him.

"Rifle."

"What?"

"It's a rifle, not a gun."

"Well, I've got it."

"Okay, Gus. You go with my group."

"Good. Let's hit it."

"Not just yet. Jericho's got us scheduled to fit in with some other things that are going to happen."

"Like what?"

"They only tell me my part," George told him.

"Well, hell. In that case, I can't wait any longer. I'm going outside and find a tree."

"Good luck," Tu said.

PRIMAVERA BASE
0230 HOURS LOCAL

"Your calling me every fifteen minutes will not get us any closer, *Presidente*," Armand Calvera said.

"I know," Silvera said, "and I apologize. Still, it is most important."

"I will call you the minute I know something."

Silvera replaced the microphone and surveyed the base through the window in front of him. It was light outside and visibility seemed decent, though the wind was increasing in intensity and windblown flurries of snow danced across the runway and the revetments where ground crewmen were preparing aircraft. The windchill index was at -40 degrees Fahrenheit, and Silvera felt sorry for the maintenance personnel required to be out in it. All of the fighters were on the ground undergoing maintenance and weapons change-outs, to increase the proportion of offensive ordnance they would carry. Only two of the KC-130s were airborne to extend the radar coverage.

He scooted his chair around to look over at the desk where Suarez and Tellez sat, planning the morning's strikes. He knew he had been lax about making decisions in the past few days, but Silvera had allowed the two pilots to prevail, and the Front for South American Determination would now assume an offensive stance. Their resolve would be known to the world.

Ricardo Fuentes, who had been keeping people out of bed in Argentina and Chile with his faxes and telexes, crossed the floor with his latest batch of paper and sat in a chair next to Silvera.

"Do you hold our salvation?" Silvera asked, pointing to the papers.

The young man's face suggested otherwise.

"Come on, Ricardo. Tell me."

"There are twenty-four Russian MiG-29s, sixteen MiG-27 bombers, and six Ilyushin transports, along with some aerial tankers, at Christchurch."

Silvera shook his head sadly. "Do you suppose that under the guise of evacuating their bases, those MiGs will visit us?"

"The Chilean foreign ministry was told that New Zealand would not allow the airplanes to land with weapons aboard, except for one hundred rounds of cannon ammunition for each warplane. I don't know if we can rely on the information, Juan."

"I don't believe we will."

"And then, an airplane out of Rio de Janeiro has identified an American aircraft carrier task force of nine ships. They are probably two days away from mounting air operations against us."

Silvera sighed. "Do you recall telling me, Ricardo, that the American administration would be too weak-kneed to act? That they would gladly allow the United Nations to resolve the situation we created?"

Fuentes was a trifle pale-faced this morning. He didn't answer.

"Tell me again of this weak-willed American president."

Fuentes cleared his throat. "He would not have acted on his own. I suspect that he is being pressured by his military leaders and other nations to act, Juan. The killing of the Russians and the Frenchmen was too much for them to bear."

"Ah, but, Ricardo, the hostages were our aces, were they not? That was part of your plan."

Fuentes shrugged. "We had the example of the Americans held hostage in Teheran as a guide. No one acted then."

Silvera was afraid that his own reservations—that the Western nations would not cave into terrorism even when multiple nationalities were involved—were surfacing. These people would allow more to die in order to achieve the destruction of the Front for South American Determination.

He reached over and plucked at the papers Fuentes held. "And what other surprises do we have in store, Ricardo?"

"Most of the rest of it refers to rumors of the moment, Juan."

"You're sure?"

"There is one report of a radio directive aimed at Eights Station."

"Which says?"

"The personnel have been directed to abandon the station, to attempt survival on the ice for several days."

"I see. They anticipate our move, do they?"

"It appears that they do," Fuentes admitted.

Silvera pushed himself up out of his chair and walked to the desk where Suarez and Tellez were calculating fuel requirements and bomb loads.

The two of them looked up at him.

"Eights Station is out."

"Why?" Tellez asked.

"They are abandoning it. Our attack would have no impact."

Tellez did not seem to care. "How about the Americans' Siple Station, then? Or the United Kingdom's Halley Station? Siple is sixteen hundred kilometers away, or Halley is twenty-one hundred kilometers. I can reach either easily, but it seems to me that the British are due for an awakening. This man Bentley seems to be in charge of operations against us, and perhaps he should have a reaction from us that hits close to home."

"We will attack no other stations," Silvera said.

"But, *Presidente*. . . ." Suarez began to argue.

"Our threats do not hold anyone in awe, Colonel. In two days, we will have Russians swarming around us from the west and Americans from the north. Our only recourse is to hold off the United Nations forces for long enough to allow Calvera to complete a well. And as Major Tellez has pointed out, defending the drilling sites is not sufficient. We must attack their carrier."

"Finally," Tellez said.

"With every available asset we have," Silvera said.

"When?" Suarez asked.

"As soon as possible."

GYPSY MOTH ONE
0315 HOURS LOCAL

King George Island was now behind them, and the *U Thant* was between Elephant Island and the Falklands. On a heading of 192 degrees, crossing the tip of the peninsula on an angle toward the south-southwest, Primavera Base was 450 miles away.

In an obvious abandonment of her covert nature, the *U Thant* had reversed course and was now headed west. It was supposed to be obvious to the C-130s flying radar patrol for the FSAD, anyway.

Cady knew that his Harriers could reach Primavera Base in about forty minutes. He also knew that Silvera's Mirages and Tornados could reach the UN ship in half that time.

"It's going to be touch-and-go," he said.

"Are you having second thoughts, Colonel?" Hermann von Stein asked. "This is your plan, after all."

"No, but using the ship as the bait seems less admirable, the more I think about it. My first responsibility is to protect this ship," Cady said.

"I have faith in your operation, and I have faith in my defensive systems," the German officer said. "Proceed with the mission."

Cady looked at Baker, Anderson, and Nakamura, who were sharing the table in the wardroom with Cady, von Stein, and Purgatory. The three squadron leaders all nodded their concurrence.

"Okay. Go ahead, Archie." Cady sipped his coffee.

It was an early breakfast and the table was strewn with coffee mugs, plates, and paper. The smell of bacon permeated.

Baker finished chewing a mouthful of scrambled eggs, then said, "All right, CAG. First, the two LAMPS helos will maintain their regular alternating patrols, as is normal. We have, however, removed the antisub weaponry and provided them with four Sidewinders each for air defense.

"The three Jerry Can tankers are ready to accompany your strike force.

"All of the Sea Apaches are armed for air defense. Falcons Eight, Nine, and Ten will fly close-in interception support for the carrier, refueling hot on the flight deck as necessary. The remaining six helos are ready for launch at any time."

"Good, Arch. You can brief your people and take off as soon as we're through here. Nikki?"

Nakamura sat up in his chair, glanced at his notes, and said, "Yes, sir. The 2nd Squadron is broken into two elements of two aircraft each. Tiger Barbs Five and Six will fly high air patrol for the ship, alternating returns to the ship for hot refueling if necessary. They are armed with four AMRAAMs and two Sidewinders each. As with the Sea Apaches, they will be under control of the ship's radar intercept officer."

Nakamura looked to von Stein, who nodded.

"Lieutenant Orlov and myself will fly the defense suppression mission utilizing HARM missiles. The two of us will have eight missiles between us, in addition to Sidewinders for aircraft defense. After the attack pass, we will join up with the others."

The Texas Instruments AGM-88 HARM (High-speed Anti-Radiation Missile) had an 11.5-mile range, could make Mach , and delivered a 145-pound warhead against defensive radars. Operating from either the aircraft's radar or the missile's own seeker head, the missile prioritized threats and selected the targets of greatest peril first.

Cady said, "Pack Rat reports nine SAMs still in operation."

He passed out maps of the defensive battery placements as identified by McNichols's analysts.

"He's sure of that number?" Anderson asked.

"Pretty sure. They finally got the Aquacade in the orbit they want, and they're getting both radar and infrared data."

"How about AA?" Nakamura asked.

"Twenty units. They're marked on your maps," Cady said. "We sure as hell want the air base radar, if we can get it, and let's remember to ignore the three SAMs and six ZSU-Quads located near the drilling sites. We don't want to screw up Dave George's plans. Unless he calls us in for a strike. That's still an option."

"All right," Nakamura continued. "We will leave here and join up with Jerry Can. . . . ?"

"Three," Baker said.

"Three. Then we will head west and loiter one hundred and fifty miles west of the base for as long as it takes. Jerry Can will shuffle back and forth to the ship for fuel if required."

"Fine, Nikki. Okay, Phil, the 1st Squadron?"

"We'll be in three elements," Anderson said, "as soon as I get Gypsies Three and Six back on the deck and turned around. They will recover when the Tiger Barbs relieve them of air patrol duties.

"You are flying strike with AMRAAMs, Shark, and will take on any defensive fighters we run into. Stein is the second wave of HARMs, all by himself. He's loaded with four antiradiation missiles, plus two Sidewinders. Olivera, Sifra, Mikkelson, and myself make the bomb run. We're taking off overweight with external tanks, one AMRAAM each for the return sortie, and a variety of Paveway hardware. That includes the SUU-54/B Pave Storm cluster bomb, GBU-10 cluster bombs, and Mk 83 one thousand-pound demolition bombs. Waypoint Two, one hundred and forty miles east of Primavera, is our loiter point, and Jerry Cans One and Two will keep us from getting thirsty. After we get the go signal, we zip in, deposit the hardware, and exit north on zero-one-two, hoping for the best."

The Paveway laser guidance kits, developed by Texas Instruments, allowed conventional bombs to be outfitted for guidance by laser designators. The units, which included a laser seeker, a small computer, and four steerable control surfaces, were mounted to the noses of conventional weapons. If Cady had been thinking ahead, he could have sent a designator along with George and had the ground party light up a few targets. The problem with that, however, was that the targets were spread all over the landscape, and George might not have been able to get into a position from which he could select all of the primary targets.

"Got your targets selected?" Cady asked.

"On the map, Shark. I'll brief with each aviator before we go."

"Again," Cady said, "nothing goes down on the wells unless George calls for help."

"Roger that, CAG."

"Eddie, wrap it up for us."

Purgatory handed copies of his latest meteorological maps around.

"We get what you prayed for," he said. "Within the next hour, and sixty miles south of here, just before you reach the continent, you're going to encounter thirty-knot winds out of the southwest, gusting to forty-five knots. That's going to kick up ground snow into a blizzard that will suppress ground travel and make things difficult for the boys on the AA and SAM batteries if they have to go visual. I'm looking for zero ceiling and a top at around five thousand feet. Off the coast, out your way, Nikki, you should have clear skies until you go inland. There's some scattered cloud cover over the peninsula and to the west ranging from fifteen to seventeen thousand feet."

Cady didn't think that any of his aviators appeared particularly enthusiastic about the conditions, but they were sure as hell helpful in a land where the cover of night wasn't available.

He provided the frequencies for command and flight element usages. "In addition, we'll need to monitor George's frequency. You'll each have an encryption unit in the circuit so George doesn't come to you scrambled.

"Then, finally," he said, "there's the kick off time. We can only afford to loiter for about four hours before the fatigue factor makes things dangerous for us. If we don't have a go signal from Pack Rat by 0750 hours, we're going anyway at 0752. Plan B then applies, and we take on whatever we meet up with. Questions?"

There were none.

"Arch, can you brief and be off at 0400?"

"That, we can do, CAG."

"That's the initiate time, then," Cady said. "I'll tell Eames."

"Let me tell her," Baker said. "She's my girlfriend, after all."

Cady nodded, but he was just a little put out by the request. He didn't know why.

PRIMAVERA BASE
0340 HOURS LOCAL

Suarez had sent Nightdog Two farther to the north, to check on the ULCC, and when the KC-130 reported back that the ship was now headed west, 730 kilometers away, with two fighter aircraft flying patrol, the last degree of uncertainty vanished from his mind. No crude oil carrier reversed directions in the middle of a voyage.

He and Tellez had dressed in balaclavas, fur headgear, and parkas in order to walk the flight line and check on each aircraft. Most of them were already prepared, their weapons uploaded. The Mirage damaged by the Sno-Cat had had its wing panels straightened and was declared airworthy. The Tornado with the damaged engine that had kept Tellez from downing the Harrier bomber had had its turbine replaced and the final wiring and plumbing were underway.

All along the flight line, start-carts were running, channeling warm air into the cockpits, and portable propane space heaters roared, blowing hot air into enclaves of canvas surrounding airplanes. Ground crewmen having to use wrenches and screwdrivers with their gloves off carried pained expressions. A radio was being changed out on Jaguar Eight. Puma Seven had a problem with its flap control, and the left side actuator was being replaced. Jaguar Ten, the last to land from air patrol, had blown a tire, and was resting on jacks as the wheel was removed. Two trailers with high-speed pumps and de-icing fluid were parked near the end of the taxiway, ready to spray aircraft as they stood in line for takeoff.

Tow tractors with strings of empty dollies were parked behind the fighters. Suarez's inventory of ordnance was getting low in some areas. The last of the Sky Flash and Matra Super 530s had been up-loaded on the Mirages, and the remaining pylons had taken Matra R.530 missiles.

The eight Mirages were going as interception aircraft, to meet the expected challenge by the Harrier jump jets.

The six Tornados were armed with twelve Kormoran anti-ship missiles and twelve Matra R.530 air-to-air missiles.

Suarez pulled back the flap on an eight-foot-high canvas shield and stepped out of the wind into the revetment where his Mirage waited. Tellez followed him.

The canvas wall provided little protection. The wind whistled overhead, and the snow fluttered from overhead, settling on the skin of the airplane. The two of them stood and watched as the 1700-liter external tanks were removed from Suarez's aircraft. They were going to have all of the tankers airborne, and they would not hamper themselves with external tanks.

Over the wind roar, Suarez said, "I do not like sending all of the aircraft, Major. We should leave two or three for protection."

"You do not believe in your ground defenses, Emilio?"

"Of course, I do. Still, something could go wrong. It always does."

"If we had better intelligence gathering, Emilio, I might agree with you. However, we have no idea how many Harrier aircraft or helicopters are available to protect the carrier. Not one of Fuentes's friends in Chilean or Argentinean intelligence has ever heard of this United Nations aircraft carrier, much less can give us any idea of the defensive capability she might carry. We cannot take the risk of approaching her too lightly, not if we want to keep Calvera drilling for two days. We must use all that we have."

Suarez reluctantly nodded in agreement. He had sensed that Silvera was near the end of hope, and if in the next few hours, they did not smash the carrier completely, they would be out of time.

And where then would be his aspirations? What kind of publicity would attend to the name of Suarez de Suruca? How proud, how envious, would be his brother and his sister?

No. He would give all that he had to give to make the Front for South American Determination the success that Silvera envisioned for it. And if the objectives were not met, no one could cast dishonor on his name. He would have died in a cause celebrated by historians as aspiring to just treatment not only for his homeland, but for all of the continent of South America.

Suarez looked upward at the snow swirling overhead.

"This storm is not going to abate, Roberto."

"Nor is it going to stop us," Tellez said. "You understand that this is the last chance we will have?"

"I understand."

"At 0600 hours, then, we will make the best of it."

FALCON ONE
0400 HOURS LOCAL

All nine of the Sea Apaches were on the flight deck, five aligned along the catwalk and four on the fore and aft elevators. On the hangar deck below, the three Jerry Can choppers were ready to be lifted to the deck for their missions. The single LAMPS helicopter was flying twenty miles ahead of the carrier, and her replacement was undergoing maintenance on Hangar Deck 2.

The *Dover* was out there somewhere, too, Baker knew, probably feeling lonely with her sister gone missing.

He couldn't help thinking that this would be the first time he had had all of his assault helicopters off the ship at the same time. It was a thought that made him feel uneasy.

"It's not like we were deserting her, Major," Decker said, thinking along the same lines.

"It feels like it, Henry."

The ship felt steady enough on the sea, but the winds were strong, twenty knots of gust added to the movement of the ship, which was making twelve knots. The stationary rotors bounced up and down in the airflow.

Beehive, Giovanni Este, turned them over to Charles Adams.

"All right, my friends, you've got Shaker on this end. Listen carefully now. I want rotors turning on Falcons Eight, Nine, and Ten. I've got to get you guys off 'cause there's a couple Gypsies that want your deck space. Come on, kiddies."

In minutes, the three Sea Apaches were up to speed, and Adams directed them off the deck in sequence.

"That leaves my next package. Let's have the two forward elevators go first. Turn 'em over, please."

Baker was on the starboard forward elevator, and he went through his checklist quickly, got the turbines fired, and checked the instruments.

"How are you reading, Falcon One?"

"In the green, Shaker."

"Falcon Five?"

"Positive signs, Mr. Shaker. I'm eager."

"Off with the two of you, then, One to starboard and Five to port."

Baker eased in collective, putting the nose down to absorb the oncoming wind, and rose from the deck.

"Why is it, Major, that this is what we do best? Wouldn't it be better to take a limo to work in Fleet Street, or something?"

"Can you imagine yourself in a bowler hat, Henry?"

"Let's go a little faster."

Ten minutes later, the six Sea Apaches were in formation at five hundred feet above the sea, headed for an angry continent. Baker set the pace at 160 knots. The outlying island and the tip of the continent were twenty minutes away.

GYPSY MOTH ONE
0425 HOURS LOCAL

Nakamura's Tiger Barbs took off first, two of them taking up the air patrol for the *U Thant* just vacated by Gypsy Moth aircraft. The Gypsies were on Hangar Deck 1, getting a fast turnaround. Their last useful act before recovery had been to chase off the KC-130 that had moved in to watch over them. One Super Sidewinder was all that was required to send the tanker pilot south at top speed, probably requesting a change of underwear.

Cady hoped the crew chiefs weren't going to get overzealous about minor mechanical problems and ground either airplane. He needed them all.

Nakamura and Orlov, once they were airborne, disappeared quickly to the west, ahead of the carrier. In minutes, they would overtake and pass Jerry Can Three.

Cady waited beside his Harrier, standing on the hangar deck, as he watched Gypsies Two and Three being rolled onto the elevators. The deck aft, near the elevators, was crowded with maintenance and ordnance personnel. Yellow "REMOVE ME" streamers trailed from the missiles and bombs slung beneath the wings of the aircraft. The ordnance officer, a female captain from the Ukraine, strode purposefully from plane to plane, keeping a suspicious eye on every weapon and every pair of hands. She wasn't about to allow an accident on her watch. On the deck above, her assistants would pull the streamers and safety pins on the ordnance just before takeoff.

As he waited, the hatchway aft opened, and Terri Eames appeared. She looked around the cave of the hangar until she spotted him, then walked across the deck to the Harrier.

Before she could speak, Cady said, "Thanks."

"Thanks? What for?"

"For the good word with Monmouth."

Her eyes watched his face closely. "I don't know why anything I would say should carry any weight with the captain."

"It does, Terri, believe me. Sam values your insights."

"I don't want to play God with anyone's life."

"But you do, everyday. And trust me, we all appreciate it."

Cady waved his hand toward the other aviators standing near their planes.

He was aware that many of the men and women were watching them. The elevators started upward, and Gypsies Two and Three along with Phil Anderson and Miguel Olivera disappeared.

She acknowledged his comment with a nod and said, "I came down to wish you Godspeed."

"Thanks," he said, then decided to throw her own tactics from their earlier meeting back at her. "You don't like military aviators, do you?"

"Nope," she said, and grinned at him.

Cady didn't know where to take it from there. He hadn't expected an honest response.

"But we can talk about it, sometime, Jim. Come back."

"I will."

"Don't do anything foolish."

"I made some promises."

She touched the back of his hand with her fingertips, then turned and walked back to the hatchway. More than a few eyes followed her exit.

Cady's crew chief, the Indian, grinned at him.

Cady decided that the balance of his life was going to be shrouded in confusion.

Just when he had thought he had his life remapped and was going to be a responsible adult figure.

FALCON ONE
0429 HOURS LOCAL

The South Shetland Islands were many, and once Baker had seen a few of them, he tended to think of them as muddy. Summer melt had revealed real earth in great splotches, and ice floes filled the waterways between islands.

"You see anything that appeals to you, Henry?" he asked on the internal communications system.

"No, Major, I do not."

"Well, then, do you want to try darts?"

"That bit of nothing just ahead is Bridgeman Island," Decker said. "I suspect it's as good as anything else. We go much farther, and we probably won't be able to see anything, anyway."

Ahead, toward the peninsula, wasn't very inviting. A band of white was rising above ground level and towering over them. Even twenty-five miles away from the peninsula, they were beginning to lose visibility in the growing flurries at their altitude of a thousand feet.

"We'll take a look," Baker said, then added on the frequency assigned to them, "Falcons, stick close to me."

The Sea Apaches followed him as he dove toward the island and circled a five-mile square area. There were a lot of birds and, on the northern shore, a pack of a dozen seals, but nothing remotely humanoid.

"Looks good to me, Henry."

"I question your artistic view, Major."

Baker picked a patch of white snow, rather than a muddy field which might act like quicksand, and settled the Sea Apache onto it gingerly. The surface absorbed the undercarriage without totally collapsing, and he allowed the full weight of the helicopter to sink onto it.

Nothing caved in.

The rest of his element landed around him.

Everyone shut the turbines down.

"Because you question my artistic values, Henry, I think it only fair that you stand the first watch."

"I knew that would happen, no matter what I questioned," Decker told him.

Baker shut down most of his electrical systems, loosened

his harness, found his parka behind the seat, and draped it over his chest. It was going to get cold in the cockpit soon.

He slouched down in his seat, found a crook between the seat and the cockpit coaming for his head, and was asleep in four minutes.

PUMA LEADER
0602 HOURS LOCAL

Tellez's heavily-laden fighter-bomber left the runway sluggishly, but once he had airspeed and had retracted the flaps and gear, began to respond with its typical agility.

He climbed to two thousand meters, above the ground blizzard that was building force, and put the Tornado into a wide orbit.

"All systems are showing green, Major," Umbrago told him from the backseat.

"We'll take that as an omen, then, Miguel."

Five hundred meters above him, and to the east, Tellez saw the Mirages in orbit, looking much like eagles on a rising thermal.

And above them, already moving north, he saw two of the KC-130 tankers. They would enter a holding pattern a hundred miles south of the ULCC. It wasn't likely that they would be needed, but if the Mirages or Tornados got into a prolonged skirmish, the tankers would be available.

Below, he could barely see the runway through the cloud of snow, but after a few seconds, discerned a shadow lumbering off it and into the air. Primavera Control cleared Puma Five and ordered Puma Three onto the runway.

Seven minutes later, in the clear skies above the ground storm, the six Tornados joined, and Tellez lined them up off his right wing.

On the radio, he called Jaguar One.

"Puma One, Jaguar One," Suarez responded.

"Puma Flight is assembled. You may initiate hostilities."

Suarez did not respond, but the Mirages peeled off on a heading of twelve degrees at their briefed speed of seven hundred knots, and Tellez led his Tornados onto a track five hundred meters below them, advancing the throttle until he was holding 575 knots.

The *Cornucopia* was 725 kilometers north, and the Mirages were supposed to get there first.

DEFENSE INTELLIGENCE AGENCY
0611 HOURS LOCAL

McNichols had been up for most of the night, again.

At one time, he'd thought he might grab a half-hour's catnap, but when he went to his office, found Pam Akins in his cot. He went back out to the communications center and spread out on a desk, but was unable to sleep on the hard surface, so he got up again and went down the hallway to shave and pee.

When he got back, he found that Jack Neihouse had gone out for a couple boxes of donuts, and McNichols poked into one of the boxes and came up with a soft, chocolate-covered raised donut. He filled his mug with coffee that was four hours too old.

With his prizes in hand, he settled into a chair at a desk in the second row. He looked up at the left console screen and saw dozens of targets that hadn't been there when he went down the hall.

"Jesus, Jack! Look at that!"

"Oh, hell, Cam. They're going to do it."

"Get a count," McNichols said as he picked up a phone and punched the direct-dial button.

"Fourteen of them."

The Aquacade radar could see pretty well through the scattered clouds over the peninsula and even penetrate the flying snow fairly well, but not fully. The radar returns around Primavera had mostly disappeared among ground clutter except for the active radar being used by the air base. To the east, and out of view of any other radar, the satellite was showing two helicopters and six Harriers orbiting. Out over the sea to the west was one helicopter and two more blips

The *U Thant* and her air patrols were clear of snow and showed up well in the Drake Passage. A container ship was moving east some seventy miles north of the ULCC, and an eastbound freighter was fifteen miles south of her.

"CIC, Eames."

"Terri, baby, Cam."

"They launched," she said.

"All fourteen of their fighter-bombers. We're showing two transports orbiting to the north and to the west, plus two more that I assume are tankers."

"They're all headed our way?" she asked.

"Looks like it at the moment."

"I can't believe they'd not leave a couple to protect the base."

"If I see any turn back, I'll let you know."

"Thanks, Cam."

She hung up on him.

Story of his life.

DRILLING SITE #6
0614 HOURS LOCAL

Armand Calvera was near tears.

They were 125 meters below the lava at this site, and

for thirty of those meters, the petroleum sign had been increasing steadily.

But for the last ten meters of drilling, all traces of petroleum had vanished entirely.

He could not believe it.

He had been so certain.

His hearing was numb from the hours of cacophony he had endured on the platform. He could not take it any longer. His body was fatigued from lack of sleep, from noise, and from worry, and he felt as if he might collapse at any moment.

Calvera picked up the last sample, pushed through the flap of the derrick, and descended to the ground. He walked across the frozen surface, rutted from the passage of vehicles, to the manager's shanty.

Inside, in the warmth from the stove, he placed the sample on a side table, next to dozens of others collected over the past days. He shed his coat and then sat down at the table. His geologic charts were spread over its surface and he pored over them, very aware that the rig's foreman was sitting up in his bunk watching him.

The foreman knew.

He asked, "Nothing, Dr. Calvera?"

"There has to be a pocket! It's there. I know it is!"

"We just missed the fault, that is all. Perhaps the other rigs—"

"No! It's here!"

The results of sampling at Sites 5 and 7 pointed toward Site 6 as the fault line that would trap oil and gas in the spongy structure called a pool. He no longer had hope of a strike at either of the offset wells.

It had to be at Site 6.

Or not at all.

Calvera kept his face turned away from the foreman. He felt a tear trickle down his left cheek.

How could he tell Silvera?

He would not.

NINE MILES NORTHEAST OF PRIMAVERA BASE
0617 HOURS LOCAL

"Raccoon, Jericho."

Dave George heard the call in the earphone he had plugged into his right ear. He didn't want the radio speaker alerting people who should not be alerted.

Speaking softly into the microphone, he acknowledged the call.

"Fuzzbuster," Eames said, uttering the code word he had been wanting to hear.

He clicked the transmit button twice and then shut off the radio and checked the time on his watch.

Gustav Brelin looked at him.

George whispered, "Twelve minutes from now, they'll hit the base."

"So, we go now?"

"We go now, Gus."

George and Brelin were sprawled on top of a shelter half resting on the snow behind a large boulder. He scanned the area directly in front of him, but could see only the single FSAD sentry that had been posted at the top of the ridge overlooking the middle drilling site. The muted roar of the rig's diesel engines could be heard rising from the chasm.

The sentry appeared miserable, his shoulders hunched against the cold. The snow was blowing fiercely, and the wind-chill was down to around seventy below, Brelin had told him.

The others from George's team were scattered around both sides of the ridge top, and they had two antiaircraft units and one SAM battery in the sights of their LAWs, weapons replaced from new stores when the Seahawks picked them up for relocation.

Bascom's team was three hundred yards to the south, perched over another rig, and Suslov's team had found another drilling rig four hundred yards to the north.

The earphone of the squad radio was snug in George's left ear, and the whisper mike was pressed against his cheek by his balaclava. He pulled it away from his face and spoke, "Two, Three?"

He got clicks in response.

"Eleven minutes to kick-off. We go in two."

Bascom and Suslov both responded with clicks.

"I'll do this one, Gus."

"No. This one is for Zip."

They waited.

When the second hand came around for the second time, George said, "Now, Gus."

Brelin was prone alongside the boulder, his captured Kalashnikov rifle pulled tight against his shoulder, the stock resting in his left hand.

It barked once.

And the sentry pitched over face-first into the snow. The body didn't move, and George figured he wasn't going to be miserable any more.

Almost simultaneously, the antitank weapons rimming the canyon fired.

George couldn't see more than fifty yards in any direction, but two predominant explosions on either side of the canyon told him that the two antiaircraft guns had been hit. Seconds later, the chunk-chunk-chunk of more detonations rolled along the cliff top. Suslov's and Bascom's teams had also hit pay dirt.

"Raccoon One," came over his earphone, "Seven. One SAM in flames."

The SAMs were on the valley floor, and his man had hit at least one of them. It helped when the enemy was only looking to the skies.

"Let's go, Gus!"

The two of them leapt to their feet and went charging along the canyon rim, dodging boulders, sliding on the ice, until they reached a spot away from the camouflage cover over the derrick. They dove for the edge and landed on their stomachs. Far to his left was a fire that raged beyond the curtain of snow. He could hear ammunition rounds cooking off. On the other side of the canyon, another fire glowed in the snow, and more exploding ammunition could be heard.

Peering over the side, George saw men spilling out of the derrick covering and diving from the doorways of the buildings.

They were in panic, unarmed. Obviously, someone had believed the ruse that the SEALs had left the ice.

Brelin rolled away to fasten one end of their rappelling rope to a rock outcropping. George grabbed the other end and tossed it over the side. Checking the safety on his M-16, George slung it over his shoulder, grabbed the rope, wrapped it around his calf and boot, and slid over the side.

A minute later, and a hundred feet lower, he released the rope and unslung the rifle. Brelin slid down next to him.

Across the ravine, he saw more of his men appear in the snowfall. They started advancing up the canyon, staying to either side of the road.

They encountered no defensive fire, and they held their own.

Fifteen yards from the rig, Corporal Angelino called out in Spanish, and within two minutes, the workers and soldiers had responded to his demands, forming up in a circle in front of the drilling rig, their hands on top of their heads.

A few weapons had been tossed aside, and George's team members moved in and secured them.

"I think these guys have lost the will to fight, Gus."

"Damned sorry lot," Brelin told him.

He and George left the protection of a boulder and trotted into the end of the box canyon.

George saw a man standing in the doorway of a shanty. An old man. He walked over to him and asked, "Are you in charge?"

The man spoke English. "Who are you?"

George gestured with the muzzle of his rifle, letting the menace of a bullet in the gut make his point.

"I am in charge. My name is Dr. Armand Calvera."

"Step back."

The man stepped back inside, and George and Brelin followed him in.

Two tables were littered with core samples, mud samples, and papers. Brelin rifled through the papers.

"Geologic reports and maps," Brelin said. "Just what we want, Commander."

"Good. We'll take them along." One of the objectives of this mission, he had been told by Monmouth, was to capture documentation. Otherwise, they would have sent the bombers in.

Brelin opened a briefcase that was resting on the floor and swept all of the documents into it.

"All right, Calvera, grab a coat and get your butt outside."

They took their prisoner out of the shed, forced him in with the others, and herded them down the road. Corporal Angelino fired up one of the two Sno-Cats that were parked next to the diesel shed, backed it around, and followed them down the road.

When they were a hundred yards from the derrick, George called, "Sergeant Tu!"

"Yes, sir."

Tu turned back, raised his forty-millimeter M79 grenade launcher, and lofted a grenade high into the air. It arced casually onto the snow-covered camouflage sheeting.

The grenade exploded with a dull thump.

And the sheeting began to split.

Tons of snow poured down.

The wooden sheds cracked, split, and flattened under the load.

The diesel engines died, and over the idling Sno-Cat, George could hear jet engines in the distance.

TIGER BARB TWO
0629 HOURS LOCAL

Nakamura had finished topping off his tanks from Jerry Can Three five minutes before he got the "Go" signal. Eames also told him that there were no defensive aircraft over the target, and he could not believe that, though he did not question it.

"Tiger Barb Four?"

"Four," Orlov said.

"We're on our way."

"Roger."

They had been holding in a figure-eight pattern at four thousand feet, and Nakamura rolled out and found a heading of ninety-five degrees, which should put him right on top of Primavera.

He boosted the throttle until the airspeed on the HUD registered 650 knots.

Orlov stayed with him, fifty yards off his right wing.

As he closed on the peninsula, Nakamura lost altitude, and by the time he reached the pack ice, the AGL altimeter reported five hundred feet.

The Harrier had been originally conceived as a close-support aircraft, assisting ground troops in all kinds of weather and terrain. The United States Marines and several NATO countries used it in that role, but the United Nations variant, the Harrier III, had an expanded set of expectations, avionics, and equipment. Now, Nakamura reverted to the original concept.

He was sneaking in on Primavera at low level, to avoid being caught by enemy radars. The irony was that to sneak in using his ground mapping radar, he had to emit electromagnetic radiation that could pinpoint him, if anyone was looking.

The weather, however, dictated his use of Terrain-Following Radar. Just off the ice pack, he entered thickening blankets of snow and switched on and engaged the TFR. The E-scope came alive, showing him the zero command line, called the "ski toe." It appeared to be a ski tip emplaced on the screen face. If obstructions appeared and penetrated the ski toe, the aircraft would be automatically commanded to pull up by the E-scope, the HUD, and the cockpit flight director to avoid the barrier. He clicked the rotary switch to select the minimum safe altitude as five hundred feet. He retarded the throttle and bled off speed to 450 knots.

Since the terrain beyond the ice pack was relatively undulating, without major changes of altitude, and since he was using a medium altitude, he selected an easy ride. The airplane's up-and-down movements would be less harsh. A hard ride would allow him to maintain a low two hundred feet of altitude, with the aircraft prepared for sudden and abrupt changes in attitude.

"You still there, Four?"

"Here, TFR engaged."

"Copy."

He couldn't see Orlov any more.

"Four minutes," Nakamura said. "Arm missiles."

"Roger. Arm the missiles."

The hard part of this flight was believing in the radars and the computers. It required great faith in electronics. He could see nothing outside the canopy, and he had to rely on the electronics to keep him from flying into the side of a cliff. It helped to stay busy, making sure the HARM missiles activated and powered up.

The Harrier suddenly pulled up, shoving Nakamura hard into his seat. After a second, she leveled off, then began to lose altitude again.

He wished he had been able to see the rock or hill or mountain.

"Four, radars."

"Roger."

Nakamura switched his attack radar from standby to active.

The screen lit up with the base. He picked out the air base's major radar, on top of the cliff, immediately, and manually assigned it to his first missile. For the other missiles, he selected their "AUTO" modes. They would arm themselves for radars with the highest threat priority.

Within seconds of activating his attack radar, his RHAW screen began identifying search radars, displaying "S" symbols.

Eleven miles from the target, the "S" symbols began to blink out, to be replaced by "A"s, "8"s, "9"s, and an "11" as enemy radars tried to lock on him.

A sudden beeping in his ears told him he was in peril. "LOCK-ON" lit up on the instrument panel.

Nakamura released the safety switch and committed the missiles.

One by one, they dropped off the pylons and streaked off ahead of him.

When the last missile released, Nakamura punched out chaff and flares, to attract the oncoming missiles, rolled hard

to the left, defeating the TFR for a few seconds, and headed
north.

He lost the "LOCK-ON," but he didn't know how. Either
the missile chased his decoys or one of the HARMs killed
the radar guiding it.

He clicked the minimum safe altitude selector down to two
hundred feet and selected hard ride. It might be rough, but it
was better than being up there where any remaining SAMs
might find him.

GYPSY MOTH ONE
0632 HOURS LOCAL

The first element had a three-minute head start on the
second, and the second element preceded the third by one
minute.

Cady hung back behind the other five Harriers, but still
making 450 knots. He was fifteen miles from Primavera.

Originally, he was to have gone in as escort to Stein in the
second element, prepared to take on any aircraft defending
the air base. With Pack Rat's information that there were no
airborne defenders, though, Cady had lost part of his job.

It was all right with him. He would be able to save his
missiles for later.

He cut off the TFR and began climbing, heading for five
thousand feet as he scanned the radar scope and the RHAW
screen.

Stein was also carrying an electronic countermeasures pod,
and just before the first element was due to hit, he initiated
jamming that would interrupt or confuse the enemy tracking
and guidance radars as well as clutter the radio frequencies
that the FSAD had been using out of Primavera.

Not very many SAM launches were made before the active

symbols on his RHAW began to vanish, either hit by incoming HARMs missiles from Nakamura and Orlov or shut down by the crews trying to avoid the antiradiation missiles. The main radar atop the cliff winked out. Primavera Base was now effectively blind.

A minute after the fusillade of missiles from Nakamura and Orlov, a few SAMs and ZSU-23s came back up, hunting for targets.

"They found me," Stein yelled on the radio, "and here you go, suckers! Missiles away. Star's going north."

The threat receiver screen went almost blank as defensive radars shut down again or were killed.

Cady punched his button number four.

"Raccoon, Gypsy One."

"Raccoon here, Gypsy."

"You need any help?"

"Hell, no. Unless you want to herd prisoners. We've got bunches of them. Just level that base for me."

"Roger that, Raccoon. Gypsy One out."

On his radar screen, Cady saw the blips of Nakamura, Orlov, and Stein turning to the north. Five miles from Primavera, the next four Harriers were at 1500 feet, heading straight for the base.

The aviators were going to have a time of it in this snow, he thought. They were using laser range and targeting finders, and when they popped over the cliff, they were going to have to light up their targets quickly, release the first wave of bombs, then circle to the south and come back for the last pass. On the second pass, they would have more time to locate targets.

"Thirty seconds," Anderson said on the radio.

Cady stayed behind them, now at five thousand feet, and went into a right 360-degree circle. He scanned the radar screen looking for bogeys. One was off to the west, coming east, but at 340 knots. That would be one of the C-130s, and if he wanted to venture closer, Cady would be happy to welcome him.

His RHAW showed a few antiaircraft guns coming up again, but no SAMs.

The flight of planes began sounding off with "bombs away" messages.

"Hot damn! This is Raccoon, guys. We're three miles north of Primavera, and you just lit up the city. Explosions everywhere! Fires! An ordnance dump went up like July Fourth. Come on around, again!"

Four minutes later, the Harriers dropped the last of their bombs, then climbed as they continued north.

Cady brought his Harrier up another five hundred feet and cleared the ground blizzard. He dawdled along as the remaining aircraft joined on him.

"Let me have your conditions," he asked.

They all reported in green, except for Gypsy Six, Jasper "Tiger" Mikkelson, who had flak damage to the fuselage and was leaking fuel.

"Jerry Can Two, Gypsy One."

"Gypsy One, Jerry Can Two."

Gail Alhers and Mikhail Makarov were over a hundred miles to the east, northbound.

"Think you can find Gypsy Moth Six?" he asked.

"I can find anything, anyplace, anywhere, Gypsy One."

"Go for it, then. Tiger, slow to three hundred and rendezvous with the tanker. If you get any reds, eject and she can pick you up."

"Roger that, One," Mikkelson said.

"The rest of you," Cady said, "start your pre-attack checklists."

DEFENSE INTELLIGENCE AGENCY
0645 HOURS LOCAL

"Un-fucking-believable!" McNichols yelped.

"Try me," Eames told him.

"I don't think there's anything left of Primavera. Our radar and infrared sensors are showing fires everywhere. No detail, but almost all of the defensive radars are gone."

"How about aircraft, Cam?"

"Nothing down. There's a Harrier dragging his tail, but I see a helicopter on an intercept course. The rest are all coming at you."

"Do you have a position on the FSAD aircraft?" she asked.

"The Mirages are just clearing the tip of the peninsula, love. The Tornados are fifteen miles behind them."

"Thanks, Cam. We've been emissions quiet, but in about a minute, I'm going to hit them with everything I've got, and I'm going to be busy."

"Talk to you later, Terri. Luck."

PUMA LEADER
0647 HOURS LOCAL

The radios from Primavera were silent now, but for a few minutes, they had been screaming that the drilling rigs were under attack, then static cut everything off.

Suarez, in a crisp but obviously anguished voice, tried to reach the base, but was unsuccessful.

Tellez depressed the button for the tanker's frequency.

"Esso Four, Esso Five, Puma Leader."

"Go, Puma Leader."

"Take your tankers to a heading of three-five-zero and orbit two hundred kilometers north of the carrier."

"Roger, Puma. On the way."

They would be happier closer to the mainland of South America than to the Antarctic continent.

"Puma, Jaguar One."

"This is Puma One."

"We have just initiated attack radars, and we count two fighter aircraft and four helicopters."

"Yes. There may be some behind us if they attacked the wells and jammed the radios."

"They cannot catch us," Suarez said.

"That is true. Why don't you shoot down those aircraft that you see for us?"

"We will do just that. Going to three thousand meters. Jaguar One out."

Tellez went the other way and led his flight downward, leveling off at two hundred meters above ground level. The whiteout seemed total, but he knew they would emerge from it in a few minutes.

PRIMAVERA BASE
0648 HOURS LOCAL

Silvera felt catatonic.

He did not feel like moving.

Or talking.

Ever again.

Around him, men were in panic, abandoning their posts, running for the door, though where they would go from there, Silvera did not know.

Through the window and the dense wall of snow, he could see the glow of fires everywhere. Fire was the devil for those living in Antarctica. It was difficult to fight. Behind the runway, the residential buildings that he could see were all on fire. Most of the defensive batteries were not answering their radio calls because of the static, and those that were contacted on landlines were reporting that they were out of action.

No one answered calls at the drilling sites.

Ricardo Fuentes was tugging on his sleeve. "Come, Silvera. We must get out of here."

He shook his head. "What is the use, Ricardo?"

"Come on, damn it! The pilot said he can still get the Mystère off the runway. We must go before it is totally destroyed."

Silvera stood up and allowed Fuentes to shove his arms into his parka. Then he followed him dumbly through the door, slogging through deep snow to where the Falcon business jet was idling its engines.

THE PALOMA
0649 HOURS LOCAL

The captain of the freighter *Paloma* had already decided his course. He was not stopping for anyone or anything until he saw the lights of Rio de Janeiro. As soon as he cleared Antarctic waters, he would abandon the two patrol boats secured to his starboard side and let them fend for themselves.

The ULCC *Cornucopia,* which was the target Captain Enriquez had designated for him, was steaming westward nine kilometers off the port bow, and the captain intended to maintain that separation as they passed in the Strait.

Then the bridge lookout shouted, "Captain! Look!"

He stepped forward to the bridge windows and followed the pointing finger.

Eight warplanes had cleared the coastal islands, heading

straight at him. Or hopefully, over him and toward the crude oil carrier. They were high in the sky.

"And behind them, sir!"

Barely visible were another six dots emerging from the ground blizzard, coming fast, growing larger by the second. The second group was much lower.

The captain had a change of heart.

Here, his friends and allies were going to have their victory.

Plus, if any of those pilots saw him not doing his job, then the court-martial proposed by Captain Enriquez might come to pass.

Even if it were a hastily called court-martial in some dark alley, five thousand kilometers from here.

"Tell the patrol boats to drop their lines and proceed with the attack. When they are clear, come left rudder fifteen degrees."

UNS U THANT
0651 HOURS LOCAL

Captain Samuel Monmouth hit the General Quarters alarm himself, and the Klaxon began to blare all over the ship.

The defensive crews were already in their positions, however, and at the sound of the horns, the tank hatch covers forward folded back and the guns rose into firing position. The hatches covering the Vertical Launch System slid aside.

Like the rest of his crew, Monmouth was wearing his helmet, his armored vest, and his life vest. He felt bulky.

Pressing the button for the intercom, he said, "CIC, Bridge."

"CIC, sir."

"Commander von Stein, you may open fire at your discretion."

"Aye, aye, Captain."

FALCON ONE
0652 HOURS LOCAL

From the left side of his canopy, Baker had watched the FSAD aircraft approach. They were crossing the nose of the helicopter at a right angle, some four miles west of where the Sea Apaches rested in the frigid cold of Bridgeman Island.

"Sorry you didn't get a chance to nap, Henry."

"I am, too, Major."

He waited until the Mirages had gone by, and when the Tornados passed into the frame of the front windscreen, where he thought the helicopters would be out of the cone of any operating infrared seekers on the Tornados, he depressed the transmit button.

"Wind them up, Falcons."

All around him, the turbine engines whined into life. In seconds, his own instruments were showing the RPMs coming up, the exhaust temperatures climbing into operating ranges.

"Mind turning on the heat, Major?"

"That was the next item on my checklist, Henry."

It was cold in the cockpit, and the beginning stirrings of warmed air were welcome.

"Everyone ready?"

"Two."

"Four."

"Five."

"Six, on line."

"Seven."

Baker still missed the gap of Falcon 3. He was afraid, too, that he might soon have a few more gaps.

"Take care," he said as he pulled collective and lifted off.

They put the noses down and screamed northwestward at top speed, staying a hundred feet off the sea.

"We'll light them off in about ten seconds, Henry."

"I'm ready. I've already got an infrared lock, Major."

"Combat spread," he said on the radio. "Let's get 'em, Falcons."

He pulled the nose up and began climbing toward the tails of the low-flying Tornados.

Decker fired the first Super Sidewinder.

JAGUAR ONE
0653 HOURS LOCAL

Emilio Suarez was thirty kilometers from the ship, in a dive going through three thousand meters at five hundred knots, when his infrared and radar threat receivers began to chirp.

Suddenly, there were radars everywhere. Attack radars from the ship lit up, looking as powerful as anything he had ever seen before.

He tried to ignore them and brought his nose down a rifle, lining up on a single Black Hawk helicopter flying to the left side of the ship, five kilometers away from it. His wingmen began to peel off, heading for a group of three Apache helicopters.

"Jaguar!" Tellez called. "We are being attacked from the rear!"

What!

Impossible, he thought. There had been no other aircraft.

He almost lost his concentration, but the lock-on warning from the Sky Flash missile jerked him back, and he committed the missile, then rolled hard to the right.

"Jaguars, go to one-eight-zero. We must protect the bombers."

UNS U THANT
0655 HOURS LOCAL

Eames had the main console, directing air operations, and Hermann von Stein sat next to her, directing the ship's defensive systems.

There were radar targets all over her screen, but the IFF beacons in the planes identified them for her.

The wave of Mirages had launched several missiles, attempting to clear the air defenses in preparation for the attack run by the Tornados.

Luigi Maroni was on her right, ready to assist, to call actions she might miss.

"Tiger Barbs, Jericho."

"Tiger Five."

"Come left to zero-nine-zero."

"Five, roger."

The two Harriers were at five thousand feet, ready to pounce on the second wave of attackers.

"Missiles in the air, Terri," Maroni said. "Hunting the close in Apaches."

"Falcons Eight, Nine, and Ten, heads up!" she called on the radio.

On the screen, the symbols for the Sea Apaches split up, taking evasive maneuvers. They didn't have the same missile range as the Mirages.

"Damn!" von Stein yelped. "The LAMPS just went down."

"You'd better go early," Eames told von Stein.

"Sergeant O'Hara, trial engage."

"Trial engage, aye, aye, sir."

The Aegis Mk 10, working off the SPY radar, started selecting targets.

"Eight missiles selected," O'Hara called out.

"We'll take four from each VLS."

"Four from each launcher, aye, sir. . . . ready!"

Von Stein committed the launch.

FALCON ONE
0659 HOURS LOCAL

Baker's attack had scrambled the Tornados. They were scattering in every direction, climbing for the safety of altitude,
pursued by hungry Sidewinders.

Most of the missiles missed their targets, confused by coun-
termeasure decoys, but Falcon Five's shot clipped the wing on
a Tornado, spinning it out of control, and the pilot ejected
himself and his navigator before he ever knew whether or not
he could regain control.

"Very nice, Five," Baker complemented him.

He had seen the LAMPS Seahawk explode in a bright flash,
but he didn't have a comment for that.

Decker launched his second missile as Baker rolled right,
trying to center himself on a Tornado that was in the vertical,
his afterburners a streak of white behind him.

"They've got a couple air-to-air missiles hung, Major, in
addition to the antiship."

"Good eye, Henry. But it means they could turn on us,
does it not?"

"That would be my supposition."

He was about to make an appropriate suggestion to Jericho
when he saw the launches from the ship. In a steady stream,
two S-2 Aegis missiles at a time leaped from the port and
starboard vertical launchers, climbing high, selecting their targets and leveling out.

The Mirages, which had turned back to help out the Tornados, suddenly didn't care about the Tornados. Baker could imagine that every one of them was showing a missile locked-on and homing.

The Mirages were all over the sky, dipping and swaying, trying to shake the surface-to-air missiles.

Baker leveled off, watching his Sidewinder miss its fighter-bomber target. The Tornado had climbed nearly out of sight, headed east, much too fast to pursue. He turned back toward the ship.

"Boom!" Decker yelled. "Mirage down. And there, Major, another!"

Almost like clockwork, the ship's missiles began catching Mirages. Baker and Decker counted five down within seconds of each other. The remaining three Mirages shot overhead for the south so fast Baker couldn't count the missiles left on their pylons.

But he'd bet they still had most of them.

The Tornados were still a problem, however.

As Baker recalled his Sea Apaches from their scattered positions, he saw the Tornados regrouping to the east.

"Jericho, Falcon."

"Falcon One, this is Jericho."

"You might expect a pass on your stern."

"We see them, Falcon."

And Baker's eye caught something he hadn't expected to see.

Two patrol boats and an old freighter, hell-bent for the side of the *U Thant,* maybe a couple miles away, and ten miles away from Baker.

And all he had was air-to-air missiles.

"By the way, Jericho, you've got a surface attack coming at you, your bearing one-eight-zero."

"Uh . . . thanks, Falcon."

Beside her, Hermann von Stein was aligning S-2 Aegis missiles with Tornados as new targets, but Eames was concerned with the symbols on the screen designating the *Paloma* and the two patrol boats, unidentified. The freighter's data box showed she had been flagged for monitoring, but Eames had forgotten all about her. Where the patrol boats had come from, she didn't know.

Falcons Nine and Ten were out of position, to the southeast. The vessels were too close to initiate firing of Tomahawk missiles from the VLS launchers.

"Falcon Eight, can you intercept the boats?"

"No missiles, Jericho, but we've got some cannon rounds left. On our way."

She watched the radar track of the Sea Apache as it turned on the boats and picked up speed.

And almost immediately, the symbol tumbled, then disappeared from the screen.

"Eight's down," somebody called.

"Hermann," she said, "I need your guns."

Von Stein took one look at her screen, saw the boats, then spoke into his headset, "Port gun, engage hostile vessels now. Free to fire."

"Here come the Tornados," Maroni said.

Tellez knew that a stern attack presented him with the smallest target, but he did not think he had time to go around and try the starboard side. It would give the Apache helicop-

ters time to get position on him, and while they weren't a
strong threat, they had still knocked Puma Six down.

As he dropped the nose to begin his run, he was surprised
to see the freighter and patrol boats making what he considered a suicide attempt on the behemoth. He had no idea where
they had come from.

"Can you believe that, Roberto?" Umbrago asked.

The freighter was unarmed, but he saw that the patrol boats
had opened up with their deck guns. He thought he saw a
torpedo being launched.

And then a gun on the forward deck of the ship began
firing and heavy geysers spouted all around the ships. In less
than a second, both patrol boats erupted in flames.

The freighter, apparently with damage on the bridge, veered
off-course.

The torpedo struck home, though, and he saw the detonation at water level.

"Sixteen kilometers," Umbrago said. "On course. I have
the target illuminated, dumping data to the missiles."

The targeting reticule was placed directly on the stern of
the ship. He was holding 450 knots at two hundred meters of
altitude.

Steady.

Missiles suddenly appeared from nowhere, launching out of
the ship's deck.

"This is a very lethal crude oil carrier, Miguel."

Tellez fired two Messerschmitt-Bolkow-Blohm Kormoran
antiship missiles. They ignited immediately on their booster
rocket motors and dove for the sea. By the time they reached
their twenty-meter cruise altitude, the main rocket motor had
taken over. As they closed on the ship, the active radar head
would take over, then lower the strike altitude to five meters.
The 165-kilogram warhead was designed to penetrate the hu

before detonating, then sending sixteen individual slugs pene-
rating interior bulkheads. It was a devastating weapon.

As soon as the missiles were clear, Tellez rolled hard to the
left.

"Come, Pumas. Launch and follow me."

He shoved the throttle into afterburner.

UNS U THANT
0711 HOURS LOCAL

Monmouth watched as more missiles departed the VLS
launchers, arcing backwards and passing over his head.

He was monitoring the CIC on the overhead speakers, and
he heard Eames directing the two Tiger Barb Harriers to an
attack profile on the Tornados.

"Cancel that, Tigers. We have ten incoming missiles, ID'd
as Kormoran. Launch on the incoming missiles."

"Tiger Five, roger."

The intercom sounded off, "Bridge, Damage Control."

"Bridge."

"Compartments one-two-six, one-two-seven, and one-two-
eight are flooded, but sealed off. We have small leaks in one-
two-five which will be contained shortly. We are counting two
dead, six injured, one unaccounted for."

"Thank you," Monmouth said and released the intercom
talk bar.

The compartments were residential and storage spaces.
They could survive the torpedo damage.

He wasn't sure about ten Kormorans.

He briefly considered turning the ship, but the missiles
would be here before the bow even started to swing.

Four more missiles rose from the forward deck, standing
momentarily on their rocket flames, then whisking away.

The Tiger Barb Harriers flashed by overhead, and Mon
mouth saw the streaks as they launched all of their AM
RAAMs and Sidewinders.

The stern seventy-six-millimeter Oto guns began firing, th
dull staccato thuds vibrating through the deck.

Despite the ship- and air-launched missiles and the rada
controlled guns spitting 120 rounds per minute at the Kormo
rans, Monmouth felt particularly impotent.

He waited for the impacts.

On the overhead speakers, Eames's voice continued to issu
in a steady and surprisingly calm fashion: "Falcon One, detai
or sink that freighter . . . Tornado down . . . Falcon Nine an
Ten, search for survivors of Seahawk Five and Falcon Eigl
. . . second Tornado hit . . . incoming missiles engaged . .
one out, two, three . . . four down . . . another Tornado . .
fifth-sixth-seventh Kormorans . . . up to the guns now . .
eight . . . nine . . . and ten!"

The wave of relief that swept across the bridge was palp
ble. Monmouth heard audible sighs, and realized that one
them was his own.

"Gypsy Moth One, Jericho."

"Go, Jericho."

"You have three Mirages and two Tornados headed yo
way, the Mirages at angels six, seven-zero-zero knots, and tl
Tornados at angels three and climbing, Mach one-point-two

"We'll be happy to meet them, Jericho."

PUMA LEADER
0722 HOURS LOCAL

After evading the missile that had locked on to him, Tell
jockeyed the fighter until he could look back at the ship.
raised his visor and pulled his oxygen mask free.

Not one of the Kormorans got through the fusillade of mis-
.les and gunfire directed against them.

"This is a bitter pill to swallow," Umbrago said.

"It is an amazing ship," Tellez said, impressed with the
eapons that had been brought to bear against them. Even in
efeat, he could admire the power and the technology of his
iemies. The ULCC had been completely deceptive; no one
ould have expected the devastating and overwhelming fire-
ower she could raise.

Tellez thought that perhaps he had reached retirement age.
he minor insurgencies that were likely to hire him in the
iture would be unable to afford the weapons required to
iunter such technologies.

The strategy was well-handled, also. Tellez was certain he
cognized the technique of the lead Apache pilot; it would be
e man he had encountered the week before. The attack by the
sault helicopters had completely disrupted the raid on the
ip, drawing the Mirages away from their assignments.

Enrico Salazar, in Puma Five, pulled up alongside him and
oked over at him. His visor was raised, and his face was
le.

Tellez grinned at him. Salazar was a survivor, also.

"Roberto! Bandits at twelve o'clock! Three thousand me-
rs, six hundred knots."

"Yes. This will be my friend, the Harrier pilot."

Tellez spoke to Salazar on the radio. "Five, prepare for air
mbat."

PSY MOTH ONE
23 HOURS LOCAL

Cady had been monitoring Jericho, as had the others in the
ght of seven Harrier jump jets.

On the radio net, Solomon Sifra said, "It is too bad the did not attack the ship earlier. The war would have been com pleted much sooner."

Cady had the targets Eames had designated on his rada screen, three Mirages thirty miles ahead and two Tornado twenty miles behind them. If he hadn't been taken out by on of the ship's missiles, one of the Tornado drivers was a gu who liked to shoot down unarmed civilian craft.

Off his left and right wings, he had six Harriers, Stei Nakamura, and Orlov each armed with two Sidewinders an the balance of them with one AMRAAM apiece. Cady ha four AMRAAMs. Mikkelson was now about fifty miles be hind, escorted by Jerry Can Two.

They were in a slow descent, about to penetrate the stor below.

"Listen up," he said on the frequency. "Flip, you take Gy sies Three and Four and the Tiger Barbs and engage the M rages. Gypsy Five and I will check out the Tornados."

"Roger that, Shark."

Anderson climbed out of the formation, and the others fe into trail behind him. The Mirages were at six thousand fe above the storm, and Anderson led his formation into a clim to get above them.

Sifra rolled in on Cady's right wing.

"Five, let's go button three."

"Gone."

Sifra checked in on the new frequency. Getting off the p mary channel would keep things from getting confused soon as the action started.

The Tornados were maintaining three thousand feet of al tude, staying down in the storm.

"Five, these were the bombers. They're going to be lig on air-to-air."

"Roger that, Shark."

"You take the guy on the right. I've got the left."
"Five."

JAGUAR LEADER
0727 HOURS LOCAL

There was no longer any static on the radio frequencies used by Primavera, but Suarez could not raise anyone there. He began to have grave reservations about the amount of damage resulting from the UN raid.

He should have left an air cover, have refused to go along with Silvera's insistence on a major strike against the ship.

Was the president all right?

He felt as if he had failed in his responsibilities to the Front for South American Determination and to Silvera personally.

The attack on the ship had turned into a fiasco. He kept reliving the rout and anguishing over it.

And ahead of him, as shown on his radar, the Harrier aircraft had split up, with five airplanes climbing to meet him and his two remaining wingmen.

"Puma One, Jaguar One. Do you see the Harriers coming for you?"

"I do, Jaguar. There are but two, and they will not take long to obliterate."

Tellez was his typical, confident self. Did he not realize what might be waiting for them at Primavera?

Suarez still had two Matra Super 530 missiles, and he armed them.

"Jaguars, we will take the formation head-on, and scatter them. Shoot down what you can and break through for Primavera. We will do a hot refueling and rearmament, then take off immediately."

The Mirages acknowledged him, and Suarez put the nose down a little, to meet the climbing Harriers.

Thirty-two kilometers of distance between them. They were closing at over 1300 knots.

Precious seconds sailed by.

On the radar screen, the UN airplanes did not waver. They came at him like an unstoppable freight train.

He finally saw them, five silhouettes spread wide apart, backlit by the storm clouds and raging, windblown snow below them.

His missiles warned him that they had targets selected.

They exchanged missiles almost simultaneously.

Suarez fired his Super Matras the second that he saw missiles ignite from several of the Harriers.

And then both fighter groups began the dance of evasion.

Suarez shoved his throttle to afterburner, ejected flares, and pulled the stick back to his belly, going vertical.

Counting one . . . two . . . three.

Pulled the nose over and rolled inverted.

Looked up through the canopy and saw both of his wingmen hit at the same time. One Mirage cartwheeled through the sky and disappeared into the clouds. The other disintegrated in one blinding burst of yellow-red flame. There were no parachutes.

To the south, he saw one rolling Harrier hit, coming apart in a dozen pieces.

Then they were all around him, climbing after him.

He had no more missiles.

Suarez rolled upright, banked to the left, found a northerly heading, and watched anxiously as the airspeed climbed past Mach 1.5.

They could not catch him.

On the radio, he asked, "Esso Four, where are you?"

GYPSY MOTH ONE
0729 HOURS LOCAL

Cady heard Phil Anderson report to Jericho on the command net that David Stein had gone down, but he was concentrating on prepping his missiles, aligning his targets, and trimming the airplane in the turbulence of the storm, and he let it slide by in the back of his mind.

With the speed available to them, the Tornados could probably have blasted right past Cady and Sifra, but they chose not to do so.

When the lead pilot made that decision, Cady was certain it was the same pilot he had engaged before. The man would not run from a good fight.

"Five, I'm going to switch targets with you."

"What? Why, Shark?"

"I know this guy, and he's mine."

If Eames was listening, she'd probably be pissed at him, he thought. Taking unnecessary risks again. Playing hotshit aviator.

"Five, roger."

He could no longer see Sifra's fighter. The whiteout was complete, and he could barely discern his own wingtips.

On the RHAW scope, however, Sifra's active radar was shown, and Cady estimated him at two hundred yards of separation. In these conditions, it would be easy enough to force a midair collision, and Sifra was taking no chances.

"I'll make the move," Cady warned, then abruptly pulled up from his dive.

The Harrier was doing six hundred knots. He leveled off at 3500 feet, then to test the hostile pilot, he rolled right, hauled the stick back for a short count, then centered it and rolled upright. He was heading almost directly east.

The Tornados split up, with the lead ship following him to the east.

This was the asshole.

Twenty-two miles apart.

Cady banked hard to the left, and when the tone of the AMRAAM reached fever pitch, punched off one of them.

The missile streaked away, and in anticipation of the Tornado's evasion, Cady went vertical. The strong winds buffeted the airplane hard. He heard vibrations that he hadn't been aware of before.

Four thousand feet . . . five.

He popped out of the storm, rolled inverted, and tugged the nose back down into the maelstrom.

He found the Tornado again, along with two missiles headed his way. Judging by the release distance, they were probably Matra R.530s. They didn't have the range of the Super Matras.

He popped chaff and flares.

Banked hard left.

Dove.

The missiles passed above him, chasing the decoys.

Rolled right and started climbing again.

Found the Tornado.

Eight miles away.

"Five's got one!" Sifra shouted.

Cady didn't respond.

The two of them came at each other head-on, holding their fire.

Cady still had three missiles, and he figured the Tornado for another pair.

The AMRAAMs were screaming at him.

He held off.

Six miles.

Five.

Fired one.

Held his course and attitude.

The Tornado released his missiles.

The AMRAAM was converging on the screen, homing.

The Tornado broke right, disgorging flares and chaff.

Cady led him, counted to two, listened for the lock-on tones, fired his remaining missiles, then hit the flare and chaff buttons before breaking to the left.

It was close.

The missiles detonated on his flares fifty yards behind him, and the shrapnel peppered the tail of the Harrier. The stick and rudder pedals shuddered.

He rolled upright, noted that he was down to four hundred knots and 2500 AGL, and rotated the stick, feeling for damage to the control surfaces. It felt a little iffy, but he was going to have to live with it. The rudder pedals felt spongy. Something was loose.

He was going to have to live with the Tornado pilot, too, who had dodged all of his AMRAAMs.

Shoving the throttle to the stop, Cady began climbing to the east, where the other Harriers had joined up after their engagement. He wanted to be above the storm if it came to cannons. He also did not want to face the Tornado head-to-head. He had done that before, and he didn't like it.

He was pretty certain the Tornado would come after him.

As he topped the storm, still headed east, Cady realized the other Harriers would probably have spent all of their missiles.

He punched button two. "Flip, what's your missile status?"

"Zero, Shark. But bring him this way. Five guns are better than one."

"He probably won't come."

A glance at the radar screen showed the Tornado in hot

pursuit, about nine miles back, Sifra coming around behind him, and Anderson's group turning toward Cady.

Sifra couldn't catch him, and Cady wasn't going to risk the other Harriers.

He banked right, diving back into the snowstorm toward the south.

And started counting. He was holding five hundred knots, but the Tornado was probably topping Mach 1 by now.

He kept his dive shallow, then leveled out just below the top of the storm. The buffeting tossed him against his harness. He armed the Aden guns.

If the son of a bitch was mad enough, maybe he'd forget what he was chasing. He'd just been shot at by four missiles, so maybe he was mad.

Cady tested his controls again. They felt sloppy. He might have a loose hinge joint in the rudder.

He got ready for a VIFF (Vectoring in Forward Flight), and watched the active radar of the Tornado closing on him on the RHAW screen.

Six miles.

Coming in hard and fast.

He'd be opening up with his guns in seconds.

Four miles.

Cady shifted his left hand from the throttle to the vectoring lever.

Aimed the nose down and started to dive at high speed.

Rolled to the right.

One mile.

The Tornado began firing. Cady saw the streaks of tracer passing over his wing.

He hit the lever.

The Harrier, on its side, jumped sideways, slowing immediately.

The Tornado shot past him, a flash of suddenness in the snow.

Cady slammed the lever back, rolled upright, and cut loose with the guns, oscillating the nose to cover a wider area. He chased after the phantom until his cannons came up empty.

He hit vitals.

An instantaneous peach glow in the wall of snow ahead of him suggested a fuel cell.

On the radar screen, the Tornado took a long time to slow, and split into two images, tumbling toward the ice four thousand feet straight down.

On the squadron channel, Anderson said, "Jesus, Shark, that was nice."

Cady reduced power, rolled into a left turn, and began to climb out of the snow. If he never saw snow again, he'd be happy.

"Let's go home," he told the others.

PRIMAVERA BASE
0740 HOURS LOCAL

Commander David George and his SEALs had ridden into Primavera Base on three commandeered Sno-Cats, acting like American cowboys, driving their motley herd of captured drillers and soldiers on foot ahead of them.

George thought the enforced short march would at least keep the prisoners from freezing to death.

When they arrived at the station, fires were still raging out of control, and most of the defensive force had abandoned their weapons in order to fight fire.

He ordered one team of SEALs to secure the prisoners in

the open, in an empty aircraft revetment, and then took the rest of them to the operations hut.

They met no resistance from the twenty or twenty-five men crowded into the hut, seeking warmth.

With his M-16 at port arms, he stepped inside, with Suslov and Brelin behind him, and surveyed the men massed against the far wall. Some were wearing officer's insignia and he took them to be part of the command staff or operations officers. They looked back at him with defiance in their eyes, but he knew they weren't going to do anything about their feelings.

With Corporal Angelino interpreting for him, George told them, "I'm the new mayor of this burg, and I don't like what I see. We're going to do three things right off the bat. One, you're going to bring in your men from the field and have them stack their weapons. Two, you're going to organize them to put out the fires. And three, you're going to clean up the fucking mess you guys made. You accomplish that, and maybe I'll arrange for you to go home again."

He looked over at Brelin. "Anything you want to add, Gus?"

"No, Commander, that'll do for starters."

FALCON MYSTÈRE
0750 HOURS LOCAL

Juan Silvera and Ricardo Fuentes stood in the narrow aisle of the airplane, just outside the pilot's compartment, so they could be near the radios.

Fuentes was pasty-faced. He had already vomited once from airsickness. The acrid tang remained in the air. The escap-

route from Primavera had been in very turbulent air, going far to the east before turning north.

"It is no use, Señor Silvera," the pilot said, "Buenos Aires Air Control says that we may not land anywhere in Argentina. If we attempt to land, we will be shot down."

Silvera turned to Fuentes. "You get on the radio telephone and call your boyfriend in the energy ministry. You *will* get that decision reversed."

Fuentes inched into the compartment and took the handset from the copilot. He dialed a telephone number that he probably knew by heart.

When he had the connection, Silvera grabbed Fuentes's wrist and turned the handset so that he could hear both sides of the conversation.

"Carlos, it is Ricardo."

The response seemed particularly cold to Silvera. "Yes?"

"Carlos, they will not let us land."

"Yes, that is true."

"You must do something!"

"Do you have with you two hundred million dollars to return to the treasuries of two countries, Ricardo?"

"Carlos. . . ."

"Do you?"

"You know that I do not."

"Goodbye, Ricardo."

Fuentes dropped the handset.

Silvera shook his head sadly, then asked the pilot, "Can we reach Navarino Island?"

After consulting his gauges, the pilot said, "I do not think so, Señor."

"We must try."

Silvera went back and sat in his seat.

He did not think he would see Lucia again.

JAGUAR ONE
0755 HOURS LOCAL

Suarez had located the KC-130 tankers far north of the UN ship, topped off his tanks, and then ordered the airplanes to return to Navarino Island. He didn't know where else they could go.

He flew alongside the tankers, but not as much of a protector. He was unarmed except for a few rounds for the cannons.

His life was in ruins.

He could recall vividly the day they had flown out of Navarino Island. Such ambition! Such hope for the future! He had had pictures taken of himself in front of this very airplane.

The pictures would not now go to his family at the *Rancho de Suruca*. He himself would never return to the region of his birth. There was no place in his entire country where he could hold his head high.

He must slink about like a weasel.

But Emilio Suarez de Suruca knew that it was not in him to complete his life in disgrace.

He rolled the right wing up and over and dove away from the tankers.

GYPSY MOTH ONE
0812 HOURS LOCAL

Cady, being Cady and also Commander Air Group, had dropped out of the formation and gone back to escort Tiger Mikkelson and Gail Alhers.

Mikkelson's Harrier was spewing fuel about half as fast as Jerry Can Two could top it off. Though both Mikkelson and

Alhers were worried about fire resulting from free-flowing JP-4 and hot exhaust nozzles, they were in high spirits. They had listened to the clashes of the Gypsy Moths and Tiger Barbs with superior aircraft.

Cady stayed with them all the way back to the carrier and circled as both were recovered by Shaker Adams. The other aircraft were already below decks. He was getting low on fuel himself, but had enough to wait while the deck crews cleared the flight deck of Mikkelson's damaged Harrier.

The *U Thant* looked almost like a ULCC again. The guns and missile hatches had been closed. She was almost dead in the water because, on the port side, a scaffold had been rigged and lowered to water level where men in wet suits were fighting the high waves and fitting temporary patches in place over the hole created by the torpedo.

Several hundred yards away, also dead in the water, was the freighter *Paloma,* her bridge all but nonexistent. She had been ordered to follow the *U Thant.*

Cady circled both ships at a thousand feet of altitude, waiting for a clear deck.

"Gypsy One, Jericho."

"Gypsy. Go, Jericho."

"Shark," Eames said, "we have an unidentified bogey at three-five-four, three-one miles, fifty feet AGL, Mach 1."

Cady was already rolling onto the heading as he asked, "Headed your way?"

"Roger. We're bringing the guns up, but it may not be quick enough."

Two minutes later, Cady saw the aircraft, which slowly became a Mirage as it neared him. Like his own plane, its pylons were devoid of weaponry.

He threw the Harrier into a 180-degree turn and thrust the throttle as far forward as he could get it. Losing altitude in the turn, he rolled level in parallel with the Mirage, which was on his right side.

He didn't have one cannon round left, and he regretted his decision to spend them all on the Tornado.

The Mirage pilot didn't even look at him. His head was straightforward, his eyes focused on the carrier.

Cady waggled his wings. He waved from the cockpit.

There was no response.

He knew what was coming.

Looking ahead, he saw the *U Thant* blossoming in his windscreen, helpless on the surface of the sea.

He wagged his wings one more time.

The carrier was ten miles away.

Split seconds at this speed.

Cady eased in stick and pedals and slid sideways toward the Mirage, rising slightly above it. The turbulence coming off the fighter rocked him violently.

When he felt as if he were about in the right place, he nudged the stick forward and slammed the bottom of his fuselage into the canopy of the Mirage.

The effect was instantaneous.

The French-built fighter nosed down and plowed into a twelve-foot high wave. At nearly seven hundred knots, it was like slamming into concrete, and the airplane came apart in a hundred pieces, disappearing quickly behind him.

Cady's Harrier bounced as the uplift from below vanished. He fought it, retarding throttle, trying to get the speed down quickly and keep the nose up.

The ship was still directly ahead of him, a mile away.

He was too low to bank. The wave tops slapped at the wings and fuselage.

He kicked in some rudder.

The Harrier slewed.

The rudder parted at the hinge line and was whipped away

He was skidding across the sky.

The nose dipped.

And the Harrier jump jet hit the surface of the sea, skipping like a flat stone on a pond for nearly a mile before the left wing caught a wave and she flipped end over end over end.

15 DECEMBER

Cameron McNichols wore his gray pinstripe, a nice Mara tie that Pam Akins had selected, and his Reebok running shoes. He had almost tossed the black loafers that pinched his toes, but had instead deposited them at a Goodwill store

Sir Charles Bentley had insisted that McNichols deliver his own after-action report to the Security Council. He wanted them to know McNichols.

He had complied grudgingly. McNichols did not need acclaim.

He had reported, as objectively as he could, on the fatality and casualty counts for both sides of the conflict—devastating for the FSAD—on the aircraft and vessel losses, on the documents captured by the SEALs which suggested the greed motive, but which was unfulfilled since the wells had come in dry. He had only his own suspicions to rely on in regard to the source of funds to underwrite the Front for South American Determination, and he did not report his conjecture.

He recommended continuation of the Peacekeeper Committee and possible expansion of its activities. He admitted that he was biased toward the committee.

Afterwards, Sir Charles, Julia Highwater, and Justin Albrecht took him to lunch at the Four Seasons.

"That wasn't so bad now, was it?" Sir Charles asked him after they were seated and drinks were on the way.

"I've had better days," McNichols said. "I get butterflies."

"Nonsense," Julia Highwater said. "You did very well, and think we'll land funding for another year of operation."

"How would it be, Cameron," Sir Charles asked, "if we were able to secure funds and an arrangement with the National Security Agency to support our own information agency?"

"I think we could justify the need for you, Sir Charles."

"Would you consider directing that agency?"

"You mean full-time? Jesus, if I had to work more than half-time, it'd kill me."

"Think about it, please."

McNichols would think about it for about a half-second if it came to pass.

"And Cameron, I meant to ask you, have you met that major yet?"

"Major?"

"The one with the nice voice."

"I don't think it'll work out, Sir Charles. She says she's married."

"Ah. It happens."

To her job.

As he was to his.

INS U THANT
305 HOURS LOCAL

When Cady finally came out of it, he saw white.
A white jacket.
He squinted his eyes and looked up at Jan Gless.

"How are you feeling, Colonel?" she asked.

He had to think about it. He felt as if he could move most of his extremities. His body felt a little numb. His stomach felt empty.

He looked to his left and saw that his arm was in a cast Fiberglass. Also white. He was getting tired of white.

"Hungry," he said.

"Good."

"What the hell happened?"

"Just a second."

She went to an intercom and talked to someone, then came back to stand beside his bed.

"You suffered a major concussion and mangled your arm broke the forearm bone, when you ejected. There'll be some scarring."

"Of my brain?"

Gless smiled at him. "I don't think so. Just the arm."

"Jesus. I don't remember any of it."

"We've kept you under for quite awhile. It may come back to you, it may not. The parachute didn't open fully before you hit the water."

"Who got me out?"

"Gail Alhers. Her helicopter was still on deck when you went in."

"I owe her."

Cady remembered something, but couldn't quite grasp it . . . oh! He remembered he was glad he hadn't tossed Ja Gless's cosmetics overboard. Eames had been right; he didn't want the doctor mad at him.

The door opened and Monmouth, Eames, and Baker came inside. He thanked Gless as she left.

Monmouth shook his hand. "Thanks."

"Thanks?"

"For my ship, but goddamn it, Jim, you have an unorthodox way of doing things."

He looked at Baker, who said, "You do get your prey, one way or another, Shark."

"Do me a favor, Arch?"

"Name it."

"Send a couple dozen roses and a case of whatever it is that Norwegians drink to Gail Alhers."

"Done."

Eames stood near the bulkhead and just smiled at him.

Monmouth said, "We're in Rio, Jim, debarking our passengers, who are exceptionally glad to leave this cruise, and reinforcing our temporary repairs to the hull. Then, we'll limp back to Norfolk for some permanent rehabilitation. While that's going on, you get a month off. I'd like to have you spend part of it in Maine with me. There's nothing like a roaring fire, a loud surf, and a little snow."

Cady was thinking more along the lines of white beaches, Mai Tais, and bikinis.

"I appreciate that, Sam, and I'll sure think about it."

Eames gave him the dirtiest look he had ever seen.

"But hell, yeah, it sounds good. Count on me."

Monmouth and Baker chatted a little longer, then left the room.

Cady tried to sit up, but a sharp pain in the back of his head made him reconsider.

"Want some water, Colonel?" Eames asked.

"Please."

She helped him get the glass from a side table and waited while he sipped from a bent straw. It was the best water he'd ever had.

"Jan Gless said I'm going to be all right," he told her.

"I know. She's told me all about you."

"Everything?"

"Probably."

He looked at her, and he still couldn't guess where she was coming from.

"You apparently thought it was important for me to go up to Sam's place in Maine?"

"Uh huh. I'm going to be there, and I thought we could talk."

"Oh," Cady said. "Did you know that our talks always leave me addled?"

"Sure. I wouldn't want you to think that you'll ever have me figured out."

She sat on the edge of the bed and took his good hand in her own and held it tightly.

Cady suspected that she was always going to be right.

BRANDEIS BASE, ANTARCTICA
1500 HOURS LOCAL

David George, as provisional commander of the remains of Primavera Station until a United Nations team arrived, had some power, and he commandeered a Bell JetRanger and its pilot for the afternoon.

He, Gregori Suslov, and Sergeant Tu flew to Brandeis Base where only three of the former residents had returned to join Gus Brelin.

Gus met them with exuberance and brought them inside his hut for a double shot of brandy before the services.

It was a short memorial service, with Brelin officiating in his brusque manner. Counting the helicopter pilot, who had not known Zip Andover, there were only eight of them to stand around the plaque that Brelin had carefully carved in a four-inch-thick slab of solid oak. In Antarctica, it would never rot, and it was mounted on a steel pole to the east of the camp.

It read:

BENEATH THIS TIMELESS SURFACE
RESTS THE ASHES OF
PAUL "ZIP" ANDOVER
A MAN OF HIS WORLD, AND OURS

About the Author

William H. Lovejoy is a successful author of high tech thrillers, espionage novels, and mysteries. He lives with his wife Jane in the Rocky Mountains of northern Colorado where he is at work on his next novel.

THE WINGMAN SERIES

THE SEVENTH CARRIER SERIES
by Peter Albano

THE SEVENTH CARRIER (3612, $4.50)
The original novel of this exciting, best-selling series. Imprisoned in a cave of ice since 1941, the great carrier *Yonaga* finally breaks free in 1983, her maddened crew of samurai determined to carry out their orders to destroy Pearl Harbor.

**THE SECOND VOYAGE OF
THE SEVENTH CARRIER** (2104, $3.95)
The Red Chinese have launched a particle beam satellite system into space, knocking out every modern weapons system on earth. Not a jet or rocket can fly. Now the old carrier *Yonaga* is desperately needed because the Third World nations — with their armed forces made of old World War II ships and planes — have suddenly become superpowers. Terrorism runs rampant. Only the *Yonaga* can save America and the Free World.

RETURN OF THE SEVENTH CARRIER (2093, $3.95)
With the war technology of the former superpowers still crippled by Red China's orbital defense system, a terrorist beast runs rampant across the planet. Out armed and outnumbered, the target of crack saboteurs and fanatical assassins, only the *Yonaga* and its brave samurai crew stand between a Libyan madman and his fiendish goal of global domination.

QUEST OF THE SEVENTH CARRIER (2599, $3.95)
Power bases have shifted dramatically. Now a Libyan madman has the upper hand, planning to crush his western enemies with an army of millions of Arab fanatics. Only *Yonaga* and her indomitable samurai crew can save the besieged free world from the devastating iron fist of the terrorist maniac. Bravely, the behemoth leads a ragtag armada of rusty World War Two warships against impossible odds on a fiery sea of blood and death!

ATTACK OF THE SEVENTH CARRIER (2842, $3.95)
The Libyan madman has seized bases in the Marianas and Western Caroline Islands. The free world seems doomed. Desperately, *Yonaga's* air groups fight bloody air battles over Saipan and Tinian. An old World War II submarine, *USS Blackfin*, is added to *Yonaga's* ancient fleet and the enemy's impregnable bases are attacked with suicidal fury.

TRIAL OF THE SEVENTH CARRIER (3213, $3.95)
The enemies of freedom are on the verge of dominating the world with oil blackmail and the threat of poison gas attack. *Yonaga's* officers lay desperate plans to strike back. Leading a ragtag fleet of revamped destroyers and a single antique WWII submarine, the great carrier must charge into a sea of blood and death in what becomes the greatest trial of the Seventh Carrier.

REVENGE OF THE SEVENTH CARRIER (3631, $3.99)
With the help of an American carrier, *Yonaga* sails vast distances to launch a desperate surprise attack on the enemy's poison gas works. But a spy is at work. The enemy seems to know too much and a bloody battle is fought. Filled with murderous rage, *Yonaga's* officers exact a terrible revenge.

Available wherever paperbacks are sold, or order direct from the Publisher. Send cover price plus 50¢ per copy for mailing and handling to Penguin USA, P.O. Box 999, c/o Dept. 17109, Bergenfield, NJ 07621. Residents of New York and Tennessee must include sales tax. DO NOT SEND CASH.